Uncommon
Pleasure

Uncommon Pleasure

ANNE CALHOUN

HEAT | NEW YORK

ROM
Calhoun

THE BERKLEY PUBLISHING GROUP
Published by the Penguin Group
Penguin Group (USA) Inc.
375 Hudson Street, New York, New York 10014, USA

USA / Canada / UK / Ireland / Australia / New Zealand / India / South Africa / China

Penguin Books Ltd, Registered Offices: 80 Strand, London WC2R 0RL, England
For more information about the Penguin Group visit penguin.com

This book is an original publication of The Berkley Publishing Group.

Library of Congress Cataloging-in-Publication Data

Calhôun, Anne.
Uncommon pleasure / Anne Calhoun.—Heat trade paperback ed.
p.   cm.
ISBN 978-0-425-26289-4
1. Man-woman relationships—Fiction.   2. Soldiers—Fiction.   3. Erotic fiction.
4. Love stories.   I. Title.
PS3603.A43867U53 2013
813'.6—dc23
2012031811

PUBLISHING HISTORY
Heat trade paperback edition / March 2013

PRINTED IN THE UNITED STATES OF AMERICA

10 9 8 7 6 5 4 3 2 1

Cover photograph by Claudio Marinesco.
Cover design by Jason Gill.
Text design by Kristin del Rosario.

For HelenKay Dimon.
As always, for Mark.

ACKNOWLEDGMENTS

I'm forever indebted to HelenKay Dimon, whose kindness and friendship at a pivotal moment in my career resulted in the kind of good fortune I can only pay forward. Similarly, this book would not be in readers' hands without the diligent efforts of Laura Bradford and Leis Pederson, and I thank you both. Robin Rotham, B, Jill Shalvis, and Alison Kent provided crucial support and encouragement. Going above and beyond, Alison helped me correctly plate a car in Galveston County, while Walt Stone provided insights into a petroleum geologist's work; any errors are mine. Finally, thanks to Kristi, who said Sean would drink Shiner Bock, and has been along for the ride since the beginning.

CONTENTS

Over the Edge

Chapter One

As the engine wound down the helicopter's rotors lost speed, slowly thwapping at air saturated with late afternoon sunshine and humidity. Braced against the trunk of her car, Lauren Kincaid watched Ty Hendricks emerge from the helicopter. Acknowledging that he'd set off a purely physical response in her body wasn't enough. She wanted to know why.

It could have been his hair—blond, too long, finger combed back from his face—or perhaps his eyes—dark chocolate, with spiky blond lashes. It could have been his square jaw, or the broad shoulders straining at the seams of a plain gray T-shirt as he spoke a few words to the chopper pilot, then hoisted his duffel over his shoulder and crossed the helipad.

But it wasn't any of those things.

It was the way he walked, utter confidence in his long-legged, loose stride as he cleared the helipad and set off down the aisle between two rows of cars and trucks left by Gulf Independent Petroleum employees working offshore. He inhabited his body as if it existed only to accomplish what he set his mind to, nothing more. He didn't dress it or accessorize it or sculpt it. He used it— hands, arms, hips, legs—and based on the torque he applied to a wrench the length of her arm to work loose a recalcitrant bolt, she had no doubt he could be unspeakably brutal if he chose.

His jeans were faded to pale sky blue and worn white at the seams from years of keeping him decent, nothing more. The T-shirt lacked ads for microbreweries or sports teams or Jesus, no funny slogans. He'd tucked it in, hooked his phone and Leatherman on a worn brown leather belt fastened with a dented silver buckle. She'd spent a lot of years in the company of men, from gruff, gravel-voiced career NCOs to PhDs who hadn't seen daylight since Bush was president. She could tell a man's man from a ladies' man, knew within seconds when a guy puffed up like a rooster to hide insecurities and when an insecure front hid a sweetheart of a guy.

Ty Hendricks was no sweetheart. He'd been offshore for thirty days, and pent-up need simmered in his industrial-strength body. Lauren hadn't felt a man's body, hard and demanding and maybe even brutal, against hers in a very long time. Illicit desire, long-suppressed and therefore all the more potent and volatile, zinged through all the right places.

He crossed the lot, his worn brown laced-up engineer's boots crunching gravel underfoot, and paused by the back of a crew-cab pickup to swing his duffel into the bed and head home. He had his key in the door lock before he paused, bent his head in something that looked suspiciously like resignation, then cut her a look with those melting eyes.

She'd spent four days on an oil rig with Ty. A development geologist for Gulf Independent, her two-day trip to log the hole the drilling crew just finished drilling coincided with the end of Ty's thirty-day shift. Two bridges to clear before she could log the hole turned forty-eight hours offshore into ninety-six and gave them plenty of time together. She'd caught him watching her with those shadowed eyes often enough.

"Dead battery?" he said.

Her Lexus IS 250 had four thousand miles on it, and if the battery had died, the dealership was going to get an earful. "Nothing's wrong with my car. Would you like to have dinner with me tonight?"

The T-shirt strained over his shoulders as he braced his elbows on the side of the truck's bed and let his hands dangle. There was no glint of gold on his ring finger, but that didn't mean much. Wearing any jewelry was dangerous on a rig.

His expression didn't change. "Dinner."

"Yes. Dinner," she said with a small smile. "After four days of gray mystery meat and iceberg lettuce I'd kill for a decent salad."

A breeze off the Gulf tossed his hair in his eyes, but he didn't move. "You don't want to have dinner with me."

She lifted both hands to tuck a fluttering strand into the heavy knot at her nape, watched his gaze flick to her breasts, sparking a hot, tight clench low in her belly. "Actually, I do."

He straightened, put on a pair of wraparound shades that hid his eyes. "No, you don't."

That wasn't *I'm in a relationship*, or *I'm seeing someone*, or *I have plans already*, and his blunt statement raised her hackles. She'd grown up having the circumstances of her life—frequent moves in the middle of the school year, making friends only to leave them months later, the only place that felt like home her grandparents' farms in Kansas—dictated by her father's meteoric rise to general in the United States Army. Once she was in charge of her life, it was a point of pride to know what she wanted, why she wanted it, and then go after it.

"Fall's coming," she said, glancing up at the faded blue sky. "This is one of the last warm nights we'll have for a while. I'm going to go home, shave my legs, and put on a dress, then I'm going to

McGuigans. They have a bar on the patio and a Thai chicken salad I like. That's where I'll be around seven if you feel like eating something at the same time I'm going to eat something." She was interested, not desperate, so she clicked open the locks on her Lexus and pushed away from the trunk. "Trust me, Ty. I know exactly what I want."

Dark blond eyebrows rose ever so slightly above his Oakleys, but he said nothing. She slid into her car. A push of the button started the engine, and within moments cold air blasted from the vents, chilling the sweat at her hairline, hardening her nipples. She backed out, and in the rearview mirror she saw the door close and brake lights flash on Ty's truck before she headed across the causeway connecting Pelican Island to the mainland.

Maybe she'd misunderstood the looks that lingered a little too long, attributed sexual interest when he saw only an oddity, a five-foot-ten female geologist working in the male-dominated oil industry. Whether he showed or not, she'd still be going to McGuigans, but she hoped he showed. She wasn't just curious about Ty Hendricks. She wanted to know what it was about him that sped up her heart, made her aware of her body, and his, brought to the surface a very primitive female yearning. She knew exactly what she wanted.

She wanted Ty.

The unexpected conversation with Lauren Kincaid in the parking lot sent a fairly predictable sensation coursing down Ty's spine. After four tours and months of working two- to four-week jobs on isolated, confined oil rigs, he recognized the purely physical need for a woman that he suppressed when there was no chance in hell of having one.

She'd stood out from the moment she got out of the helicopter with the rest of the crew assigned to log the well and not just because all loggers wore the same color jumpsuits. Ty noted endless legs and a full, wide mouth, then tried to dismiss her from his mind. Work relationships were too complex to make the payoff worthwhile, and a woman like that would want more than he would give.

Until he'd seen her standing by her car, realized she was waiting for him, and thirty days of repressed need became a physical ache, sitting low and tight in his spine, hardening his cock. But physical need wasn't enough; he had numbers to text if he wanted to get laid. No, what got him under the tepid trickle of water that passed for a shower in his hotel room then digging through his duffel for clothes both clean and suitable for McGuigans was simple curiosity.

How would that mesmerizingly calm woman look in a dress?

The setting sun bled orange and red into the Gulf, the tips of the waves gilded silver as he drove to McGuigans, parked the truck in one of the lots near the beach, and walked the rest of the way to the bar. His phone buzzed with a text message. As he walked he flipped it open to see New op 8 am my office from John Langley. Good. Work, lots of it, helped mute the memories.

So did alcohol and sex.

The two-sided bar separated the restaurant from the back patio. Lauren was sitting on the patio side at the end of the bar, and when he saw her something very primitive flickered to life under the curiosity. Each of the four days she'd been on the T-22 she'd restrained her hair in braided twists just under the back strap of her hardhat, but now her hair streamed over bare shoulders and down her back.

He wanted to see that silver-brown silk caught on her wet lips, sliding against his thighs to pool in his lap.

A bottle of beer sat in front of her, and her long fingers trailed in the moisture sliding down the green glass as she watched the flat-screen TV over the bar. The Thursday-night college football game was on, the commentary competing with the music barely audible over conversations. He'd been out of the Corps over a year.

Civilian life should have felt normal, but crowds, noise, and no personal space still set his nerves jangling. Ignoring the internal clamor, he turned and worked his way down the bar to her. Something tipped her off to his presence, because she looked over her shoulder at him, her eyes wide with something he could only identify as *not flirtation*.

For a long moment silence stretched between them, tinged with the same heat currently climbing her throat to her cheeks. "I didn't think you'd come."

He signaled the bartender for a beer, then said, "I eat."

She turned on the bar stool to face him, and all mental activity halted as her outfit registered in his brain. Lauren Kincaid's idea of a dress was what his mother would have called poor judgment and his grandmother would have called a disgrace, but some years all a cotton farmer's wife had was her respectability. He was the only member of his extended family to leave Camden County, Georgia. The Corps, travel, and life experience shone a different light on their attitudes. That perspective transformed him from local boy to outsider, and made it hard to go home even before his last tour. Now it was worse. He knew he was different, and they knew he was different. No one knew how to bridge the gap.

The disgrace was the color of the sweet, milky chai tea he drank with the Afghan villagers, and thin straps exposed virtually all of her shoulders, neck, collarbone. The fine silk lay against the gentle slope of her breasts and her flat belly without the ridge that normally accompanied a bra or panties. He'd bet the next round that under her expensive-looking dress she was bare all the way down. With her legs crossed the skirt rode up to midthigh, revealing a good three-quarters-of-mile-long, smooth, tanned legs.

Breathe, Hendricks.

Under his gaze the pink staining her collarbone and cheeks darkened, and she bit her lip, looked away, then her eyes met his again.

Her position on the bar stool left her head below his as he leaned against the bar and began sharing body heat, the first step in the dance. Despite the air-conditioning blasting away inside the bar, heat radiated from her, and a clean, simple scent rose into the air between them. A hint of lip gloss, and dark shadow on her blue eyes that turned them storm gray. The pink on her cheekbones was all him, though, and by the time he was through with her mouth, that color would be all him, too.

Blood surged south, but there were manners and rules to this game. To cover his response, he looked out at the patio area, saw a table for two being cleared. "Let's eat," he said.

She picked up her bottle of beer and uncrossed her legs, all it took to get her feet flat on the floor. He led the way, spending the time it took them to snag the table trying to think of something else to talk about besides food and sex.

"How did the well look? Worth casing off?"

The corners of her mouth lifted, but whether she was laughing at his conversational gambit or enjoying the diversion, he couldn't tell. "Preliminary logs look good," she said. "There's a solid pay zone around fourteen thousand feet. Everyone's waiting on orders, and I need to finish my analysis on reserves, but it was worth the trip out."

"Even if you were out there twice as long as you should have been," he said.

The waitress arrived with menus. "Anything else to drink?"

"We're ready to order," Ty said, then glanced at Lauren. "Unless you've changed your mind."

"No," she said.

"A Thai chicken salad for the lady and a french dip and fries."

The waitress tucked the menus under her arm, scribbled on her order pad, and disappeared.

Lauren picked up her bottle of beer and took a long swallow.

"Rigging down to clear the same bridge twice doesn't make for the smoothest logging run," she said. The driller all but yanked the drill string up through the sensitive sand section, a move that would at best partially collapse that part of the hole and at worst cause an underground blowout. "I thought for sure the driller would swab the hole, but he didn't."

"You got lucky," Ty said. "Last run he did swab it. The geologist had to fly back twice to get four thousand feet logged. He was pissed. He send you instead?"

She smiled again. "He's got a wife and two kids, hates to be away from them. I'm happy to go in his place."

"Nobody waiting at home for you?"

"Just my dog," she said lightly, her fingers trailing through the condensation again. "You?"

Where was home anymore? His sisters, brothers-in-law, and father waited for him to come home to Georgia, but that wasn't going to happen. There was no one here. "No," he said shortly.

"Dave said he'd fire the driller and give you his job," she said, continuing with the work-themed conversation.

Ty shifted in his seat. The temperature hovered near eighty-five, and the indoor air swirled around his booted feet, doing nothing to cool his upper body. She'd know the job as driller paid more, had better hours, and he could pick his crew, but he didn't want to go there. "He tried. I turned him down," he said shortly.

She said nothing, just tilted her head and studied him. "You're not from around here," she said.

"Neither are you." He was out of practice with dating and casual conversation, but remembered it wasn't supposed to sound like a verbal fistfight.

"My parents are from Kansas, but my dad is career Army and we lived all over the world," she said easily. "After two years in

England we had to break my sister of her English accent, but the rest of us just sound like Midwesterners. You're from . . . ?"

"Georgia," he said.

"You do pronounce all the vowels in a word," she said.

"Just talking," he said, lifting one shoulder. As the silence stretched between them she idly rubbed her instep against her calf. The thin silk of her dress slipped down to pool at the tops of her thighs, but she made no move to push it down.

The sexy dress, the hair, the makeup all made her look a little younger, a little less professionally polished, but none of it changed the fundamental confidence and competence she radiated. She was studying him the same way she'd pored over the logging reports and the mud samples when she arrived, and the scent of her skin or maybe whatever she'd washed her hair with drifted into his nostrils, mixing with his blood like oxygen.

They may not have much to talk about, but he'd bet his truck Lauren didn't want to talk.

The waitress came back with their food. He ordered another beer, and for a while, they ate. She used her knife and fork to eat her salad, cutting the fancy, dark green leaves into bite-sized pieces, watching foot traffic go by as she ate.

"They ebb and flow like the wave patterns," she said after a while. "Watching the ocean from the helipad is still my favorite part about being on a rig."

He finished chewing a mouthful of fries as he looked at the pedestrian traffic. At the back of his mind he wondered what it must be like to see only this moment, not a steady stream of possible threats or unwary victims. "I felt the same way about being on the deck of an aircraft carrier," he said.

"I should have known," she said, "but I thought with that hair, no way. Navy?"

"Marines," he replied.

A light flicked on behind her eyes. "NCO?"

"Staff sergeant," he said. The montage of images he could never fully turn off brightened and sharpened in his mind—the acrid stench of high explosives, smoking rubble, bodies laid out under shrouds. Children wailing.

"How long have you been out?"

He startled. "A year," he said, then before she could make a reply, added, "Twelve years in. Four tours, two in Iraq and two in Afghanistan."

Her smile faded as her eyes sharpened. She tilted her head and considered him, her fingers toying with the liquid slipping down the side of her beer bottle. "So, Ty, what's a former Marine doing working as a roughneck on an oil rig?"

That was the million-dollar question he didn't want to answer. "Gotta do something."

She waited, like she expected something more, details, an explanation, a lifelong fascination with drilling into the earth's crust in search of a nonsustainable fuel source, and when the silence grew, her smile slowly disappeared. The girls he picked up the first night off the rig usually chattered more than Lauren did, so he'd reached the end of his small talk capabilities. But her storm gray eyes met his without flinching, and the living, breathing, beating thing hovering in the air between them swelled in his ears, drowning out the high-pitched laughter in the background, the street traffic, everything.

He braced his elbows on his knees to reach down and brush the back of his finger over the delicate knob of her ankle, thin, silky skin over bone. She blinked slowly, watching him move his finger an inch higher to stroke the hollow above her ankle. Slow, small moves on a patch of skin no bigger than a Post-it note, nowhere near an erogenous zone. Not too much pressure, just enough to register intent, purpose.

Her mouth softened as her breath eased from her and his body felt the chemistry like he'd hooked himself up to a battery charger. "Tell me what you want, Lauren."

"You."

No playful flirtation, no licked lips or flicked hair or sexy bump-and-grind on the dance floor at No Limits. Objective stated, terms agreed to, decision made. "Pretty bold," he said.

"Welcome to the twenty-first century," she said softly.

Twenty-first century or not, the primitive male urge to claim flared in the muscles and bones of his arm, and he shifted his finger up the swell of her calf, to her inner knee. Shivers raced along the taut skin of her thigh and, more to the point, hardened her nipples under the thin layer of silk, catching his attention.

"What do you want, Ty?"

Oblivion. Hot, dark, mindless oblivion. "I want to know what you're wearing under that dress," he said, then drew his finger over her knee, letting the bump of her kneecap break the connection, transforming the movement into an open palm as he stood. A quick glance up at his face, then she put her hand in his and followed him out of the restaurant.

"Where?" she asked as they cleared the front door.

"Your place?"

"Not a good idea," she said. "I've been gone for four days so my dog's a little possessive right now. Plaintive whimpers aren't my idea of mood music."

She probably had one of those sleek silver dogs, a Weimaraner, and he didn't feel like dealing with a big, growling, overprotective guard dog. "I'm at a hotel," he offered. He owned his truck free and clear, hell, he had the money to buy a house outright, but there was no point putting down roots when he might crew out of Louisiana or go overseas. This way there was no roof to repair, no pipes to burst, no lawn to mow or windows to clean. Nothing to take care of. Nothing depending on him.

"Perfect."

"It's a local place that rents by the week. By the interstate," he clarified when she continued to look bewildered. "It's not gonna win any travel awards."

"I just got off an oil rig," she said patiently. "I don't expect a five-star restaurant and turndown service."

Nothing about this was following the standard operating procedures, but the breeze plastered that fine silk dress to her breasts and thighs, and his brain shut down. "Fine."

"I'll follow you."

Chapter Two

Getting from bar to hotel with a woman who was both sober enough and smart enough to drive herself was a unique change to his typical first night off the rig. Come to think of it, he was both sober and alert enough to note a flash of discomposure over the worn cream stucco, dented green shutters, and anemic landscaping. The emotion disappeared when he put his hand at the small of her back to escort her up the stairs to his room, because the whisper of silk over skin as she moved left no doubt she was naked under the dress.

He pulled the key card from his front pocket, opened the door, and led her inside. She let the door close behind her, leaving the west-facing room in an odd gold-dipped darkness as he went through the automatic motions of dumping keys, wallet, and sunglasses on the scratched veneer dresser.

When he looked up she was still standing by the door. The weird light from the setting fall sun lay against her like she'd been painted with it, highlighting the curve of her mouth, the drape of silk over her breasts, the sleek muscles in her arms, the jut of her hip bone against the fabric, the slightest hint of her mound.

While he stared at her she let her purse drop to the floor at her feet. The casual, almost taunting move set off something dark and primitive inside him. He stepped close and gripped her wrist, turned her to face the door, flattened her palms at shoulder height, then covered her hands with his.

She went stock-still, but when he leaned into her she pushed back with hands and hips, pressing her ass against his cock, her back into his chest. He neither gave way nor pushed back, simply let her strain, and fail, to move him. Her hot, wracking shudder told him all he needed to know. She'd tested her strength against his, liked the way the struggle tasted. She'd liked losing, too.

In a flash he revised his assessment of Lauren Kincaid. A whole range of possibilities lit up in bright, hot, digital clarity in his mind's eye. Mysterious, unspoken places they could go. Steamy, secret things they could do. Starting right now.

"We have a problem," he said.

She cut him a glance over her shoulder, first meeting his eyes, then her gaze dropped to his mouth. "What?"

"This dress." Their cheeks aligned, and the musculature of her nape and shoulders that looked so sleek and strong at the restaurant was now newly vulnerable and bare inches from his mouth. He bent his head, his breath coming in soft, hot gusts as he used his unshaven chin to nudge the spaghetti strap of her dress to a precarious position on her shoulder, then watched a shiver race over her skin. "This dress looks very, very fine, and if I get my hands all over it, it's not going to look so fine."

To demonstrate he laid his palm flat on her shoulder, then ran his hand down her bare arm, calluses and rough spots rasping against her skin. No amount of cream or oil softened his hands, and he'd given up trying.

"Oh," she managed. "I'll take it off."

She reached for the hem, but he gripped her right hand and brought it down to her thigh. His hand on hers, he encouraged her to work the silk up her leg, until he could lay his palm flat on her thigh, his thumb in that secret, delicate hip crease, and leave it there while he licked and nibbled at the sensitive spot where her neck and shoulder joined. Trapped between his body and the door, she stared straight ahead at the diagram explaining the location of the emergency exits, not seeming to breathe, then her throat produced a low, soft sound. Her nipples hardened, her shallow breaths sending the silk shifting over the peaks.

She shifted, her quadriceps trembling under his hand. He turned his fingers inward to grip her thigh, each movement slow and dark and hot. Then he drew his hand up, the thumb moving to her hip bone, palm flat against her mound.

"No underwear," he said, stating fact.

"No," she agreed, her voice almost inaudible.

A dark, molten heat simmered low in his belly, and his hand tightened on her hip bone. "When I come off the rig, Lauren, I want a woman. Bad." With his booted foot he widened her stance. "Did you want a man tonight?"

"Yes," she whispered.

"And if I'd stayed away? Would you have gone home with someone else?"

"No," she said, her soft, hot body a distinct contrast to her firm voice.

"Choosy," he said, amused.

"I know what I want," she said.

That gave him pause. "You wanted me."

She gave a brief nod. He wouldn't ask why, because it didn't matter. Here she was, face-first in his door, his hand under her skirt, her excuse for a dress hanging on her body by one shoulder strap and her tight nipples. Great. Fine. Go with it.

"Hold your dress up." Tone and wording snapped together to form a command.

Her breath caught in her throat. She bent slightly, groping blindly for the lace hem, pushing her ass against his erection, then pulled her dress to her hips. Forearm flat against the door, curved over her back, he nudged forward and brushed his thumb over the outer lips of her sex. The way this worked for her astonished him. He used one hand to sweep the fall of hair over her left shoulder, then cupped the back of her head and tilted it forward, exposing the bumps of her spine to his mouth. Teeth, tongue, lips, and within moments she sagged back into his body, the hot, sweet pressure eroding what passed for control after a month offshore.

"Tell me what you want."

"More," she whispered.

"More what?"

"More anything."

Lots of room for inventiveness in that statement, so he said, "Pull your skirt all the way up," and urged her hands to gather the fabric, leaving her bare from the waist down. He took in the view while he automatically unbuckled his belt and unzipped his cargo pants, then pushed down just far enough to free his cock. Each bump of his knuckles against her bared ass and the zipper's rasp sent a tiny shudder through her.

He put his feet outside hers, forcing her legs close together as he tucked his erection between her thighs. Fuck, oh fuck, they were a near perfect fit. She gathered her skirt in one hand, slapped the other against the door, and pushed back, wriggling to get him inside.

"No," he said, low and rough, pinning her hand to the door

with his, weaving their fingers together to keep her where he wanted her. "Close your legs around me. Tight. Fuck . . . like that. Oh, that's good." And it was. He was snugged up against her hot, wet sex, trapped between her taut thighs, bareback, pinning her body to the door, and her pulse was pounding under her ear. He found a rhythm he liked, measured and steady, paying attention to her breathing, the way her muscles quivered, the way she choked back the soft whimpers.

With a low moan she let her forehead drop to the door by her forearm and ground down against him, pushing back. With his next thrust he forced her forward, and then they were simulating sex, his abdomen pressed hard against her bare buttocks, the door thudding into the frame from the combined impact of their bodies. She was strong enough that he had to work to keep her in place as he thrust into the hot clasp of her thighs, felt sweat and her juices slick him up. Sweat shone on her shoulders. In the back of his mind he wondered why the AC hadn't kicked on yet, but no fucking way was he stopping for climate control now, because Lauren was winding tight; soft, pleading noises were trapped by her teeth clamped on her lower lip.

He spread her slick, silky folds, exposing her clit and stroking his fingertip over the swollen nub. She tried to spread her legs, that primitive female response awakening base impulses of his own. He tightened his legs around hers, using his body to control hers, her movements, her pleasure. Somehow both tight and soft, she let out a pleading little gasp, then began to quiver as he thrust in time to his strokes along the side of her clit, his cock clasped between her thighs as he rode her, and the edge. Her nipples strained against the silk. She pressed her thighs together, muscles in her bottom and stomach tensing and releasing as she squirmed and shifted.

"Ty, please!"

"No." He could be just as blunt as she was. Her head tipped

back, came to rest on his shoulder, baring the flushed length of her throat. "Gotta make you hot and wet," he said, his attention focused on his tanned hand, fingers dipping into her creamy folds. "After you come, I'm going to fuck you hard."

Lauren Kincaid must have one hell of a visual imagination to go with that analytical mind, because she came. Her eyes dropped closed, shudders wracked through her body, reverberating into his, and fuck, when he made that happen when he was inside her, it was going to rock his world hard, maybe as hard as he'd just rocked hers. Only when she went limp did he let go of the wrist he'd pinned to the door.

He waited a beat to make sure her knees and the door would hold her, then stepped back. Two seconds to turn the AC up full blast and grab a condom, then he took up position behind her and smoothed on latex. The promise of oblivion tormented him, just beyond his reach. He stepped back into her, this time tapping her ankle to spread her legs apart and nudge into those soft, swollen folds. He had both hands on her hips, forward momentum powering him inside, when she went up on tiptoe against the door and gasped, "Wait! *Wait!*"

Chapter Three

Lauren didn't think he'd wait. She really didn't. Every muscle in his body was taut against her, fingers tight on her hips, ridged torso braced against her back so she had nowhere else to go, the door flat and warm against her breasts and cheek. She tried to soften, relax into the sharp sting that threatened pain.

He stopped.

A shudder ran through his body, but he stopped, the thick head of his cock wedged just inside her. A moment passed, giving her time to register the teeth of his zipper against her ass, his lightweight khaki pants against her inner thighs, the way her leg muscles trembled from exertion. She ran thirty miles a week, and he'd reduced her legs to noodles.

A groan snared in his throat, but he stepped back, putting space between them. Lauren sank down to flat feet and turned to face him, her dress slithering down her thighs as she did.

"It hurt," she started.

"Yeah, I got that." He considered her for a minute, his face expressionless. He stepped close, and her heart kicked hard against her breastbone. His eyes were heavy-lidded as he stared at her, hands on his hips, thick shaft jutting from his opened pants. "Take that off," he said, lifting his chin at her dress.

The room seemed to shimmer a little as she hesitated. He stepped forward, took her chin between his thumb and forefinger to peer into her eyes. His gaze swept over her swollen mouth, the flush still standing high on her cheeks, heating her throat.

Without looking away from her eyes, he slid one rough fingertip under the thin silk strap and popped it free from the bodice. The fabric slithered down, lace rasping over a nipple desperate for any stimulation at all. "Unless you want to drive home naked, take it off."

She went still, drowning in the primitive electricity crackling in the room. His whole demeanor was utterly arrogant Southern male, but behind his dark eyes flashed something naked and vulnerable she might call need, so she kicked out of her shoes as she reached for the hem, pulled the dress over her head, and dropped the fabric in a puddle beside her purse. His gaze swept her like a physical caress, from mouth to breasts to sex and down the length of her legs. With his hand between her shoulder blades he guided her to the bed. He braced the two thin, limp pillows upright against the headboard, then sat back and pulled her down to straddle his lap.

The pace had slowed, the moment stretching between them like hot, soft taffy, so she reached for his shirt collar and fisted her hands in the fabric, popped the first mother-of-pearl snap on the shirt, slid her hands down and popped the next. He quirked an eyebrow at her as his hand stroked her thigh. The darker brow disappeared into the blond hair tumbling into his eyes.

"I like to look, too," she said, then released the next snap. Darkly tanned skin appeared in the widening gap. He wasn't heavily muscled; there just wasn't an ounce of fat on his body. As she unfastened the last snap and spread the fabric wide to expose his torso, smooth, flat pecs gave way to a delineated abdominal wall, the skin abruptly lightening just above a thicket of darker blond hair. His erection arced over his belly. Lethal power. This was no bodybuilder, playing around with weights and spotters and reps.

"Oh my," she said, her gaze focused on his cock. It wasn't especially long, but it was thick. Very thick. Dark red.

"Told you I wanted a woman."

The dark, blunt words sent lava pulsing through her veins to pool between her legs. A woman. A hot, wet, available body. Some analytical corner of her mind, still operating under the spell he was weaving, considered this. *Getting laid* implied an act. Simple release. A *woman* hinted at something else. He craved more than getting off. He wanted the dark dynamic of stripping a woman of her clothes and pushing his cock into her body. Using the slick, clinging grip of her pussy. Tonight, she was his to use. The thought sent sensation coursing through her. Despite the orgasm, the hot, dark scenario against the door wasn't sex, and she had needs, too. She wanted a man, a dark, edgy, demanding man, inside her, and for a good, long time.

He pulled his shaft back from his belly and, other hand on her hip, guided her up so she was centered over him. Then those dark brown eyes snared hers. "Been a while?"

She nodded, straddling his big body, and waited for his cock to stretch the slick, anticipatory walls of her pussy. The waiting was torture of a completely different kind. Pressure, promise of a ride like she'd never had, made her shimmy.

His hands tightened on her hips, holding her still. "Longer than four days."

This was another man entirely than the one she'd seen on the rig, and in the parking lot. She hadn't expected him to be careful with her. Heat seared her skin, and her heart threatened to pound its way up her throat. Rather than answering she reached for his broad, heavy shoulders to support her weight, leaving her body exposed to his hands and eyes. He laid one big hand on her neck, idly caressing her pulse, pounding just under her jaw, while his melting chocolate gaze slid over her skin, striking sparks the trailing hands stroked into flames. He looked for a good, long time, making her wait, then he said, "Ride me. Slow. Just the tip. Don't rush it."

Low, quiet, even-voiced commands, the tone of a man accustomed to authority. She set a slow, shallow pace while he slid his palms along her waist and up to cup her breasts. The rough scrape of his palms over her skin made her undulate, as there was nothing tentative or gentle about his grip. He squeezed the firm flesh, avoiding her nipples until she arched into his hands. A slow, firm pinch had her gasping, sinking a little lower on his cock.

"Not so fast," he growled.

His words were faint against the blood roaring in her ears, lost in the rhythmic surge and drag as he stretched her, nerves popping and firing into an all-consuming ache each time she sank a little lower on his cock. As if from a distance she heard desperate, pleading little gasps, but when the walls parted, she arched her back and took him as far inside her as he could go and cried out in sheer pleasure.

Ty's hands tightened on her hips. "Fuck," he growled. "Do that again. Right fucking now."

She dragged her eyes open to meet his. A muscle leaped in his jaw as she rose until the tip caressed the very edge of her sex, slid down again, made the same limpid, helpless noise as her sheath clung to him, quivering, slick.

"Okay?" he ground out.

"Fine. Better than okay," she whispered, lost in the glimmering sensation. Again. Again. Again, the angle perfect, gliding over the sensitive bundle of nerves. Heat and pressure sparked under the edges of her skin, and his hands tightened on her hips.

"You sure?"

He was different. Protective. Under the mask of arousal the lines of his face changed, the rakish twist of his mouth softening. He almost looked like someone else. "God, yes."

Then the world spun as he tumbled her to her back and drove deep into her. She cried out even as she flattened one hand at the small of his back and gripped his shoulder with the other as he adjusted the tilt of her hips in a possessive, preemptory move, then surged into her. Every stroke slid over the hot ache building inside her, the hard ride she'd wanted coming harder and faster as he pinned her down, and—

Ohgodohgodohgod

—were those noises coming from her? The tension fisted deep, almost unbearably. The bed was squeaking, thunking against the wall in counterpoint to his soft grunts, her erratic gasps and wordless pleas. Her legs drew up until her heels were digging into his ass, the impact of flesh on flesh sharp in the dark, quiet air. He cupped the back of her head and tipped her face into his shoulder, trying to stifle her cries as she reached the peak—

A fist thudded against the door. Ice flashed through her veins, and he froze above her, sweat trickling down his jaw. He looked as utterly staggered as she felt, like they were a combustible chemical experiment halted, explosions arrested just before some new compound was created.

"Hey, buddy!" came a male voice from the hallway. "Jesus fucking Christ! I can hear her down the goddamn hallway!"

Indeed, her moans still hung in the thick air, trapped in the plastic curtains and the thin, maroon and green quilted polyester bedspread that lay half on the bed, half on the floor. Torn between humiliation and laughter she stared up at Ty.

Another pounding underscored a muttered *goddammit*. The security chain rattled in its mooring. "Lady! You okay?"

Humiliation won.

Ty looked over his shoulder, his long hair tumbling forward, then withdrew and slid back inside, slow and hot and relentless. "Better answer him," he said, and just like that the emotionless bad boy was back.

"I'm . . ." The word *fine* died in her throat as Ty stroked in, slow, arrogant, silent as the grave. The bed frame gave a soft squeak, or maybe that was her when he bottomed out. "Stop that," she begged in a stage whisper. "I can't think when you do that. I'm fine," she said, hoping her raised voice was steady enough to make her knight in shining armor move on to the next damsel. "Just . . . just got carried away."

"You sure?" Suspicious this time. In her mind's eye she could see the guy, hands on his hips, glowering protectively. Probably middle-aged, balding, heavyset, a lifetime of smoking in his voice. Probably he had a wife and daughters. Probably he had a conscience.

Unlike Ty. Another slow, deep stroke and the heavy weight of his shaft slid over nerve endings that didn't give a damn about noise and propriety and protective strangers. Her pussy spasmed, and Ty laughed, soundless except for the movement of his chest against her.

"Go on, Lauren. Tell him how you are. Want some help? You're slick and hot and primed."

She turned her head and sank her teeth into the biceps nearest her mouth. Ty's eyes widened in mock outrage. A wicked gleam in his eye, he shook his head *no-no-no*, and Lauren couldn't remember what the guy outside the door said ten seconds earlier. "I'm fine," she called firmly, then licked Ty's sweat from her lips.

A cough outside. "All right, then. Sorry to bother you folks." Finally, finally, footsteps thudded down the stairway.

"He's sorry *he* bothered *us*?" Lauren said. "Oh my God."

"You're loud," Ty said. "It's hot as hell."

The searing emotional connection must have been her imagination, a product of endorphins and oxytocin. She shifted awkwardly, as far from an orgasm as she'd ever been. "Just . . . oh God. Just finish," she whispered.

He bent his head and bit down on her earlobe before asking, "That's what you want? You want me to just finish?" His voice was low but completely audible in her ear. Compelling. "Can I use you like that, Lauren?"

He'd rewired her nervous system, because his breath against her ear and his voice shot a wicked current straight to her nipples and clit. "It's fine . . . just . . . finish."

Challenge gleamed in his heavy-lidded brown eyes as he started to move again, still slow, still measured, and Lauren was out of the mood enough to keep her eyes open and watch his face as he focused on satisfying his own need. She'd thought he'd let go and get it over with, but he was watching her, adjusting. When a stroke sent heat cracking through the pit of her belly, he gripped her thigh with his free hand and repeated the move. Despite the slower, measured thrusts that didn't set the mattress singing, oh so slowly the tension built again. His gaze swept her torso, lingering on her peaked nipples, the quivering in her abdomen, and suddenly need snarled, grew teeth and claws. Her nails dug into his biceps.

"Still want me to just finish?"

"Don't you dare!" she gasped, biting her lip in an effort to stifle the damned noises in her throat.

Her body clenched around the release threatening to make her implode, strained with the effort of holding in her response, but a hitching, breathy gasp still filtered into the room, blending with the low whir of the air-conditioning unit. Her heels dug into the backs of his thighs and her body was trapped, pinned under Ty as he plunged in and out of her. Sweat gleamed on his skin, and the heavy muscles of his shoulders and torso bunched with the effort. She wriggled and squirmed under him, made him hold her down, made him keep her in place, felt his growled curse rumble through his torso as he well and truly pinned her to the bed with hands, hips, and chest, and took her.

She closed her eyes as the tight fist at her core flung open, sending her whirling into the abyss. Sound forced itself from her throat, and without warning Ty's hand clamped over her mouth, stifling her breathless moan. Shudders wracked her, slowly subsided. When they ebbed, she opened her eyes just enough to see him grit his teeth, let his head drop back. Agony washed over his face as his cock throbbed inside her once, twice, the pulsations coming in time to the grind of his hips against her. His features softened from brutal to harsh as he bent forward and took his weight on his elbows, the hand covering her mouth slipping in what could have been a caress of her ear, then her hair, but probably wasn't. His chest heaved, and sweat plunked against her collarbone.

She pushed at his ribs and he slid out, backed off the bed, and walked to the bathroom. Wrung out, she rolled to her side and curled up. The muscles of her inner thighs trembled sporadically, and her shoulders eased as she tucked her arm under her head and sank into the ebbing pleasure.

The toilet flushed in the bathroom. Water ran in the sink, then the door opened. He'd zipped his pants. As she watched he shrugged out of the shirt and tossed it toward his duffel, then braced a shoulder against the frame and folded his arms while he looked at her. He stayed in the doorway, and it occurred to her that he wasn't likely to get within five feet of the bed until she'd left it. She got to her feet, sent a mental threat to her knees to steady up, then walked past him into the bathroom. "Excuse me," she said.

In the bathroom she wet a washcloth and cleaned up, taking her time as she swiped the cloth behind her neck, down her throat, along her belly. Between her legs. She splashed water on her face, combed the worst of the tangles from her hair with her fingers.

When she emerged he was sitting in one of the room's two chairs, her dress pooled in his lap as he deftly reattached the shoulder strap to the bodice with a needle and thread.

The night was one surprise after another. Astonished, she perched on the edge of the rumpled bed and watched him. His big, rough hands took neat stitches in an ecru thread that almost matched the lace, no less. It took less than a minute, then he snapped the thread with a quick jerk of work-roughened fists, stuck the needle back in the travel sewing kit, and held out the dress.

Ty Hendricks was a six-foot-tall, hard-muscled, prowling contradiction.

She took her dress from his outstretched hand, pulled it over her head, and twisted her hair into a loose knot at her nape. She was decent to get home. "Thank you," she said.

He tore the plastic bag from around a paper cup next to the brown plastic ice bucket and poured a good two inches of whiskey into it. His throat worked as he swallowed, then he sat back, arms dangling from the arms of the chair. All sign of the connection arcing between them during sex had disappeared from his angular, expressionless face. "Want a drink?" he asked carelessly, without meeting her eyes.

A women's magazine she'd flipped through in her doctor's office contained the theory that a man's walls crumbled when he was having sex, an idea her scientifically trained brain considered and discarded in the time it took to close the magazine. But living, breathing proof of the hypothesis was sitting in front of her, walled off like a compound, proving her wrong. She smoothed her palm absently over the silk dress and considered him, but, drink offer aside, he couldn't possibly be less inviting. "Thank you, but no," she said. She picked up her purse from the spot where it had landed by the door and rummaged through it. Cell phone, keys, credit card, driver's license. She was good to go.

She'd gotten exactly what she wanted. Going back to his room with him should have satisfied her curiosity as well as her body, but as the room's shadows sidled toward him, making a home in his dark eyes, neither was satiated. Every cell in her body remained on high alert, attuned to the chemistry still crackling between them, to the odd emotional resonance swirling in and out of the shadows. But she had no idea how to go about illuminating what haunted him, and twenty minutes of conversation over dinner taught her how unwelcome her efforts would be.

"Good night, Ty," she said quietly, stepped out into the hall, and let the door close behind her.

Chapter Four

The briefing started at eight. Ty pulled into the parking lot of Langley Security at 7:58 a.m. He downed a fast-food sausage and egg biscuit in three bites, finishing just as John Langley's black Ford Explorer parked beside him. Ty got out of his car while John and his girlfriend, Lucy Monroe, emerged from the SUV. John wore slacks, a dress shirt, and a tie, which meant he was due at a sales presentation at some point during the day. Lucy was dressed for her day as a partner with a local accounting firm in a slim, fitted black jacket and a skirt that ended just above her knee, killer spike heels, and the amber necklace she wore almost daily. Her hair was pulled back in a sleek ponytail, her makeup demure, her manner consummate young urban professional.

Ty knew better. At John's request, six months earlier Ty had picked Lucy up in a bar for a night of sex she thought would drive John away, but had instead changed their relationship entirely.

John handed Lucy his keys as he nodded a greeting to Ty. "Top desk drawer," he said to Lucy. Flipping through the keys, she hurried past Ty up the sidewalk leading between cedar chips and low bushes to the door of the redbrick building. "Hello, Ty," she said over the sharp snap of her heels against the cement.

Ty and John shook hands in front of Ty's truck. "Her car wouldn't start this morning."

"She still driving the Prelude?"

"Yeah. She bought it when she graduated, and she won't give it up. This time it's the water pump."

They followed Lucy into the building, through the reception area, and into John's office/war room. He and John had served in the same rifle platoon for the duration of their time in the Corps, and for a while they'd been closer than brothers. Ty headed for the makeshift commissary at the back of the room and made coffee while John and Lucy rummaged through John's mess of a desk.

"You always leave this until the last minute," Lucy chided, but there was more amusement than irritation in her voice.

"I tried to get here last night," John said. Based on the rough lick of laughter in his voice, Ty knew exactly what kept John at home. He tucked a filter in the cup and scooped coffee grounds into the filter as images of Lauren Kincaid flashed like lightning in his brain.

The sex had been hot. Wet. Only a couple of inches shorter than him, she'd tucked his cock snug between her thighs, lubricated her grinding, swiveling search for ecstasy with sweat and her slick fluids, making him work to keep her trapped between his body and the door, and that was before he got inside her tight pussy. He'd been well on his way to losing his mind when the knock came on the door, but the way she trembled under him, offering up her body so he could "just finish" flicked a switch inside him. She'd been just nervous and hesitant enough to activate a whole bunch of primitive centers in his brain he'd rather not acknowledge.

And that was that. Hot. Different. Done. Especially after he asked her if she wanted a drink like what they shared was just a fuck. He'd get used to it eventually, ruining relationships even when his instinct was to nurture them. She'd walked away without a backward glance, too. Not that he cared. Except he couldn't stop thinking about her, and the 180 degree turns between *hold her* and *discard her* were giving him mental whiplash. She had depths and textures he'd barely begun to explore. In another lifetime he'd take his time reconnoitering everything she knew she wanted, maybe teach her a thing or two she didn't know she could want. But that lifetime was over.

"Shhhhh," Lucy said. Ty resolutely kept his back to the two of them as he closed the filter cup and ran water into the carafe. "Last night is still last minute! Quarterly taxes are due tomorrow."

"You updated all my records two weeks ago," John said reasonably. Ty heard a drawer close. He turned around to see Lucy stuffing a manila folder full of receipts into her leather briefcase.

"That's not the point."

"Good thing I'm marrying my accountant," John said.

"Is she more patient than I am?" Lucy said.

"No, but she'll let me make it up to her," John said.

Now that he was looking for it, Ty saw the diamond glittering on Lucy's left hand, and despite his efforts to not feel a goddamn thing, happiness lifted his spirits for a moment. "Congratulations," he offered as he crossed the room to shake John's hand again, then bent to give Lucy a swift kiss on the cheek.

She let her hand linger at his shoulder. "Thanks, Ty. How are you?"

"Fine, Luce," he said. The delight gleaming in her eyes dimmed for a moment, and he hated to see that. He took care of people, or used to, not the other way around. "I'm good," he said firmly. "Coffee?"

"No, thank you," she said. "I like my stomach lining intact. Lunch?" she said over her shoulder to John.

"One," John confirmed, and made no bones about watching his girlfriend—*scratch that*—fiancée, hurry toward the door, tall and slender and firing on all twelve cylinders. The office door opened just as Lucy reached it. Two men with buzz cuts, dressed in khaki cargo pants and polos, stood on the other side. One was Sean Winthrop, the lieutenant who took command of the rifle platoon just as Ty's enlistment period ended. The other man didn't even look familiar.

"Excuse me," Lucy said with the same Southern poise Lauren reached for last night.

"Allow me, ma'am," the stranger said, stepping to the side to hold the door open for her. She swept through. All four men watched her cross the parking lot and climb into the Explorer. Her skirt hitched up enough to reveal a flash of stocking and garter belt before she slammed the door, started the truck, and shot out of the lot.

"Anyone got dibs on that hot piece of ass?" the door-holder said.

Sean shot him a narrow-eyed look as John said, quite mildly, "That hot piece of ass is my fiancée."

The kid all but came to attention. "Sorry, sir."

"You don't need to apologize to me," John said, still deceptively bland as he focused on his e-mail. "You need to apologize to her, but I don't want your death on my conscience, so I'll accept your apology on her behalf."

"Yes, sir. Thank you, sir."

"Knock off the sir. I'm a civilian."

"Still working for you. For the moment. Sir."

Not bad, Ty thought. John must have agreed because he nodded. Sean crossed the room to give Ty a handshake and a quick, hard hug. He was Ty's height, with blue eyes unusually brilliant against his tanned skin and close-cropped blond hair bleached nearly white by a year in Afghanistan's relentless sun.

"You out?" he asked Sean. Ty'd chosen not to reenlist after the last tour, but last he heard Sean still had a year to serve. Had he really gone that long without talking to him?

"On leave," Sean replied. "Just finished a deployment in Afghanistan. Not sure what's next."

"You've got options?"

"Resign my commission, continue with the platoon, or take a reassignment to Quantico."

Where the Marine Corps Officer Candidate School was, along with the command center that developed strategies for combat, among other things. Quantico was a plum assignment for a young officer moving up the chain of command, and Sean had the brains and education to go with the combat experience . . .

Ty gave himself a hard mental shake. Used to be personnel assignments were his specialty, but this wasn't his company, or his op, and that's the way he liked it. "So yeah, you got options," Ty said, and left it at that.

"Chase Duvall," Sean said with a nod at the runaway mouth. Ty shook his hand and waited until after he'd seen him in action to pass judgment.

"Huddle up," John said, stepping over to the large table that occupied most of his office. A whiteboard hung beside the table, and the four men clustered around a computer screen displaying a satellite image of a business park, three-story brick buildings clustered around the inlets and curves of a man-made lake with a fountain in the center. A blacktop path encircled the lake. Park benches sat under flowering trees, among bushes and annuals, landscaping that far outstripped the sickly shrubs outside his hotel.

"Standard surveillance operation," John said, then brought up photographs of two men and a woman. "These individuals work for Reynolds Freeman, the pharmaceutical firm, and are suspected of selling information to a competitor. The company did some basic e-mail tracking and turned up enough dirt to justify digging deeper.

I've got a team watching homes and the most likely contacts at the competitor. I need to know when they get to work, when they have lunch, who with, when they leave. We're compiling evidence for a possible court case here."

The specifics were for the new guys. Ty had done this before, knew the drill, could do it in his sleep. Chase and Sean nodded, Chase chewing away at his thumbnail as John pointed out the front door, loading dock, cafeteria door leading to the lake. Sean had his arms folded across his chest and was studying the images. "If we see them leave during the day, do we follow or just note it?"

"For now, note it, and call in. I'll take it from there," John said. "Ty's lead on this one, so you'll work with him to organize schedules."

Ty shot John a look John returned with the same calm, level gaze. After a moment, Ty spoke. "There are about a dozen companies working out of that business park," Ty said without breaking eye contact. "Pay attention. Lots of coming and going, lots of entrances and exits. Don't get distracted."

"When do we start?" Sean asked.

"Right now," John said.

"Equipment's in the closet in the reception area," Ty said with a jerk of his head. Sean and Chase filed out.

Ty closed the door behind them. "What the fuck? You know I don't do lead. I'm back on the T-22 in four weeks and this will go on longer than that."

"Good thing it's not a hundred degrees out like it was last month, because you're going to be sitting outside for those four weeks," John said, then got serious. "I need you on this. It's a big subcontract for me, a foot in the door. If this goes well, I've got more work than I can handle. Hell, if you'd just buy in we'd take this operation to the next level. The game's getting bigger. More complex. I could use you."

He used to get a big charge out of teaming up with John to put together personnel, intelligence, equipment, and terrain to pull off risky, complicated operations. During their time in the Corps they'd talked frequently about going into the rapidly growing industrial security business together, but shit happened, and when the time came, Ty backed out. John went ahead without Ty on board as personnel specialist, dragging Ty into operations when he wasn't working. Ty kept waiting for John to quit on him. So far he hadn't.

"Not gonna happen." He tilted his head toward the front room. "Ask Winthrop. He's thinking about getting out, and you know he's good."

"He's not out yet, you stubborn motherfucker," John said, but without any heat. "You can't keep ignoring life."

"Watch me," he said, then opened the door to find Sean and Chase back-to-back in John's meticulously organized, ultrasecure room containing the high-tech surveillance gear. He watched them dig through the toys and mulled over the way fate liked to bitch slap him.

Gulf Independent was headquartered in that business park. He'd spend the next four weeks watching Lauren Kincaid come and go from work.

Chapter Five

The normally crisp edges of numbers and letters had begun to blur half an hour earlier. When Lauren's eyes slid involuntarily to soft focus, she sat back and pulled off her glasses, then opened her drawer and retrieved her soft-sided lunch box. "I'm going to go sit outside," she said to her coworker, Danelle, over the low wall separating their cubicles. "Want to come?"

Danelle was slumped down in her chair, gazing fixedly at the monitor as she alt-tabbed between two chat sessions and an Excel spreadsheet full of formulas and complex macros. "You don't have to go down to the courthouse again?"

Thanks to a screwup with the bank and the title, it had taken Lauren three trips to get her car plated. Inefficiency brought out the cranky bitch in her, and so the conversations with the county clerks became regular break room fodder.

"Sorry to disappoint you, but no. The car's finally plated."

"I'm in the middle of this, so I'll pass. It's cooler than it was, but find a bench in the shade. You got too much sun on the rig."

Lunch box in hand and moving on autopilot, Lauren walked down the hallway, rubbing the grit from her eyes. She took the stairs to the first floor, cut through the cafeteria's seating space, and headed out into the midday heat, intending to space off into the distance and think about a puzzle of a different sort than locating, logging, and casing off a productive well.

The night with Ty.

The sex had gone exactly as she'd hoped, but nothing else had. Everything—his entire demeanor, the bottle of whiskey, the sight of him in that dismal hotel room—felt wrong. But he was a grown man, a seasoned Marine, perfectly capable of taking care of himself.

Except he wasn't taking care of himself. But Ty and his rootless life were none of her business. He wouldn't thank her for meddling, even if she could think of a good reason to go back to his room. Worse, odds were good if she knocked on the door she'd overhear someone else's good time. The memory of the interruption still made her blush. Eventually, her curiosity would fade.

The benches farthest away from the door were all occupied, so she settled for a spot in the curve of the man-made lake, the edges of the growing tree barely shading it. The shaded benches nearby were more desirable, and therefore full, with two women gossiping on one, and a man and woman on the other, sharing food. A single man dressed in lightweight cargo pants, a pale blue button-down shirt, and lace-up boots occupied the last bench, a Texas Longhorns cap shading his eyes from the late September sun.

Ty. The hat covered his slicked back hair and obscured his forehead and eyes, but she'd seen the line of his jaw and the Oakley shades under a hard hat too often to mistake him. "Hey there," she said. "Can I join you?"

At the sound of her voice his head jerked up, his eyes completely unreadable behind the shades. "Sure," he said, gathering the newspaper and brown paper bag strewn over the ends of the bench.

"What are you doing here?" Roughnecks rarely had a reason to come to the company's headquarters.

"Lunch break."

"I meant, did you have a meeting about the driller job?"

He shook his head, not even bothering to look at her as he did, and his demeanor settled the question of whether or not she'd made the right decision to turn down his offer of a drink. She sat down, opened her lunch box, withdrew the Tupperware container holding her turkey sandwich, and took a bite, all the while relaxing her eyes by focusing on the horizon and making her mind go blank. She could play the ice princess when the situation called for it, and was dressed for it in a sleeveless sheath dress and summer-weight cardigan, her hair restrained in an intricate knot by two polished mahogany sticks.

When she was halfway through the sandwich he sighed and pulled a pen from the pocket of his cargo pants, then wrote on the newspaper and held it out to her.

Look in my right ear.

Surprised, she swallowed the mouthful of sandwich then peered behind him and saw the tiny, clear earpiece, the type the security detail for the president wore. She pulled back and looked at him, brows lifted. He pulled out a touchscreen phone with a keypad that slid out from under the phone and looked at her until she gave him her phone number. He thumbed away at the little keypad. A moment later her phone buzzed with an incoming text.

I'm working.

"Doing what?" she said, then thought the better of it and texted him back.

Will your mic pick up my voice?

Not if you're quiet.

She glanced at him, saw a dark teasing little smile lifting the corners of his mouth. "Very funny," she said, her voice low.

Your volume is appropriate.

The man picked a fine time to get a sense of humor. "How do you know?"

His big thumbs shifted deftly over the tiny keyboard. My partner would ask me who I was talking to if he could hear you.

"Okay," she said, but she was putting pieces together. Former Marine, earpiece, a business park housing technology and oil industry firms. "And your work has nothing to do with committing industrial espionage related to Gulf Independent, right?"

The answer was short and came without hesitation. No.

She looked at him for a long minute. Behind the mirrored shades he could have been looking back at her, or at the lake or a person or a doorway into the building. If pressed she wouldn't have been able to say why she believed him, but believe him she did. "I trust you," she said.

The words seemed to hang in the air, then he turned away from her to scan the lake, then the door leading from the building. Several minutes passed before he picked up his phone again.

You shouldn't.

"Because in addition to working in industrial espionage, you're an old-fashioned Southern bad boy?" she asked. "Hard-drinking, hard-partying, looking for the next score?"

You like bad boys. The text neither confirmed nor denied her assessment and came with a single dark blond eyebrow arched over the sunglasses.

She shrugged, went with it. "On occasion," she said. "They certainly have their uses."

A muscle in his jaw jumped, as if the idea of being a one-night stand in her life didn't sit well. Be careful. We break hearts.

Real bad boys didn't worry about hearts getting broken, but maybe he was just protective. Except it didn't fit. Nothing about this fit, right down to the tension in his shoulders. "I went to high school in Texas and college in Virginia. I know the type." And despite his best efforts, she had a hunch he wasn't that type at all. "You can trust me. I'm not going to get my heart broken."

She finished the healthy portion of her lunch and brushed the crumbs from her sandwich onto the pavement. Three tiny, dusty birds hopped over to squabble over the bits of bread. She'd run eight miles that morning, earning her treat for the day, a chocolate chip cookie. Chocolate and sugar blended on her tongue, and the sensation of sweat trickling down her back sent her body back into his hotel room. She remembered taking his weight, the slow lick of flame under her skin as he moved inside her, the breadth of his shoulders, the way he used hands and hips to control her. The way he'd waited when she cried out, then taken her body's resistance and molded it into a dark, seething ache, used that beautiful, hard body to satiate her.

The way he disappeared into himself a split second after it ended. Being with Ty was like drinking salt water. Every sip stirred the need for more, and more. "You make me curious, Ty," she said.

Don't waste the energy.

She smiled because she liked complex things. Puzzles. Projects. People. "That's too bad, because if I were curious, I'd invite you over tonight."

She didn't need to see his eyes to tell they'd sharpened. His whole demeanor ratcheted up a notch, muscles tightening, breathing shallow. His hips shifted on the bench, and she reflected on the simple pleasure of teasing a man, watching him get hard for her, knowing she'd pay for it later.

"I thought we were pretty hot," she continued. Incineratingly hot. "Worth a second round. If I were curious. If I'm not . . . Gretchen needs a bath. Oh, and there's a *Toddlers and Tiaras* marathon on tonight." She gave him a smile. "Help me out?"

He brushed his thumb absently over his phone's keypad before replying. Address?

Without a word she entered her home address in her phone and texted it back to him. "Any time after seven," she said, then stuffed her containers in her lunch cooler and zipped it shut. He wasn't looking at her when she walked away.

She'd said any time after seven. It was nine thirty when he rang her doorbell. Flowering pots of geraniums stood on either side of the old oak door, and dog bones decorated the welcome mat. After a moment Lauren appeared, her slender figure distorted by the lead glass panes in the window, and the moment she opened the door, he knew he shouldn't have come to her home. She wore a thin gray T-shirt and a pair of shorts made from a thick cotton material. No bra. The length of her smoothly muscled legs drew his attention to her bare feet, the toenails painted a brilliant blue.

"Hey," she said.

"Hey yourself," he replied and lifted a six-pack of bottled beer.

She opened her mouth, probably to automatically thank him, but at the sound of nails skittering against the tile she turned and shifted her weight. Ty braced for the big guard dog, then looked further down to the wriggling, barrel-chested tube of a dog, with a black face and ears and a dark brown body. Using her ankle, Lauren kept the dog from escaping. "Come in and shut the door," she said.

"That's your dog?" Ty asked as he closed the door behind him.

"This is my dog," she said. "You sound surprised."

"I was expecting one of those gray dogs. A Weimaraner. Not a wiener dog."

"She prefers dachshund," Lauren said, putting a German guttural into the pronunciation as the dog peered at Ty from behind her ankles. "Or doxie if she's feeling flirtatious. Come here, sweet girl," she said fondly as she slid one hand under the little dog's butt and the other behind her forelegs and lifted her into her arms. "Why did you think I'd have an eighty-pound gun dog?"

He wasn't sure if he'd offended her, so he tried to explain. "It's what came to mind when you said you had a dog. I pictured big, useful. Something you went running with, or played Frisbee with. Silvery, kind of like your hair."

"Gretchen is very useful. She makes me feel better after a bad day, and my hair is a dull ash brown," she said.

"It catches the sunlight like polished steel does."

The uncensored words were almost poetic, and when they eddied into the tiled foyer, he felt his face heat. This wasn't about romance, and based on their previous encounter, he wouldn't have to sweet-talk her into anything. She shifted her dog a little higher in her arms and kissed the top of her head. "Ty, meet Gretchen, my non-Weimaraner."

Obligingly Ty lifted his hand to scratch her head, but Gretchen cowered back in Lauren's arms. He blinked, then said, "What did I do?"

"She doesn't respond well to men, especially big men. The humane society caregiver said she had a sprained back when she was left in the overnight drop box, and she preferred female attendants. Best guess is that a man or maybe some teenage boys abused her," she said, stroking Gretchen's back. "I thought maybe if I was holding her . . . well, we're working on it. Come on in."

In the kitchen she set Gretchen on the floor. Ty followed, the six-pack in hand, and while he'd taken off his boots in the foyer, Gretchen still hid behind Lauren. "Bottle opener's on the fridge," she said. "She'll feel safest if I put her in the laundry room," she said.

The dog scurried as fast as she could down the hall. Lauren cajoled her into her kennel, then the click of the metal latch slid home as he popped the tops off two bottles of beer. When she returned, he offered her one, they clinked the bottles together, and she tipped the bottle back.

"Want to sit down?" she offered.

His parents raised him with a firm hand and an eye toward manners, habits not yet broken by his new personality, so he said, "Sure," and followed her into the living room to settle at one end of the sofa while she curled up at the other. They both had another swallow of beer while he looked around. The kitchen was at the north end of the house, with the dining and living rooms sharing the same large, rectangular space. A rug under the dining room table delineated the dining space from the living room. A sofa and two armchairs clustered around a large stone fireplace, and big sliding glass doors opened to the backyard. Pale cream walls were covered with black-framed photographs of her family, and the bright red and orange throw pillows added color to the dark brown leather sofa.

"Nice house." And he shouldn't have come, because every passing moment confirmed his opinion that Lauren wasn't the kind of woman he usually hooked up with the first night off the rig.

"Thanks," she said, and he could hear the pleasure in her voice. "I bought it a couple of years after I got the job with Gulf Independent. I was straight out of college and needed to save up the down payment. It was a real fixer-upper. The kitchen hadn't been renovated since 1957, and the whole house had to be rewired to bring it up to code. I did some of the work myself . . ."

He was looking at her, just looking, sprawled out at the opposite end of her sofa, and her words trailed off into silence. His hair, still damp from a shower, slid forward to lie against his cheekbones. "I'm not here to talk about your house, Lauren."

The words were intended to reestablish boundaries, focus on the chemistry crackling between them. She cocked her head and looked at him, a mysterious little smile on her face. "So that means you don't want to talk about the driller job, or what you were doing at the business park today."

He shrugged, then finished the bottle of beer and set it on the floor beside him. "I'm not taking the driller job," he said. "A friend, a fellow Marine, has a security business. I work for him when I'm not on the rig. Taking the driller job would end that."

"Post–nine-eleven, the security business has been growing," she said. At his sharp glance, she added, "My dad was in Army intelligence. I know what kinds of work sharp former military types go into. Is your friend's business doing well?"

"Real well," he said. "We were supposed to go into business together, but plans change. He still wants me to buy in."

"Sounds like it would be interesting work," she said. "More interesting than running pipe on the T-22."

"I sat on a park bench for six hours today, and when I wasn't sitting on the park bench I was sitting in a truck," he said dismissively.

"You have a degree?"

He did. It took him five years of online classes and campus courses when he was stateside, but he'd gotten the degree. It was nobody's business but his if he wasn't using it. "International relations."

"And field experience in two of the world's biggest hot spots. Partner work wouldn't involve sitting on a bench for hours a day. Planning ops, maybe. Sales meetings. Strategic thinking and planning related to your client's industry or political situation."

She was too fucking curious. Seven years ago, when he started college, that had been his goal. Now he had no goals other than getting a second beer and getting laid, so this trip to her house wasn't a total waste. "Don't waste the energy wondering about me. I work, I sleep, I eat, and I'm off the rig, so I want to fuck as much as possible. Then I'll leave. Next time I'm in town, I won't call. Still curious?"

She considered him for a few seconds, his brusque words hanging in the air. "Yes, I'm still curious," she said.

The curiosity was going to burn her eventually, because she wasn't the type to keep emotions from the questions she asked. God knew his answers were nothing but the emotions he'd learned to loathe. Time stretched as raw, edgy energy poured from him, then he got to his feet, using movement to push away feelings he couldn't bear.

"Now's good."

Chapter Six

She led the edgy, wound-up former Marine down the hall to her bedroom. He stood just inside the doorway, hands on hips, eyes ticking off the details of the room while she drew the sheer curtains. It was an old-fashioned room, pretty bare, but she'd left it that way to show the bones of the house, the light against the hardwood floors and original trim around the doors. A chenille spread covered the oak spindle bed, and a cheval glass mirror stood in the corner. The oak dresser across from the foot of the bed matched. The set looked old but was new; she was too tall to sleep easily in an antique bed. She had braided rugs on either side of the bed, but otherwise the polished wood gleamed in the moonlight.

He crossed the room to her nightstand and glanced at it. "Twenty-first-century woman, right? What's in the drawer?"

She added the occasional moments of humor to her growing list of things she liked about him. "Help yourself," she said, because questions of trust seemed key to Ty Hendricks. He told her not to trust him, then looked almost hurt when Gretchen recoiled. Definitely a hot-button issue.

He pulled out her red leather restraints, tossed them to her, then strode back down the hall. Pure sexual heat blended with a sense of freedom. The unassuming way he chose the cuffs from the modest assortment of toys in her nightstand told her he was comfortable with sex outside the realm of plain vanilla. More to the point, he didn't shy away from having her under his control. He hadn't missed her body's shuddering, female response when she'd struggled between him and the door at the hotel. That visceral flash of memory, and the way he moved across the helipad, so completely self-assured and all man, surfaced as he walked out of the room, and her blood heated and thickened to molten lava.

When he returned he held one of the chairs from her dining room table. He set it down in front of the oval mirror, eased into it, and gestured her to stand between his knees. When she did he held up his hand and beckoned for her to give him the restraints.

She dropped them in his hand and felt her heart start to pound hard against her breastbone, slow, sledgehammer-like thuds. She watched him turn the cuffs over, examining them, getting familiar with them.

"Red?" he asked as he deftly unfastened the snap hook hanging from one D-ring. "Really?"

"I like color in my accessories," she said.

A wry smile. "I noticed. Wrist."

She held out her right wrist, then the left, waiting docilely as he slid the leather over her hand and drew the loose end tight before fastening it in the buckle. There were two ways this could go down. He could fasten the cuffs in front of her, turning the scenario playful and giving her some measure of independence. Or he could fasten them behind her, placing her completely at his mercy.

Hands on her hips, he turned her to face the mirror and then fastened the cuffs behind her back. Even without removing a stitch of clothing, vulnerability washed over her in waves. He peered up at her through the hair tumbled in his eyes, and for a charged moment the carefully indifferent facade faltered. Without thinking she bent her head. He reached up to release the clip holding her hair in a floppy updo. The strands slid forward, into her face, and his hand followed, long fingers caressing her cheek before his thumb brushed over her mouth.

His rapt attention on her mouth made her think she was about to end up on her knees, but he turned her and seated her facing forward on his lap. She let her legs drop to the outside of his. Her ass rested directly against the thick erection, her hands wedged against his hard abdomen. The short-shorts exposed her leg from inner thigh to the arch of her foot, and her breasts pressed against the T-shirt's thin fabric, nipples erect.

He stroked the backs of his hands down her bare arm, sending shivers down her spine. She shifted a little, his body hard and strong under hers. Then he tucked his bristly chin into her shoulder and slowly tugged up her shirt, exposing belly then bare breasts, his movements smooth, unhurried, his gaze focused on her.

"No bra?"

"I'd given up on you," she admitted. "This is what I sleep in."

"I shouldn't have come," he said, almost to himself.

"Why not?"

He didn't answer, stroking the sides of her breasts with the backs of his curled fingers. The promise of his touch hardened her nipples, as did his focused gaze.

"What's with the mirror?" she asked, her voice soft, high-pitched as she sank into the scenario.

"I'm a man," he said absently. "We like to watch."

He lifted her shirt over her head to catch at her elbows, then flattened his palms on her collarbone and swept them down, rasping her nipples, her abdomen, again, again, again, until she was arching into each stroke, desperate for the rough contact. Her breasts heated, grew heavy at the rough touch of his palms, and when he pinched her nipples, her bones seemed to dissolve into her blood, running as thick and lazy as warm honey. Sensation pooled between her thighs, turned her hot and liquid.

His gaze followed his hands as he cupped her breasts and plucked at the nipples, stroked down to the edge of her shorts. Her lips parted, and she arched into his hands. She whimpered, and he slid his hand under the elastic waist of her shorts to circle her clit with the tip of his middle finger. The movements were obscured by the fabric, but glowed on her mental map of her body. The touch was rhythmic, light, close enough to the bundle of nerves to make her thigh muscles tremble and her eyes drop closed, but not close enough to do more than maintain her on a simmer.

Her leg rose as she sought a way to shift into his hand, but he followed the movements with ease, and the hot snares of frustrated desire tightened around her. The hand not occupied with her clit rose back to her breasts, where he stroked the soft underswell of one, plucked at the nipple, pinched it before repeating the pattern at her other breast.

She arched away from him, then sank back against his hard body, unthinkingly jerking at the restraints. The soft leather, warmed from their shared body heat, gave not an inch as the snap hook held firm.

"Want more?"

"Yes," she whimpered.

"Too bad."

She let her head drop back against his shoulder and pressed down hard against his erection.

"It really works for me when you squirm like that," he said. He lightly bit down on the curve where her shoulder met her neck. "It works for you, too, doesn't it? You like not being in control."

She tried to sit up, even get her feet flat on the floor to get some leverage, but he just widened his stance. "A gentleman wouldn't mention that," she gasped.

"You sized me up for four days, Lauren. You knew what you were getting."

Another firmer bite on her neck, then he set his teeth and tongue to work on the nape, ratcheting up the tantalizing pressure between her legs. Shivers raced down her back, counterpoint to the heat building in her breasts. A gasp slipped from her throat.

She felt his bared teeth against her nape. "So fucking hot."

The tilted angle of his head sent his blond hair tumbling into his face, but she could see his eyes plain as day when he looked up from her body and met her gaze in the mirror. Tiny, secret, electric movements around her clit, sometimes closing the circle and drawing a pleading gasp from her throat, always widening again while she arched and writhed. A fine sweat gleamed on her face and body, her hair clinging to her mouth and collarbone as he drew the tension out into sexual torture.

"Please, oh please," she whispered.

"I'm gonna get mine, right?"

Electric shock straight to the brain. "Yes," she said. *Anything.* She'd promise anything.

With the pad of his middle finger he stroked her swollen clit, the pressure firm, relentless. She let her head fall back against his shoulder, her body drawing into a taut bow anchored by her head against his shoulder and her ass grinding into the cradle of his hips. The build was as hot and fiery as the burnoff from a runaway well and narrowed her focus to his finger against her clit until the tension exploded into blackness. Shudders wracked her, easing slightly with each subsequent pulse until she lay limp against his hard body.

Opening her eyes just a little she saw her breasts quivering with her rapid pulse, her abdomen rising and falling under Ty's arm. Ribbons of electric heat fluttered along her nerves; her nipples throbbed in the cool, dark air of the bedroom. Her clit fluttered under his motionless finger, and her thighs trembled from exertion.

She opened her eyes a little wider and met his gaze in the mirror. Pure male satisfaction simmered behind those dark eyes, but then his cock pulsed and shifted under her ass.

"Time to get mine."

The sight of Lauren Kincaid sprawled on his lap, gleaming and disheveled after a breathlessly powerful orgasm, sent a disquieting mix of emotions cascading through Ty. He liked watching this confident, assured, collected woman splinter into shards under his hands, but that felt too much like a connection, so he pushed it aside for a simple, base dilemma. Should he continue this torturously arousing game, or situate her on her knees on the bed with her face in the sheets, and fuck her until he exploded deep inside her?

This wouldn't last more than the next couple of weeks. There would be plenty of time for quick, anonymous fucks when this was over.

He reached up and smoothed her hair back from her face, then laid his palm flat between her shoulder blades and pushed her to her feet. "I thought these shorts all came with PINK on the ass," he said as he pushed them down her long legs.

A breath of a laugh huffed from her. "I am not the kind of woman who goes around with derogatory slang for female genitalia on my butt."

She wasn't. There was nothing little girl-ish about her sexuality, what she wanted, how she responded, and that was part of the problem, but his cock had more pressing needs than labeling Lauren Kincaid or the way possibilities opened up around her. He wanted her completely naked, so he unclipped the snap hook, pulled her top to the floor, then refastened it. His gaze leisurely examined her body, the sexily toned curve of breast and hip, the trimmed thatch of hair between her thighs, the lean muscles of her legs. His finger-tips trailed down her abdomen, brushed her damp curls, then traced the line of her right quad. She looked down, away, then back at him, as if she'd never watched arousal build in her body, watched it shimmer and dance between her and the man in her bed. Her hesitation made him want to take his time. Show her something about herself.

"You a runner?" She nodded, her cheeks flushed, her mouth swollen, lips parted. He looked at it and mentally added another possibility to his list: a slow, thorough blow job with Lauren in the cuffs. *Tempting.*

Very tempting. It was exactly what he should do, avoid the con-nection of being inside her, feeling her open to him in every sense of the word. But he wanted the visceral satisfaction of feeling her hot and wet, quivering around him, so he lifted his hips to extract his wallet from his pocket, then opened it and pulled out a condom. "Let's test your endurance."

She waited docilely, watching in the mirror as he unbuckled his belt, popped open the button fly on his cargo pants, and pushed them down his hips. He rucked up his shirt and smoothed the con-dom down his shaft.

He'd undressed the bare minimum to get serviced while she stood stark naked except for red leather cuffs and her hair, and it didn't feel right. After a moment he pulled his shirt over his head, watched her mouth slacken a little, her gaze soften.

"Turn around." She did, waited again while he looked up and down the length of her back. "Look over your shoulder."

Again, she obeyed, eyelids fluttering when she did. Her shoulder blades jutted like bird wings over the length of her spine, the column of muscle, bone, and flesh broken only by the bright red and silver restraints holding her wrists folded one atop the other at the small of her back. Then he put his hands, tanned dark and work-rough, on her ass and guided her to straddle his hips.

"Keep watching." When she shifted, losing her balance as she focused over her shoulder at the darkly erotic sight of her body spread open for his, he added, "I won't let you fall."

Something in his tone caught her attention, turned her face to his. "Look," he said brusquely, with a firm squeeze to her ass to reinforce the command.

She did as he ordered, strands of hair catching on her damp mouth and cheek as she did.

"Good," he praised, his grip firm on the cradle of her hips. A little nudging, then the jolt of pressure as the tip of his cock pushed into wet heat, demanding entrance. When he was sure she had her balance, feet flat on the floor, poised above him, he gripped her restrained wrists and used the leverage to pull her down.

They both watched the straining shaft disappear into her body, the walls of her pussy tight, pulsing a little as she stretched to accommodate him. Her head tipped back as a low moan drifted from her throat. "Slow," he said. "So slow I feel you ripple around me every time."

His words bound her as effectively as the leather, weaving a spell that wound around her nerves, up her spine, into her brain. She moved as he demanded, rising and falling on his cock, and he could indeed feel the spasms each time she came to rest against his wide-spread thighs. All too quickly the sensation built, tension and need seething in the tip of his cock. He let his head drop back, surrendering to the slick tug and glide of her tight sheath. His heart pounded against his sternum, making him light-headed, so he lifted his head.

Her mouth was right there. He could have kissed her, because her mouth was right fucking there, lips soft and hot and moist, and fuck, he was drowning in the sensation of her, but he wouldn't give in to that need. He clamped one hand on her hip to control her movements and fisted the other in her hair to tip her head back and ravage her throat. She gave a trembling little moan when he tugged on her hair, but she never stopped moving.

In the mirror he watched his hand glide over her ass cheek, into the cleft where he pressed the pad of his middle finger against her pucker. Her cunt gripped him like a fist, and she pulled back to look at him.

"No?" he asked.

She didn't answer with words, instead made a sound that was part laugh, part moan, and all arousal. He pushed firmly, not quite penetrating. She undulated, inside and out, pure yielding flame in his arms. Her motions slowed but gained strength as she leaned forward to work his cock over the bundle of nerves inside her, her hands gripping the opposite forearms with white knuckles.

"Fuck yeah," he said. "Come for me."

Her tight little nipples scraped against his bare chest with each rise and fall of her torso, tightening the hand in her hair. When she gasped and went over in a series of soft, hot shudders he drank in her helpless cry of release. It surged down his spine and straight to his cock, and just like that, he was trembling on the verge, gritting his teeth against shooting off like a teenager. His eyes slitted, he stared at their reflection in the mirror, saw Lauren fiddle with the snap hook, release her hands, and grip the back of the chair.

Feet flat on the floor, she lifted herself almost all the way off and slid back down. Leverage put power into the move, and she thudded against his pelvis, forcing a groan from his throat. He was so hard, granite hard, balls aching, electric tension seething in the tip of his cock, and he couldn't swallow, much less breathe. She did it again, slow and confident and sexy as hell, and he stopped thinking, just watched his hands pull her hair and grip her ass as she rode him, sheathing his cock in sweet, luscious heat. Again. Again.

His hands were fists, his entire body rigid, sweat streaming down his ribs when she leaned forward and whispered, "Come for me, Ty."

Release hit him like a body blow. She gasped when he held her hard against him and ground up into her body, reality disappearing for a few precious seconds into oblivion. All that existed was the rap of his heart in his ribs, the ebbing tide of arousal as his muscles slackened, and Lauren's mouth on his jaw.

Kisses. Slow, soft, sweet kisses, the kind he hadn't felt on his skin in a lifetime. They'd started just under his ear, measured the length of his jaw, each one flicking a little spark at his skin. She reached the corner of his mouth, her breath warm and moist, the temptation of her lush, full lips millimeters away. Without warning anguish slit him open from throat to belly, but feeling that emotion here was worse than feeling the connection that strengthened every time they were together. *No connections.* This was a hookup. Meaningless.

He tilted his head away from her. "You should get off."

The fact that he felt her lips curve against his face only confirmed his suspicion he was going insane. Then she got to her feet. Without looking at her face he lifted a hand to her hip to make sure she was steady, then he got to his feet and headed into the bathroom he'd seen off the hall on the way to the bedroom. He ditched the condom, washed his hands, zipped up. Splashed some water on his face. Searched his brain for a reason to leave.

Realized he didn't need one. Hell-raisers never did. They just walked, but to walk he needed his shirt.

When he came back Lauren had one wrist cuff off and was working on the other. The pink flush on her throat was still visible, but fading quickly, and damn, she was strong. The muscles of her abdomen were defined, like the sexy cover of an exercise magazine. He could watch her all night long.

"Takes all the fun out of it if you can get free on your own," he said, bracing one shoulder against the doorframe.

She flicked him a look through the tangled fall of her hair, her eyes stormy sea gray under languid satisfaction. "You want to go there? Because that involves quite a bit of trust," she said.

Between the implication that this was about anything other than casual sex and his gut response to anything less than complete trust from her, he went rigid for a second. Fortunately, she was fumbling with the stubborn buckle, so she didn't see his involuntary reaction. He had to act like this didn't matter, so he went to her, deftly unfastened the buckle and tugged the loosened leather over her hand. She looked up at him. Still naked, she stood with her back to the windows, and shadows and her hair hid her face. The scent of sex and sweat clung to her tanned skin.

Sometimes the release didn't satisfy the need. Sometimes even the hottest sex only tempered the ache rather than cured it. Each time worked her further under his skin instead of getting her out of his system, and that drove careless words from his mouth. Made it sound like none of this touched him, like he wasn't dreaming about her, watching for her. "Two more weeks, Lauren. We can go wherever you want to go. You want more, you know where to find me."

"I do," she said lightly.

For a split second he thought she meant *more, right now*, maybe *always and forever*, and he had to remind himself he was no longer in the *always and forever* business. Just the *live in the moment* business.

"On the sixth bench from the door," she continued. "I'll keep your offer in mind."

He blinked, shocked by getting out-hell-raisered by a geologist, but that was what he wanted, a woman who didn't want anything, didn't need him, felt nothing, like he did. Being alone was better than letting someone into the mess inside him.

Right?

Right.

Tumultuous emotion roiled inside him. He snagged his shirt from the floor and tugged it on. "See you around, Lauren."

Chapter Seven

Lauren laced up her running shoes with quick jerks, scrambled to her feet, grabbed a plastic bag full of diced hot dog, and hauled the door open. To her utter shock Ty's truck stood in the driveway. He was halfway around the hood, his keys in his hand, when she stepped onto the front porch.

"Ty," she said. "Did you text?" When he paused, clearly shifting gears, she looked at his feet. He wore jeans, a polo, good boots with thick lug soles. Good for walking, and she bet he'd know how to turn a neighborhood upside down. "Never mind. Gretchen ran away again. Help me look for her? Please?"

It was his turn to blink. "Again?"

"If I leave her loose in the backyard she digs her way under the fence. If I attach her collar to her chain, she sits on the deck and ignores me, when she's not looking at me with her big, sad brown eyes. I try to watch her, but if I'm weeding in the garden, sometimes I get lost in what I'm doing, and she gets away."

He looked like he was considering wisecracks about her useless little escape artist dog, but all he said was, "It's a nice night for a walk."

She stood at the end of her driveway and looked around as if seeing the scenery for the first time. It was a beautiful clear fall night, the breeze not cold or strong enough to chill her bare arms. Crickets chirped, and leaves rustled in the trees. At the back of her mind she knew this wasn't why he'd come to see her, but concern for Gretchen trumped everything else.

"Getting dark," he said, and opened the toolbox on his truck and pulled out a big, heavy flashlight.

"I searched the western end of the neighborhood already, Gretchen," she called as she set off down the sidewalk. "Gretchen, come!"

"Does that work?" Ty asked, clearly amused. "Or is it the hot dogs that get her back?"

"She follows commands when she feels like it, and I'm not above bribery. I need to manage her weight, but hot dogs work better than carrots. I tried those the last time she got out of the yard, and got nothing. Mrs. Lacross two streets over found her under her bush. I think it was a hydrangea. Or was it forsythia? I can't remember. Anyway, she got her out from under the bush with two hot dogs. I know a better tactic when I see one, so I adapted. I just have to find her and coax her out."

"And this happens how frequently?"

"She's following her instincts," she said defensively. "Dachshunds were bred in Germany in the 1600s to go after small game— rabbits, foxes, rats—and they'd follow animals into burrows and then fight them to the death, including badgers. *Dachs* is German for *badger*."

"No kidding," he said.

She smiled at the new respect in his voice. Trust a man to find a fight to the death in an enclosed space admirable. "No kidding," she said. "They've been turned into lapdogs, but their instinct is to dig and roam. She's just being who she is. I can't blame her for that."

"You go to a lot of work for one little dog."

They stood by Mr. Minnillo's corner lot. Rosebushes lined the terraced slate slabs leading to his front door, and peonies bowed along the picket fence enclosing the yard. She'd found Gretchen under the peonies a few weeks ago, but not tonight. Lauren let the white, scented blooms droop, straightened, and looked at him. "Did you have pets growing up?"

"Not to speak of," he said. "We had farm dogs and barn cats. But there was always a dog to take fishing or a litter of kittens to tempt a girl into the hayloft."

His voice got lower, slower, the drawl more pronounced when he had that one thing on his mind, and despite her worry, the image of a younger Ty without the dark shadows in his eyes, exploring the edges of his sexuality in a hayloft, sent dusty, summer-hot lust flickering through her. She swallowed, looked away from the answering heat in his heavy-lidded eyes. "We didn't have pets," she said, and the memory firmed her voice. "Not even cats. When you change posts every twelve to eighteen months and the health regulations vary from country to country, keeping anything that lived longer than a hamster wasn't going to fly. I've wanted a dog my whole life. Gretchen isn't perfect, but she's *mine*."

He looked around. "I figured you for a condo downtown in one of those loft buildings, not in an old, established neighborhood," he said. "No kids on bikes, just old folks on porches. You're probably the only single woman around. Why did you buy here?"

"It's fifteen minutes from work, and because it's an old, established neighborhood," she said. "Look around." He scanned the neighborhood over her head, but she got the feeling he'd already taken its measure. "What do you see?"

"I see the opposite of base housing," he said.

She shifted the bag of hot dogs to her other hand. "Exactly," she said simply. "This is what people do when they put down roots. They get a house and a dog. Many of these houses have been owned by the same people for forty years. They raised their children here. Weekends and summer vacations the street is full of grandkids on bikes, high on sugar cookies and getting spoiled rotten. They know how to do things I never learned to do because we moved all the time. Mrs. Leddershin can name all the trees and flowers and bushes and flowering shrubs in all the yards in Galveston. We didn't even grow plants in flower boxes on the bases. When Dad earned offbase housing, Mom flatly refused to deal with the yard, so Dad got one of his aides to mow for us. Problem solved."

"What did your mother do?"

"Raised us, then eventually got a PhD in seventeenth-century English literature. We were in Virginia long enough for her to go ABD—all but dissertation—then write her dissertation from wherever Dad was stationed. She teaches classes online now. What did your mother do?"

"Cotton farmer's wife," he said laconically.

"So she did everything," Lauren said. At his raised eyebrow she said, "My grandmothers on both sides were farmers' wives. Kansas. They remembered growing up during the Depression. You couldn't save enough money or have enough food. They both had big freezers in their basements, and they could talk about meals someone made decades ago. And when they weren't cooking or cleaning or sewing they were helping in the fields. Dad joined the Army because his choices were farm or go into the Army. Mom jokes that she married Dad because he didn't want to farm and swore she'd never have to grow or can or pickle or preserve anything. She never has."

"But now you do."

"We moved ten times in the twelve years I was in school. I wanted roots. I saw my run-down fixer-upper among all these gorgeous yards, and I was sold. After I moved in I knocked on doors, pleaded total ignorance and begged for help, and now I can grow tomatoes and peppers and roses."

Professor Stekel looked up from his front porch swing. "I haven't seen her, Ms. Kincaid," he called.

"Thank you, Professor," she called over Ty's amused huff. "Retired oceanographer. He trains carrier pigeons now."

"And now you have roots," he said, glancing back at the professor, then around the neighborhood again. She remembered the single duffel in his hotel room, the basic toiletries in the bathroom. He could up and disappear from the hotel room, from Galveston, possibly from the face of the earth, in under a minute.

"I do," she said. "Is all your family in Georgia?"

"My mom died a couple of years ago. My dad's still there. My sisters, their husbands and children are still there, growing cotton. The girls were smart, though. They got jobs with benefits." He pulled back low-hanging honeysuckle draped over a white picket fence and peered behind it. "You think she'll be in the bushes?"

"That's where I've found her every time," she said. "Why didn't you go home after you left the Corps?"

"I like the ocean," he said without inflection, then shone the flashlight toward the trellis at the garage end of the Gileses' driveway. The powerful beam picked up a rolling trash can, a recycling bin, and three bags of yard waste.

Lauren groaned and put the back of her hand to her forehead. "I've found her in the bushes every time except the one time she got into the Lucases' garbage. Tomorrow's garbage day."

He followed her to the end of the block, to a house with great bone structure, peeling paint, and a yard bordering on overgrown. "The Lucases are in their eighties, and neither one of them likes the stairs. They just drop the garbage over the porch railing and the guy who runs the route walks back to get it. Every couple of weeks she makes pork chops or leg of lamb, and the bones go in the . . ."

They rounded the corner, Ty's flashlight held cop-style, clasped in his fist at shoulder height, illuminating coffee grounds, tea bags, half-eaten sandwiches, tissues, and clumps of rice smeared with a mixture of mold and cream of mushroom soup strewn in a semicircle at the end of the driveway. A trail of gristle and grease led under the overgrown shrubbery lining the driveway.

"Trash," Lauren finished. "Oh, Gretchen."

They hunkered down by a quivering, rustling bush, Ty using his big body to block the path to the street while Lauren parted the branches. When the beam from the flashlight hit Gretchen she shrank back against the fencing, jaws clamped around a gnawed pork chop. Her tail whipped between her legs. She didn't release the pork chop, but she didn't growl, either. The stench of rotting meat and barbecue sauce made Lauren pull her T-shirt up over her nose.

"What am I going to do with you?" she said into the cotton.

"Careful when you grab her," Ty said as she moved to do just that. "She may be pretty protective of that bone."

Lauren gripped Gretchen's rib cage just behind her forelegs and gently tugged her out onto the driveway. Still crouching by Gretchen she said, "Drop it."

Gretchen released the bone and looked up at her so apologetically Lauren could do nothing but sigh.

"Or maybe not," Ty said.

She picked her up, supporting both hind and forelegs, and held her close. "Holy cats, you stink," she said, keeping her voice singsong and soothing, then turned to Ty. "I need to tell Mrs. Lucas what happened. Would you—"

Before she could finish the sentence Ty shifted the flashlight beam to illuminate the path into the backyard and the stairs to the porch.

The steps shifted under Lauren's weight. With a muffled curse he braced himself against the short edge along the driveway, and the wooden structure stabilized.

"No wonder they don't like the stairs," she said as she knocked on the door, but Ty was already examining the posts.

The porch light flicked on and Mrs. Lucas's lined, cheerful face appeared in the door. "Oh dear," she said when she took in Gretchen, and the state of Lauren's T-shirt.

"Mrs. Lucas, I'm so sorry," Lauren said. "I need to take her home, but I'll come back later and clean up the mess she made."

Ty's voice came from beside and below her. "Ma'am, do you have a shovel in your shed?"

"Mrs. Lucas, meet Ty Hendricks," Lauren said. "He's a friend of mine."

"How kind of you, young man. I believe we do," Mrs. Lucas said.

"You don't have to do that. I can do it," Lauren called over her shoulder.

"Stay there or you'll send that porch crashing to the ground," was all he said. The deck shifted back to the left, then the flashlight beam swerved to the stepping-stones set between the porch and the shed. The door creaked open, and a moment later Ty emerged pulling a plastic trash can on wheels. A shovel handle and several lengths of two-by-four stuck up above the edge of the trash can. Mrs. Lucas produced a clean bag. Lauren held Gretchen with one arm and held open the other side of the bag with the other hand, and in moments the trash was back in a bag. Ty pushed the can against the porch, then wedged the two-by-fours into the soft earth next to the rotting supports.

"That should make the porch a little more stable, ma'am," he said. "You can just drop the bag into the can. Discourage the critters some."

Georgia infused his accent, making Lauren smile as much as she could while holding a wretched, smelly dog. There were times he reverted to the man he used to be, to the man buried under that world-weary, I-don't-give-a-fuck attitude he wore like an exoskeleton.

Mrs. Lucas took a few hesitant steps onto the porch, and her face lit up. "Why, that's much better!"

"It's only temporary," Ty said. "I don't recommend you take those stairs."

"Thank you, Mr. Hendricks," she said formally. "I do appreciate it."

"My pleasure, ma'am."

After Mrs. Lucas went inside, Ty returned the shovel to the shed and secured the door behind him. Lauren waited for him in the middle of the driveway.

"Thank you," she said. "You really didn't have to do that."

"No big deal," he said. "I've cleaned up worse messes."

"Latrine duty?" she guessed.

"Based on the smell, I was thinking of the last time my buddies got trashed at Hooters and puked up beer and wings all over the interior of my truck."

Ouch. She changed the subject. "Mrs. Campbell across the street said her son needed service hours for his church youth group," she said. "Maybe she can talk them into rebuilding the porch as their service project."

Ty considered this as they turned the corner. "They have any building experience?"

"Two summers of service projects on a reservation in the Panhandle," she said. "Their leader worked construction before he became a youth pastor."

He nodded as if it was now his responsibility to make sure the job was done right, but when he caught her looking at him, his expression closed off again.

They strolled back down the street to Lauren's house, Gretchen perfectly content to ride in her arms, her belly hot and silky soft against Lauren's arm. Ty didn't say much, kept his gaze resolutely forward. She glanced over at his face, saw shadows under his eyes as well as in them, and two deep grooves bracketing either side of his mouth before they stepped into the darkness between streetlights again. A wave of recrimination swept through her. He'd clearly needed something other than being drafted into a search for her escape artist dog, but there was no getting around the stench clinging to Gretchen, and by default, to her.

When they climbed the steps to her front door, she kept it light. "This isn't how you planned to spend your evening."

He lifted one shoulder. "Better than a sharp stick in the eye," he said.

"Not by much," Lauren said.

"You've never had a sharp stick in your eye," he said.

"You've got me there. I need to bathe my dog, and myself, but you're welcome to come in and wait."

A quick shake of his head. "You have an early day tomorrow," he said.

"Meetings with an alternate energy business partner," she said . "How did you know?"

"Your car's been in the parking garage at six every day this week."

Her eyes widened, and she halted in the act of digging in her pocket for her keys. "Have you been keeping an eye on me?"

It was the wrong thing to say, because he stepped back again, just outside the glow of her porch light. "I'm keeping an eye on everything that goes on in that business park," he said, widening the distance between them physically and emotionally.

"Right," she said. "Come back anytime, Ty," she said softly.

He looked at Gretchen, still snuggled in her arms, and for a moment even the darkness couldn't hide the ache seething under his skin. She waited, holding her breath, knowing she couldn't cajole him across the threshold into her home and have it mean anything at all, but all he said was, "I'm glad you got your dog back."

Then he left.

Ty dug his keys out of his pocket and climbed into his truck. Lauren and the ridiculous little trash-smeared sausage dog watched from the front porch as he turned over the engine and backed out into the street. In the rearview mirror he saw the front door close and the porch light flick off. He felt a disquieting blend of relief for having escaped before he gave anything else away, and disappointment. He'd wanted a woman, wanted *her*. And he hadn't had her. He'd have felt awkward waiting around while she gave Gretchen a bath, like she'd take care of the dog, then take care of him. The alternative, helping her bathe the dog like they were a couple laughing in a commercial, would have felt worse.

Neither option worked when his mission in life was to avoid feeling at all.

Coming over unannounced was a mistake. In the months he'd been working on the rigs, he'd made a point of not seeking out a woman for anything more than sex, and not seeking out the same woman during his next shore leave. The single night in his hotel should have been enough, but seeing her at the business park, not in a bar or in his bed, changed the game, made her real, unique, and against his better judgment, interesting.

He stopped for a red light and worked his shoulders to pop the kink in his neck. He didn't want to know anything more about Lauren than where, when, and what turned her on, made her shudder and strain under him. Even seeing her as a professional in her tailored dresses and colorful accessories crossed that line between casual hookup and woman with feelings. When he could see her as a woman who wanted sex, nothing more, which was how he'd seen her in the Gulf Independent parking lot, he was fine. But then she joined him on the bench, invited him over because she was curious. And then, like an idiot, he went to her house and had sex with her again. Saw her home, her dog, the calm, knowing look in her eyes before he sought oblivion in her body.

Every time he saw her he got what he wanted, and more than he bargained for in new facets of Lauren. There was the petroleum geologist, logging the well. There was the sexy woman in her slip of a dress, naked underneath, explosive chemistry. There was the homeowner. Now there was a caring, devoted dog owner, a woman who didn't give up because things were hard.

Bad news for him.

The stomach-turning stench and mess on the driveway would have sent most women into hysterics, or at least unleash a steady stream of bitching and griping. Lauren didn't flinch. That dog was hers, and if she had to get greasy, rotten meat on her hands to take care of Gretchen, she would. And she'd take care of the Lucases, too. He knew exactly how Lauren's night would play out. Bath for Gretchen, shower for herself, and then, with her hair loose and damp over her shoulders, dressed in the T-shirt that was as soft as her skin and the tight cotton shorts, she'd pick up her phone and call the neighbor with the son who needed service hours. She'd gently suggest the son approach his church youth group about building a simple porch. It wouldn't take long. A group of teenagers and a capable supervisor could do it in an afternoon, no problem. The neighborhood would be a slightly better place because Lauren lived there, cared, got involved. He used to do the same kind of thing.

This was getting worse, not better. She knew he'd gone over for a booty call; she was too smart not to know that. Instead of getting offended and telling him to fuck off, she enlisted him in a search for the dog, and instead of walking away, he helped. Idiot that he was, he helped look for the damn dog, and went above and beyond to stabilize the porch. She was pulling him back into the world he wanted to ignore, making him feel all the things that he didn't want to feel.

He pulled into the parking lot of his hotel, cut the engine, and took the stairs to his room. Once inside he let the door close behind him, but just stood there, hands on hips, surveying the room. Even the light muted by the crooked lampshade didn't hide the circular stain under the window, the scratched veneer on the dresser, the television secured to the wall with a cable, or the cigarette burns on the counter in the bathroom, but this was enough. He didn't need anything more than fast food, a cheap place to sleep, whiskey, and sex. He didn't need a house, or a dog, or a partnership with John, reminding him of who he used to be. He especially didn't need a woman like Lauren liking him, beginning to depend on him, thinking about him as anything other than a great lay.

He tossed his keys on the tiny table. The momentum carried the keys to the floor between the chair and the dresser. "Fuck," he muttered, but let them lie there as he twisted the cap off the bottle of Jim Beam and poured two inches of liquid into a thin paper cup. This should have been simple. Most guys seemed to alienate women with very little effort. A forgotten date, a missed birthday, the suggestion that *Yes, your ass does look fat in those jeans* and they were out. The divorce rate in the military was around 80 percent, and the breakup rate before the marriage happened even higher. Most posts had a wall of shame plastered with pictures of girls back home too weak to last the deployment.

Thinking of deployments brought Sean to mind. As far as he knew, Sean didn't have a girlfriend waiting for him, or maybe there was a girl, but it ended early in the deployment? Either way it was over. He could do something for him, something memorable. Take him to a strip club, get him drunk, get him laid. Women were easy to find, easy to fuck.

But while Lauren had practically fallen in his lap, she wasn't easy to categorize. The sex . . . He couldn't just close his eyes and get lost in the sensation until the itch was scratched. He'd been thinking, aware, into it on so many levels, and the aftermath genuinely sucked. She wasn't forgettable. The way he missed her when he walked away, when his shift didn't coincide with her lunch hour. He didn't want to miss her. He didn't want to feel anything for her other than the overwhelming desire to roll her onto her back and fuck her until her legs wound tight around his hips, until she was utterly helpless under him.

So he'd gotten in his truck with the intention of making it as clear as possible that he saw her as a sex partner, nothing else. Giving her a good reason to dismiss him, ignore him, avoid him. Thanks to the most useless, troublesome dog he'd ever know, the plan backfired.

Sure. Blame the dog.

He swallowed the rest of the whiskey, refilled the cup, and thought about the two people he spent the most time with these days. Sean, too reserved to hit the bar scene and find a girl for the night, and Lauren, with her storm-blue, all-seeing eyes, the bold, twenty-first-century woman so thoroughly engaged with her life.

He could do this. He could make her walk away. She was a woman, emotional, getting attached, half blind because she kept seeing a man who didn't exist anymore, and she was curious. That was the key, her stubborn curiosity. The next time they met on the bench, he'd turn that inquisitive curiosity against her, so she'd get gone and leave him alone. He looked around the room, at the jeans and T-shirts stuffed haphazardly in his duffel, at the travel toiletries in the bathroom, at the bottle of whiskey, and in that moment, he knew how to make her walk.

Chapter Eight

Lauren knew an hour-long search for Gretchen hadn't satisfied whatever need, physical or emotional, that drove Ty to her house. He'd come looking for her, for whatever reason he admitted to himself, and ended up elbow deep in garbage while he looked for her dog. She couldn't have come up with a better way to rub his nose in what he went to great lengths to avoid.

But he'd pay a price for a need suppressed. Ty was edgy, restless, and his hold on the facade he used like a shield was fragile and easy to disrupt. His pain was so vivid to her, shifting under the surface of his skin in waves of anguish and shock, and the emotions only grew with each encounter. Sex seemed to provide a release he could accept, but he hadn't gotten sex the last time he saw her. He'd gotten Gretchen, and a neighborhood, and an elderly couple with a rickety, rotted porch.

Yet he'd agreed to help a woman in distress, and she couldn't help but think that was the real Ty under the sharp, spiny attitude he so frequently projected. A walking, talking contradiction.

Something was going to blow. Soon.

These thoughts occupied her mind while she sat in interminable meetings for the second straight week, this time with a different prospective business partner. The conference room windows looked out over the lake, and during dull spots in the week of strategic planning meetings she'd watched the surveillance operation taking place on the business park's campus. At least three men were involved, including Ty, and they seemed to rotate shifts and spots but always watched the main exits and entrances between about seven a.m. and five p.m. It was likely that they arrived based on when their targets left home, and left when the person or people they were watching left. The duration of Ty's stay was unpredictable, a tactic that made sense. Sometimes he stayed for an hour, and if he arrived earlier in the day he stayed longer, opening a laptop to make it look like he was working outside in the sun and breeze. Maybe regular meetings with a woman who worked at the business park would help with his cover.

Today the senior executives were at an off-site team-building exercise with the leaders of the newly acquired company, and Ty was on the bench at lunchtime. He lifted the ball cap, smoothed back his long blond hair, and something about his solitary position, the slant of his shoulders tilted her heart. She collected her sunglasses, phone, and lunch. "I'm going to lunch," she called to Danelle.

"So early?"

It was odd. She usually ate around one, but there was no telling if Ty would be sitting outside at one. "I want to sit outside before it gets too hot."

She hurried down to the nearly empty cafeteria and bought two bottles of water from the lone cashier. The smell of tuna casserole hung in the air as she walked through the seating area and out to the lake. When the door opened Ty looked up from the folder open on the seat beside him. He had one elbow propped on the back of the bench, fingers tapping a rhythm against the middle slat.

The fingers stopped midtap when she walked down the path. His face, what she could see of it, was expressionless, but after a moment he shuffled the papers together and closed the folder, making room for her. She held out the bottle of water and when he took it, sat down, crossed her legs at the ankle, and tucked them under the bench.

"Hey," she said as she unzipped the cooler.

He got out his phone. Thanks.

"It's hot out today." A hint of a smile, no more, as she opened her Tupperware container filled with leftover Chinese. She got a forkful of rice into her mouth without spilling it on her dress and chewed while she considered her next move. "How's the operation going?"

Can't talk about it.

"What happens when you go back out on a rig? Someone else steps in for you?"

He nodded.

"Does that disrupt the team's cohesiveness?" At his lifted eyebrow, she added, "Daughter of career Army intelligence officer, remember? It matters. People aren't interchangeable engine parts. Teams develop a rhythm together."

Another moment when he just looked at her, then down at his phone.

A text appeared on hers. They make it work. Why do you care?

She filled in the rest of that sentence in her head . . . *when I so clearly don't want you to care about anything related to me.* "I'm curious," she said quietly. "About you."

I told you not to be.

"My dad will tell you I'm not very good at following orders," she said. That got her an arched brow, but nothing else. She ate another bite of rice. "Once I figured out dating troublemakers got under his skin, that was the only kind I liked. Dad says it wasn't age but my teens that turned him gray. In college he was stationed in Virginia, so I had a steady stream of NCOs and junior commissioned officers escorting me to sorority functions." She finished a mouthful and added, "You probably already know this, but if you want to turn a sorority upside down, bring a man in uniform to a function."

That got a laugh. A real laugh, and she wasn't sure who was more surprised by the rough, rusty sound, him or her. Then his attention turned inward, and he spoke quietly. "Nothing. I'm going quiet for a couple of minutes."

He pushed a button on his cell phone, looked at her with those dark, dangerous eyes, and spoke. "My partner can't hear us now."

She made a vague gesture near her ear. "You running all that through your cell phones?"

"With a few upgrades," he said ambiguously. "Not worried about what happens to curious cats?"

"I think that phrase is more about alliteration than truth. My roommate in college had a cat that was fascinated by candles. She'd burn her whiskers, but she never died from investigating the flame. I'd rather get burned living my life than calcify living someone else's," she said.

She snapped the lid back on the empty container and reflected on him, their almost-conversations, the way he melted in bed with her only to harden right back up afterward. A classic wounded warrior. She knew that type, watched women wait for the man they loved to physically come home from the war, then mentally. Most did, eventually. Some of them never made it, living in a hellish stasis between who they'd been and who they were. She didn't want Ty to disappear into that run-down hotel room, to keep turning his back on life, on who he was and what he could be. He had to be about her age, thirty or a little older. Too young to have those grooves carved on either side of his mouth, too young for those dark, weary eyes, too young for all work and no play.

Too young, too smart, too full of potential to give up on, as much as he wanted the rest of the world to do exactly that.

When he spoke next it was with a studied casualness that set her radar quivering, and she steeled herself for whatever might come next. "I've been meaning to ask you . . . how about helping out a friend of mine?"

"Sure," she said, secretly pleased he'd asked. "With what?"

"Sean's just back from Afghanistan, and I mean just back. As in his leave started a couple of days ago. He's kind of an academic type. Very smart. Very focused. Not easily distracted. And not the kind of guy to pick up a girl in a bar for a one-night stand. So . . ."

The words hung in the air, and between his studiously cocky body language and the brazen insinuation, Lauren almost laughed. "Are you suggesting I fuck your friend to get him back in the saddle after his deployment?"

Ty's mirrored sunglasses never wavered from her face, but the lines around his mouth deepened, and she wondered if he had any idea at all how much he gave away. "Yeah. That's what I'm asking."

"Not much to be curious about there. We already know I'll fuck near-strangers," she said blandly, and based on the way his jaw dropped she'd actually managed to shock the world-weary Ty. "What's in it for me? Where's the uncharted territory?"

All the muscles in his face went still, and she didn't need to see his eyes to feel the intense focus on her. Did he think she'd run screaming in horror? When he didn't say anything, she added, "I'll do it. Or him, as the case may be, but on one condition."

"Which is?"

"You have to be there, too. You, me, and Sean." She stowed the container in her lunch box. Sure, she'd gone there in her dreams, but she never would have considered living out this fantasy. With Ty, it was easy to cross that line and meld dreams with the reality of him. "I've always wanted to try a ménage. A guy in his situation deserves a night to remember."

"Wait a second, that's not—"

She cut off his backpedaling. "This happens with you, or it doesn't happen at all. And I want to meet him first. Somewhere neutral." She pulled out her treat, peanut butter chocolate chip cookies. "Want one?"

He looked at the cookies, then at her.

"I brought extra, for you," she said, holding out the plastic bag.

With an air of *Why the fuck not* he took one, ate it. "You make those? They're good."

"I did," she said. "Peanut Butter Sensations. My grandmother's recipe. Have another one."

He did, sitting forward, elbows on knees as he ate. The traffic around the lake picked up as noon grew closer. The silence had stretched on long enough for him to look at her. She didn't need special equipment to measure and sell the play between them. It was off the charts. And if the dark passion between them was all he'd let himself feel, then she'd work with it.

"Why do I have to be there?" he asked.

"I'll answer that if you tell me why you're working on the rigs," she said, and brushed the cookie crumbs to the birds.

"Great pay," he said without hesitation.

"In security work contracts routinely run hundreds of thousands of dollars and that's just the retainer to secure the company's services," she said mildly. "You don't need to be a roughneck to make very good money."

He shook his head, but he didn't offer another explanation for working as a roughneck.

"Come on, Ty," she said. "Be curious. Don't you want to know what it would be like?"

He turned to face her. "I know what it's like," he said, and the rough bite to his voice sent a jagged electric shock straight to her clit.

"Well then," she said. "I guess you'll be in charge."

A clear indicator of her trust in him, if he recognized it for what it was. Heat rose up his throat and into his cheeks, but he looked down at the blacktop path for a long time before he spoke. "Let's go dancing Saturday night."

"You dance?" she asked with a little laugh.

"Yeah, I dance."

Curiouser and curiouser. "Where?"

"No Limits. You know it?"

No Limits was the city's hottest dance club and bar. Dress code was suggestive. Dance moves were provocative. Hookups were expected. She'd have to dig through her closet for something suitable. "I know it."

"Nine Saturday." He cut her a look. "I'll bring Sean."

If this was the only way he'd relate to her, she'd go with it. After all, she was curious, and she trusted Ty. "Then I'll be there."

Somewhere along the line in the past two weeks, Ty had lost control of his life. In a contest of who could be more casual about sex he was getting one-upped by a petroleum geologist, and the results were driving him out of his fucking mind. She didn't play by the rules of standard relationships. According to those rules, when he was a rude, insensitive, arrogant asshole who wanted to share her with his friend, she ditched him in a huff. Maybe he'd even get slapped. Southern women still slapped men. It was practically guaranteed in state constitutions. He'd seen it happen in bars.

She wasn't supposed to call his hand and tell him it was a three-some or nothing at all. He could have said no, walked away. He still could. Introduce Lauren to Sean, get them interested in each other, and bail. Except acid rose in Ty's throat at the thought of Sean with Lauren, exploring that lean, graceful body. He didn't want to need Lauren, but he didn't want anyone else to need her, either.

In the end, he wouldn't back down. So here he was at No Limits, drinking and dancing hard enough for the background noise of wailing children to nearly fade from his mind. Then he saw Sean shoulder his way through the crowd to the bar, and it all came back. He countered the flood of memories by gripping Lauren's hips and turned her, back to his front, and nodded Sean's direction. "That's him."

Without breaking rhythm to the dance music Lauren looked at Sean. From his position behind her, his cheek against hers, one hand splayed on her belly and the other just under her breasts, Ty could see her gaze skim the crowd, felt her body pause momentarily when she found the other man. "Tall, blond hair, wearing the dark green button-down?" At his nod she eased back into the dance, swiveling her hips against his erection. "That's not an academic type," she said with a laugh.

"He's a Naval Academy graduate and a Rhodes Scholar," Ty said. The slow, thumping beat merged with his heartbeat, and he could feel the blood moving through his veins. Both hands lifted to link behind his neck, giving him access to her body and a clear view down her shirt, unbuttoned to the clasp of her bra. Her hips grinding slowly against his cock and the sheen of sweat on her breasts stole his ability to form words.

"*Smart* doesn't always equal *geeky academic*. Either way, he's really late," Lauren said. "I was starting to worry."

Sean was actually ten minutes early. Ty told him to meet them at ten, because maybe she'd have come to her senses between now and then. He'd wanted to give her an out. The desire to have an hour with Lauren by himself, her body rubbing against his, her hair sliding loose over his arms as they danced, was just a side effect. Now that was over. He took her hand to lead her from the dance floor, but she tilted her head in the direction of the restrooms. "Give me a minute?"

He made his way to the bar, exchanged the all-purpose *Hey* with Sean, and ordered a shot of whiskey. Sean had some kind of fancy beer in a bottle in front of him. He studied the crowd intently, as if searching for someone, then relaxed.

"Where's your girlfriend?" he asked.

He'd better make things clear before Lauren joined them. "She's in the head, and Lauren's not my girlfriend."

Sean paused in the act of lifting the bottle to his mouth and cut him a glance. Some guys joined the Corps to stay out of jail, get out of a nowhere town, or because they had no other options. That was John. He'd come from less than nothing, wanted to use the Corps to leverage himself up and out of poverty. Some longed for the days of gladiators and knights, when the study of war was an all-consuming, legitimate calling for a man. That was Sean, disciplined and intense, a straight-up warrior in thought, word, and deed.

"Okay, how'd you meet this woman who's not your girlfriend?"

Ty snapped out of his useless introspection. "She's a geologist. She logged the well we drilled on my last shift. We hooked up."

Not true. Something about you made that smart, clear-eyed, sexy woman pick you out, keeps her coming back for more, and she won't tell you what it is. He signaled the bartender for another shot, and added, "She's real curious," tarnishing a simple statement with cynicism to keep the protective instincts at bay. The point of this was to teach her a lesson about trusting him.

"About what?"

"Lots of things, but tonight she's curious about being with two guys at the same time." No point in telling Sean he'd baited her into it.

Sean's eyes widened. "No shit?"

"No shit. That's her." He tossed back the shot, felt the burn but no glow.

Sean watched Lauren make her way through the crowd toward them. Her hair, loose around her shoulders and upper arms, glinted silver and brown under the lights, and the crisp white sleeveless blouse clung to her skin.

"You, me, and her." It wasn't a question, but Ty nodded anyway. "What happens?"

"That's on me. Nonnegotiable rule is that nothing happens that she doesn't want." Sean raised a brow, as in *No shit, Sherlock*, so Ty added, "You up for it?"

An uncharacteristic bitterness twisted Sean's mouth. A part of Ty's mind he thought he'd eradicated warred between thinking this was a bad idea for Sean, and thinking it was exactly what he needed when Sean said, "Why the fuck not?" more to himself than to Ty. "Has she done this before?"

Good question, one he would have asked in another lifetime. Ty shrugged, as if the thought of Lauren with not one but two other men didn't ache like newly formed scar tissue. "None of my business."

"Have you done this before?"

The jaded feeling swamped him again. "Jesus. You're a lieutenant, not my mother."

Sean looked at Ty's empty glass, then at the cluster of glasses on the bar by his elbow. "If this is on you, you might want to ease up on the shots."

Lauren's breathless, smiling arrival saved him from a suitably obscenity-laden response, and if he didn't order another whiskey, it was because he had to introduce Lauren to the man she was going to fuck later. Lauren shook Sean's hand, her considering look nicely masked by the smile. She got the bartender's attention and asked for water. "You want one?" she said to Ty.

"Yeah," he said, and drank it when it came. Then signaled for another glass.

"How do you know Ty?" Lauren asked Sean. Her skin gleamed with sweat, and her eyes were bright, shining with a patina of dancing and alcohol. She was smart to choose water.

"We served together," he said. "Ty was the guy who held everyone together. Personal problems, girl problems, grudges, whatever. He was magic with the friendlies, too. We'd go through the same villages again and again, trying to form relationships, strengthen ties while we were on patrol, and Ty was the guy who learned Farsi so he could make conversation. I remember this one time—"

Sean had been very careful to deemphasize his officer rank and present Ty in the best possible light, but the sludge inside him crawled up his throat. "Knock it off," he broke in. "She's already sleeping with me, and playing nice with the locals has a low CDI factor," he said, then tried to distract her by wrapping his arm around her shoulders to pull her in for a kiss. She bit his lip hard enough to make him yelp, then gave him an insincere smile.

Sean froze with his beer halfway to his mouth as he watched this. Lauren turned to him and said, "I grew up on Army bases, so I know what CDI means. Chicks Dig It. The average male thinks things that go boom have a higher CDI than the hard work of diplomacy."

He gave Ty a glance that said *You are so in over your head.* "You don't seem like the type to go for that."

"I'm not, and he knows it. Since you mentioned it, I noticed the same thing on the rig. The other workers looked to him for advice or just a shoulder, but it makes him really uncomfortable when you bring up what he used to be," she said to Sean in a tone so mildly amused it took Ty a second to realize that she'd just stripped away the illusion that he was hiding anything from her. "Let's dance instead."

She took Ty's hand, but he stayed put. "Kiss that and make it better, first," he said, tapping his lower lip with his index finger.

"Does it hurt?" she asked, a hint of *poor Ty* in her voice.

"Yeah." Everything hurt, especially watching Lauren and knowing he couldn't risk what she had to offer. Standing in a club full of people who were drinking and dancing their pain away, maybe fucking it away later with a stranger. Grief and despair were everywhere, covered with the thinnest veneer of life.

"We're even, then," she said, too low for Sean to hear as she leaned in and flicked her tongue against the edge of his lip. Another slow swipe, then she gently kissed the throbbing spot. Fingers woven with hers, he bent her arm behind her and pressed their clasped hands against her tailbone, pulling her against him for a hot, slow kiss.

It wasn't an apology, and he knew it.

Sean watched, color high on his cheekbones, not looking away. Lauren broke the kiss, turned to Sean, and tipped her head toward the dance floor. "Shall we?"

Sean looked around once more, and a memory bloomed in Ty's brain, something about a girl who liked to dance, but Sean just drained his beer and followed them to the dance floor. His hand clasped with Lauren's, Ty broke a path through the crowd, Sean brought up the rear, and somewhere along the way, his fingers had linked with Lauren's, too. The DJ spun up Sheena Easton's "Love Bizarre," and the rhythmic beat thumped through Ty's feet and into his chest. He let it pound rational thought in the background and bring the sheer animal lust front and center in his brain. The dance floor was packed with people dancing together, dancing alone, dancing in packs. This was No Limits. The wilder, the dirtier, the more blatantly sexual the better. Ty saw a man hike up his partner's short skirt to grab her ass, exposing the red thong she wore as he pulled her hard against his thigh. Another woman had her hand down the front of her girlfriend's black leather shorts, attracting attention from several guys in the vicinity.

Might as well set the mood now. Ty turned Lauren to face Sean, and within a few bars of music they'd found space for hands and legs. She put one hand on his shoulder and the other on his hip, fingers flexing to bring herself in close. Ty watched arousal flare in Sean's eyes as he got into the swing of things and shifted Lauren so one thigh slipped between hers, his hand at the small of her back to hold her steady, even though Lauren was tall enough to fit perfectly between them. Maybe there was more to Sean than Ty knew.

Ty slid his arms under Lauren's and flattened his palms on her rib cage, just below the swell of her breasts, aligning his body with hers from chest to hip, and in seconds the three of them grooved to the beat, hips and shoulders shifting and swiveling, as synchronized as a parade ground drill, and a hell of a lot hotter. The position brought his abdomen in close contact with Sean's hand at the base of Lauren's spine. He could feel Sean's fingers flexing and shifting with Lauren's movements, watched Sean's mouth soften, the hair at his temples grow damp with sweat.

Moving with the beat, Lauren lifted her arms and broke the hold, then turned to face Ty. A bolt of lust shot down his spine and into his balls at the languid heat in her eyes. Her hair clung to her cheeks and neck; without thinking, he slid his fingertips over her hot face, gathering the hair and gripping it in one fist at her nape before he kissed her, hard and hot and deep. With his other hand he gripped her ass and pulled her tight against him. Her arms looped around his neck, and her pussy snugged up against his thigh. Without hesitation Sean stepped into her back, pushing Lauren firmly against Ty. Sean's hip joint shifted and worked against Ty's hand on Lauren's ass as they swiveled in time to the beat.

Right now everything was making him hot. Everything. The music, the way Sean's presence was slowly turning Lauren inside out, her rhythmic, uninhibited grind against him.

Sean's hands moved up Lauren's rib cage, not stopping until they cupped her breasts. Lauren's mouth opened on a sigh Ty felt against his jaw. Sean leaned in, murmured something in her ear.

"Very okay," Lauren said with a low, sexy laugh. Ty kissed her again, felt the aroused resilience of her lips, the languid wet heat of her mouth when his tongue swept inside. Her pussy would feel just as hot and sweet around his cock.

Ty unfisted the hand at Lauren's nape, gripped the base of her skull, and used his thumb to tip her head. "You like him?" he asked.

She peered at him, hot desire in her eyes and a delighted little smile on her face, and nodded.

"Want to fuck him?"

Maybe Sean heard him, maybe he didn't. Either way his hands worked over Lauren's breasts, fingers stroking her nipples. A shudder rippled through Lauren.

She nodded again, then lifted her mouth to his ear. "And you."

Sean's gaze met his over the top of Lauren's head.

"Let's go," Ty said.

Chapter Nine

They'd all driven separately and met at No Limits. When they left Ty walked not to his truck but to her car with her while Sean headed for a gleaming Mustang. One member of the bar's security staff, a sharp-eyed, off-duty Galveston cop, threw them a quick, assessing glance, a visual sobriety check honed by years of experience, then watched Sean's car pull in behind hers before returning to a conversation with a group of women waiting behind the velvet rope.

"What about your truck?" she asked Ty as he slid into the passenger seat of her car.

"I'll get it later."

The drive to her house took only fifteen minutes on nearly empty streets, the lights from Sean's car steady in her rearview mirror. Time should have tempered the lust-saturated mood. But when Ty worked his palm under her skirt, then wriggled an index finger under her thong to gently stroke her clit, Lauren swallowed hard.

"I can't focus when you do that," she said.

One corner of his mouth lifted briefly, accenting the deep grooves carved into his face. "I'm in charge, right?"

A moment's consideration was all she needed. She trusted Ty, felt the feedback loop humming between them strengthen with every action, every word spoken or unspoken. She didn't need to tell him that condoms were mandatory and if she said stop, it stopped. "Yes."

She pulled into her garage and killed the engine. He wasn't smiling, his gaze dark and heated with a purely masculine admiration. His damp hair grazed his cheekbones, and the faint scent of sweat rose with the heat simmering off his big body.

She had no idea what was coming. She'd assessed risks and rewards, wondered what it would be like, fantasized about it. But reality was here, in the form of not one but two Marines, and the one sitting in her car, radiating sex and masculinity, didn't seem to be playing at all. Without hesitation he'd accepted the role as the man in charge, reinforcing Lauren's growing confidence that he was falling back on his core character.

Sean's car pulled into the driveway, and the engine shut off. Lauren opened her door and slid out, then crossed the garage to the door leading into her kitchen. She cut Sean a glance. He moved with an easy grace as he got out of his car and braced either arm on the car's roof and driver's door, and a hot little flutter flared low in her belly.

Sexual attraction, however potent, didn't outweigh common sense. "Up to date on your physicals, Sean?" she asked, clear and calm.

He met her gaze without blinking. "Yes, ma'am," he said.

"Anything I need to know about before we go any further?"

"No, ma'am."

Honor and integrity radiated from the other man, confirming Lauren's belief that Ty's personnel skills were wasted on the rigs.

She looked at Ty and nodded. One corner of his beautiful mouth curled up in amused respect. "Go inside, get your dog settled."

Gretchen greeted her at the door, tail whipping back and forth, paw lifted in anticipation. Lauren let her out the sliding doors into the yard, kept a close eye on her as she sniffed bushes and explored the vegetable garden for rabbits. Sean wasn't here to round up her escape artist dog. When she bounded up to the door, Lauren coaxed her into the laundry room, gave her a treat, and closed the door on the bewildered brown eyes.

Just outside the door to the garage Ty murmured to Sean in a low tone. His drawl slid like hot honey along her nerves. The interior of her house was cool, dark, and silent, the furniture shadowy shapes under the moonlight streaming through the big windows lining the backyard. She felt like a stranger in her own home, listening to Sean's softer, brisker tones ask a question, then give assent.

Ty was running this show. Sean would follow his instructions. She'd obey them both.

The garage door began to lumber closed. She dropped her keys and ID on the counter and walked down the hallway to her bedroom. Dark floors, braided rugs, the chenille spread covering both bed and pillows, and moonlight draped in swaths over bed, floor. She tugged the sheer curtains closed, muting the moonlight but giving her a measure of privacy.

At the sound of boots on hardwood Gretchen's disappointed whines cut off, and Lauren heard her scamper for the safety of her bed in the laundry room. Lauren turned to face the doorway, her heart pounding in her throat. The two men filled it, Ty taller and broader through the shoulders, Sean with hair the color of moonlight, his deceptively lean body masking potent strength. Despite the difference in size, he was as strong as Ty, and as they both moved into her bedroom, Ty hanging back while Sean continued toward her, she went still. They'd divided her attention, and she looked from Sean to Ty and back again before Sean wrapped his long fingers around her upper arm and guided her away from the window, toward the bare wall. A very primitive tension heated the cool air around their bodies, and she felt very keenly the thin cotton of her blouse, the thong she wore under her skirt, the fact that she was barefoot to their boots, the fact that they both outweighed her by sixty pounds or more. Then she was no longer thinking, just observing like prey in the wild, and her heart tripped into double time as sensations registered.

"Hold her," Ty said, his voice low, even, and crisp in her soft, feminine bedroom.

She recognized the voice, brusque, commanding, ensuring there would be no doubt or hesitation. It took all responsibility on the speaker.

In one smooth move Sean wove his right arm between her shoulder blades and her upper arms, gripped her left upper arm with his right hand, and backed into the wall. The action restrained her hands and arms, pinned her tight against his body, and left her breathless as she looked up into Ty's face. She arched away from Sean, writhed to test his strength, his resolve.

He didn't flinch. He gripped her arm harder, pulled her shoulders farther back and at the same time crossed his other arm over her collarbone, effectively controlling her movements and arching her breasts toward Ty.

Dark brown eyes met hers, then flicked over her parted lips. Her nipples thrust against her top as Ty considered the vulnerable front length of her body. She was tall enough that the balls of both feet were still on the floor, but barely. Sean was securely braced, his rubber-soled, sturdy Doc Martens gripping her floor and keeping her off balance. Her breasts rose and fell rapidly. Sean exerted little effort to hold her, his breathing even, if a bit shallow. Like the dancing earlier, movement felt good. The shift and press against a harder male body felt good.

The inability to break free felt even better.

Ty's gaze focused on the gap in her sleeveless blouse as he reached for the buttons and slipped them through the buttonholes. She'd half expected him to rip it open, but as the seconds passed the deft, negligent touch of his rough fingers sank into her consciousness. She wasn't going anywhere. He didn't have to be rough to do exactly as he pleased for as long as he pleased.

He parted the white cotton, draping it over her shoulders, exposing her torso from throat to the waistband of her skirt. He slid one rough fingertip along her bra strap, then tugged it down, his face a study in concentration as he repeated the maneuver with the other strap. Her silk bra cups snagged on her nipples before he arranged the fabric under her breasts, lifting them. Her nipples were taut, dark pink, more exposed than if she were naked.

Their breathing wasn't synchronized. Her own inhales were sharp gasps for air as her rational mind battled her reptilian brain's response to Ty and Sean. Strong and solid behind her, Sean breathed a little rapidly, but steadily. Ty was breathing slowly and deeply. Only his pulse, visible at the base of his neck, and the thick thrust of his cock in his pants gave any indication the circumstances affected him.

Then he flicked a whip-strike glance at her. Heat wicked through her at the intent arousal in his dark eyes, and a hint of something else. She undulated in Sean's grip, felt him adjust his stance and tighten his grip.

A faint smile lifted the corner of Ty's mouth, then he stepped forward and cupped her breasts in his hands to stroke his thumbs over her nipples. For a moment she remained stiff and resisting, then heat spread along her skin, softening her spine, making her eyelids droop. Her head lolled back against Sean's broad shoulder, and she breathed deep to arch her breasts into Ty's hands. In response he pinched the nipples, rolling them between thumb and forefinger until her jaw relaxed, her lips parted, and a soft, helpless little sound drifted into the room.

"Damn," Sean said.

She felt the word, heard the aroused tone as he shifted his weight to press his cock against her ass. Already so hot. Going to get hotter, she thought as Ty's fingers sent electric shocks coursing along her nerves, to her clit. He stepped into her body, pressed his erection against her mound. The movement re-created the scene on the dance floor, and she shuddered at the pressure. She tipped her head from side to side as need expanded in her pussy.

When the purposeful press and release stopped and his hands lifted, her nipples throbbed in the cool air. She opened her eyes to find Ty watching her, his expression darkly aroused. Then he pulled his shirt over his head and dropped it on the floor, and her mouth went dry. The cool, angular moonlight added an air of menace to his heavily muscled shoulders and abdomen. He pulled a condom from his pocket, then put his hands to his belt. She blinked rapidly, watched him release the buckle and fly, shove his cargo pants and shorts low on his hips, and roll the condom down his shaft. Then he closed the distance between them.

Both hands landed just above her knees, and his palms began a slow, purposeful ascent, gathering her skirt as they went. Deft fingers wound into the thin elastic strips at her hips and tugged. Fabric gave way without a protest, and the silk dropped to the floor beside them. Then Ty slid his forearms under her thighs, lifting her feet right off the floor as he gripped her ass in his palms. She gasped, the sound high-pitched, startled, and very, very aroused as her legs spread, leaving her open to him. A hitch in Sean's breathing registered at her back as Ty aligned the head of his cock with her wet, swollen folds and pressed inside.

Her pussy spasmed as his thick shaft stretched her soft channel. Her head lolled back against Sean's shoulder, and her eyes closed as she dropped through conscious thought, into pure, molten sensation. Ty took possession of her body in one slow, hot thrust. The pressure of his pelvic bone against her clit sent another high-pitched sound into the air. A growl rumbled in the muscled chest behind her, and Ty gave a rough little laugh in response.

"We're just getting started," he said. The words could have been meant for her, or for Sean, or for the room in general, but he moved. He gripped her ass, leaned his naked chest against her breasts, and pulled out. The drag of the head of his cock along millions of awakened, desperate nerve endings made her cunt ripple around him, spurring another laugh.

"This is gonna be good," he said. "So good."

He fucked her, slow and steady, the rhythm far more important than intensity. Sean's rough cheek snagged in her hair and scraped her ear as he looked over her slight curves and watched his friend fuck her. Ty's cock gleamed with her juices as he slid in and out, and the angle and weight of her body ensuring perfect pressure on her G-spot.

"He's watching me fuck you. Feeling it," Ty added. Each thrust bumped and ground the length of her back, ass to shoulder blades against Sean's torso. At the words he gave a little groan and tightened his grip on Lauren. "Is he hard?" Ty asked.

"Yes." Sean's erection felt like an iron shaft at the base of her spine. Sweat dampened his arms and hers, making her skin slippery in his grip. The plunge and slide of Ty's hips, the soft huff of his breathing nearly drove her insane. First she whimpered, then she gasped, arching in Sean's grip, squirming against Ty as the pleasure expanded, filling and tightening the soft, swollen tissues around his cock.

This wasn't gentle lovemaking on a soft bed with satin sheets and roses. This was a hard man at her back, restraining her for the equally hard, insistent man at her front. It was shoulder strain from the position, skin slipping in a tight grip, and helplessness in the face of superior strength. It was being outnumbered, two aroused men, one willing woman, no rules, only instincts. Ty made her wait, measured out rhythm and speed until she was quivering on the verge.

"Guys like to watch," he said when her involuntary gasps peaked in pitch and frequency. "But he gets more than a good show. Think about that. What are you going to do for him?" He leaned in, put his lips right against her ear, never breaking rhythm, and murmured, "What do I get to watch?"

All the possibilities flashed through her brain in the instant before orgasm swamped her. Rough, crashing waves surged from her center and from a distance she heard her desperate cries of release as her cunt pulsed around Ty's hard cock. When she subsided, he pulled out and lowered her feet to the floor, then nodded at Sean, who released her, keeping one hand at her waist until she found her footing.

Curiosity led her to trouble, took her deeper, might even break her heart, but at least she'd die satisfied. She plucked strands of her hair from her mouth and cheeks, then looked at Ty.

Hands on his hips, brown eyes dark and heavy-lidded, he assessed her, then gave her the same brusque nod he'd directed at Sean.

"Strip. Then get on your knees."

Chapter Ten

Ty had never seen anything as hot as Lauren Kincaid, flushed and damp with sweat after Sean held her so Ty could fuck her into a screaming orgasm. Never. Her hair shrouded her face until she skimmed it back, lifting her bared breasts and sending a bolt of lust searing down his spine. Her lips were parted, swollen, that dark shade of pink that made him think of her nipples, her sex after he'd worked her over. It touched some animal portion of his brain he rarely accessed but was in the game now, driving the blunt words.

He wanted to see her on her knees, sucking Sean's cock. Keep it sexual. Take her beyond the limits. He wanted to drive this composed, controlled woman further than she'd ever gone before.

Lauren shrugged her shoulders, and her top dropped to the floor. Behind her Sean yanked his shirt over his head and set his hands to his belt and zipper, but Ty stopped him with, "She'll do that." He stayed close, crowding Lauren as she reached back to unhook her bra and tug it down her arms, leaving her torso bared to him. As she moved the shafts of moonlight illuminated her breasts, the strong, sleek muscles in her arms and shoulders, and his cock jerked as lightning speared down his spine, into his balls. When she reached for the side zip on her skirt he spoke again.

"Turn around."

Holy Christ, this worked for her. He knew it from the way her mouth softened, the glance she flicked at him before she turned to face Sean. Sean's gaze lingered on Lauren's body as she released the button and zipper. The skirt dropped to the floor, and a tight, soft huff eased from his throat. Ty knew what Sean saw, the long, lean curves that spoke of strength, endurance, a capability that made her surrender all the more arousing.

He nodded at Sean to go ahead, watched him lift his hands to her hair. Sean never bragged about quantity experience, but there was some quality there because he gathered it and swept the moonlit mass to stream over one shoulder, exposing the line of her cheek, jaw, and throat. Then he flattened his palms on her shoulders and pushed. A shudder rippled under her skin as she dropped to her knees. Ty remained on his feet behind her.

"Go on," Sean said. There was an edge to his nearly soundless voice as he looked down at Lauren.

Alert to the nuances in the room, Ty looked at him and mouthed, "Take it easy."

Sean gave him a level gaze that gave away nothing. Ty's people-radar pinged once, then went silent when Lauren lifted her hands to Sean's belt, opening the clasp without any fumbling. Sean braced one hand against the wall by the door and put the other on his hip as she popped open the button fly and hooked her fingers in shorts and pants to work them down and release his shaft. She flicked a quick glance up, then gripped the hard shaft and licked the precome off the tip.

"You want her to use her hands, too?" Ty asked, remembering the bright red leather restraints in her nightstand.

"Yeah," Sean said. "Suck it. Nice and slow."

Dark pink stained her cheekbones as Lauren swirled her tongue around the tip then opened her mouth, fisted her hand at the base of the shift, and took Sean's cock in her mouth until her stretched lips met her fingers. She pulled back, cheeks hollowing just a little. The muscles in Sean's abdomen jumped, then released as she went down, nice and slow, just as he'd ordered. With her other hand she cupped his balls, fingers gently rubbing at the sensitive patch behind them. A few moments of this and Sean's head dropped back against the wall, eyes closing. "Oh, fuck," he said, then tipped his head forward. The hand on his hip lifted, then closed hard around the loose fabric of his cargo pants. But as Lauren kept the pace Sean reached forward to comb through the silvery waterfall of hair, then tighten his fist in it.

Ty went to his knees behind Lauren, snugged up against her back. "Easy," he said, directing the word to her. Sean also took it to heart because he relaxed a little, visibly reaching for control. *Good. Better all around.*

"Make it last for him," he said. "This is every guy's wet dream, a girl on her knees, sucking his cock like it's her favorite lollipop. Don't rush it."

Lauren obediently eased up, and the tension plateaued. Ty took advantage of her lifted arms and kneeling position to run his fingernails from her knees to the crease of her thighs, where he curled his fingers into the damp skin and urged her legs apart. She'd be sensitive from the recent orgasm, so he didn't touch her clit immediately. Instead he brought his flattened palms up her flat stomach to cup her breasts and brush his thumbs over her nipples. She gave a delicate little shimmy as she went down on Sean, and he knew he had her attention.

"Don't think about what I'm doing," he said. "Focus on him. Please him." But he couldn't miss the way anticipation trembled under her skin even as she maintained rhythm. The hand encircling Sean's shaft slid to flatten against his hip bone as she started taking him deeper into her throat. Her mouth was wet with saliva, lips stretched and sliding along the taut, flushed skin. Ty felt his own cock jerk as the images seared into his brain, but he kept his fingers busy on her breasts, alternating light strokes of the undersides with pressure on the nipples. When her legs spread of their own accord, pressing against the insides of his thighs, he knew he had her.

"Do women like giving head as much as men like getting it?" he asked.

A laughing little whimper escaped her mouth, then she went down.

He pinched her nipples. "You can't imagine the wet heat, the pressure against the tip when his cock nudges into the back of your throat," he said, timing the words to coincide with exactly that moment. "And then you pull back, go down again, and if you're good, if you're really, really good, the orgasm starts to climb up his shaft. Is she good?"

"Jesus Christ," Sean gritted out. "Fucking awesome."

The academic veneer had totally disappeared, Ty noticed. The hand gripping Lauren's hair shifted to press fingertips to skull and guide her movements, but he'd picked up on the undercurrents in the slow tempo. There was no need to rush: the normal boundaries pushed into a darker, hotter realm. Sean could take his pleasure from Lauren's mouth, and from the looks of things, he'd settled in to do exactly that.

Ty skated his hands down Lauren's damp torso and made a wide circle around her clit with the tip of his middle finger. He put his palm flat on her inner thigh to emphasize the openness, then worked the tips of two fingers just inside her, stroking the wet, slick flesh he knew to be most sensitive. The touches weren't intended to get her off, but rather to get her desperately aroused. She writhed in his grasp, lost rhythm for a moment until Sean's hand in her hair refocused her.

"It's not your turn, Lauren," Ty murmured. "I'm just playing, keeping you ready for the next round. Suck him."

Stifled grunts choked from Sean's throat with each slow, sure movement of Lauren's head, every muscle in his abdomen tight under the strain. His jaw was set, eyes closed, hips thrusting into her mouth. Ty withdrew his hands from Lauren's pussy. She whimpered, then whimpered again when he pinched her nipples, and flat-out groaned when he simply cupped the soft mounds, leaving the sensitive, wet peaks to cool in the air.

"I'm gonna come," Sean ground out. "Right fucking now."

His fingers tightened around Lauren's head, and Ty rolled her nipples as Sean's body jerked in release. He heard her swallow in rapid succession and her body tremble in his hands before Sean's arm went limp. Lauren's head dropped back against Ty's shoulder as she gasped for air. His head bowed, Sean eased back against the wall, and Lauren wiped the back of her hand across her wet mouth.

The movement hit Ty like a body blow. She turned to look at him, her eyes glazed, her lips so swollen and stretched. "Like the show?" she asked.

Another body blow. In response he laid his fingers along her jaw to turn her mouth to his and kissed her as he ground his cock against her ass. "What do you think?"

"I think everyone's come except you," she said.

"I'll get mine," he said. He looked up at Sean. "Ready for another round?"

"Two minutes, tops," Sean said.

Semper fi.

Languid desire coursed through Lauren's veins with each slow, hard heartbeat. She'd passed arousal and now floated in an ocean of molten need. Ty asked if women found blow jobs as arousing as men, and the answer was *It depends* . . . on the man, the circumstances, the mood, the time of the month. The stars were all in alignment tonight, because that blow job got her almost as hot as

Sean. Another slow circle around her clit and she would have come with Sean's cock in her mouth.

While Ty watched. How much of the arousal stemmed from Ty's commanding demeanor? He let down his guard like this, became the man she knew was inside. She'd seen the sharp anguish in Sean's eyes, felt uncertainty skitter across her nerves like hard-soled shoes on black ice, but Ty stepped in and managed it.

When Sean moved to shove his pants down and off, Ty gripped her around the waist and urged her to her feet. "On your knees on the bed," he said.

She obeyed, pulling the chenille spread and top sheet to the foot of the bed before kneeling in the center and watching the men strip. Ty rummaged through her nightstand, handed Sean a condom, then withdrew the lube. She quirked an eyebrow at him, but he didn't answer, tilting the power dynamics back in his favor. After Sean sheathed his still erect cock in latex, Ty said, "Against the headboard."

As Sean situated himself his gaze flicked over her, the light in the pale blue depths telling her she wasn't the only participant expanding her horizons tonight. A few more low-voiced commands from Ty and she straddled Sean's hips, her hands on his shoulders holding her poised above his erection. He cupped her breasts while Ty exerted pressure on her hips and she sank down, taking his shaft deep into her body.

The position left her vulnerable and exposed, and when Ty's fingers trailed over her hips then down into the cleft in her ass, she knew where this was going. He pressed one thumb firmly against her pucker. An answering spark of arousal flashed through her cunt.

"Ever done this before?" he asked.

She peered over her shoulder, through her tangled hair. "Which part?"

A little grin lifted the corner of his mouth, but he pressed more firmly on her anus. Her eyelids dropped closed as she clenched around Sean. "Tried," she said softly. "It hurt, so we stopped."

"Same rules apply here." The top of the lube bottle clicked open, then his fingers returned, circling her anus, applying pressure. She looked at Sean. His face was intent, serious, aroused as he slid his hands under her hair to grip her nape and jaw and pull her face to his for a purposeful kiss. When his tongue slid into her mouth heat washed through her, and her fingers tightened on his shoulders. He pulled back, her jaw still cupped in his hands, and peered at her. She smiled.

His next kiss was hot, deep, slow perfection, effectively dividing her attention. Ty kept up the slow, circular pressure, making sensation build inside her until she shimmied in their grip.

"Stay still," Sean said.

One hand dropped to her hip to make sure she did. She whimpered a protest but followed his command because she couldn't do anything else. Sean kissed her with a focus that shocked her, and it only grew worse when Ty's free hand drifted to her clit and began to mimic the circles against her anus. Sean's mouth on hers, his fingers now plucking her nipples, Ty's hands on her clit and anus, Sean's cock inside her, Ty's sliding against her tailbone. Her brain sparked and crackled like a downed wire, then shut down completely.

Until Ty slid one finger into her anus. She tore her mouth from Sean's and moaned, not from pain but from the sensation. She'd heard it could be incredible, knew it was a possibility in this scenario. She trusted Ty to take it slow and gentle, but . . . oh God.

Sean took his role as distraction quite seriously, because he pulled her mouth back to his and continued to torment her nipples, and though she tried to remain still, eventually the focused sexual attention had her grinding down on his cock, trying to get additional pressure on her clit. Then Ty slid a second finger into her ass, and this time Sean leaned back.

"I want to see this," he said, his voice low and rough.

He kept his hands on her breasts, and Lauren, drifting in a heated, supercharged zone of pleasure, trailed her fingers along his muscled arms until her hands covered his as they worked at her breasts. Ty's fingers in her ass didn't hurt. Instead the steady, stroking movement rubbed over newly awakened nerves, and his meticulous attention to her clit ensured her entire body trembled with arousal. Each time her pussy spasmed as need built inside her, she was dimly aware of Sean's answering sharp inhale. He tucked her hair behind her ear, and she sensed the moonlight cool and bright on her flushed face.

"God damn," he said.

Could need show that clearly on her face? What must she look like with her body coaxed past normal definitions of pleasure and propriety?

Ty's response was a low, dark chuckle. "Yeah. Just wait."

When Ty added a third finger, she tipped her head back and gasped, "Just do it. I don't . . . I need . . . just do it. Please."

She couldn't stand it anymore. She needed more than teasing fingers on her nipples and clit. She needed movement, sensation, release.

Ty's fingers slipped from her ass, replaced by the broad head of his cock. He wrapped his arm around her waist, holding her still, still delicately stroking her clit with the middle finger of his other hand. She felt pressure, stretching, then sharp sensation as the tight ring of muscle succumbed, and the head of his cock slipped inside. She gasped, her hands lifting, fingers splayed as the line between pleasure and pain thinned and sharpened. Sean's hands left her breasts, and his fingers wove through hers, giving her something to grip, but she stayed taut, arched like a bow.

Then Ty's free hand slid along her arm, under her wrist to break Sean's grip. He guided her hand behind his head, to the sweat-damp, tangled hair at nape of his neck. She fisted her hand in his hair and pulled his cheek alongside hers. The rasp of his stubble across her hot, sensitive skin should have been too much. Instead it softened her, broadened the plane of pleasure. She drew a shuddering breath, and the hand at her waist slipped up to splay at her collarbone and throat.

They stayed like that for a long, thrumming moment as she absorbed the new sense of fullness. Then she said, "More."

Ty's warm palm closed around her throat, his long fingers pressing on either side of her jaw and his mouth hot and soft against the corner of her mouth. He slid deep inside, his breath halting at her helpless little moan. His low, stuttering groan of pleasure as she tightened around him and ushered him in trickled over her breasts, down her abdomen, into her pussy.

His heart slammed against her back, the thuds hard enough to reverberate through his breastbone and into her skin. "Does it hurt?" he asked.

"No," she said, her voice nearly soundless in the dark, still air.

His hand flattened against her mound to hold her still as he withdrew, the movement careful and slow enough for the pressure to glide over nerve endings eager for stimulation, paused for a heated moment, then slid in again. "Now?"

"Doesn't hurt," she gasped. "Feels . . . amazing."

"Good," he said. This time when he pulled out two fingers slipped back down on either side of her clit, and when he pushed back inside a shock wave of pleasure surged through her sex. She was so full, Sean's cock thick and hard inside her, Ty's moving purposefully in her ass, and the pounding of her heart against her breastbone made it nearly impossible to breathe. Sean remained still under her and let her glide up and down on his cock at her own pace. Behind her, Ty's thrusts would have been gentle if they weren't so achingly teasing, forcing her to feel every stretching glide into her ass, the waves of pleasure pulsing out to merge with the sensation in her pussy and clit.

Careful could be devastating.

Ty set a relentless rhythm, and before long the pleasure swelling under her skin broke in a wave of sensation so intense she dissolved, no longer enclosed by the edges of her skin. From a distance she heard sharp, high-pitched cries, knew in some remote corner of her brain she made the noises, but all she could process was the glimmering, relentless pleasure. Seeking an anchor, she reached behind her to fist her hand in Ty's hair and turned toward him. When he bent to her, pressed the corner of his mouth to her parted lips she moaned, low surrender echoing in her throat. The ache built again, this time with an intensity that frightened her. She gripped Sean's forearm, fisted her hand in Ty's hair, and let the dark, swirling vortex suck her down.

Ty's movements were less restrained now, taking on an edge of seeking his own satisfaction. She was dimly aware of Sean's hand on her hip as he arched into her, the angle and movement stroking over her G-spot. Her nipples throbbed mercilessly, sparks flaring under the skin as each thrust made the small mounds bounce from impact.

"Oh God," she moaned into Ty's mouth. "Oh God!"

She was shaking, trembling on the verge of an abyss, her heart thundering in her ears when the wave swamped her. She shattered, release pulsing from her core through the edges of her skin, obliterating her, body and soul.

Behind her Ty plunged deep, hips hard against her ass cheeks, then went rigid. Hard grunts punctuated each pulse of his cock inside her. Sean's hand gripped her hip tightly enough to leave marks as he gritted his teeth and jetted into her. Once again asynchronous breathing filled the air, her own gasps high-pitched and relieved, Sean's huffing from his chest, Ty's bent head sending air gusting over her shoulder. Sean patted her hip in a movement so sweetly tentative she smiled, while Ty's arm grew heavier and heavier at her waist. Then his hand drifted over her hip and down. He gripped the base of the condom and gently pulled out of her ass, backing away from her. Sean offered his hands to balance her as she lifted herself off him and sat at the foot of her bed, not sure if her legs would hold her just yet. When Sean got up, she stretched out in the warm spot left by their bodies, let her eyes drift closed.

Sounds behind her, water running in the bathroom, a short, murmured exchange between Sean and Ty, then a big, warm hand on her hip.

"You okay?" Ty's voice. Ty's hand. *Of course.*

"Do you want to know why you had to be here?" she said, drifting on the endorphin rush.

The hand on her hip flexed briefly in hesitation. "Yes," he said.

"Because he's a nice guy . . . and very, very hot . . . thank you for that, by the way . . . but for me this is all about you. I trusted you to make this amazing, and it was."

It wasn't just the oxytocin talking. She'd finally figured out what drew her to Ty from the moment she saw him on the rig. He buried honor under attitude, shoved trustworthiness aside for hard words and an *I-don't-give-a-fuck* temperament. Underneath the emotionally distant, hard-drinking shell was the good, decent, honorable core inside that made him everyone's confidant, the guy you went to when you didn't know what to do. The guy you trusted with your questions, your doubts, your life, because he'd keep them safe.

Not many guys had that, but most of the good NCOs she'd known growing up did. Sean was all officer, but Ty . . . Ty took care of the people around him.

Under the hell-raiser, that was Ty.

She still didn't know why he was doing his considerable best to eradicate that man, but she was patient. She could wait until he was ready to talk.

Low voices wove into the fabric of her consciousness, the pleasure ebbing from her body, the relaxed breaths, the steady thump of her heart, and enveloping it all was the sweet darkness of sleep. The front door opened. Closed. Sean was leaving. Still drifting, she pillowed her head in the crook of her arm and waited for Ty to return. She'd get up then, get dressed, take him back to No Limits, or maybe ask him to just spend the night . . .

Gretchen's sharp yelp woke her. Lauren sat up, chilled to the bone by the cool air blowing from the vent onto her naked body. The moon had dropped lower in the night sky. Shadows licked at the edges of the room. She looked at the clock on her nightstand. Three a.m. She'd slept for ninety minutes or so.

Alone. Ty hadn't come back.

She got to her feet and pulled on her robe, belting it as she walked through the living room to the laundry room. The walls held the still emptiness of the moon and the silent neighborhood. When she opened the laundry room door, Gretchen looked up at her accusingly. Lauren crouched and gave her a conciliatory rub, then hurried to the front door, Gretchen at her heels. The fact that she was moving freely in the house confirmed what Lauren already knew: the men were gone. A quick peek out the window in her front door showed an empty street and driveway.

Something shifted in her throat, not quite sadness, not quite disappointment. She straightened, clutched the V-neck of her robe to stop the scent of sweat and sex from drifting into her nostrils because the postsex endorphins were gone. She'd known exactly what she was getting when she waited for Ty in the parking lot. She'd thought the hell-raiser persona he wore so well was a cover, the NCO his true self.

She'd been wrong.

"Come on, girl," she said. "Time for bed."

Gretchen trotted down the hallway ahead of Lauren, happiness evident in the smug spring in her step. A shiver rolled down Lauren's back, so she stopped in the bathroom to take a quick, hot shower. Just to warm up, she told herself. It was hard to fall asleep when she was cold. The hot earth scent of satiated lust clinging to her skin and hair had nothing to do with it.

Chapter Eleven

Ty slumped into Sean's passenger seat and shook his hair back out of his face. The motion dislodged images from the carefully ordered lockboxes in his brain, and his muscles went rigid.

The look on Lauren's face when she realized Sean's grip was unbreakable.

Her complete vulnerability, all the more powerful for her strength and confidence.

That searing moment when they were both inside her, and she surrendered, completely and unconditionally.

Her hands had lifted as if searching for stability in a world made soft and hot by pleasure. Sean gripped them first but a hot possessiveness made Ty break the hold, lift Lauren's arm behind his head, exposing the whole front of her body to him. But when her hand fisted in the hair at the nape of his neck, connection crackled between them. The room was too dark to see her face, but he heard her gasps loud and clear, the pitch riding the edge between pleasure and pain. He used to love that edge, sought it out by pushing himself to the limit physically, finding the endorphin rush in the agony of a hard run or swim, the upwelling of satisfaction that came afterward.

No. It was more than that. What he'd just felt with Lauren was the surge of connection he felt as part of a team, the daily experience of life with people he trusted and who trusted him. He hadn't felt that for a very long time, hadn't wanted to feel it for even longer, but twenty minutes ago, with Lauren he'd been there. It wasn't about the physical act. It was about the emotions borne from the physical.

Physical, emotional, it was all about Lauren.

He'd been so caught up in the mind-blowing sex that he'd slipped into his old way of being, into the man he used to be. Like a moron he couldn't just walk without checking on her, and she said the fateful words.

I trusted you. This was all about you.

Lauren felt it, too, and that made it all worse, the emotions exploding one after the other like a series of timed charges against the night sky of his soul. So he walked. Followed Sean down the hall, out the door, and into his car.

"What the fuck are you doing in my car, instead of in her bed?"

He framed his lie in a context that would suit Sean's sense of honor. "She was falling asleep. I didn't want to wake her up. Drive."

Sean turned the engine over and shoved the gearshift into reverse. "So she's gonna wake up alone."

Ty ignored him, counting streetlights as Sean navigated out of Lauren's neighborhood.

"After what we just did."

She was a big girl. She knew the rules of this game. She wasn't his responsibility.

Seven lights and a stop sign slipped past before Sean spoke again. "I'm starving. You mind if I drive through somewhere?"

He could eat after that? Ty didn't think he'd care about food for the rest of his life. "Whatever."

Sean pulled into the late-night drive-through at Wendy's and stared at the brightly illuminated menu board. "That was different," he said absently.

Ty didn't want to rehash what just happened, but he had to say something. "Yeah." If different meant hot, devastating. A strange mixture of exhilaration and apprehension turned in his gut. He wanted to hit something. To his utter amazement, he wanted to cry.

A girl's sleepy voice buzzed from the speaker, asking for their order. "A triple stack combo with bacon, extra large, and a Coke," Sean said, then turned to Ty. "You want anything?"

"I'm not hungry," Ty said.

Sean looked at him, but Ty refused to meet his gaze. "Why'd we do that? Why did you let me fuck a woman you care about?"

"I don't care about her."

"Great," Sean said, switching gears without blinking an eye. "If you don't care we can compare notes. I'll start, because goddamn, that was the best blow job I've ever had. Of course, it's been almost a year, but objectively speaking, Lauren was incredible. That thing you were talking about . . . the back of her throat thing . . ." Sean shook his head. "Nice soundtrack."

He knew Sean was baiting him. Knew it, because Sean didn't talk like this, and his face was as red from sheer embarrassment as if he'd run ten miles, but Ty still clenched his jaw against the anger boiling inside him.

"It was probably for the best that Lauren was on top, because even after the blow job my control wasn't all that great. The whole thing was so fucking hot. Every time you got a little deeper in her ass she'd tighten around me, and when Lauren came—"

If Sean didn't stop using her name, Ty was going to make him bleed. "Give it a rest, Winthrop."

Completely unintimidated, Sean just looked at him. "Make up your mind, Hendricks. You either don't care, or you do. I've heard you and John and the other guys after shore leave. Marines fight in pairs, and they fuck in pairs. Girlfriends are off-limits, but you said she's not your girlfriend, so she's just a piece of ass, right? An exceptionally talented piece of ass," he said meditatively. "So go on, tell me what you thought."

"I think you're in danger of losing your teeth to my fist."

Still completely unconcerned Sean said, "How was her ass? Come to think of it, how do you talk a girl into that? You think Lauren would be up for another round, let me get some practice in?"

Ty swung around in the passenger seat, fist balled at the end of his cocked arm before he saw the drive-through girl leaning toward the window, a bag of food in one hand and an extra-large drink in the other. Her eyes were wide, like she'd heard the whole fucking thing.

Sean held his gaze for a long moment. "Don't care, huh?"

Jesus *Christ*. "Take your goddamn food before we get arrested for corrupting a minor."

Sean turned to face the window and hesitated for a split second. Then he reached for the food, set the bag on his lap, and put the drink in the holder between him and Ty. "I know why I was there," he said conversationally as he dug in the bag, then crammed four french fries into his mouth. Chewed. Swallowed. "Get the LT laid after fifteen months overseas, and in a completely fucked-up, guy bonding way, it was thoughtful. But maybe you should have considered what Lauren meant to you before you did it."

He tipped his head back against the headrest and closed his eyes. "She doesn't mean anything to me," he said, a lie that he might have been able to pass off as the truth before What Just Happened.

"Bullshit," Sean said through a mouthful of burger. "Remember that hot little thing about me watching you fuck her, you watching her go down on me? I was there. Watching. You care about her. It was all over your face, in the way you touched her. And in the end, when she lost all control, she turned to you. Not me."

The absence of engine and tire noise registered, and Ty opened his eyes. Sean was parked outside No Limits. "She just knows me better. Emotions have nothing to do with it," he said. He reached for the door handle, suddenly bone tired and sick at heart.

"You can keep denying it," Sean said quietly, "but it won't change reality. That's the shitty thing about reality. Doesn't change just because you want it to."

He got out and slammed the door, strode across the lot to his truck, and peeled out of the parking lot. Back at his motel, away from Sean's relentless questions, he cut the engine and let his chin drop to his chest.

What the fuck did you just do?

On one level the night worked. Sean was clearly back in the land of the living, or at least in the land of the sexually active. But his objective with Lauren was to turn her curiosity about him and about sex against her, and there he'd failed. Spectacularly, if she did that because he was there.

Behind the closed door of his hotel room he stripped where he stood, leaving the clothes in a pile by the door, his keys and wallet in his shoes, and turned on the shower. One benefit to showering at two in the morning was an abundance of hot water. He twisted the dial into the red and stepped under the spray. Pain bloomed where the water struck his skin, and rivulets burned down his back and abdomen.

He didn't care. He didn't. But whatever it was surging inside him, hot and anguished and sharp-edged, was too much when the point was to feel nothing at all, and like a snake hidden in the back of a hole, anger bloomed at Lauren, curious, stubborn Lauren, who didn't back down from a challenge. He'd have to go further, he realized. Lauren wasn't picking up signals she should read clearly, that he didn't give a good goddamn about her, and that this was over.

Tomorrow he'd make himself crystal fucking clear.

Somehow she'd known that, come Monday, he'd be on the bench, but when Ty strolled onto the lake path and took up position on the bench just before noon, Lauren's stomach wound into a hard knot behind her rib cage. She'd watched him often enough over the last two weeks to read his body, his demeanor, and even across the lake and three stories up she could feel the tension humming under his skin. He seemed bigger, broader, somehow spoiling for a fight.

She was going to give him one. She gathered her sunglasses and lunch box. "I'm going to lunch," she told Danelle.

"You sound like you're marching off to do battle with the county again," Danelle said. "Based on the way you've been pounding those keys, you need a break. Sit in the sun for an hour. It will improve your mood."

She had a feeling her mood was going to get worse, not better, but that didn't stop her. A quick trip through the nearly empty cafeteria for a bottle of water, then she pushed open the door leading to the path, strode past the first five benches, and stopped in front of Ty and his folders of paper. The ends of her pink silk scarf danced in the fall breeze, and she wished she'd worn a sweater. Goose bumps rippled up her arms, and for the first time in Ty's presence the shivers weren't accompanied by a little rippling thrill in her belly.

He looked at her for a long moment, unsmiling, his jaw set. Then he gathered the papers he'd just spread on the green slats and made room for her. She unzipped the soft lunch box, her movements brisk, jerky. "You didn't have to leave. I would have driven you back to the hotel in the morning."

Her phone buzzed. You were asleep.

"Enough with the texting. I'll bet my car Sean's on the other end of that audio feed, and after Saturday, we don't have any secrets." A muscle jumped in his jaw, but he put the phone away. "I wasn't asleep. I was waiting for you. Why did you leave?"

"No reason to stay," he said.

She huffed out a bitter laugh. "Right. Because that was just about sex."

"Exactly," he said easily. "Sean said you were awesome, by the way. Best blow job ever. His exact words. Definitely the most memorable night of his life. But I knew you would be." He turned and gave her a picture-perfect bad boy smile. "Thanks, darlin'."

Without a sound, her lungs emptied of air, and a hot flush rose up her neck. When she woke up alone Saturday night she'd expected him to be casual about it Monday, but not vicious. Not cheapening her.

Based on prior experiences on this bench, she knew what she was supposed to say next. To spite him, lash out at him, she'd tell him she thought Sean was awesome, too. A nice guy, and would Ty give her his number? She knew Ty wanted to drive her away as clearly as she could read the signs of a nearly unbearable tension in him, the veneer micron thin. He looked like he'd been through a forty-eight-hour stomach flu, skin pale and drawn under the tan, grooves pronounced in his cheeks, and suddenly she didn't have it in her to keep playing games with him. He was following his own instincts, trapped in a dark hole and in a snarling, locked-jaw, torn-flesh fight to the death with himself, and those fighting instincts would take her down, too.

"I'm glad one of us got something good out of what we did,"

she said quietly. Struggling for composure, she opened the Tupperware and pulled out half a turkey on whole wheat. Took a bite.

He lifted both arms to spread wide on the back of the bench and let his legs drop open as he glanced casually around the lake. "Sometimes you can't overcome instincts. Sometimes wounded animals don't want to be healed. Sometimes in the twenty-first century it doesn't pay to be curious."

He twisted her words, used her flirtatious, life's-an-adventure attitude to backhand her with his contemptuous tone, and despite her best efforts, the verbal blow generated an involuntary flinch. "Did you mean to teach me a lesson, Ty?" she asked, only a slight tremor in her voice.

A second passed, stretched into a moment while she met his gaze. Maybe the question was so obvious he wouldn't bother to respond. Maybe he had the good sense not to respond at all. Either way he just looked at her, mouth in a grim line, eyes hidden.

"It worked," she said quietly. "I no longer care to know another thing about you."

It was a lie. She'd always be curious about him, the facets and depths she'd barely begun to explore, but she wasn't a masochist. Drawing a deep breath, she sat back. The slats on the back of the bench bit into her shoulder blades as she took another bite of her sandwich. Swallowed it dry and sipped from the water bottle to get it down her throat. Ate a carrot stick. Stared fixedly at the lake. She would not run, so she continued on to her treat, a cupcake, slowly peeling the paper back from the bottom, separating the frosted top from the cake bottom, eating both, then brushing the crumbs onto the ground. A robin fought the ever-present sparrows for the crumbs while she snapped the lids back on the plastic containers holding her sandwich and carrots, zipped them into the soft cooler, got to her feet, and walked away.

No backward glance, no regret in her steps. An expert in

standoffishness taught her the walk, tall and proud, shoulders back, stride loose and even. She walked away from him, knowing he'd won. He wanted to destroy himself, and he meant to do it.

Alone.

Ty watched her go, tall and slender in her gray wrap dress and pretty pink scarf, and felt the bottom drop out of his stomach. A faint crackle in his earpiece, then Sean's shocked, disbelieving voice. "Jesus Christ, Hendricks, that was cruel. What the fuck is wrong with you?"

This was who he was now, so he said nothing, because there was nothing wrong with him. Nothing at all. He'd wanted this, and he'd gotten it. She'd been under his skin a little, sure, but actually, he owed her, because now he knew exactly how far he had to go to drive good people away. The casual ones left after a month or two of ignored texts and phone calls. People like John and Sean and Lauren, he had to work harder to move them.

Now he knew exactly how hard. Push a boulder up a mountain hard. *Right. Fine.* He could do this. "There's nothing wrong with me. After Saturday I'm done with her. She needed to move on."

Move on she would, based on the way hurt shifted behind her eyes, pushed at the muscles of her face, but never quite settled or broke free. He saw plain as day the moment when she decided there was nothing more to be curious about. A spike of pain drove straight through his ribs when her expression closed off. He'd known her two weeks, and it hurt that bad. Worse was coming. John and Sean were brothers, the bonds formed under fire in Afghanistan. He hoped the end would come quickly. He dreaded the pain.

"Hey," Sean said, his voice shifting from disgusted to alert. "Did you see Richards leave? Because his car's pulling out of the lot."

Adrenaline shocked Ty to his feet. He scanned the benches

around the lake, then trotted along the path toward the building and around to the loading dock. Richards's car was gone from the shaded employee parking garage. "I didn't see it." *Because I was watching Lauren learn to hate me.* "His car's gone."

"Fuck," Sean muttered. "I'll call the other team. Maybe they can pick him up."

"Check and see if the other guys' cars are still in the garage," Ty said, his mind racing. He held his phone to his ear, as if he wanted to stand in the shade while conducting a conversation, and angled his body so he could see both the doors into the cafeteria and the garage. Sean's SUV with borrowed plates prowled through the garage until it reached the top floor, then circled down.

"Both cars are still there. Any chance they left with Richards?"

Ty put his hands on his hips and bent his head. He'd been entirely focused on Lauren. Santa Claus could have come out the cafeteria door with eight tiny fucking reindeer and a merry band of elves, and he would have missed it. "Yeah. There's a chance."

Silence, then, "I'll call it in."

Fuck the chain of command. It was Ty's responsibility to report his mistake back to John. Sean knew it. "I'll do it," Ty said.

He called John, who said nothing more than a terse *okay* and sent a team out to replace them. Ty skirted the side of an anonymous brick building, left through one of the business park's side entrances, heading out into the suburban office sprawl. Sean picked him up a couple of blocks away. They drove in silence to John's office, but Ty didn't miss the tight clench of Sean's jaw, the jerky way he handled the car's gearshift, knew it wasn't over the egregious, rookie surveillance mistake, but Lauren.

"Look," he said. "It's none of your fucking business."

Sean said nothing, just took the corner into the parking lot at a tire-screeching veer. He got out, slammed his door hard enough to rock the heavy truck, including Ty's added weight, and strode into the building. Ty got out of the truck and walked into John's office. Looked like this was his lucky day. He could end relationships with everyone who cared about him in the span of a couple of hours.

Both the door to John's office suite and his personal office were flung wide open. Even if they weren't, Ty would have been able to hear Sean's outraged bellow through closed doors. "What the fuck is wrong with him? He's gone from being the guy who held every-thing together to the guy who fucks it up six ways to Sunday!"

"What happened?" John said mildly when Ty leaned against the doorframe separating the reception area from John's office, but Ty could see the nerves. He remembered John's focus on the business that was his future, the diamond glittering on Lucy's finger that made John's success her future as well, Sean with thirty days to recover from a deployment and decide what to do next.

The fracture inside him splintered, sending shards of emotion into the numbness.

"Richards left, and I missed it," he said.

The words hung in the air.

"How?"

The single word was clipped with frustration and disbelief. Ty missed nothing. Nothing. He hesitated for a second, reluctant to bring Lauren into this, because it would mean remembering what he'd said, what he'd done to her.

Like you're not going to replay that brutal scene every night for the rest of your life.

"He was busy being a fucktard to a woman."

Sean normally sounded like a walking thesaurus. Ty leveled a look at him. "It's none of your fucking business."

"The fuck it's not my business. You made it my business," Sean snapped.

Based on Sean's narrow-eyed glare, he was figuring out exactly what Ty had done Saturday night to all of them. You had to work pretty hard to sever the bonds of brotherhood formed in the Marine Corps, but he'd almost managed to do that. He wedged a crowbar into the splintered fragments of his soul, spoke words he knew would end everything. "Do you get this emotionally involved every time you fuck a woman? You've got a long, hard road ahead of you."

"The fuck I do," Sean snapped back. "I know a class act when I see one. Give me a week, and I'll make her forget you exist."

The surging acid in his stomach crawled up his throat at the idea. "You're new to this, so I'll help you out. Rule number one of fucking in pairs is never take another Marine's sloppy seconds."

"Jesus Christ, Ty!" John said, genuinely shocked.

The Academy veneer disappeared from Sean's face, eerily blank as he surged toward Ty, fists clenched. Ty squared up, ready for the fight, but John put himself between the two of them and shoved them apart. "Step back! Not in my goddamn office!" When they separated, John turned to Ty. "Tell me what's going on."

Ty shook his head. Sean hauled in a breath and jammed his fisted hands onto his hips. "Tell him, or I will. All of it."

Ty folded his arms across his chest, trying to ease the pain from the splinters digging into his lungs. "I met a woman on the rig. We hooked up a couple of times. She works in the same business park, and when I saw her today I ended it. Winthrop got some action with her, and now he thinks he's her big brother or something."

The words landed in the room with the splat of a flat basketball hitting concrete, and the moment Ty heard them, pain that had been physical drove into his psyche. John didn't move, just kept his gaze focused on Ty. Sean fisted his hands on his hips and turned away, but neither of them matched Lauren's poise when she cut him dead. She wasn't just a woman he met on the rig. They hadn't hooked up. It had been so much more than that, and every time he tried to make it small and cheap and ugly, he shattered inside. But he was so lost in his interior wasteland that it never occurred to him that his drive to sever ties would hurt the people around him more than he could bear.

John and Sean trusted him with their lives.

His screwup today could end Langley Security's bid for a bigger piece of the corporate espionage pie.

Lauren saw right through his posturing bullshit and came back for more.

This is not who you are. That's why it doesn't feel right. Try all you want. This is not who you are.

Caring too much, getting too involved, had torn him apart. The sound of children wailing in terror never, ever went away. Not caring was worse. It shredded his soul, and everyone's around him.

John had the weirdest expression on his face. Sean's eyes widened as he took a step toward Ty, and then Ty found himself looking up at the two of them because he was on his ass, back to the wall, and someone with his voice was saying *I can't do this. I can't. I can't.*

"Get some water," John barked. Sean bolted for the cooler in the empty receptionist's office. "Hey," John said, hunkering down in front of him. "Hey. It's okay."

"It's actually not okay," Ty said. His voice shook. "Life is a fucked-up nightmare."

"Well, sure," John said sagely, his forearms on his knees. "But it's what people say in this situation. *It's okay.*"

Ty laughed, a hard, sharp crack of laughter that sent the thick wedges of pain through his ribs, into the tense air in the office, and buried his face in arms. He took two deep breaths, surprised in some dispassionate part of his brain that he could breathe around this spear of pain, then accepted the cup of water from Sean.

"Is this about the village?" John said quietly. "Because that wasn't your fault. That was nobody's fault."

"Oh, Christ," Sean said as he spun away, shoved his hands over his hair. "Last night I told her . . . I didn't think . . ."

Ty cut Sean off. "Fuck that, John," he said flatly. "Fuck. That. Twelve people died. We killed women and orphaned children. It was our road, our territory, our bombs. Somebody has to be at fault. I made them feel safe. I told them they could trust us. And they died."

A special ops team was under fire, pinned down in the mountains, calling for air support, and somewhere the communication flurry of e-mails, video from drones, text messaging, and calls someone got the air strike coordinates wrong. It was a mistake, a miscommunication, but that was an excuse, not an answer. He'd talked to the extended families that comprised this village, sat with them, drunk their tea, eaten their bread, told them they could trust Americans, that they would be protected. He'd believed in their mission, wanted their trust, spent months offering his and earning theirs. Then he'd walked through the stink of burned flesh and mortar rounds into the rubble of their homes, heard the wails of children, watched them shrink back from him.

"Who'd you talk to about this?" John asked.

He shrugged.

"No one? Jesus, Ty, I thought . . ."

Ty hated the self-recrimination on his face. "I'm not your responsibility."

"The fuck you're not. If I'm yours, you're mine. That's how this works." In a softer tone, he added, "There are people you can talk to. Good people."

"You didn't talk to anyone," Ty scoffed. "We all saw crazy bad shit. I can handle it."

"You're fetal on my office floor, you've pissed off Winthrop, and from what I can piece together, you've been an asshole to a woman you liked enough to fuck more than once. You think you're handling it?"

Ty considered flattening him, but Sean brought him a second

cup of water, this time holding it out like a peace offering, so he drank that instead. Then he balled up the paper cone and chucked it at the trash can. He knew what to say. He'd heard guys say it a thousand times. "Goddamn it. I eat. I sleep. I don't drink when I'm offshore. I am fine."

He knew when guys were lying, too, and he'd go back again and again, listening until they talked. Personnel issues were his specialty, in that other life the bombs destroyed as thoroughly as they'd flattened the village.

"Sure you're fine," John said easily, "if that's all you want out of life."

He wished it was all he wanted out of life. The problem was, acting like he didn't want anyone or anything to matter to him didn't seem to stop people and events from mattering to him. "It's supposed to be enough." He looked up. "Jesus, Sean, stop looking at me like I've got a gun in my mouth and my finger on the trigger."

"Then do something about this."

Sean's voice, all officer, cracked into the room, and apparently Ty was still a United States Marine because his spine straightened at the tone.

John continued in a more reasonable tone of voice. "Ty, you were the guy who united us as a platoon in boot camp, the one who listened when guys got dumped because they were gone, the one who carried water and batteries when other guys couldn't. You kept the most boot Marines walking for each other. Jesus, did you think you could stop yourself from caring about people? That wasn't you before. It's really not going to be enough for you after. What we saw, what we did, it changes us. It's how you know you are okay. If it didn't . . . life would be a fucked-up nightmare."

Ty said nothing.

"If the positions were reversed, what would you tell me?" John asked.

A bitter laugh. "You fucker. I'd tell you to talk to someone."

"Good advice. Take it." As if that settled things, John stood up and held out his hand.

Maybe it did.

Ty let his breath seep from between his lips, then took the proffered hand. John, his friend, his brother-in-arms pulled him to his feet. He pushed his hair back, settled his hands on his hips, and looked at John. "I'm sorry about today. It's on me, and it won't happen again."

"Team two picked them up a mile from Richards's house. The time frame's right for him to have driven straight there from work. Forget about it."

Relief swamped him, and when it receded he felt a little cleaner inside, as if the ecosystem of his soul was healing, new growth emerging from a year of self-imposed solitude and sorrow and guilt. "Yeah. Okay, good."

"Make an appointment."

"I will." *Eventually.*

"Make an appointment and tell me when it is so I can take you," John amended.

The stubborn son of a bitch reminded him of Lauren. "I can go by myself."

"You can, but I'm going to go with you," John said amiably. "Or Sean will, until he makes up his mind what he's doing with his life. You're not in this alone."

"Damn straight," Sean said. He was leaning against John's desk, arms folded across his chest.

Ty swallowed hard against the thick lump in his throat. Blinked. His friends just watched while he turned away and got himself under control.

"Call Lauren," Sean said unexpectedly, and shrugged when John and Ty both looked at him. "I don't know her that well, but somehow I don't think she'll break when you tell her the bad shit."

He thought about that for a long moment, what he'd said, her face when he'd taken her trust and thrown it away like a dirty piece of trash. He owed her an apology and an explanation, but he didn't have a Marine Corps-strength relationship forged into steel with her. Whatever you could call what they had, it bloomed as fast and potent and velvety-soft as a hothouse flower, and as fragile.

"I fucked that up but good," he said quietly.

An awkward silence settled into the room. "One thing at a time," John said.

Ty nodded. "One thing at a time."

Chapter Twelve

Two weeks later Ty settled onto his bench for his surveillance shift. It was one in the afternoon, and the humidity from a late fall hot spell trapped the sun's light and rays like a wet blanket. Shards of light reflected off ripples in the lake as the ducks paddled listlessly from the island in the center to the edge. He snugged his wraparound glasses against the bridge of his nose, pulled his A&M ball cap lower on his head, and waited for Lauren to appear.

Sean's low voice resonated in his ear. "What's with the A&M cap? I thought you were a Texas fan."

"Switching up my look."

"You want to switch up your look, get a haircut."

Ty waited until two women gossiping about a coworker passed him before he responded, but Lauren's appearance in the door leading to the cafeteria stopped the words in his throat. While she no longer sought him out, she still ate her lunch outside. She emerged from the dining area on the building's first floor, found a spot at random, sometimes passing him in search of a bench, ate, and went back inside. She never rushed her meal, never looked even remotely uncomfortable, never looked his way. Sometimes she brought an e-reader with her, holding it in one hand while she ate. The birds always got her crumbs.

He got nothing, exactly what he deserved.

Today she didn't have an e-reader with her. Today she had a man.

He was about her height, wore a nice pair of slacks, a button-down shirt, and a blazer, in this heat, for fuck's sake, and he did all the right things. He held the door open and let her walk through it first, gave her the seat with more shade, made sure she had room for her lunch box as they went through the ritual of opening sacks and arranging food for consumption. She crossed her legs at the ankle but tilted her knees toward him, a listening posture, her head cocked as she chewed. He spoke for a while, then asked a question and listened just as attentively as Lauren talked, her hair neatly restrained at the nape of her neck with two sticks that gleamed in the sunlight. He nodded, offered her a french fry from a foam box, gave her a napkin when mustard oozed out of her sandwich onto the bench.

Ty wanted to hurt him. Slowly. Painfully. Permanently.

"You haven't talked to her yet, have you?"

Sean again. After Ty missed Richards leaving they rearranged the surveillance positions. Now the guy in the truck parked at the edge of the lot where he could watch the lake and the cars. "You're like my fairy fucking godmother, Winthrop," he said.

"Bippity boppity boo," Sean said, startling a huff of laughter from Ty. "Don't be a pussy, or you'll lose her forever. She's strong. Trust her."

She was steel-like, sunlight glinting in her ash-brown hair, reflecting off the silver ring she wore on her right hand. He was back in where he felt comfortable, with John and Sean and a few other guys in the area. He'd found a veterans' group, gone to the first meeting wary and walled off, and to his surprise helping other guys helped him, too. But asking for Lauren's forgiveness, laying himself open to her, involved a depth of vulnerability he wasn't sure he could take. He'd charged enemy positions without a second thought, but after what he'd said to her on this very bench, he couldn't bring himself to sit down next to her at lunch.

He sat and watched them finish their meal. Watched her split her cupcake with him. Watched them get up and go back inside. She'd never glanced his way. Not a taunting look, or a curious one, or a sly, sneaky one. He'd wanted nothing, and he'd gotten nothing.

The hard knock of his heart against his sternum told him the uncomfortable truth. Sex couldn't heal him, but Lauren's strength and confidence, her roots, and the way she saw him pulled him back from the edge. Lauren wouldn't let him get away with being anything less than whole and himself.

Maybe you don't want to be let off that hook.

He didn't. If he had, he would have cut ties rather than making himself hateful and difficult. He'd pushed and shoved, lashed out inexcusably, but he couldn't move good people. John and Sean were the brothers he never had, would be until the day he died. Maybe, just maybe, there was a chance Lauren would put him back on the hook, hold him to the standards of honor and decency until he could hold himself there.

He finished out the shift, rode back to John's office with Sean, gave a routine summary of a routine day. Got in his truck and went back to the hotel to take a shower. Dressed. Sat in front of the TV without seeing it, until the sunlight shifted enough to tell him it was evening. Got back in his truck. Drove to Lauren's place. He wasn't thinking much. All the while he paid attention to that quiet space inside, his sixth sense, his radar, listening for the ping that told him to walk away.

The driveway and street in front of her house were empty, so it wasn't likely she had a guest. He parked on the street and walked up her front steps and knocked on the door.

An indistinct babble of words preceded her as she flew at the door and hauled it open. She had her car keys in one hand, and behind her a bowl of peaches sat in the middle of her dining room table. Mrs. Kennedy's peaches, waiting to ripen and be turned into pie. *Roots*. A house, a dog, neighbors she helped and who helped her. Her jeans were muddy to the knee, and the skin covering her shoulders and collarbone, exposed by her low-cut tank top, gleamed with sweat. Desperate expectation widened her eyes, then melted into despair when she saw him. She lifted the back of her hand to her forehead. "Ty, I can't—"

"How long has she been gone?"

At the words a strong ping registered on his internal radar, but not one of warning. Instead, the vibrations reverberating through him affirmed what he'd always known and tried to ignore. *This is who you are.* So he tried again. More bluntly and emphatically, using words of one syllable and his NCO voice. "I want to help you find her. Let me help."

Lauren looked at him, as if trying to decide whether he was worth a second chance. "I was in the garden, pulling weeds. I . . . I got distracted. It was warm and sunny and a really nice evening and for the first time since . . ."

He could fill in the *since* himself, knew this wasn't a second chance. She'd just tabled the discussion until after they found Gretchen.

". . . I wasn't thinking about anything but what I was doing. Pulling weeds. I kept an eye on her for a while, but she was curled up in the sun by the deck, and I just . . . I got distracted, and when I remembered and turned around, she was gone."

"How long ago?"

"A couple of hours."

"Okay," he said. "We've got this. You have treats?"

"I've been all over the neighborhood," she said. "I'm out of hot dogs. I was just about to go to the store when I thought I should call some of the people who live farther away to find out if they've seen her. I don't want to call and search at the same time. I'll be distracted, and it's getting dark. It will be easy to miss her."

He pulled his keys from his pocket. "I'll go. Call your neighbors."

He made it to and from the store in record time, and when he came back, Lauren was waiting on the porch, her cell phone in hand, two empty plastic bags, a flashlight, and a pair of scissors beside her. He flung himself out of the truck but she still met him by the hood, scissors at the ready when he opened the grocery sack.

She peered inside, then said, "How many hot dogs did you buy?"

"Every package they had," he said. "You're getting your dog back."

They hunkered down in the driveway, and Ty pulled out his pocketknife and sliced into a package. While he used the knife to slice and chop right on the cement she wielded the scissors, and in a minute they had a mound of cut-up hot dogs. Lauren divided them between the two bags, and wiped her hand on her jeans. Ty got his Maglite from the toolbox on his truck.

"I've already looked everywhere," Lauren said. "I called six people in a four-block radius. No one's seen her."

Her despairing tone sliced into his heart. "She's mobile. Curious. She could have retraced her steps, found a different hiding place. Hey," he said, and tipped up her chin with his knuckles to avoid smearing her with hot dog grease. "We'll find her."

They set off in opposite directions down the block. Eventually the deepening twilight made every shift of leaves into a small, barrel-chested dark brown dog with floppy ears and a whip of a tail who never materialized. When Ty's phone vibrated he was standing on the corner, his bag still full of hot dogs. The streetlight buzzed on as he pulled the phone from his pocket to see a message from Lauren.

No luck. Do you have her?

The text was full of hope, and he hated to disappoint her. No. I'm sorry.

It's okay.

But it wasn't. She loved Gretchen, would never give up on that dog, and he couldn't bear to think of her heart breaking again. Then, out of the corner of his eye, he heard the rustle of leaves, the sound slightly out of rhythm with the wind. A moment later came the slightest movement under Mr. Minnillo's rosebushes. Keeping his body entirely still, he turned his head and looked more closely at the nearest bush. Two round, dark eyes gleamed in the street-light's glare, and as his eyes adjusted to the contours of the shadows, he could make out Gretchen's round body.

"You little shit," he said, crooning like he'd heard Lauren do. "I've been by this house four times in the last hour. But you weren't coming out, were you?"

Moving slow and easy he approached the rosebush. Gretchen shrank back, so he stopped one bush before the one she cowered under, and began to lay a trail of warm, disgusting hot dogs from the bush down the path, placing piles of them a couple of body lengths apart, through the gardens, to the sidewalk. Then he sat down on the last step and blew out his breath.

"Why do you keep running?" he asked. "You don't know how good you have it, you dumb dog." He dangled his hands from his knees, and laughed at himself. "Sometimes you have to fight your instincts, Gretchen."

Behind him the door opened. "Can I help you, young man?"

"Just waiting for a dog to come out from under your bushes, sir," he said. "Sorry about the hot dogs."

"Oh, that's quite all right. You're a friend of Lauren's?"

He hoped to hell he still had that chance. "Yes, sir," he said. "But Gretchen's still making up her mind about me."

A soft chuckle. "Good luck. You tell Lauren I said hello."

"I will, sir. Thank you."

Behind him the bushes rustled, but he didn't turn around, not even when he heard the first pile of hot dogs devoured in a couple of slurps, or the click of her nails on the cement as, after a moment, she trotted up to the second pile of meat and licked it up.

She paused, so he started talking in the same soft voice. "Cut me some slack, girl. I fucked up big-time, and I could use a little help. Showing up with you might get me back in the door so I can throw myself at her feet and grovel. What do you say? Want to see me grovel?"

Nails scritched against cement, then she ate another offering. Maybe groveling was on the menu with hot dogs tonight.

"You and me, we were two of a kind. Except I wasn't letting her in, and you weren't going to let me in."

She was close enough now that he could hear her breathing. Maybe two piles left. "You were the smart one. Not getting too close to me. You knew I wasn't good for her. But I am now. Getting there, anyway. So how about you and me, we call a truce. Let me take you back to her, and I promise I won't hurt her again."

Gretchen's black nose nudged at his elbow. Slowly, like there was a scorpion, not a dachshund at his side, he turned to look at her. Another nudge, so he lifted his arm. She climbed onto his lap and sniffed at the bag. He dumped the remaining hot dogs into his palm. Gretchen's velvet tongue licked over his skin, and the hot dogs disappeared. She sniffed again, then settled into his lap and looked up at him, her brown eyes guileless, trusting. He lifted his hand and stroked the length of her sleek body from skull to tail, nice and slow, as if this was no big deal. As if she was just a dog.

Connections were already forming. People recognized him as a friend of Lauren's, asked him to say hey to her, which was, in the South, a request not handed out lightly and expected to be honored. So he should go do that. Bring her dog back to her, and say hey from Mr. Minnillo. Then throw himself on her mercy and beg for a second chance.

Keeping the length of his arm under Gretchen's body he got to his feet, cradling her like he used to cradle his rifle. Then he set off down the sidewalk, toward Lauren's house.

Chapter Thirteen

Lauren stood at the end of her driveway and watched Ty emerge from Mr. Minnillo's gate, then disappear into the darkness between streetlights. He moved slowly, almost at a stroll, and underneath her worry for Gretchen simmered the same visceral appreciation for his lanky, powerful body. She wondered if what brought him back to her door had disappeared in a two-hour search for an abused, escape artist dog that'd probably never fully trust anyone again, even Lauren.

She knew what drove him back. Guys like Ty were territorial, and today at lunchtime when he was two hundred feet away and across the lake she could feel waves of alpha male rolling at her, hackles raised, growling. Which wasn't the nothing he'd said he wanted, but twenty-first century or not, at some primitive level sex with the right man still marked a woman. They weren't going there. No more hookups, no more booty calls for wounded warriors. But of all the surprises he could have sprung, the willingness to search for her dog topped the list.

He strode into the circular spill of a streetlight halfway down the block, his slow, rhythmic stride meshing with her heartbeat. He cradled something in both arms, but whatever he held was too dark to see against his black T-shirt. The corner of the plastic bag poked up from his jeans pocket. He disappeared into blackness between streetlights again, then reappeared two driveways down. Shoulders squared, spine straight, his gaze met hers, and he smiled, so little-boy victorious that her heart leaped hard against her breastbone. He looked happy, utterly pleased with himself and the world, and then she knew why.

Gretchen rode in his strong arms like the royalty she was. She equably considered the view from this new vantage point until her brawny, six-foot-tall ride neared Lauren, then began to wriggle free. Her arms brushed Ty's abdomen and forearms as he shifted the dog to her. Gretchen promptly gave her a hot dog-scented face licking. She squeezed her and said, "Thank you! Oh Ty, thank you! Wherever did you find her?"

"She was under Mr. Minnillo's rosebushes," he said, then reached out to stroke the dog's tiny head with the back of his index finger. Gretchen didn't flinch, just turned and licked his finger. "She's probably going to be sick tonight. I used half a bag of hot dogs to tempt her out."

"And then grabbed her?"

"And then she jumped right into my lap." At Lauren's surprised glance he cupped his palm in demonstration and added, "I baited the trap. I didn't want her getting away again."

"She came to you?" Lauren asked, looking up at him.

He wouldn't meet her eyes, just kept petting Gretchen. "We made a deal, your useful little dog and me."

"And what was that?"

He met her eyes, and the remorse and hope blended in the dark chocolate depths took her breath away. "The deal was, if she let me bring her back to you I wouldn't hurt you again."

"Oh," she said inadequately. Gretchen's warm, sleek body vibrated in her arms. Night dropped warm and dark around them. Fireflies danced above the lawn, golden stubs suspended in the darkness.

"I'm sorry," he said, his voice blending with the humid air.

No excuses, she thought. The U.S. military in general and the Marine Corps in particular demanded answers, not excuses, and he wouldn't allow himself that luxury, either. It was up to her to extend forgiveness. She held all the power in her hands.

"Do you want to come in and talk about it?" she asked.

His weight shifted to the balls of his feet as he shoved his hands in his pockets, then came up with the greasy plastic bag. "Yeah. I do."

Inside the house she set Gretchen down. They washed their hands, then Lauren got glasses of ice water for the humans while Gretchen lapped at her water dish. When she'd drunk enough, she trotted into the living room, stopped at the sliding glass doors and looked inquiringly at Lauren.

"Not a chance in hell," she said. Gretchen curled up on her bed in front of the fireplace instead. "Please, sit," she urged Ty.

They settled into opposite ends of the sofa, much as they had before, her at one end with her knees pulled up to her chest, him at the other, but he didn't sprawl this time. It was as if he didn't want to break something in her living room, a picture, a knickknack. Her.

She handed him a glass. While he drank she looked him over, liked what she saw. Clear eyes, eased lines around his mouth. She couldn't heal him, never intended to. He had to do that work himself, but she could be there for him while he got reacquainted with the man he was born to be. Remembering his dig about healing wounded animals, she said, "I never thought you needed to heal, Ty. You just . . . needed to get reacquainted with yourself."

He leaned forward to set the glass down, then shook his head, gave a little huff of laughter. "You weren't supposed to be curious. You were supposed to see my fucked-up-ness and walk, not . . ."

He gestured helplessly, so she finished the sentence. "Not suggest increasingly intimate sexual experiences? Or not care?" she said.

"Both," he said with a wry smile. "Why me, Lauren?"

He sounded composed, as if he were asking her the weather forecast, but under the words ran a hint of nerves. The way he smoothed his hands over his thighs told her so.

"Why are you working on the rigs?" she asked, keeping the words gentle, not challenging.

His shoulders were broad enough to block out the rising moon when he squared up. "Because no one knows me, what I've done or seen. No one cares. Out there, all I am is a dime-a-dozen rough-neck, an interchangeable cog in a machine. I don't have to care about anybody, and nobody cares about me." He finished the water in the glass, his strong throat working as he swallowed.

When he set the glass on a coaster, she spoke. "I chose you because I liked the way you moved. There was something in the way you walked and held yourself that inspired confidence. I liked the way you looked, sure, but I really liked your stride."

He actually blushed. "That's crazy."

She shrugged. "Men like hair or breasts or legs. I like a guy who can handle himself, which is what I thought you were until we had sex, because you were totally different in bed than you were out of it. And then I was curious."

"I was an asshole."

"You were acting like an asshole. That's different from being one."

"How did you know?"

She smiled, remembering years of dating bad boys of all stripes and sizes. "Hard-won experience," she said. "Why did you come back?"

He flexed his hands, then met her gaze. "I didn't like what I'd done. Who I'd become. I'd worked hard to become that man, but in the end, I didn't like him."

The words made her lungs seize up like they did when the showers ran cold at her gym, and it took her a few seconds to catch her breath.

"If you want to tell me about it, I'd like to hear the story," she said.

He looked at her for a long moment, the dark brown eyes seemingly stripped of the protective edge he'd worn for so long. "You know this story."

"I don't know your story."

Another pause. He leaned forward, rubbed his eyes with the heels of his hands, then braced his elbows on his knees and talked to the floor. His thick hair slid forward, partially obscuring his expression. "There aren't many different reasons why people join the Corps. Money for college. Fight terrorists. Family history of service. Get out of a hick town. Wear dress blues and carry the sword for duty and honor and country. The last one's Sean, the walking recruiting poster." He threw her a look, sardonic and aching and amused, all at once. "I joined because I believed in the mission, and I thought I could save the world."

An image bloomed of Ty, young and handsome and idealistic, using kittens to tempt girls into haylofts, and her throat tightened for the boy he had been. "Oh," she said.

"There was this village, a one-donkey hamlet, a scattering of mud huts housing a few families at the base of the hill country we patrolled every week. We all knew a little Farsi, commands mostly, but I learned more so we could talk to the tribal elders. Gain their trust. And the kids, the boys at least, and a couple of little girls with their hair cut real short so they looked like boys, were learning English in school. So they practiced with me, and I practiced Farsi with them. My sisters organized school supply drives, shipped over books and toys for the kids. I'd been in their houses, drunk tea with them, brought medical supplies and food when I could. It was beyond exchanging information for supplies. We were friends.

"One night a platoon engages in the hill country, and they call in air support, except somewhere in the communication chain someone fucks up the coordinates and the village gets smoked."

She covered her mouth with her hand. At the movement he looked up, and now she could see the raw pain bubbling and popping, forcing volcanic plates of injustice and anger and helplessness against each other. "It happens. It's not supposed to, but it does. We got up there as soon as daylight broke. Half the village was obliterated. Bodies, and body parts, and what little these people owned was strewn over the ground, and the smell of high explosives and burnt meat. But they weren't mad at us. They said it wasn't us, but it was us."

He stopped for a moment, drank some water, leaned forward to brace his elbows on his knees. She waited, her heart pounding.

"The kids wouldn't come near me. The ones that survived. Three died, and the sound of them wailing as they crouched by their dead friends . . . I hear it all the time. I tried to talk to them, but they hid behind their mothers on the other side of the road. The Marine Corps is black and white, good or evil, all or nothing, and so was I. No gray areas. But after that everything was gray, and something inside me broke."

Something inside her broke at the telling. "I'm sorry," she said. "For them, and for you. I know it's meaningless, but I am so sorry."

"It's not meaningless," he said. "That's what I finally learned. Life's a fucked-up mess, but that's no reason to stop living, to stop taking care of people. In fact, the people you care about and who care about you are the only thing that make living worthwhile."

He looked at her then, and the vulnerability in his brown eyes sliced right through her. She scooted down the length of the sofa as he reached for her, burying his face in the curve of her neck, then shifted to pull her onto his lap and wrap his arms around her. Despite the uneven shudder to his breathing, his heart beat strong and steady against her ribs. She held him until the tension eased from his muscles and the embrace lost the desperate quality.

Then she pulled back and kissed him lightly on the lips. "I do care about you, Ty." And it would be so easy to do so much more than care. They were balanced on the edge of a precipice together, but he needed time. Time, and patience.

His breath eased from him, but tension still hovered around his dark eyes. "Who'd you have lunch with today?"

She laughed. "A friend."

"A friend you're curious about?"

What a Neanderthal. She loved it, laughed out loud. "He's nice enough, but he doesn't make me curious."

His hand skated up her spine and released the clip holding her hair in a floppy knot at the back of her head. It tumbled down around her face, and he brushed it back, then cupped her jaw and kissed her, a real kiss, soft and hot and wet. Languid heat simmered in her veins. "I care, too," he said when he pulled back enough to let words escape, and the potent emotion behind them made her heart leap. He sat back, blew out his breath as he considered her. "I've been making plans. Not too many. I need to get my feet under me again."

It wouldn't take long, she thought. "That seems reasonable. Care to share them?"

He took a breath, spoke decisively. "I'm going to finish out my next shift on T-22 because they're counting on me, but then I'm going to quit Gulf Independent and buy into Langley Security. Put what I learned in the Corps and in school to use."

It was a plan with permanence, a plan engaged with the people and ideals that mattered most to him, a new beginning founded on old principles of trust and commitment and honor. "I like that plan," she said with a smile.

"John and I are going to team up with an NGO to help the village rebuild. Those kids deserve a school, and they're going to get one."

"I'll help," she said without hesitation.

This time when he smiled the creases at the corners of his mouth looked like laugh lines, not the weight of the world etched into his skin. "I knew you would."

He lifted a hand to her tumbled hair and tucked it behind her ear. There was a calm certainty in his actions and in the way he held himself, as if he'd slipped into something familiar, a pair of well-worn boots, a favorite chair, a lifelong friendship. Into himself, really. He was no longer doing battle with himself. "Lie down with me, Lauren."

This answer required action, not words. She stood, then took Ty's hand and walked with him down the hallway to her bedroom. The windows were open to the cool night air, a breeze gently lifting the sheer curtains as she pulled back the spread and top sheet and stretched out. Ty followed her onto the bed, wrapped one strong arm around her waist and curved his body around hers. Their feet tangled together, his knee between hers, her leg draped over his thigh, his hand at her waist, her fingers spread over his neck and jaw. His short, spiky blond eyelashes swept down as he looked at her mouth, then he brushed a kiss over her lips, apologetic and repentant and yet utterly male, offering whatever she wanted from all he had.

She took the kiss, gave it back to him. The pulse in his throat leaped under her fingertips, and the muscles in his thigh tightened briefly, but he held himself still except for slow, exploratory kisses. She'd never kissed him like this, face-to-face, with no other goal in mind, and while she felt his cock thickening and shifting in his jeans, ached at the rasp of her lace bra over her nipples, longed to rub herself against him, for an endless length of time she lay with Ty and just kissed him. She learned his mouth, the pattern of his breath, the lazy slide of his tongue against hers, the way a closed-mouth kiss at the corner of his mouth would make his breathing halt for a second and his fingers tighten at her waist.

He was shivering, tremors eddying through his muscles when she shifted back to look into his eyes. "Hey," she said. The standard Southern greeting, all-purpose, the intent derived from the tone behind the word. She'd pitched hers to mean *Hello*, *Hi*, *there*, *Glad to see you*.

His lips curved into a lazy smile. "Still know what you want, Lauren?"

"I do. I most certainly do. I want you."

"I'm all yours," he said, and with those words she knew Ty Hendricks was finally coming home.

All on the Line

Chapter One

Of all the places Sean Winthrop had stood around waiting in miserable conditions, the parking lot of an anonymous apartment complex in Galveston, Texas, was the worst. Objectively speaking, it wasn't. The weather was decent, the waning moon setting among the stars in the western sky, and he wore cargo pants and a button-down shirt against the cool, near-calm, early morning air. He leaned against his car, not standing at ramrod straight attention while upperclassmen flung abuse and spittle at his face, waiting for Plebe Summer to begin. He wasn't in an Oxford examination hall, his stomach in knots, waiting for an exam. He wasn't even hunkered down in a near-freezing foxhole, waiting for the right moment to signal his platoon to commence another attack on a Taliban position.

At five in the morning he was waiting for Abby Simmons to walk out of an apartment that wasn't her own.

0458 became 0502, then 0515 before the door at the top of the third-floor landing opened, then closed almost immediately. She padded down the concrete steps in her bare feet, her high heels and purse dangling from one hand, her car keys jangling in the other. She wore her No Limits waitress uniform, a black skirt and a white shirt, but the shirt was buttoned unevenly and untucked. Her red hair was a wreck, the shining, soft waves from earlier in the night tousled into bedhead. A pool of light from the parking lot's streetlights illuminated her face just long enough for him to see mascara and eyeliner smudged around her green eyes, and her mouth, swollen and bare of the bright red lipstick she'd had on earlier in the evening.

Cock-sucking lips was the term the Marines in his platoon used, but he'd seen her mouth as well-used after a couple of hours of sex. She loved to kiss, loved to open her mouth and breathe into his, her tongue rubbing against his as he worked in and out of her wet—

Stop.

The state of her mouth almost sealed the deal, warning him to silence. After what he'd done ten months ago he had no business being here, half-stalking her in a parking lot, no business asking her who she'd been with, what she'd done. Howling regret had no right to use sharp claws dripping with acid to crawl up from his bowels and into his chest to slice casually at his throat.

"Abby," he said curtly.

So much for his much-vaunted impulse control.

In the act of stepping off the sidewalk she startled, regained her balance, and swung to face him. For a brief moment he was glad he'd kept his Oakleys on, even though it was the purple-tinged blackness just before dawn. He didn't want her to see his eyes.

"Sean?" She took a step closer, into the light. "What are you doing here?"

Shock and disbelief infused her voice, so she hadn't seen him at No Limits earlier in the night, watching her wait tables in Galveston's raunchiest, wildest nightclub. She used to drink and dance there, not work there.

"I'm on leave," he said. *I wanted to see you. I missed you. I made the biggest mistake of my life telling you we were both too distracted to make a relationship based on thirty days of hot sex and five months of e-mail work while I was deployed.*

And you did exactly what I told you to do. You moved on.

Those thoughts and more lay under his blunt words, but she didn't hear the subtext. "I meant, what are you doing *here* at five in the morning?"

She crossed her arms over her torso as she spoke, shoulders hunching slightly as she glanced over her shoulder at the stairway she'd just descended. She looked for all the world like a teenager caught sneaking out of a house. He flashed back to the first night he met her at No Limits. The chemistry had been instant, and lava-hot, but she'd looked so young, so impossibly young, that he'd made her show him her ID before he got a room. It was the freckles dusting her forehead and cheeks, the green eyes, the innocent cast of her mouth. He was sober enough to do the math. Twenty-three to his twenty-eight. Old enough according to the law, young enough to feel a little dirty. At first. Then it just felt right.

Until fear got the better of him.

"I'm waiting for you," he said, as if it was obvious.

"How did you find me?"

"Lisette told me where you were," he said, naming another cocktail waitress at No Limits. When he asked where Abby went, Lisette said she swapped closings with her and went home early. He'd rattled off her old address, the procedure of double-checking dates, times, coordinates drilled into him over the last year, and Lisette gave him a new one, thrown over her shoulder as she hurried off to another table. He'd assumed she'd finally moved out of her father's house.

His assumption made an ass of him.

"Why?"

She'd been young, not stupid. "I've been asking myself the same question," he said. This was a mistake. He should have gone to No

Limits the night he got home and ended this for good. But he'd wanted Abby. Red-haired, freckle-starred Abby, now leaving her lover's apartment at five in the morning.

"*You* broke up with *me* ten months ago. You sent me a four-sentence e-mail saying I was a *sweet girl*, but I had a lot of growing up to do, and neither of us had the time or emotional energy to commit to supporting each other through a difficult situation."

He'd meant to respect her wide-open, no responsibilities, no ties life, because the home front was different. Life went on there, and she didn't have to be tied to a Marine fifteen thousand miles away with no time for her. He drew breath to say something calm and rational when the door at the top of the landing opened again and a man's heavier tread thumped down the stairs.

A uniformed cop, his utility belt in one hand and car keys in the other, rounded the corner. His keys sounded businesslike, metal on metal, at least a dozen. It was the key ring of a man with responsibilities or maybe access to bedrooms all over town. He stopped when he saw Abby, then his gaze zipped over to Sean.

Big motherfucker, even without the vest adding bulk. Paramilitary haircut, paramilitary demeanor, close but not quite the rebar backbone the Naval Academy jammed up your ass to the base of your skull your first day of Plebe Summer. But the guy could handle himself. It was in the way he squared up and shifted his weight to the balls of his feet when he saw Sean.

Without moving, Sean leveled a look at him that said *Bring it the fuck on.*

"Problem, Abby?" the cop said without taking his eyes from Sean.

"It's fine, Ben," she said. Red hair tumbled over her left hand as she rubbed her forehead with her palm. No engagement ring, no gold band, just the smell of the cop's skin and sweat as a faint breeze drifted from Abby to Sean. "I know him from a long time ago."

The words seemed to be enough for Ben the Galveston Cop, who looked like he wasn't any more eager to begin his day with a take-down in his parking lot than Sean was to end his with one. More telling, Ben didn't show a hint of remorse or embarrassment at Abby's tousled condition, nor did he look proud, or cocky. He'd fucked her, she was going home, and it all meant nothing, or at least there was no shame in it.

Sean wouldn't have let another man see her like that, not for the shame of it, but because it was so personal, so intimate. Between them only.

Ben looked over to the Mustang. "That your car?"

Sean gave him the barest hint of a nod.

"Your plates expired four months ago."

"He was deployed to Afghanistan," Abby said impatiently. "He's got a grace period to get them renewed."

Still expressionless. Ben offered Sean a bare nod of his own, then spoke to Abby as he got in his car. "Text me when you get home safe."

The message came through loud and clear. Ben had the right to ask that of her, or at least offer the security of checking in with a law enforcement officer. Sean didn't, and he'd better get to the courthouse sooner rather than later. A blue Shelby Cobra with a red racing stripe and plates that read *500 HSPR* would attract attention even without a word from Ben to his colleagues.

Abby watched Ben hoist his utility belt into his truck, then leave the lot. When her attention returned to Sean, he said, "Wow. A cop. Not so sweet anymore."

Oh yeah, he was the master of impulse control and logical argu-ment. Make it personal, throw it back in her face. Except on closer inspection the shadows under her eyes weren't the smudged makeup on her lids. They were the deeper purple of exhaustion.

Her chin lifted, throwing her swollen mouth and stark cheek-bones into relief. "That's right. I'm not."

"Is he your boyfriend?" *Say* no. *Wait. Say* yes, *because* no *means booty call* . . .

"No."

And . . . that was worse, hearing the word in her mouth, seeing her freshly fucked and doing the walk of shame at five in the morning. "Jesus Christ, Abby."

"It's none of your business, Sean. You made it none of your business."

Cold, flat, and saying exactly what his conscience said thirty seconds earlier. "Right," he said. "Fine. I'm out of here."

He turned to get in the Mustang when Abby spoke. "How long are you in town?" The words were high-pitched, just rushed enough to convey a curiosity that overcame reluctance.

He stopped. "A little over a month," he said.

"Then what?"

"Does it matter?" He hauled open his car door, but Abby's voice stopped him once again.

"Why did you come looking for me? I thought *sweet* and *innocent* were too distracting for a guy with a war on his mind."

He hadn't said that, goddammit. Implied it, yes. It was his turn to rub his forehead in disgust. Fuck it all. "Doesn't matter, does it? You're not that girl anymore."

"No, I'm not," she said flatly. "I don't have time for a relationship, and Ben's not interested in one. That's who I am now. So don't you get on your high horse because I'm not the girl you left behind."

She'd stalked up to him during this speech, hands holding her shoes and her keys spread to either side as she flung the words at him like a slap. He gave up any hope that he'd spend this leave like he'd spent the last, getting the comfort he needed from the person he least expected was able to give it to him. Maybe it was just exhaustion, but she was pale under the remaining eye makeup, almost Goth in her appearance, tightly wound, and thinner than he remembered. She'd turned her back on him and was stalking toward her car, as much as a woman could stalk when barefoot and carrying her heels.

"Abby," he said, his voice pitched to command. She stopped, but she didn't turn around. "My Marines were distracted. Unfocused. Texting and e-mailing and checking social networking sites from a fucking *war zone*. I had to help us coalesce as a unit. Some were married, with kids, or had babies on the way. All of them had mothers who'd sent sons off to war. They needed me focused and there to make sure they got home to their families. The consequences, if we didn't, were unacceptable."

Days would go by without a thought of Abby. Sometimes a couple of weeks. But then he'd be hunkered down in a foxhole, and his fears would chase their tails like frantic dogs. The ever-present fear that all his planning and strategizing would be for nothing, that he'd lose a Marine, narrowed his focus to exclude everything but the immediate moment. As the countdown to homecoming entered double digits, then single, a new fear began the whirling, snarling chase in his head: that he'd made the right choice for now, but the aftermath was coming.

The starry swath of bitterly cold, black Afghan sky calmed him, giving him the uncanny sense she was right there beside him.

At that she did turn around. "We all make choices," she said, the heat gone from her voice, replaced with a heart-turning sadness. "You made yours, and no one, including me, would tell you you made the wrong one." She lifted her shoes and keys with a shrug, then looked around Ben's parking lot. "Welcome to *your* consequences."

With that she got in her Celica. The engine ground for a few seconds before it turned over, and she steered out of the lot without a backward glance.

And that was that. Except he couldn't breathe. War created a time warp in his mind, and in that frozen world, despite his e-mail,

Abby hadn't changed. Sweet, cheerful, always smiling and laughing, always ready for a good time. Just out of college and searching for a job, she'd had all the time in the world to spend with him.

With the scent of Abby's warm skin lingering in the cool dawn air, the sheer ludicrousness of his assumptions sucker punched him. Of course she changed. Of course she'd moved on. She was pretty and vivacious and just the right combination of sexy-sweet. Guys used to go down on their knees at her feet for the chance to buy her a drink, or dance with her, or just talk to her and watch her eyes gleam with the sheer pleasure of being alive. Now she looked wounded, bruised, battered. A different kind of man loved that. They either wanted to make it all better, or they wanted to go there with her. Vicariously live someone else's pain. Something about the damaged ones made the surrender all the more sweet.

You told her to grow up. *Did you really think she'd sit in limbo, waiting for* you?

Yes.

He'd told her to change; turns out he'd wanted her exactly the way she was. But she *had* changed . . . just not in any way he'd imagined.

Now what?

Now you move on, just like she did.

Cognitive fucking dissonance, compounded by lack of sleep and the total system shock of reentry into suburban life in Texas after a year at a FOB in Afghanistan. He knew the drill. Sleep, eat, keep moving. Make a plan. The next goal to tackle was Life Without Abby. He slid back into the Mustang and started the engine. His cell phone buzzed. Text from Ty Hendricks. No Limits tonight 2200 hrs.

Sean rubbed his thumb over the screen and shifted his gaze to the pale horizon. After leaving the Corps, John Langley, a former staff sergeant, had opened a security business headquartered in Galveston. Ty, John's best buddy in the Corps, was supposed to be the personnel specialist, but for reasons locked away in Ty's impenetrable self he'd chosen to work on the oil rigs instead. With his Galveston connection, John told Sean to look him up when he came home. Sean touched base with him, half expecting the contact would be a courtesy call. Instead, because the work sounded interesting, and John obviously needed experienced help, Sean signed on for a month of surveillance in an industrial espionage case. Most days he worked with Ty, who'd mastered the art of silence.

He ran his thumb over the phone's keypad. Ty was up early, or maybe he'd skipped sleeping tonight, too. So what if Abby worked at No Limits, Galveston's hottest, sexiest hookup bar? Time for a little payback, even.

He keyed I'll be there into his phone, got into his car, and floored it out of the parking lot, leaving a pile of assumptions in a shattered heap on the pavement.

After Sean broke up with her via a four-sentence e-mail sent from a war zone, Abby had imagined the reunion scenario hundreds of times. Like her, he was Galveston born and raised, so she fully expected to see him around when he was home. The grocery store. The bookstore. The park. No Limits, of course, where they'd met.

One deployment and a lifetime ago.

In every fantasy she'd been in control, dressed in something that looked both sophisticated and sexy, her hair done, her makeup subtle but her mouth a nice shade of red guaranteed to draw his eye. She'd developed three different scathing speeches specifically tailored to how he might open the conversation, because she sure as hell wouldn't. And when the cutting speeches didn't patch up her wounded pride, she'd practiced cutting him dead for condescending to her while he shredded her heart against a cheese grater.

None of her revenge-based fantasies included him scaring the living hell out of her in Ben's parking lot after a quickie, three hours of sleep . . . and another quickie. That's what she liked about Ben. She could call him at one in the morning and his bed and his body were at her disposal. If he was home, and alone. She wasn't sleeping with anyone else, but she harbored no illusions she was Ben's only bedmate.

Driving home on autopilot, her car was already in the crosswalk when the light blinked from yellow to red. She slammed on the brakes and jerked against her seat belt harness. As usual, she was too tired to be driving safely, let alone dealing with Sean Winthrop's sudden appearance out of the predawn darkness.

"Oh, God," she moaned.

No perfect outfit. No sexily tousled hair, just a snarled mess thanks to Ben's hands. Her mouth was probably the right shade of red, though, and her nipples and thighs still tingled from his morning stubble. She'd gaped like an idiot until her exhausted, sex-befuddled brain realized she wasn't hallucinating, that Sean was actually right there. And if she could see that he was bigger, bulkier, holding himself with a tense, vibrating masculine energy that was new, he was close enough to see . . . everything.

Including her incorrectly buttoned blouse. "Oh, *God*," she said.

The car behind her honked impatiently. She sat up straight and floored the accelerator before letting up on the gas. She'd gotten two speeding tickets in the last six months. One more and she'd lose her license, which meant she'd lose everything else, and Ben had made it perfectly clear from their first night together that he didn't fix tickets, bail drunk girls out of jail, or get asshole ex-boyfriends' cars towed in exchange for sex.

The car behind her sped past on the right, the driver alternating his attention between the road and his own face in the rearview mirror as he shaved his jutting jaw with an electric razor. He looked so stupid Abby almost laughed, but she was afraid if she started she wouldn't stop.

The clock on the dashboard read 5:22, and the day stretched out in front of her, every single minute booked. Get home, get Dad up, take a quick shower while he dressed, give him his breathing treatments, fix him breakfast, get to school for extra time in the lab, work at her homework, followed by her shift at No Limits. Weekends involved a whole different but equally pressing set of responsibilities, cooking, cleaning, and the never-ending homework.

Exactly what Sean thought she couldn't handle. He hadn't said as much in his e-mail, but she could read between the lines. A lot of growing up to do. That's what he said. Because a twenty-three-year-old college graduate who still lived with her father and didn't have a job wasn't nearly as mature a Naval Academy graduate and Rhodes Scholar who was about to lead twenty-two men into combat.

"I've done it," she said. "I am all grown up, Sean. As you just saw."

She wished she could have seen his eyes. Were the Oakleys in the darkness before dawn some kind of military thing he'd picked up overseas, looking cool and tough and bad? Because he'd looked all three of those things. Square-jawed and ready for action, especially when Ben came down the stairs.

She pulled into her garage, killed the engine, left her No Limits heels strewn on the passenger floorboards, and hurried up the stairs leading into the house. After the diagnosis her Dad had moved from the master bedroom upstairs to his former office downstairs, sleeping on a single bed wedged between his big oak desk and the wall. She knocked on the closed door and cracked it open.

"Dad," she said softly. "Time to get up."

His rough, phlegmy breathing halted then started again. He coughed, and she heard rustling as he started to extract himself from the covers. It would take him twenty minutes to get up, shuffle to the downstairs bathroom, and get himself dressed. In that time she'd shower, dress, start breakfast, and tidy up the main floor.

"I'm going to take a shower, Dad," she said.

A grunt was her only answer.

She raced upstairs to the bathroom in her bedroom suite and started the shower running to warm up the water. She stripped off her clothes and stuffed them into the laundry hamper. Time to do laundry.

When she turned back to the mirror she froze. Nothing so gauche as a hickey marred her neck. Ben was older than her, and if even half the rumors were true, vastly experienced. But looking at her there was no doubt she'd recently had sex. Her hair wasn't quite a rat's nest, but there was no mistaking the *man's hands in it* look. Her lips were pouty and swollen, kiss-reddened, and the orgasmic flush still stained her throat and collarbone. Her nipples were dark pink and only just softening, and the red triangle between her thighs was flattened.

She met her eyes in the mirror. "That's what all grown up looks like."

The words disappeared into the spray and steam from the shower. He told her she needed to grow up, toughen up, and she had, but he wasn't supposed to see the one thing that gave her release and helped her cope. And while she'd gotten right in his face and told him off, the memory of it made her smart. It wasn't the coolly disdainful persona she wanted to project to him. The next time she saw him, she'd leave him with no doubt that he mattered not one little bit to her.

Her dad's coughing followed her into the shower, and by the time she stepped out again, it hadn't stopped. She dressed and hurried down the stairs, mentally tabulating chores and weighing them against the time she had before she was due in the lab at school. More chores than time, as always.

Chronic Obstructive Pulmonary Disease, or COPD, a disease that caused shortness of breath and a lasting cough, now regulated her life. She'd gone to college in Houston, where her mother moved after she divorced Abby's difficult, brilliant father, but Galveston remained home. When her father was diagnosed after a lifetime of smoking and working at a chemical plant, she'd moved home to take care of him, because no one else would. But her father proved to be a combative patient, resisting the diagnosis, then the various treatments his doctors prescribed. He took his medication irregularly, or not at all. That was the first task of the day.

Her father's face was gray, his face deeply lined and puffy from poor circulation. "Ready for your breathing treatment?" she asked lightly.

Another grunt. She set up the nebulizer and measured out the medications, something he could easily do himself but refused to, then held out the mask. When he had the mask secured over his face, she got up and opened the fridge. The plate of sliced turkey breast, asparagus, and mashed potatoes she'd left for him sat on the second shelf, uncovered and drying out. "You hardly touched your dinner."

"Wasn't hungry," he said after a deep inhale.

The man in front of her bore little resemblance to the hulking, imposing figure from her childhood that dominated the house with his mood swings. His clothes hung on his frame like a suit on a hanger, jowls sagging from his jaw and neck as they hadn't even a year ago. A profound mixture of love, irritation, and fear bubbled in her stomach. "Dad, you need to eat."

"It didn't taste good. No flavor."

That wasn't her cooking. A lifetime of smoking unfiltered cigarettes had destroyed his taste buds, and his precious Tabasco sauce gave him unbearable heartburn. "Hold your breath after you inhale. Two, three, that's good. I'll make you eggs for breakfast if you'll promise me you'll go for a walk with me before I head over to the lab."

Her father had high blood pressure, high cholesterol, COPD,

and rapidly clogging arteries, and eggs were theoretically off his diet. His churlish eyes lit up. "With a side of bacon."

"With a side of orange juice, and only if you promise," she said firmly.

"You'd think you'd be more accommodating, what with spending the night out."

"I can make Cream of Wheat with a side of fresh peaches," she said brightly, holding on to her patience with her fingernails.

He inhaled again, held his breath, then exhaled and tugged the mask down. "Goddamn thing."

"Cough, Dad."

He reached for a tissue and began the laborious task of clearing the secretions the medication loosened. "The doctor said no eggs."

"Cream of Wheat it is," she said.

He looked at her, his eyes red and watering, lips wet and trembling, and a wave of recrimination swept over her. "Watch your tone, missy. Eggs'll be fine."

She pulled out the nonstick pan and spray.

"That nonstick stuff'll give you cancer," he said as he coughed again. "Cast iron and bacon grease. That's how you fry a good egg."

She took a deep breath and counted to ten, then scrambled two eggs and four whites in the nonstick pan, toasted the bread and buttered it with a spread designed to lower cholesterol, set the breakfast and a glass of OJ in front of him, then sat down at her place. He gave the eggs a dismissive snort but ate them, and the toast, and drank half the orange juice. She washed the nebulizer components, then the breakfast dishes, and ran the dishcloth over the counters in the time it took her dad to get up from the kitchen table, heading to his recliner in the family room.

"Not so fast, Dad. We're going for a walk."

"I don't feel up to it."

"I don't care, Dad. It's a beautiful morning. Just down to the corner and back. You haven't been outside in two weeks."

She took his elbow and guided him toward the front door, and the simple fact that she could shift his direction, force him to her will, made a lump swell in her throat. He already had his shoes on. She scuffed her sore feet into flip-flops and opened the door.

Her father blinked. She held his elbow until he stepped down the stairs, then he shook her off. "I'm fine."

Sunshine dappled the driveway, filtered through the big oak in the center of the front lawn. Abby made a slight production of inhaling the slightly cooler fall air and looking around. Perfect picnic weather. The lump in her throat tightened until she swallowed it down. Her father focused on his feet, his once-large stride reduced to a shuffle as he navigated the shifting sidewalk, lips pursed to control the flow of air into and out of his clotted lungs. She kept one eye on him as she looked around, using the weather to steel her resolve and hide her emotions.

"Pretty day," she said as they walked back up the sidewalk to the front door.

Her dad looked up, his eyes watery, his skin still paste gray. Usually a walk improved his color. "Lawn needs mowing."

She bit her lips, counting to fifteen this time. "I know, Dad. Not today."

Inside the house her father again cleared his lungs while Abby packed her bag to head to school. Getting back in her car brought memories of the morning rushing back. She flushed and straightened her shoulders. *Cool. Disinterested. Over him.* That was the goal. Prove, in no uncertain terms, that she was so over Sean Winthrop.

Chapter Two

The Mustang's passenger door flew open. Ty thudded into the passenger seat, shook his hair back out of his face, then closed his eyes. Sean's jaw dropped. Ty was leaving that gorgeous, smart, sharp woman alone . . . after what they'd just done? In Ty's place Sean would have her under a hot shower, using soap and touch to inscribe on her skin how he felt. What it meant. What he wanted.

Except Lauren wasn't Abby. Abby wasn't his. Lauren, however, was Ty's for the taking. That came through loud and clear during the ménage, her openness the exact opposite of Abby's *step-back-you-fucker* attitude in the parking lot. Abby used to look at him like Lauren looked at Ty, heart and soul in her eyes.

The memory squeezed his heart into his sternum.

Start with the immediate. "What the fuck are you doing in my car, instead of in her bed?"

"She was falling asleep. I didn't want to wake her up. Drive."

Lacking the authority to order Ty out of the car and back into Lauren's bed, Sean turned the engine over and shoved the gearshift into reverse. This wasn't the Ty he knew. The Ty he knew went out of his way to take care of people, especially vulnerable ones. And a woman left alone after a down-and-dirty ménage with a total stranger definitely qualified as vulnerable. "So she's gonna wake up alone."

Ty ignored him, lost in thought, or lost in some internal hell. Sean knew the feeling. After an hour of the hottest, wildest sex he'd ever had, he should have been planning the next encounter. Where to go . . . *No Limits* . . . when to go . . . *the second the bar opened* . . . what kind of girl to go after . . . *anyone who wasn't a redhead. No redheads.*

"After what we just did," Sean added as he drove out of Lauren's neighborhood.

What they just did started at No Limits, where Abby worked five nights a week. She'd hear about it. He felt like an idiot on the dance floor, danced only under extreme duress, but something about the vibe between him, Lauren, and Ty dropped his inhibitions through the floor. He hadn't been with a woman since Abby fifteen months ago, and when Ty turned Lauren to face him and she stepped into his body, soft breasts and grinding hips, the hot earth scent of lust rising from her damp skin, all he'd cared about was that he was about to *get some*, the Marine Corps' unofficial encouraging cry, along with *hoo-rah*. But when Ty asked Lauren if she wanted to fuck him, he'd come to his senses to find most of the dance floor watching them, no mean feat in No Limits.

Abby was going to hear about that, for sure. He shook his head in a motion similar to Ty's, like he was trying to dismiss a thought from his brain. He'd broken up with Abby months ago. She'd moved on. In theory he could fuck a woman on the hood of his car in broad damn daylight in the East Beach Parking Lot and it was none of Abby's business.

A fist closed around his heart. Lauren had asked if there was anything she needed to know about. What was he supposed to say? *No communicable diseases, just a broken heart, ma'am. Entirely my fault. No excuses.*

He cleared his throat. "I'm starving. You mind if I drive through somewhere?"

"Whatever."

Based on Ty's expression he didn't mind if Sean drove the car off the Pleasure Pier into the Gulf, so he pulled into the late-night drive-through at Wendy's and stared at the brightly illuminated menu board. "That was different," he said absently.

"Yeah," Ty said, his voice thick.

A girl's sleepy voice buzzed from the speaker, asking for their order. "A triple stack combo with bacon, extra large, and a Coke," Sean said. Maybe food would settle his stomach, roiling with a knowledge he'd rather bury under two pounds of grease than acknowledge. "You want anything?"

"I'm not hungry," Ty said.

Sean looked at him. Ty refused to meet his gaze. Frustrated, he asked, "Why'd we do that? Why did you let me fuck a woman you care about?"

"I don't care about her."

Thick-headed bastard. "Great. If you don't care we can compare notes. I'll start, because goddamn, that was the best blow job I've ever had. Of course, it's been over a year, but objectively speaking, Lauren was incredible. That thing you were talking about . . . the back of her throat thing . . ." Sean shook his head. "Nice soundtrack."

Some guys could do this, talk about women and sex like it was a replay of a Ping-Pong game. He wasn't one of those guys. Heat stained his cheekbones, but Ty still wouldn't look at him, so he kept going. Maybe discussing every little detail would make it real, push

Abby to the side so he could move on, and push Lauren to the front of Ty's mind.

"It was probably for the best that Lauren was on top, because even after the blow job my control wasn't all that great. The whole thing was so fucking hot. Every time you got a little deeper in her ass she'd tighten around me, and when Lauren came—"

A muscle jumped in Ty's jaw each time he said *Lauren*. "Give it a rest, Winthrop."

Sean just looked at him. "Make up your mind, Hendricks. You either don't care, or you do. Marines fight in pairs, and they fuck in pairs. Girlfriends are off-limits, but you said she's not your girlfriend, so she's just a piece of ass, right? An exceptionally talented piece of ass," he said meditatively. "So go on, tell me what you thought."

"I think you're in danger of losing your teeth to my fist."

A fistfight in the Wendy's drive-through lane sounded pretty good, given that Ty was in the process of throwing away what Sean now knew he wanted, so he launched another salvo. "How was her ass? Come to think of it, how do you talk a girl into that? You think Lauren would be up for another round, let me get some practice in?"

Would Abby go for that? Maybe she already had, with Ben the Galveston Cop who looked like he'd be up for anything.

His stomach dropped another six inches.

Fist balled at the end of his cocked arm, Ty swung around in the passenger seat. Sean held his gaze for a long moment. "Don't care, huh?"

Ty's gaze flicked past Sean, then his arm dropped. "Take your goddamn food before we get arrested for corrupting a minor."

Sean turned to get his food and froze. The girl in the drive-through window was a dead ringer for his littlest sister Naeve's best friend, but she didn't seem to recognize him, or the car, so he gave her his best *I'm-totally-harmless* smile as he reached out the window for the bag of grease and extra-large sugar water, then set the bag on his lap, and put the drink in the holder between him and Ty. "I know why I was there," he said conversationally. He dug in the bag, then crammed four french fries into his mouth. "Get the LT laid after fifteen months overseas, and in a completely fucked-up, guy bonding way, it was thoughtful. But maybe you should have considered what Lauren meant to you before you did it."

Hypocrite. Maybe you should have thought about how you'd feel when Abby moved on before you sent her a terse, near-brutal e-mail.

Ty tipped his head back against the headrest and closed his eyes. "She doesn't mean anything to me," he said.

"Bullshit," Sean said through a mouthful of burger as he turned onto the main drag and headed for No Limits, where they'd left Ty's truck. "Remember that hot little thing about me watching you fuck her, you watching her go down on me? I was there. Watching. You care about her. It was all over your face, in the way you touched her. And in the end, when she lost all control, she turned to you. Not me."

"She just knows me better," Ty said when Sean pulled into the No Limits parking lot. "Emotions have nothing to do with it."

"You can keep denying it," Sean said quietly, "but it won't change reality. That's the shitty thing about reality. Doesn't change just because you want it to."

Ty shot him a final glare, then got out of the Mustang and slammed the door, heading for his truck at the back of the parking lot. Sean stared out his window at the people lined up between the club's brick facade and the velvet rope keeping them out of the parking lot. Two big bouncers controlled access to No Limits while the presence of two off-duty Galveston cops provided a visible deterrent to fights, drunk driving, and sex in the parking lot.

He recognized one of the cops as Ben, Abby's hookup, now smiling bright and sharp as he talked to a group of women in short skirts, short shorts, low-cut blouses, painted faces and pouty lips, hair spilling suggestively over shoulders and into cleavage, more female skin than he'd seen in fifteen months. Until tonight. One hot encounter with Ty and Lauren barely made a dent in the longing pent up inside him. No time like the present.

The bar's back door opened and Abby emerged, a clear plastic bag of trash in each hand. She flipped up the lid on a commercial Dumpster and tossed first one, then the second bag inside. She walked around the side of the Dumpster and went up on tiptoe to slam the lid.

Sean's heart stopped. When he walked into No Limits just before 2200, he'd looked for Abby, twice, and hadn't seen her. Her red hair stood out like flame even in the bar's dim lighting and glowed in the lights on the dance floor. She must have had a late shift tonight.

Trash emptied, she stopped between the Dumpster and the back door, and put one hand on her hip and the other to her forehead. From his position fifty feet away, hidden in his car, he watched her. Exhaustion slumped her shoulders as she shifted her weight from one foot to the other and rubbed her forehead with the back of her hand. Feeling like a voyeur, Sean watched her as his brain turned over what he knew about the home front.

It was easy to compartmentalize life in a war zone. There was the mission, the men, and there was everything else, all lumped into *the home front*. In an era of modern warfare, with Skype and international cell phones, Facebook and Twitter, the home front seeped into the war zone. Marines talked to their wives every day, heard all about the problems at work, the broken furnace, their kids' difficulties in school. But because the complicated, powerful emotions roiling in his gut whenever he thought about Abby overwhelmed him, he'd severed his obligation to the home front in four short sentences. He'd done it for his Marines, both to set an example and to ensure that they had his undivided attention when they needed it. Or so he told himself.

But turning his back on the reality of the home front didn't make it disappear, and based on what he saw in Ben's parking lot, somehow carefree Abby's life had become trench warfare right out of World War I. After tonight he had one of two options. He could set out to fuck his way through the available female population of Galveston in an effort to replace Abby in his body and heart, or he could find out what happened and fix his fuck-up before it really was too late.

The hand rubbing Abby's forehead dropped to her hip. She straightened her spine, squared up her shoulders, and strode back into the bar, and something about her unyielding attitude resonated deep inside him. Whatever was going on, she wasn't quitting.

Step one, get intelligence. Step two, formulate a plan. He'd screwed up once. He wouldn't do it again.

Closing in on midnight on Halloween, Abby stepped up to the waitress station on the horseshoe-shaped bar projecting from No Limits's back wall and called out, "Scotch neat, Ketel One and cranberry."

Linc Sawyer owned the bar and worked as its lead bartender. He'd hear her and have the drinks made in the time it took for her to survey the costumed crowd. No Limits was packed with slutty nurses, slutty vampires, slutty cheerleaders, slutty French maids, slutty fairies, and extra-slutty strippers. The men wore the barest acknowledgments to costumes and took full advantage of the drink specials and amped-up atmosphere.

"Hey," Lisette said, adjusting her cat ear headband. "We missed you Saturday."

"I had to take Dad to the after-hours clinic, then get new prescriptions filled," she said. The gray color hadn't just been a lack of fresh air. By four in the afternoon his lips were blue-tinged, and she was on the phone to his doctor. She'd bailed on a closing shift on a Saturday night, and her wallet was already screaming about the lost tips. Her dad's disability payments barely covered the mortgage.

"How's he doing?" Lisette asked.

"Better, actually. His doctor met us at the clinic," she said, remembering her profound relief when Dr. Weaver strode through the door, unflappable and analytical in her approach, no-nonsense enough to make her dad pay attention. "She found a better combination of drugs. He's slept better the last two nights, but he still needs to gain weight and improve his lung capacity."

"Good," Lisette said, and loaded up her tray. "Hey, did that hottie from last week find you?"

Hottie from last week. Sean. "Yes, he found me," she said, "and what were you thinking, sending him to Ben's place?"

"He whipped by the door in a muscle car, driving like a bat out of hell," Lisette said. "He didn't catch you before you went up?"

Ah yes, the Mustang, Sean's one concession to typical male testosterone toys. He liked to drive, and fast, and he was absolutely fanatical about American muscle cars. "No, but he was waiting three hours later when I came down," she said.

Lisette's eyebrows shot up. "Oh?"

"Yes. It was bad. Very bad," she said. The drinks materialized on the bar in front of her. "Thanks, Linc," she called, more out of good karma and manners than any hope he'd hear her over the bar's deafening noise level.

"Maybe that's for the best," Lisette said.

"Probably," Abby agreed, not quite sure what she was agreeing to, but No Limits on Halloween wasn't the place to carry on a meaningful conversation.

She lifted the tray on her flat palm to shoulder height, turned, and found herself face-to-face with Sean. She shrieked and stepped back, bumping into an occupied stool as she did. The abrupt change of direction sent the tray tilting to the right, and the drinks tipped precariously toward a woman waiting at the bar. Deftly Sean reached out and snagged the Scotch and the vodka cranberry just as the tray clattered to the floor.

"Nice reflexes," Lisette offered with a flirtatious smile, then whisked away into the crowd.

Abby crouched to reclaim the tray, then walloped Sean on the chest with it. "You scared me half to death! That's the second time in three days!" she hissed, and added a second wallop for good measure. She might as well wallop a two-hundred-year-old oak tree. "What are you *doing here*?"

"Looking for you. Where do these go?" Sean asked without changing expression.

She blinked. She'd fully expected to see him in the bar again; everyone in Galveston knew if you wanted to hook up, No Limits was the place to do it. But she hadn't expected him to be looking for her. His eyes, visible to her for the first time in over a year, were the same piercing blue but somehow unreadable. The tan lines from the Oakleys stretched across his temples, and crow's-feet gathered at the corners of his eyes. Even his mouth looked firmer, less inviting even than it had during the encounter in the parking lot.

Something was different. Every nerve in her body quivered, seeking additional input to make sense of the situation, her brain whirling as it tried to take in both his implacable expression and his sudden appearance. A sharp whistle shocked her out of her reverie.

"I'll do it." She held out the tray.

"I've got them," he said.

"Drinks have to be delivered on a tray," Linc called from behind the bar. "House rules. And stop harassing my waitress or there's a baseball bat back here with your face on it."

She gave Sean a bright, false smile and held out the tray with a flourish. "Don't make me lose this job," she said through her teeth. She'd been a regular here, in another lifetime, and other regulars tipped her well. "I need this job."

He set the drinks down on the cork-lined tray. She brushed past him, distributed drinks, made change, accepted her tip, and looked around for the next customer.

Sean was right there. "It's Halloween. Everyone else is in costume. Why aren't you?"

He asked because when they'd met before his yearlong deployment and three months of training prior, she'd already been thinking about her costume. This year she'd remembered it was Halloween only when she pulled into the parking lot. "I'm an overworked cocktail waitress with sore feet," she said, flipping him attitude even as she looked him up and down. He wore cargo pants, a loose shirt, and running shoes that looked like they'd seen a few thousand miles. "Who are you supposed to be?"

"A Marine on leave."

A good choice to get laid. "Unless you want a drink, go away," she said. "I'm working."

"I want a Shiner Bock and five minutes of your time."

"You can have the beer but not the time," she threw over her shoulder as she edged her way through the packed house, back to the bar.

"When can I get five minutes?"

He was right behind her, clearing a path easily with his broad shoulders. "When I'm not working or in class, which is almost never. My shadow wants a Shiner Bock," she said to Linc.

"Get Ben or Steve if he's bothering you," Linc said. He popped the top off the beer and handed it to her.

The last thing she was going to do was set up another face-to-face confrontation between Ben and Sean. "He's fine," she said as she set the beer on her tray and turned.

Once again Sean was right behind her, but this time she didn't startle. "Two fifteen?" he said.

"Five even," she replied, ignoring his confirmation of when she got off work.

He handed her a ten. "Keep it," he said when she dug in her apron pocket for his change. He turned for the door before she could say thank you, leaving her in the middle of the melee, watching him go.

He even moved differently, she realized. Wove through the crowd and out the door like a cat on a roof peak, so the hardened, implacable demeanor wasn't the only change the last year had wrought in him. There was no doubt in her mind he'd be waiting for her at two fifteen a.m.

It was nearly two thirty in the morning when she walked out the bar's back door and headed for the cluster of cars at the far end of the lot, where employees parked. Ben and Steve were long gone. Linc locked the door and followed her into the parking lot, watching to make sure every waitress locked herself in her car and left his property. She'd started her shift at five, when the bar opened, so her car was in the farthest corner, behind Lisette's Blazer and Tim's F-150. Parked beside her Celica was Sean's showy Mustang.

After a sharp-eyed look between Abby and Sean, Lisette peeled out. He leaned against the driver's side door, arms folded across his chest. Abby's steps slowed.

"I don't need the bat, you know," Linc said conversationally from behind her.

"It's fine, Linc," Abby said.

Otherwise expressionless, Sean transferred his laser focus to Linc. "I just want to talk to her."

"Standing right here," Abby said to the lights overhead. "I am standing . . . right . . . here . . . and they're talking over me like I don't exist."

"Five minutes," Sean amended, then switched those brilliant blue eyes back to her. "Please."

The *please* got her. "Go on home, Linc," she said softly.

Linc looked Sean over again, then the Mustang. "Your plates are wrong. That model runs five-fifty horse."

"I know," Sean said patiently. "I transferred the plates from the previous model."

Linc lifted an eyebrow at Abby, and she nodded. He got in his car and left. There was a long moment of silence broken only by Abby's quick inhales and the throbbing pulses radiating up from her cramped toes. Finally she walked over to the Celica and hoisted herself up on the trunk.

"Your five minutes started about thirty seconds ago," she said.

"You've got half the male population of Galveston watching out for you," Sean said.

"I'm not sleeping with him," she replied, but she was too tired to put any heat into the statement. "That's what you really wanted to know, isn't it?"

He didn't deny it. "So you don't have plans tonight?"

"With Ben?" she asked. The relief of being off her feet was palpable, her feet seeming to expand inside her heels without her weight on the ball of her foot. "We don't make plans. I text him. If he's home, interested, and alone, he texts back."

His gaze skimmed the length of her legs in the short skirt, then he crossed the short distance between his car and hers. He seemed bigger than she remembered, taller somehow, as if combat expanded him two sizes. He reached for her foot, slipped off her shoe and set it on the trunk.

The position was a little awkward, forcing her to lean back and brace her hands behind her, at the angle where the rear windshield met the trunk. Her skirt pooled in her lap, revealing the lacy tops of her thigh-high stockings as he took off her other shoe. Sean was hot before, in a clean-cut, spit-and-polish, perfect-wedding-photos kind of way, the jut of his ruthlessly shaved jaw mirroring the angle of his high-and-tight. Now dark-blond stubble glinted in the parking lot's glaring lights, softened his jawline and emphasized his full mouth. She wondered what it would be like to kiss him with that sandpaper scraping against her lips.

Then he gripped her foot, thumb rubbing her instep in counterpoint to the four fingers massaging her arch, the simple movement so confident and sensual that heat cracked everywhere she'd apply perfume—the hollow of her throat, the base of her spine, the insides of her elbows.

"Oh, that's good," she said quietly. He did it again, easing strained tendons and ligaments at the same time need tugged at her nipples and clit. Her elbows bent enough to land against the rear windshield, and her head dropped forward. Through half-closed eyes she saw herself, sprawled on the trunk of her car, her skirt barely decent, the pale, freckled skin of her thighs visible between the black stocking tops and her skirt, her blouse buttons straining over her breasts.

She shouldn't need this. A night with Ben every few weeks satisfied her just fine. And yet when Sean set down her left foot and switched to her right, she didn't primly close her legs. She didn't sit up and reestablish boundaries appropriate for jilted girlfriend and jilting Marine. She didn't say the words that would prove she was over Sean, that in her life he was so last year, and totally unnecessary this year. Instead she let him rub her aching foot and watch the telling heat climb from her collarbone to her face.

He set her foot down on the bumper, then his warm palm slid up her calf to the back of her knee and stroked. "What do you want, Sean?" she asked, and if the words lacked the acid she'd imagined flinging at him, well, she wasn't the only one feeling the connection between them. His erection strained against the front of his cargo pants.

"I want to take you out to dinner," he said, his voice so low as to be almost soundless in the silent night.

She lifted both eyebrows and let her gaze drift down his torso to his erection. "Liar."

"I owe you an apology," he started.

Her bent knee dropped to rest against his waist. "No, you don't," she said, almost sweetly. "You did what you had to do. I'm over it. And I don't have time for dinner, or lunch, or drinks, or coffee. All I have time for is a hookup. That was Ben's job. If you want it for the duration of your leave, you can have it. He won't mind sharing."

There. It wasn't disdainful or disinterested, given that her black lace panties were almost visible at the juncture of her thighs, but this was better. This satisfied something dark and sexual deep in her belly, something that tasted very much like revenge.

His hand was at the back of her thigh now, almost at the curve of her buttock, stroking delicate skin made sensitive by the tight elastic right below it. Standing between her knees, he planted his other hand on the rear windshield and bent forward, his hard body almost but not quite touching hers from lips to hips. The move put his mouth less than a breath from hers. Surprised, she dropped back against the windshield, but flattened her palms against his chest. Through his shirt she felt his heart pound, hard thuds that belied his calm demeanor.

"I can have his job," he said, but it wasn't a question. "Do I fill out an application? Give references?"

Something in the low growl dared her to say yes. His hot breath gusted over her open mouth, setting the nerves tingling in anticipation. "Not necessary," she said. "I remember your work from last year."

"What are the hours? Job duties?"

His rough mouth avoided her lips to trail along her jaw and down her neck, making it very hard to manufacture an answer out of the thick, heated air in their bubble. "Whatever I want, whenever I want."

The moment stretched between them, smoldering with things unspoken and lust. This wasn't the studious, intense man who left her behind. Someone completely unknown challenged her from the darker shadows in his eyes.

"Deal," he said. "But I'm your only hookup for the next month."

"You don't make the rules, Sean. I do."

Without blinking he straightened, pivoted, and gave her his back, leaving her skin to cool in the night air. The locks on the Mustang clicked open. She shifted back to her elbows and watched him walk, knowing this was the perfect way to end it. It was her way or no way, and she wasn't promising him a thing, especially not some fake fidelity. Except . . . her body remembered Sean. Wanted Sean. Because it was different with him. It wasn't about stress relief. It was about pure need.

"Deal," she said.

He stopped, then shot her a narrow-eyed look over his shoulder. She met his gaze without flinching. Then he turned around, strode back to her, planted both hands on either side of her shoulders, and kissed her, using his lips to nudge her mouth open. The golden stubble around his mouth scraped as deliciously as she'd imagined, then his tongue slid inside, rubbed the sensitive roof of her mouth before he nipped at her lower lip. It was as good as she remembered. Better. It was better, obliterating all traces of two orgasms from twenty-four hours earlier.

"I didn't say I wanted that," she said, low and rough, as if his stubble scraped over her voice box as well as her skin.

Something resembling humor flashed in his shuttered blue eyes. "The hell you didn't."

Definitely not the same Sean she'd waved good-bye to a year ago. Definitely different, in a definitely mesmerizing way that added to the thrill of taking him down a notch or two. "My rules, Sean. Remember that, or this is over before it begins."

Without changing expression he straightened and held out his hand, palm up. The sheer possessiveness of the move, all at once male, commanding, and very gentlemanly, made her heart knock hard against her ribs. But she didn't take his hand. Instead, she slipped off the trunk of her car and picked up her keys. "I'll drive myself. Which hotel?"

His hand dropped. "I'm house-sitting for a friend. Stay close," he said.

Chapter Three

The starter on Abby's car ground for a couple of seconds, then shut off. Sean rolled down his window and listened intently to the whirring until the engine caught and headlights flicked on in his rearview mirror. The Celica was getting to that point where components would start to fail. Starter. Battery. Alternator. The noise could be any one of those things. But the engine ran smoothly as she pulled into traffic behind him.

He took the time alone in his car to assess his strategy so far. *Total failure.* That was his assessment because five minutes into the plan, the plan was fucked. Time to improvise.

The official motto of the Marine Corps was Semper Fidelis— Always Faithful. The unofficial motto was Semper Gumby—Always Flexible. Marines made do with Army castoffs, out-of-date equipment, crappy food, took the worst losses and casualties. They cobbled together successful missions out of incomplete information, personal resilience and fortitude, and unmatched physical strength.

When everything you heard in the mission briefing got fucked to hell and back under fire, you improvised.

Ergo, if he devised Operation Prince Charming, a schedule of dates geared around conversations to learn what he needed to know about Abby's new life, but Abby wanted sex on her terms, he could do that. He'd implement sections of his plan when they weren't having sex. A complex, two-pronged approach, one according to her rules, one covertly ignoring the rules, both targeting the same objective.

He shook off nerves as he led her into one of Galveston's older residential neighborhoods. Under normal circumstances women weren't his strong suit. He was a pretty typical geek, even with the black belt in hapkido, the last person in his high school class anyone thought would apply for one of the service academies, let alone thrive there. He set goals in the weight room, on the obstacle course, in marksmanship, got stronger, faster, harder, and graduated first in his class. The Rhodes scholarship made sense, good preparation for life in Washington, writing reports and memos and classified documents for generals and admirals and diplomats. But he wanted to know what combat was like before he returned to air-conditioned rooms and moved men around like they were toys on a map. He wanted to understand what they went through, and what they sacrificed in order to follow the call of duty. Now he knew the costs, both professional and personal. He'd seen it in Ty. Maybe he was seeing it in Abby, too.

Abby parked on the street in front of the house while he parked in the driveway. Sean unlocked the front door and stood back to let Abby precede him into the dark foyer that opened directly into the living room. Camilla had good taste and money; the house was decorated in mission-style furniture and Tiffany lamps. Solid. Discreet. Street light streamed through the front window, illuminating a path along the carpet, over the coffee table, and along one end of the leather sofa.

"Where's your friend?" Abby asked idly.

"Italy, doing research for her dissertation."

"You didn't want to stay with your parents?"

"I've got a job with irregular hours. Mom can't sleep if she knows I'm coming in late."

She didn't ask about the job. Fifteen months ago, before training and the deployment, she'd eagerly soaked up every detail about him. Now she just nodded.

He eased down into the corner of the sofa, rested his elbow on the arm and his cheekbone on his bent fingers, and looked at her. Really looked at her, standing there in the moonlight, her hair seemingly lit from within, her green eyes shuttered. Her freckles weren't a cute smattering across her nose; they dusted her pale skin from her hairline all the way into the V-neck created by her blouse, buttoned at the center of her breasts. Memory filled in the rest, the spray of light brown like hennaed stars across her stomach.

Time to learn a little more about this new Abby. "This is your uniform?"

She nodded. "Linc sets the standard—white top, black skirt, black shoes. Stockings are optional."

"Why do you wear them?"

At that a small smile lifted the corners of her mouth, knowing, older than before. With a switch of her hips she turned her back to him, and since she was standing in heels and he was sitting down, her ass was at eye level. Suddenly unable to breathe, he looked at the curve of her hips, draped in a skirt that ended just past the lace tops of her thigh-high stockings, then let his gaze travel down the seam along the backs of her legs. It was old-school sexy, Marilyn Monroe sexy, hot-fuck-bent-over-the-dresser sexy.

"Oh," he managed.

She peered over her shoulder at him, then lowered her lashes, all red-headed vamp. "All the girls modify the uniforms to increase tips, and most go for hella hot. You didn't notice?"

He'd noticed every other girl in the bar. It was his job to notice details, so as much as he'd love to say he had eyes only for her, the USMC spent a great deal of time and money training him to pay attention. He couldn't just shut it off. "I noticed," he said. "But you don't. Why?"

"What do you think?" she asked, giving a little shimmy.

"It's mysterious," he said. "Makes me wonder if you're wearing a garter belt."

"You had your hand up my skirt twenty minutes ago," she said archly. "Am I?"

His hand curled, unconsciously seeking the tactile memory of the back of her thigh. Stocking elastic under his little finger, the crease where buttock and thigh met animal heat tantalizingly close to his index finger, and nothing but bare, warm skin in between. "No."

One corner of her mouth lifted. "Keep going."

He'd find out if he was right soon enough. "It draws attention to your legs."

"And my ass. Which is my best feature . . ."

He drew breath to protest, then figured he'd better look at her face if the statement would have any credibility. When he did, he saw the smile, again wicked, again knowing.

". . . For increasing my tips. Which is the point of all of this," she said, making a shopping network model gesture that encompassed her body from shoulder to thigh.

"The guys in the bar think the point of all that is to make them hot."

"They tip better when they're hot," she said.

He didn't doubt it. "Know what they talk about when you walk away?"

She turned back to face him and bent her head a little, hiding her eyes behind thick black lashes. Her hair slid forward, the soft waves brushing her cheekbones. "No," she said.

"They wonder what you're wearing under the skirt. Panties? Thong? Nothing at all?"

"What do you think?"

"Before you wore cotton bikinis, sensible but slightly sexy, but that was then. Now I'm not so sure." His gaze traveled up her torso from the hem of the skirt to the buttons on her white blouse to her throat, mouth, then eyes. Even after that night with Ty and Lauren he wasn't the most experienced guy in the world, but he knew arousal when he saw it, and he'd seen it in Abby's eyes when he'd kissed her. "Show me."

She went still. It wasn't like she'd been moving before, just standing in front of him, but there was not-moving and then there was still. Prey-still. She wasn't blinking, wasn't even breathing as she looked at him, those cat-green eyes holding his. So compelling was her gaze that he missed the first movements of her fingertips, inching up her skirt. Black fabric cleared the tops of her stockings. A few racing heartbeats later black lace appeared below the skirt, covering her mound and a couple of inches of abdomen, stretching over her hips in a swath narrower than the width of his palm.

He swallowed. "Nice," he managed as blood pumped into his cock, hardening it painfully. "Turn around."

With the same switch of her hips she turned her back to him, and he stopped breathing. The lace fabric covered the swell just below the twin dimples at the base of her spine but left the lower curves bare. It was a sight to stop a man's heart, seamed stockings, an expanse of thigh, then the sweet curves that would fit perfectly into his gripping palm as he drove into her.

Soon.

"Strip for me."

Once again, that preternatural stillness before she responded. She let the skirt drop, hiding those sexy curves, then lifted her hands to her buttons. With her back to him he couldn't see what was happening, but his brain filled in the details. The first button, the one that kept her decent, then the next, just under her breasts. The white fabric loosened a little more with each button. The next, right at her navel, then she tugged her shirttail free from her waistband, unbuttoned the last button. She looked over her shoulder at him, caught her lower lip in her teeth, and shrugged. With the slight movement the shirt slid down her arms and pooled around her heels.

A single hook fastened just under her shoulder blades, and he could see the knobs of her spine from the base of her neck, just below her hair, to the waistband of her skirt. The freckles stood out against her pale skin. As he watched, shivers chased each other across her skin.

"Are you cold?"

Still peering over her shoulder at him, she shook her head.

"Keep going."

Both hands reached for her bra clasp, unhooked it. Another shrug of her shoulders, and this time white lace dropped forward to the floor. But she didn't turn around. He could see hints of the curves of her breasts, her dark nipples hard peaks in the warm air. Without stopping she unfastened the skirt's button and zipper. It dropped to the floor all too easily, leaving her in nothing but the panties, stockings, and heels.

The length of her spine, slender, erect, proud.

God. So delicate.

Then she lifted her hands to her hair, lifting and tousling it. The movement made her breasts sway slightly, just enough to draw his attention, a reminder that *delicate* didn't mean *weak*.

"Step back," he said. She did, the backs of her calves brushing the sofa's edge. He reached up, skimmed his palms over the curves of her ass, around her hips, and up to cup her breasts. Then he kissed the base of her spine right between the two dimples just above the waistband of her panties. A slight tremor rolled through her. He drew her down to sit on his lap, her back to his chest.

He brushed his lips over the smooth warm skin of her shoulder, then moved openmouthed back to her nape. He remembered everything about her, including the sensitive spot on the right side of her hairline, where slow, hot kisses with just the right edge of teeth would melt her hot and boneless against him. That facet of Abby hadn't changed. He scraped a little harder, watching with unfocused eyes the way her nipples tightened even more, her hands gripped his wrists, the hot flush bloomed on her collarbone.

She shifted restlessly, one leg drawing up a little, the hot pressure of her ass against his cock a sweet torment. Moving without thinking he kept one arm around her waist and used the other to urge her legs to either side of his, opening her to him. Her hands tugged ineffectually at his forearms but he ignored her, and after a long, hot moment she ran her crossed arms up his biceps and lifted her arms over her head and his to clasp her hands at his nape.

So right. All his.

He stroked his fingertips lightly over her underarms, then her collarbone, caressing the swell of her breasts, then the sides, then her flat stomach and the waistband of the black lace undies before retracing his route, avoiding her nipples on the second pass, too.

"Sean," she gasped. "Stop teasing me."

Her eyes were closed, her lips parted, slowly opening as need built under her skin with each caress. When he cupped her breasts and brushed his thumbs over her nipples she arched into his palms. Possessed by some inner demon he couldn't explain, he pushed the black lace down to her hip crease, just low enough to give him access without taking them all the way off. Lost in memory, he trailed the tips of his fingers across the stars diffused across her abdomen.

She moaned and shifted again, the movement pleading and hot. He stroked the curls, petted them, as he pinched her nipple with the other hand, and watched. His hand was so dark against her pale skin, darker than the freckles as he dipped under the taut-stretched elastic and spread her soft folds.

He groaned. She was hot, wet, slick enough to shut off his brain entirely. Fuck the teasing. Fuck foreplay. In one movement he surged upright, hoisted her off her feet, and strode down the hall to the bedroom.

"Sean," she gasped as her heels dropped to the carpet, but he was past thinking, his only objective to watch her face when he fucked her and made her come.

In the dark bedroom he set her down then yanked back the covers. All he had to do was nod at the bed. She shimmied her panties down and lay back on the mattress. Shirt off, pants down, condom on. Then he gripped her stocking-clad ankles and smoothed both hands up her legs, separating them as he knelt between them. He planted a palm on either side of her shoulders, lowered his hips, and nudged into place.

At the first contact her knees drew up and her eyelids closed.

"Open your eyes," he said, stopping just barely inside the slick clasp of her pussy. "Abby. Look at me." It would kill him, literally slit him from throat to gut if he heard another man's name on her lips right now.

Her eyes opened again, the green, slumberous irises shuttered against whatever she felt. He waited, searching her eyes for a hint of emotion. All he got was her hand on his hip, her fingers flexing into muscle, thumb gripping his hip bone.

He pushed forward, in, felt that indescribable moment when the soft walls fluttered around him, adjusting to his girth. A low growl rumbled from his throat, the noise deeper, prowling because a giant hand had worked fingers through his ribs, trapping lungs and heart and throat against bone. Abby's head tipped back, arching her torso off the mattress and forcing his cock all the way inside her. Her legs in their stockings drew up, heels digging into the backs of his thighs, and he thought he might go out of his mind.

He looked at her mouth, caught up in a heart-stopping memory of kissing her, spinning a web of pleasure using the sensitive nerves in her lips alone. He lowered his mouth to hers, urged her lips apart, then swept his tongue over hers before withdrawing to nip at her full lower lip, flick his tongue along the bow-shaped curve of her upper lip. She eagerly followed his mouth, but he pulled back and shook his head. The tip of her tongue slid along her lower lip before she bit it, as if searching for the taste of his mouth.

That was better.

"Please," she whispered.

And even better . . . he bent his head and took her mouth, lips pressed to hers, teeth clicking as he slanted his mouth across hers. Her nails dug into his shoulders, and for a moment all he could think about was having her body open and available under his, legs spread, breasts pressed to his chest, legs wound around his hips.

Christ, it shouldn't be, but his control was shot, blown into tiny little molten pieces. He shifted his weight to one elbow and gripped her hip with the other hand, then pulled out and plunged back in. She made a shuddering little gasping noise, high-pitched and feminine in a way guaranteed to yank him all the way back to animal brain responses. He adjusted the cant of her hips and did it again, got the same noise and the sharp sting of her nails in his shoulders.

Game on. His body set a pounding rhythm guaranteed to end this in a matter of minutes, but she was right there with him, clinging to him, making all kinds of eager, desperate, helpless noises as she wound tight around him, under him. Then she flew apart, the blood flush climbing to her face as she bared her throat in orgasmic release. He gritted his teeth and thrust through the contractions gripping his cock like a silken fist, and when the tension eased from her body, he drove into her once, twice, a third time, the orgasm exploding from him in long, sparking bursts.

She was limp under him when he withdrew, making only the slightest incoherent noise when he backed off the bed and went into the bathroom, where he dealt with the necessities and listened to the pipes rattle softly in the wall. Back in the bedroom he extracted his shorts from the pile containing his pants and shoes, and pulled them on, forming the arguments he'd use to keep her here overnight. Instead she made a soft, sleepy inhaling noise, and twitched.

She'd fallen asleep. In the sixty seconds between him pulling out and coming back into the room, she'd dropped into sleep. Keeping his touch gentle he eased down first one stocking, then the other, and draped them over the end of the bed. Then he lay down beside her, moving carefully so as to not wake her. He pulled the covers up over them both and lay back, then turned his head and looked at her, asleep in a limp sprawl next to him. The sleep of the dead. He had plenty of experience watching exhausted, overtaxed individuals sleep. His Marines fell asleep in seconds, and they dropped from awake to near-coma in a matter of minutes when the body demanded it. A day or two of missed sleep didn't usually provoke that response. It was a chronic sleep deprivation thing, and Abby had it.

The plan was in motion, and he could add two more pieces of data to his set. She was utterly exhausted, and while she'd let him into her body, her soul was closed to him. Ramifications niggled at his brain, chasing themselves in circles as the clock crawled past 0300.

Abby drifted in the gray haze of near-consciousness as a deft mouth made its way from her ear down her neck and over her collarbone to her nipple. Lazy, sleepy tendrils of desire curled down to her pussy and along her nerves to her hands, flexing against rumpled sheets. A tongue lapped at her nipple until it tightened, hardened. Teeth rewarded this appropriate response with a tug, then gentle pressure, holding the sensitive flesh for a few moments before the mouth journeyed to her other breast.

Something was wrong, the room, the weak sunlight through sheer curtains as a large male body shifted over her, broad shoulders spreading her legs to settle between her thighs. Her eyes refused to open, and that was fine with her because a tongue touched her clit, sure and confident, and a soft purring sound rose into the air.

Strong arms worked under her thighs, then a hand captured each of her breasts, squeezing the firm flesh before pinching each nipple in time to the knowing strokes laving her clit. Desire cracked through her, and she arched into the hands and mouth. So good, steady and unhurried, slow and firm, driving all thought, including *whatwaswrongsomethingwaswrong*, out of her mind for a few precious minutes. Because this couldn't possibly be wrong. It felt so right.

The slow burn became hot, pulsating fire, and the purrs took on a pleading, needy edge. Her secret lover didn't tease her or draw it out, just urged her in a steady climb to the edge and over. Soft gasps of release echoed in the dim sunlit room.

"Go back to sleep," came a morning-rough male voice.

No problem, except her brain wouldn't let go of that niggling sense that something wasn't right. She rolled over and sank back into the gray haze, now with a golden tinge around the edges. *Sunlight*. The sun was up, and she was still in bed. That's what was wrong. She pushed up on one elbow and shoved her hair out of her face as she looked frantically around the strange bedroom *wherethefuckamI?* for the clock.

7:28. Sean's borrowed bedroom.

"Oh my God! It's seven thirty in the morning!"

Sean appeared in the doorway, a plate holding fried eggs and two pieces of toast in one hand and a glass of orange juice in the other. "What's wrong?" he asked.

"It's seven thirty, that's what's wrong! I'm late for my dad's breathing treatments, I'm going to be late for class, I'm on the wrong side of town!" She scrambled out of bed and into her underwear, snagged her stockings from the foot of the bed, then looked around. "Where are the rest of my clothes?"

"Living room floor," Sean said, and stepped back to let her fly past him, no doubt enjoying the view as she snagged her heels from the hall wearing nothing but her cheeky panties. Flashes of last night were coming back to her, and holy Mary, mother of God, what had she done, suggesting Sean Winthrop become her hookup? He was brilliant at it. Too good at it, and they had a scheduling issue. She'd fallen asleep with a man who didn't have to be at work at six in the morning. Big mistake. One of several.

It wasn't like that with Ben. Oh no, it wasn't like that at all. It was hot as hell, fast, a little rough, and utterly emotionless. She felt nothing more than physical need before she went to him, then the absence of need. The perfect antidote, come to think of it, to what she'd felt a year ago with Sean.

Or last night with Sean.

She yanked her skirt up and fastened it, then hurried into her bra and blouse. *Okay. Shoes, skirt, underwear top and bottom, shirt. Purse.* She found that on the coffee table, dug her cell phone from the interior pocket, and checked it. Two messages from her dad. "Shit," she said as she jammed her aching feet into the heels and bolted for the front door, searching her purse for her car keys as she moved.

Her mind registered the beautiful fall morning as she dashed down the driveway to the street, where her car was parked. Brilliant sunlight, a nice cool tinge to the air, a gentle breeze in the yellow leaves just beginning to turn. That's why her sleep haze was tinged with gold. The bedroom faced the backyard, and two enormous golden maples rose skyward behind the house. Regret stabbed her as last year's daytime possibilities flashed into her mind. A late brunch, sharing the paper, a walk in the park, a picnic, a movie, all in this light, this amazing light.

She unlocked her car, tossed her purse on the passenger seat, jammed the key in the ignition, and turned it.

Nothing. Not even the horrible rough growl the car had made off and on for the past couple of weeks. She checked her headlights and the overhead light. Both were off. "Please," she said to the car. "Please, please, please start. I don't have time for you to act up today. Okay? Thanks."

Another turn of the key generated the same single click. "Not today. Not here," she said warningly, but the engine ignored her and the key.

A knock on the driver's side window made her jump. It was Sean, dressed in last night's cargo pants and a gray long-sleeved T-shirt that said *USMC* on it. "It's the alternator or the battery," he said without preamble. "Pop the hood release and come on out of there."

She obediently pulled the lever that would release the hood and got out of the car. He'd sandwiched the fried eggs between the two slices of toast, and still held the glass of OJ. "Eat."

She took the glass and the sandwich from him and bit into it while he reversed his car into the street and parked it nose to nose with hers. He extracted jumper cables from the trunk, popped his hood, and met her where the noses sat just inches apart.

"How old is this battery?" he asked with a nod at her car.

She shrugged. "Came with the car, I guess," she said around a mouthful of egg sandwich. She should know that. A grown-up would know her car's maintenance schedule, or at least have it written down in the glove box. He'd peppered the hell out of the eggs, just the way she liked them, and the toast was saturated with butter.

He rubbed at the nodes on top of the battery. "The terminals are corroded. Whatever else is wrong with the car, you need a new battery."

"Okay," she said. She could use a second egg sandwich, too. One cheese stick at four p.m. didn't get a woman through twelve hours of work and sex.

Sean leaned over her car, a red claw-shaped thing in each hand. "Wait a minute," she said, and inelegantly wiped the sandwich grease on her bare thigh. "Don't just do it for me. Show me how."

Eyebrows up, he handed her the red claws. "Red is positive on most cables and batteries, but always check to be sure. Positive to positive on the dead car." He pointed at the post with the + sign on her car, and she awkwardly attached the red claw to it. Then he turned to his car. "Positive to positive on the live car," he said, and watched while she did it. "Good. The other color is negative. Negative to negative on the good car." She attached that claw more competently. "The second negative goes to clean, unpainted metal on the dead car. Never to the battery, or it might explode when you start the car." She looked over her engine block, which was pretty grungy, but eventually found a shiny bolt toward the windshield and clamped the last claw down.

"Positive to positive on the dead car, then on the live car. Negative to negative on the live car, then to bare metal on the dead car," she recited.

He nodded.

"Then what?"

"Then I start my car." He leaned through the passenger window and turned the key. The car started immediately. "Give it a minute to charge," he said when she turned for her car.

She looked at her cell phone. Dad hadn't called back yet, so he'd gone back to bed or he was struggling with the breathing treatment machine himself. Either way, he'd be in a bad mood when she got home.

"What class do you have today?" Sean asked neutrally.

"Microbiology," she said, but offered nothing else. She planned to enter the accelerated degree program at the University of Texas Medical Branch's nursing school, but she needed a year's worth of prerequisites, including statistics, developmental psychology, an ethics course, and three kinds of chemistry, all with labs. She was trying for a scholarship because she was up to her cheeky-pantied ass in student loan debt already. She couldn't afford to miss one class.

"When are you supposed to be there?"

"Ten minutes from now," she said.

He looked at his watch. "Give it a try."

She slid into the Celica and turned the key. A whir, then the engine turned over. "Yes," she breathed, and got back out of the car.

"Reverse the order to disconnect the cables," Sean said.

She gingerly reached out and disconnected the ground, then negative live, positive live, then positive dead-now-live. Sean closed each hood with a sharp clang. "It could be your alternator. I assume that's original to the car, too, but based on the corrosion, you need a new battery. Get one, and see if that fixes the problem."

"Today," she said. "Right after class."

There were wants, and then there were needs. Sean was a want. A new battery was a need, and she and her dad still had money for bare-bones needs. Her problem was the time necessary to get the battery installed. She was behind on her reading, and she needed extra sessions in the lab. She was a B+/A− student if she worked really, really hard, and it had taken every single second of her spare time to earn a B in a blitzkrieg course of Organic Chemistry over the summer.

She looked up at the man who graduated first in his class from the Naval Academy, then spent two years in England at Oxford University. "Do you know where to go to get a battery?" he asked gently.

"Sears," she said firmly, and offered him the jumper cables. "Thank you."

"Keep them," he said. "If it's the alternator you're going to need them again, maybe later today, maybe in a couple of days."

"I don't even know what the alternator does, and I don't have time to find out," she said, but she wasn't too proud to refuse the jumper cables. "I'll get these back to you."

"I assumed I'd see you again tonight."

Longing shimmered inside her. It should be easier than this, blowing him off, using him for physical release, nothing more, but after last night, her body remembered exactly why she fell under Sean Winthrop's spell at the snap of his fingers. It was better, even. Before he deployed he could have passed for a desk jockey with a crew cut, but a year of leading men in combat polished off the academic gloss and unearthed the air of command and masculine confidence she'd seen flashing under his surface, like a fish in the depths of a lake, steel glinting in the right light. Now masculine confidence draped over him with the ease of finely made chain mail armor. She remembered the rough texture in his voice when he told her to strip for him, and lightning splintered deep between her thighs.

"I'll let you know," she said as she got in her car and shut the door.

He bent down and folded his arms on her open window. "My work wasn't up to your standards?" he asked. The words were mild, if she ignored the edge to his tone. "I can do better. I'm a quick learner."

What was she supposed to say? *Make it less hot? Make it less emotional?* "It's not about standards. I'm busy," she said. "Some nights I want an extra hour of sleep more than I want sex. Are you working that odd-hours job when I get off work?"

"I'm home by then."

"Then I'll come by if I feel like it."

A muscle jumped in his jaw, and his eyes were flat, assessing. Then he leaned in and gave her a quick kiss, nothing sexy or erotic to it, just the kind of quick, possessive good-bye kiss a man gave the woman in his life when they parted ways.

"Bye, Abby."

She shifted into drive and pulled away from his house. She didn't regret the sex, but she really regretted that kiss.

Forget about him. Take care of Dad, then get to class late. Better late than never. She pulled into the driveway and hurried up the steps into the house. "Hello?" she called.

The sound of a morning talk show, the kind of *superficial crap* her father had once despised, led her to him. He was in the kitchen, seated at the table, the nebulizer that delivered his medication in front of him. He didn't look up as she set her purse on the table. "Let me do that, Dad," she said quietly.

He wheezed through a couple of breaths while she connected the tubing to the nebulizer and the compressor. "Where were you?"

"I went out with a friend after work," she extemporized.

"The same *friend* you were with last week?" he said.

She measured out each medication, carefully studying the prescription information from the pharmacy, and used concentrating to avoid answering his question. Because that answer was no.

"You're going to be late for class." Now the words were accusatory.

She offered him the breath mask. "I know." She eyed the nebulizer but couldn't take the time to clean it now. She'd do it when she got home, right before his night treatment. She ran upstairs for a two-minute shower, then clipped her hair back in a barrette at the nape of her neck. Cool air against her skin triggered the memory of Sean's hot, sure mouth working over the same spot. She brushed it aside and hurried back downstairs.

"The lawn's looking ragged," her father said.

"It will have to wait until the weekend," she said. "I'm working every night this week."

"It'll be too long by Saturday. You'll have to bag it."

She shoved her books in her backpack with a little more force than necessary. The lawn was her father's pride and joy, meticulously seeded, fertilized, weeded, mowed, and edged. She could not possibly care less about the lawn, especially when prioritized with school, work, cleaning, and cooking. "I know, Dad," she said, then bent over and kissed his cheek. "I'll see you this afternoon. Go for a walk, okay?"

He grunted in response, and she took the sunny-side up view that maybe he would go for a walk. His breathing was a little easier, a little less congested today. At least he'd answered. Her car started with only the slightest hesitation. As long as it got her to class, she'd deal with it later. It was much the same strategy she was using with Sean . . . take advantage of him now, deal with the emotional consequences later.

Except it never worked.

Chapter Four

Sean pulled into Langley Security's parking lot shortly after ten a.m. and parked the Mustang next to Ty's big red pickup truck. He strode through the unoccupied reception area, into John's generously sized two-room office. Ty leaned against a credenza at the back of the room. While John maintained the grooming standards, with his hair cropped close to his head and his jaw cleanly shaven, Ty's blond hair hung nearly to his jaw.

"Get a haircut, hippie," Sean tossed at him as he strode into the room. He'd thought about how to act around Ty, and the obvious answer was to pretend nothing happened and continue with the lame jokes about his hair. Ignore the ménage, Ty's emotional meltdown afterward, all of it.

"Fuck you." Ty threw back as he skimmed both hands over his hair to get it out of his face.

"Halloween's over. You don't have to pretend to be that pretty boy from *Lost* anymore."

That got an amused grunt from John as he looked from Sean to

Ty and back again, assessing the mood, the temperature in the room. Sean poured himself a cup of coffee, as much to have something to do with his hands as the need for caffeine, and said in a quieter voice, "Did you talk to her yet?"

Without looking at him, Ty gave him a single head shake, the movement discouraging further inquiry. Sean left it at that. Just because he'd gotten up Sunday morning with the gut-certainty that he wanted Abby back and developed a plan that would deploy every resource at his disposal to get her before he reported for duty didn't mean Ty would take the same approach. Ty worked out of Galveston, the same city where Lauren lived and worked. He didn't face the same pressures Sean did. Sean had less than a month to get back in Abby's good graces, and he knew what he wanted. Ty needed time and space to think things through.

The team ran through the report from yesterday's activity, adding notes detailing Richards's sudden departure and trip to his house. Everyone signed the logs, then they divvied up the day's surveillance shifts and duties.

"Stay alert," Ty said, looking around the room and nailing each of the operatives with a glance. "Learn from my mistake. Never get distracted. Never let your guard down."

Everyone's spine straightened a little, and Sean covertly studied Ty out of the corner of his eye. Employees, team members, Marines, whatever you called them, they listened to Ty. There was just something about him. If he'd stayed in the Corps he would have made gunny for sure, maybe even gone through OCS and made the jump from enlisted to officer. Sean could see Langley Security's leadership team coming together—John for the business side, the marketing and sales, the accounting, Ty for the personnel expertise. Between the two of them they could put together the strategy and tactics, if Ty made the commitment to the company.

Keeping Abby's hectic schedule in mind, Sean took a later shift that would follow one of the principal suspects through his evening routine. "You make that appointment?" he asked Ty as the group split up.

"Wednesday afternoon," Ty said. "John's going with me."

"Good."

Next he drove to Sears and picked up the right battery for Abby's Celica, then drove to the campus. Online he'd found the location for microbiology classes and the nearest parking lot. Finding Abby's car was simply a matter of driving up and down the rows until he found the little red car, parked in the corner of the lot, under a tree. A rectangle of faded paint sat dead center on the back bumper. What the hell had she done to the paint? Backed it into a sponge covered in paint thinner?

He had a case of socket wrenches in the back of his car. Three minutes with a clothes hanger and he had the driver's door open and the hood popped. Fifteen minutes, total, and Abby had a new battery. He closed the hood, relocked the door, and drove home, where several boxes of books from an online retailer waited on the front steps. He carried them inside, opened all the boxes, and stacked the books on the coffee table according to subject.

Stack the immediate: industrial espionage research, specifically the pharmaceutical industry.

Stack the future: Virginia and Washington, D.C., guidebooks, Civil War histories, memoirs, and relevant public transportation maps. Quantico was home to the Marine Corps Combat Development Command, where he'd apply what he'd learned in combat to strategies for the future. He'd never lived there, and the possibilities in a two-hundred-mile radius for history and culture were nearly endless.

Stack the potent: love poetry. The Persian mystic Rumi, anthologies of history's greatest love poems, and Shakespeare's sonnets.

Glass of tea in hand, he took the most recent espionage book and the sonnets to the back porch, and sat down to read until it was time to go to the business park. He was two hundred pages into the industrial espionage book and taking a break to wrestle with the structure of the sonnet when the side gate to the backyard opened, and Abby walked through it.

"Hey," he exclaimed, surprised by her sudden appearance. He shoved the book of sonnets under the hardcover. "What are you doing here?"

"Returning your jumper cables," she said, and held them out. He accepted them, watching her face, trying to make eye contact, but she transferred her attention to her purse. "How much do I owe you for the battery?"

"Excuse me?" he bluffed.

"You replaced my battery," she said as she came up with a black leather checkbook cover, transferred it to her left hand, and began to dig through the shapeless brown bag again. "Unless someone else replaced it while I was in microbiology class. I took statistics last semester, so I can calculate the odds of some random stranger replacing my battery on the very day I discovered it was dying. The odds, if you're interested, are vanishingly small. How did you get under the hood?"

"I broke into your car," he said, giving up on all pretenses. She wore dark jeans that clung to her lean hips and legs, and what appeared to be three tank tops, layered over each other, in complementary shades of blue and green. It was the first time he'd seen her in broad daylight in over a year, and the sight made his heart skitter wildly in his chest. The shorter haircut left her neck and shoulders bare, and the sunlight filtering through the big maple trees dappled her freckled skin with fall gold.

She came up with a pen, opened the checkbook on the railing, and said, "That's what I figured. How much do I owe you?"

He told her. "How did you know?"

"It started slowly when I left my house this morning, just like it did last night, but when I got in it after class, it started right up, like someone goosed it. Var*rooooom*," she said as she tore the check out of her checkbook, then flipped to the register to make the notation. "Thank you."

He accepted the check when she held it out, then folded it and put it in his wallet. "Abby, are you going to look at me once during this conversation?"

"I hadn't planned on it," she said, and turned to leave the way she came.

"Why not?"

She stopped, then hitched her bag higher on her shoulder. The movement caught the straps of all three tank top straps and pushed them up, revealing a plain white bra strap. The jeans, he noted distantly, hugged the heart-shaped curves of her ass in a very delicious way.

"I don't need you to do things for me," she said to the lilac bushes growing under the kitchen window. "I don't need *anyone* to do things for me. I need to learn how to do them myself. Now I don't have that chance."

Semper Gumby. "You're right." He waited a second. She didn't turn around, but she didn't leave, either. "Do you have time for me to show you how to replace your battery?"

"No," she said, but she looked over her shoulder at him as she said it. "I'm so far behind on everything I'll never catch up. But I still want you to show me."

He followed her down the stairs to the stepping-stones that led through the garden gate, and reached past her to open the gate for her. At the slight contact between his chest and her shoulder she startled and looked up at him, but swept through and kept walking toward the street where her car was parked. She unlocked the car and popped the hood once again, paying close attention while he gave her a crash course in battery replacement and tried not to be too obvious about how distracting the low-cut tank tops were when she leaned over the engine.

"Where did you get those?" she asked, pointing at the case of socket wrenches he'd pulled from the Mustang's backseat.

"My house. Dad's got a full workshop in the garage."

"Maybe my dad has a set," she mused.

"Most places won't charge you too much to replace your battery, and then you'll be sure it's done right." He peered through the windshield at the thick textbook on the passenger seat. "How late were you to microbiology?"

"An hour," she said. "I'll get notes from a friend."

"And why are you taking microbiology?" he asked cautiously. The plan hinged on finding out who this new woman was.

"I couldn't find a job," she said bluntly. "Apparently majoring in liberal arts wasn't a good choice in the worst economic downturn in nearly a century. I'm going back to school to get a nursing degree. I want to do a one-year intensive program, but I need to get the prereqs out of the way before I can apply."

"Do you *want* to be a nurse?" he asked. The Abby he remembered loved books and movies, and had been the entertainment columnist for the college newspaper.

"I had fun in college, read all the great books," she said. "Now I want to do meaningful work. After a few appointments with my dad I developed an interest in geriatric nursing."

There was his in. "What's wrong with your dad?"

She lifted her chin. "He has COPD. It's a chronic, progressive lung disease. I'm taking care of him."

All he knew about Abby's father was that he was twice-divorced and almost completely uninvolved in his daughter's life, despite the fact that she lived with him. "How's he taking it?"

"He's angry," she said emotionlessly. "Angry because smoking unfiltered cigarettes for forty-plus years finally caught up with him, and his mortality's staring him in the face. Angry because he can't do anything he used to do, like get dressed in less than twenty minutes, or go to work. Angry because the lawn looks terrible without him spending hours on it every weekend. Too stubborn to do anything that might make him feel better, like breathing exercises and taking a walk. And, I think, with two failed marriages and his sons barely speaking to him and a granddaughter he never sees, desperately afraid he's going to die alone. Or maybe with just me for company."

He stared at her. "Jesus, Abby," he started.

"I have to go," she said, and opened her car door. "I work at five."

"You coming over tonight?"

The words were out before he could stop them, before he could think through voicing his eagerness, but New Abby was humming away at a speed that didn't include falling in love any time soon. She looked at him, gave him the full force of those pale green eyes, the look pure challenge as she dismissively lifted one shoulder.

"Come over, Abby. I'll make it worth your while," he said.

"Better than sleep?" she asked, but the teasing lilt in her voice held an edge. "I am absolutely desperate for some sleep."

A soft laugh huffed from him as he leaned over the car door. Her gaze dropped from his eyes to his mouth, then she licked and bit into her lower lip. He knew that signal, knew it well, knew the way to seduce Abby was her mouth. So he kissed her, the car door a grievous barrier between his body and hers as he urged her lips apart and rubbed his tongue against hers as nonchalantly as she'd shrugged off his invitation. Her jaw opened in hesitant stages, then she leaned a little closer . . . and he backed away.

"I'll be fast," he murmured. "Then you can sleep. If that's what you want. Or I'll be slow. Whatever you want, Abby. Think about it. Let me know when you come over."

The knock on the front door came at two twenty. Sean pulled on a pair of boxer shorts just in case it was some drunk friend of Camilla's who didn't know she was out of town. Just in case it wasn't, he palmed a condom on his way down the hall.

It was Abby. He opened the door, and she ducked under his arm. "You have to set your alarm for five," she said. "I can't be late for class again."

"Fast or slow?"

"What? It just has to go off. I don't care how the thing buzzes, but it better be loud because—"

He kissed her, the old-fashioned, movie kind of kiss, both hands to her jaw to hold her mouth for his, but mostly to shut her up. "Fast or slow," he repeated, trusting he'd made the context clear with the explicit, hard kiss.

Her purse landed on the floor with a thud. "Fast. Now."

Giving her another rough kiss, he backed her to the sofa then spun her around, his touch demanding, careless. She dropped to her knees on the cushions with her forearms braced on the sofa's back, and he knelt behind her as he shoved her skirt up, tugged her panties down, and tortured himself with a couple of skin-to-skin thrusts against her ass. When he had the condom on he snugged up behind her and reached around to part her folds in search of her clit.

And found her slick, swollen, beyond ready for him, a lightning-quick assessment confirmed when his cock slid into her pussy with a mind-searing ease. "Abby. Fuck."

She tilted her hips back and looked over her shoulder at him. "You told me to think about it. So I did." He pulled out and drove back in, forcing a gasp from her throat. "All night. You know what

No Limits is like. Sex everywhere. I watched couples grind on the dance floor—oh God—and thought about you."

She stopped talking as he stroked in, paused, pulled out. Her head dropped forward, and her breath caught. The skin of her ass pressed soft and hot against his lower abdomen. She was slick enough for him to hear his cock stroke through her moisture with each gripping stroke, and she smelled of sweat and desire. Sensory overload. All circuits shut down.

It took no time at all. He braced his forearm next to hers on the back of the sofa, touched the tip of his finger to her swollen clit, set a ruthless pace. Pure animal movement did the rest. She tightened around him, ass and thighs tensing as she hurtled into orgasm with an anguished cry. His breath forced through clenched teeth as he jetted into her.

With a relieved, satisfied little sigh she nuzzled her cheek into her folded arms. He dealt with the condom as quickly as he could, but when he came back to the sofa she'd slipped down into a sleeping ball of Abby. He swept her up in his arms to carry her to the bedroom, but misjudged the width of the hallway and bumped her head on the corner.

"Ow," she muttered, but she didn't really wake.

So much for Prince Charming. He turned sideways to walk down the hall and set her down on the bed. She rolled over and tucked her hands under her chin, not even waking as he covered her up.

This wasn't going to work. At her pace of life he'd need a year to get her back. He lay awake for a long time, strategizing, before sleep claimed him, too.

"Thirteen more minutes." The clock read 2:47 p.m. Abby rubbed her gritty eyes and bargained with her tired brain. "Thirteen more minutes and then you can take a nap."

Her body was no longer stupid enough to fall for blatant lies. She had another fifty pages of reading for her Ethics class tomorrow, a short paper to write in response to the reading, and an entire chapter of Microbiology to outline. She really should schedule another session in the lab to review the previous week's work. At least this semester she only had one science-intensive course. The semester she'd done anatomy and physiology *and* statistics, she'd been terrified she'd flunk out of school and into a job at McDonalds.

"Twelve minutes," she muttered. She blinked hard, then read the same sentence about the history of relational ethics twice, understanding only the conjunctions before the text blurred together on the page. She groaned, closed her eyes, and rested the heels of her hands in her eye sockets.

As brief as they were, nights with Sean tilted her teetering world beyond the tipping point. Apparently she could make do on four hours of sleep, too much coffee, and fear-based adrenaline, but three hours of sleep and her body began to whine. *So tiiiiiiired. Must sleeeeeeeep.* So like a good girl would, like a girl who texted Ben once a month or so, she'd come home after work the last three nights and gone to bed for her usual four hours of sleep.

That shut down the whining, but added a deeper ache to the sustained, low-level exhaustion. Desire simmered low in her belly. Her clothes chafed her skin, the seam of her jeans rubbing against her clit at the most inopportune moments, her nipples teased by any bra at all—cotton, lace, silk, it didn't matter. It was as if her body knew when Sean's leave was over that would be the end of fabulous-Sean-sex, and she should get as much fabulous-Sean-sex while she could.

"Stop it," she said to her body. "Stop *needing.* You're not going to get enough sleep or enough sex or enough of anything for a long, long time. I can give you coffee. That's it."

She walked downstairs and made coffee. Her father sat in his recliner in the family room, staring at the television. His breathing wheezed, then he coughed his typical rattling, phlegmy cough.

"You okay, Dad?"

"Stop fussing," he rasped, but the effort of getting the words out only made him cough harder.

The doorbell rang. Abby ignored it and started toward her father, then retreated when he irritably waved her off. The wet, hacking coughs followed her down the tiled hallway as she hurried to the door.

Sean stood on the other side, dressed in cargo shorts, running shoes, and a shapeless, worn gray T-shirt with the Naval Academy logo on the chest. A backpack hung from one shoulder, and for a moment her only wish in the world wasn't for sleep or sex. It was for the clairvoyance that would have told her to study in something other than a pair of ripped yoga pants rolled low on her hips and a green cami.

"I should be used to you showing up out of the blue," she said.

At a particularly deep, horrible cough, his gaze flicked over her shoulder. "Is this a bad time?"

"That depends on what you want," she said flatly, all but daring him to suggest sex while her father hacked up the contents of his lungs.

"Company while I do some reading," he said, hoisting the full backpack as evidence. "That's all."

This wasn't in the rulebook, him showing up at her house, wanting nothing more than to be in her presence, but she simply couldn't bring herself to send him away, much less shut the door in his face. So she opened the door wide, and he stepped into the foyer.

"Go on upstairs," she said. "Do you want some coffee?"

"I'll help you get it," he said.

"Dad won't want you to meet him like this. He's having a bad day," she said, and gave him a little push for emphasis. "Second door on the left."

He climbed the stairs while she hurried back down the hall. The coughing fit was tapering off, leaving her dad with watery eyes, gasping for air. She waited for him to finish clearing the mucus from his lungs, took the small trash can full of tissues into the kitchen and emptied it, then crouched by his chair and patted his shoulder.

"Okay, Dad?"

He shook off her hand. "Who was at the door?"

"A friend coming over to study. We'll be upstairs." He nodded, his gaze focused on the television show he never would have watched before. "Do you want me to make an appointment with Dr. Weaver?"

"No."

"Dad, she said if you weren't—"

"No. Go away."

She stood and stalked back into the kitchen, poured out two tall mugs, added cream and sugar to hers, and headed up the stairs. Sean sat on her bedroom floor, his backpack open beside him, books and notebooks strewn around him, his laptop open on his lap and plugged into one of the sockets. A moment's embarrassment coursed through her, because the room was a FEMA-declared disaster area, dirty clothes piled in one laundry basket, clean clothes in untidy stacks in another, her closet door wide open on the jumble of shoes and unevenly hanging formal dresses. She'd redecorated when she moved home after college, supposedly just for the summer, but she was glad the room was now an adult, if dusty, scheme of royal blue and white. Microbiology, chemistry, anatomy and physiology texts and her laptop occupied every available inch of her desk. Beside the floor, the only other flat, unoccupied surface in the room was her bed.

He wisely hadn't chosen to sit there, but perhaps the fact that it was unmade and strewn with a tumbled assortment of blue and red pillows had something to do with it. She left the door wide open.

"I can make space at the desk."

"Abby, trust me. I've worked in far worse conditions than a carpeted bedroom floor in an air-conditioned house," he said and reached up for his coffee.

"You're really here to read."

He nodded, and the gleam in his eye was only slightly artful.

One leg tucked under her, she eased into the desk chair and sipped her own coffee. "What are you working on?"

"An analysis of the pharmaceutical industry, the players, trends, competitors, leadership, what's in FDA testing, that kind of thing."

She blinked. "Is that for the Marine Corps?"

"No. I'm freelancing while I'm on leave, and the job relates to a smaller drug company. I don't know anything about the industry, so this is background research."

"That sounds interesting."

"So far the job consists of sitting down. Front seat of a truck, outdoor bench in a business park, front seat of a car outside a guy's house."

"And now it sounds boring."

"After getting shot at for a year every time we stepped outside the perimeter, sitting in a car without random gunfire is actually kind of nice." *Getting shot at* made her heart stutter and her breathing stop. He gave her another only slightly artful smile, and added, "It's no picnic, but I'll take it."

She ignored his lead. "You need to do research to sit on a bench?"

"Not really, but you never know when something you've learned might come in handy."

The sight of him on her bedroom floor, surrounded by books, highlighter, and laptop at the ready, jolted a memory loose from her exhausted brain. Sean, in much the same pose and clothing but on a picnic blanket in the park, surrounded by books about Afghanistan that were getting as broken-spined and dog-eared as military strategy books. With her head pillowed on his thigh she'd read her way through magazines and novels while he systematically crammed the contents of about twenty thousand pages of text into his brain.

She'd fallen in love with him on that blanket, fallen hard, fast, and apparently alone. The blanket now occupied the back corner of her closet, the green-and-blue plaid wool folded carefully to keep intact the grass and twigs from their last picnic.

He nodded at the stack of books on her desk. "Don't let me distract you."

"I won't," she said. It was his turn to blink at her firm tone.

For a few minutes she had to fake intense fascination with relational ethics, but then the caffeine spurred productivity. She finished the Ethics reading, wrote her response paper, and turned to the Microbiology outline. Exactly ninety minutes into the silent study session Sean's watched beeped. He got to his feet and stretched, methodically cracking everything from his neck down to his toes, then looked around the room.

"What's with the alarm?"

"People are most productive in ninety-minute sessions. Then it's best to take a break and do something else for about twenty minutes."

The *something else* they would have done last year hung in the air above her bed until Sean walked to the window. "The lawn could use a trim," he commented.

"It's not up to Dad's standards," she agreed ruefully, but he'd moved on to the pictures on the walls and shelves.

"I never saw your room last year."

She hadn't wanted to rush into anything that might spook Sean, like meeting her bad-tempered father, although in hindsight their intense focus on each other to the exclusion of family and friends was a missed sign. A very few pictures were arranged on shelves around the room, mostly candid shots of her with friends on spring break. He examined each one carefully, starting with the picture of her with all her college friends, then switched his attention to the last photo.

"Who's this?"

"My half brother Jeff, his wife, Lindsey, and their daughter, Mikaela." She yawned, stifling the sound with her hand.

"Want to take a quick nap?" he said without looking at her.

Was she relieved or disappointed he didn't ask more questions? "Desperately, but I've still got a whole chapter to outline."

"You'll write a better outline when you're rested."

It sounded so tempting, lying down in the middle of the day, in her sun-warmed room, falling asleep to the sound of Sean's breathing. "I'll get more coffee."

"I'll wake you up in forty-five minutes."

She laughed. "I can't afford to sleep for forty-five minutes. Thirty, max."

"Deal," he said quickly.

"We aren't negotiating," she said.

He just smiled. "You'll feel more alert."

"This is temporary, Sean," she pointed out gently. "Classes are over mid-December. I'll sleep then." Until it all started up again mid-January, and that was just her last semester of prereqs. Then the actual coursework began, practicums and clinicals. She should get a CNA license, for the experience, but the pay was abysmal compared to what she made at No Limits, the perfect topic for an Ethics paper.

"But I want you to sleep now," he said just as gently. "You look so tired, Abby."

"I am tired. I can afford to run a sleep deficit right now. I can't afford to get used to—"

"It's just for now, Abby," Sean said. "Nothing to get used to. Just a little extra sleep today."

Why not? her sleep-deprived, stressed brain asked. Why not enjoy everything Sean Winthrop offers for the duration of his leave? Why not have sex and get extra sleep with someone else in the room who will wake you up if you sleep through the alarm?

"Thirty minutes," she warned. "You have to wake me up in thirty minutes."

"I will."

He didn't lie down beside her, or tuck her in, or sit by her side and stroke her hair, or do anything else lover-ly or boyfriend-ly. He set an alarm on his watch and stayed on the floor while she curled up on her side and closed her eyes. Dappled sunlight splayed against her closed eyelids, magnifying sounds. The television downstairs, volume rising and falling with the transition between commercials and content. Her own breathing, too shallow to please her yoga teacher. The sensation in her mind of doors closing as sleep crept up on her. Sean's breathing, steady, slow, deep . . .

Sean's hand on her forearm. A gentle squeeze. "Abby." *Sean's voice.* "Abby, honey, wake up."

She blinked and surreptitiously checked for drool. None. She'd slept too deeply to drool. Like something out of a dream, Sean knelt on one knee by her bed, his elbow braced on his thigh, his summer sky eyes unguarded. In that defenseless moment she smiled at him, then memory returned. The clock showed exactly thirty minutes after she'd lain down on her bed. She sat up, cross-legged, and stared blankly out the window.

That felt too much like trust. A promise made and kept, no matter how small, laid the foundation for trust. *Honey* felt too much like lovers. She cleared her throat. "I need more coffee," she said. "You?"

The guarded expression darkened his eyes. "Sure. Feel better?"

She couldn't bring herself to lie. "Yes."

"Good."

She refilled their coffee cups, then set to the Microbiology reading. When she was in the middle of outlining the mechanisms of pathogenicity Sean asked, "When do you have to be at work?"

"Seven," she replied without looking up. "I needed to get caught up on homework so I swapped the late shift with Lisette."

He stowed his books in his bag as his laptop powered down. "Six for me," he said. "Gotta go."

"You really came here to study," she said.

"I did," he said without looking up from his position on his knees, wrapping the laptop cord around his broad palm before stowing it in one of the backpack's many pockets. Sean was terribly organized. "It's one of my best memories from leave last year."

Ouch. She had, perhaps, forgotten to consider that Sean was a person, a rather complex one, and in that complexity lay his unmatched ability to hurt her. "It's not what we agreed to," she said, the words no less ruthless for their soft tone.

"I know," he said, and bent to kiss her swiftly before his electric blue gaze held hers. "I owe you. For this, and several other things I've done that we didn't agree to. Take what you want from me later."

And then he was gone, leaving only his unique scent and heat in her room, and a vague restlessness in her heart.

Chapter Five

Sean was pleasantly surprised to be home for Election Day. Usually he voted with an absentee ballot, but today he walked into his elementary school at midmorning, after the early morning voters and cameras, and before the lunchtime rush. He checked in with the elections' official, stepped inside the curtained polling booth, and exercised one of the freedoms he'd just spent a year defending. The booth beside him housed a young mother, alternating between cooing at a baby in a carrier on her chest and admonishing a younger child who was ducking into Sean's booth while his mother was distracted.

"Lucas, come back here," she stage-whispered.

Face solemnly composed, Sean looked down at Lucas, dressed in shorts and a train T-shirt, and made a shooing motion at him. The little boy peered up at him, wide-eyed, then crawled back under the curtain to his mother. Ballot cast, Sean exited the booth and accepted his I Voted Today sticker.

"How's the turnout?" he asked the volunteer as he slapped the sticker onto his shirt just below his collarbone.

She shook her head. "In an off-cycle year we're lucky to get 10 percent voter turnout. It may be a little higher because of the bond issue for the school district, so 15 percent?"

The young mother turned up with her kicking infant strapped facing forward on her chest and her young son vocally negotiating for two stickers, his mother's and one of his own. Sean watched the byplay and mentally contrasted the election process in Afghanistan, with heavily armed guards at polling stations, an all-male voter registry, and the suspicion of rigged elections.

Next stop: Langley Security. The door to the outer office was closed and locked, so Sean pressed the buzzer. "It's me," he said when he heard a click. The locked door buzzed, and he opened it.

"What's up?" John asked.

"I came by to give you this," Sean said as he handed him an 8x11 manila envelope, taped shut, no markings on the outside. "I read up on the pharmaceutical industry last week. These are my notes. Some of the younger guys you've got working for you might not know much about the background. If you think this will help them, go ahead and distribute. If not, just shred them."

John opened the envelope and upended it. The binder-clipped packet slid into his hand. "Notes? These are your *notes*? There's"— he flipped to the last page in the packet—"216 pages of single-spaced notes here."

"There's some analysis in there, too. Nothing fancy. Not what I could do with a couple of weeks and a few phone calls," he said. "And access to SEC filings. That would help. I can e-mail you the document if you want it."

"Huh," John said as he skimmed the first few pages. Then he looked up at Sean, his gaze assessing. "I'll take a look at it. Thanks."

"No problem." It was the kind of work he'd do anyway. He was a serviceable platoon commander, but his real strength lay in his ability to assimilate and analyze enormous quantities of information.

Make connections between seemingly unrelated incidents and individuals. Look for patterns where previously none existed, then deviations from those patterns. A geek, really. A geek who could run a six-minute mile, a geek with an expert marksman status, a geek who'd taken twenty-two men to war and brought them all home again, but really just a geek.

He'd geeked out big-time in Abby's bedroom, showing up with a backpack full of books and his laptop. But while being her secret lover satisfied a year of pent-up physical need, there was no way night after night of incredibly hot sex would establish the long-term emotional connection he wanted. Time was running out.

"How's Ty seem to you?" John asked.

"Better," Sean said. "More relaxed and more focused at the same time."

"Good," John said. "Has he talked to Lauren yet?"

"Based on the way she ignores him when she comes out for lunch, I'm going with no," Sean said. "She walks around him like he's part of the park bench."

"Or maybe he talked to her, and she told him to fuck off."

"I don't think so," he said, not that sleeping with a woman made him an expert on her. "She doesn't seem like the type to hold a grudge, but after what Ty said to her a couple of weeks ago, he better tell her the truth and hope she's feeling merciful." He shook his head. "He was in really bad shape. I should have noticed."

"We all should have. It turned out okay, in the end. What about you?" John asked. "Adjusting okay after deploying? Your family's here. Got a local girl?"

Sean shrugged. "I'm fine," he said, avoiding the girlfriend question.

John tucked the binder-clipped stack of paper back in the manila envelope, then slid it into the briefcase by his desk. "I'll look at this tonight."

"Later," Sean said.

Next stop was Abby's house. He rang the doorbell again and waited while Abby's father shuffled into view from the living room. An oxygen tube was strapped under his nostrils and the tank rolled beside him. He squinted down the hall then waved his hand for Sean to come in.

"Mr. Simmons, I'm Sean Winthrop, a friend of Abby's," he said as he closed the front door behind him.

The old man's eyebrow went up, but the sardonic effect was spoiled by a rasping, hacking cough. "Friend? You're that Marine she was head over heels for last year. I saw pictures, not that you bothered to come over and meet your girl's father. Then you go off to Afghanistan, and she's over the moon about it. Ribbons made a big mess. She's not here."

Sean wondered if Mr. Simmons needed more oxygen, because the last few sentences seemed to have come from another dimension altogether. "Yes, sir. I'm here to mow the lawn."

The noise Mr. Simmons made could have been the last gasp of a dying man, a grunt of disbelief, or just the tail end of a cough. "You're too good to mow my lawn."

The ridiculousness of arguing for the job of mowing a lawn wasn't lost on Sean, but he rose to the challenge. "No, sir, I'm not," he said seriously. "I mowed lawns every summer from the time I was nine until I left for school. I can give you references." Fifteen-year-old references. God help him if Mr. Simmons asked for them.

"The mower blades haven't been sharpened, and it probably needs oil. Abby can start it and push it, but she doesn't know jack about taking care of the machine."

Had her father taught her, back when he was healthy? His father showed him how to mow the lawn and take care of the mower, just as he'd taught all of Sean's sisters, and hadn't mowed the lawn in nearly twenty years. "I'll take a look at it first, sir."

"She's not going to be happy about this. Wants to learn how to do things herself."

"Yes, sir," Sean agreed. "I'll show her how to sharpen the blades and add oil another time."

"Don't bother. She said when it quits she's buying a reel mower. Better for the environment. Quieter, too."

The yard had to be damned near an acre. She needed a riding mower, not a human-powered reel mower from nineteen-ought-fuck, but Sean kept that opinion to himself. "Is the mower in the shed or the garage?"

"Shed." Mr. Simmons dug out a key ring and handed it over. "Set the deck at three inches. Abby's been scalping it to stretch times between jobs. Hard on the grass."

Sean unlocked the shed and pushed the mower into the sunshine. The blades were dull enough to be dangerous, so he sharpened them, then added oil and gas and yanked on the starter cord. The engine roared to life. Then, just because, he mowed the front and backyards into perfect double spirals, edged the sidewalk and front path, uprooted all the crabgrass encroaching from the neighbor's yard, and trimmed the hedges. By the time he was finished his T-shirt and shorts were soaked with sweat, but the yard looked good. Really good.

"Not bad," Abby's father said grudgingly. "Needs fertilizing."

"It's a little early yet," Sean said.

Mr. Simmons grunted again. "Abby'll appreciate it."

Sean wasn't so sure about that. He handed over the key ring, got in the Mustang, and headed over to his parents' house. As long as he was giving girls a break, he might as well cut their lawn for Naeve.

The knock on his door came at two thirty a.m. He stumbled down the hall and unlocked the door to let Abby in. "I'm giving you a key," he said and reached for her hand to pull her down the hallway, into bed. "Come on."

"I'm not coming in," she said, but the yawn ruined the sharp tone.

"Why not?"

"I saw the lawn. I'm not going to reward you breaking the rules with sex."

"I didn't think you'd see it until tomorrow. You said you had lab, then work."

"I forgot my laptop cord at home," she said. In the darkness her eyes looked more shadowed than usual, her skin so pale as to be almost translucent. "You're breaking the rules, Sean. The rules were what I want, when I want it. Nothing else, nothing more. I can do these things myself."

"I know you can," he said gently. Just as gently he took her hand and tugged her through the living room, down the hallway.

"I'll pay you for the work. You edged and trimmed. That must have taken hours."

She was nearly asleep on her feet. In the bedroom he went to work on the buttons of her blouse. "I don't want your money, Abby."

"I'm too tired to be a good fuck tonight," she said through another yawn.

"I don't want sex, either," he said, and unzipped her flirty little skirt.

Her skirt landed in the pooled semicircle of her blouse. "You have to want something. Why can't I figure out what you want?"

He unfastened her bra and pushed it down her arms. "Right now all I want is for you to get out of those heels," he said, hunkered down to slip each stocking down and off, then straightened to tug one of his USMC T-shirts over her head. Half asleep on her feet, she didn't protest at all, just got into bed.

"My feet hurt," she said sleepily.

"I know. Go to sleep."

"What do you want, Sean?"

The words came from the far side of awake, echoing her question in the parking lot two weeks ago, and she wasn't going to let this go. *Good.* Keep her thinking, keep her interested, keep her attention. "Go on a picnic with me," he said.

"Hmmmm?"

"Make that great wild rice salad with the walnuts and the cayenne pepper and go on a picnic with me. That's what I want. Time with you."

"That's not sex. This was supposed to be about sex. Now you're mowing my lawn and studying with me. You're breaking the rules, Sean. Rules do apply to you. Just because you show up again and you're all sexy-hot-Marine doesn't mean you don't have to follow my rules."

Half-asleep Abby did say the most interesting things. He hid his smile in her hair. "Have sex with me while we're on the picnic," he said.

"Okay."

He wasn't sure that constituted informed consent, but hell, it was just a picnic, not a chandelier-swinging sex act.

Paying careful attention to her schedule, Sean sent Abby on her way by six on Friday morning with a key and an extra twenty minutes of sleep by not waking her up for a departure quickie. When he showed up at Langley Security for the daily debriefing, John and Ty were waiting for him. A full seabag sat on the floor by the door. Sean looked at John, then at Ty. "You're leaving?" he said. "Did you talk to Lauren?"

"Yeah, Mom, I talked to her."

"And you're leaving anyway? She didn't . . . She wouldn't . . . What happened?"

"Aren't you the romantic? Easy there. It's all good," Ty said. He

was relaxed in a way Sean hadn't seen in the three weeks he'd
been on leave, shoulders low, breathing easy, the tense-to-the-
point-of-breaking demeanor gone. "I owe Gulf Independent another
month. The chopper leaves in a couple of hours. After that I'm done
for good."

Sean looked from John to Ty. "You're buying in?"

"Yeah. Chief Operating Officer specializing in personnel." He finished his coffee and looked Sean straight in the eye. "My first recom-
mendation was to get you off surveillance and on board as a partner."

"That was before he read your *notes*," John added.

Sean blinked. "You want me? For what?"

"Research and strategy," John said. He picked up the file containing Sean's background research. "Ty can get us the right people.
You can get us data. Information. Intelligence. The pieces of the
puzzle operatives need in order to do their jobs. You've got the connections and analysis training."

"What's the offer?" he asked automatically. Get data. Get information. Do a gut check.

"Equal partnership. Three-way split," John said, gesturing from
himself to Ty to Sean. "You bring something to the table we don't
have, and we need."

It was an unbelievable offer. Totally unexpected. The money
would blow military pay out of the water. "Based out of Galveston?"

"For the time being I'm keeping the headquarters here, but it's
a global industry. You could work from wherever you think you'd
be most effective, or wherever the job demanded. New York. D.C.
London."

He could be home, for good. He could resign his commission,
remove the constraint rushing his timetable with Abby. But he'd
never been in this for the money, and his gut, the intuitive instinct
he'd honed razor sharp over the last year, balked at the thought of
a job left undone. He'd asked to deploy, volunteered to take another

lieutenant's assignment so he could stay stateside with his wife and new baby. The bonds of loyalty to the Corps were ironclad before he spent a year fighting alongside the men whose faces now personalized strategy. The debt of loyalty only grew.

But what about Abby? This isn't going well, and you know it . . .

Sean shoved his hands in his pockets and looked at them. "I need to think about it."

"That's fine," John said easily. "Did I mention that in the last week I've gotten three calls from three different individuals asking for drastically different services? You want challenges and strategically significant jobs all over the world? They're all coming down the pike."

John could sell ice in the middle of a snowstorm, but Ty'd clearly told him Sean's weak spot. "I'll make a decision by the end of the week," Sean said.

Ty was watching him, his gaze slightly narrowed, a small smile lifting the corners of his mouth, and Sean remembered the way he studied the men in his platoon, understood them. Maybe Ty understood and maybe he didn't. Either way, Sean's decision just got a lot more complicated.

"I gotta go," he said. "I rotate on for Chase at 1600, right?"

John nodded.

"Lunch plans?" Ty asked easily.

"Yeah."

"Girlfriend?"

"Not exactly."

It was just like last year, if not quite as warm. The high was supposed to be around sixty-five, but the cloud cover made it feel cooler, almost fall-like. As a result the park was nearly empty. Sean parked the Mustang in the far corner of the lot. As they walked to a spot near the tree line along one edge of the park, Abby shivered in her khaki skirt and short-sleeved blouse, and wished she'd brought a sweater.

"Here," Sean said, and handed her edges of the blanket. Together they spread it out on the ground, anchoring one corner with the cooler containing the wild rice salad she'd made and the sandwiches, potato salad, chips, sodas, and cupcakes that were his contribution.

"This isn't the same blanket," Sean commented as he flipped it open and spread it on the ground.

"I couldn't find the other one," she lied. She pulled her keys from her skirt pocket but dropped them before she could get them in her purse. On his knees on the blanket, Sean picked them up, and zeroed in on a plastic picture frame-chain holding a picture of her crouched down by her niece.

"I thought you weren't close with your half brothers," he said as he studied the picture.

"I'm not," she said. "I called Jeff when Dad was diagnosed, and Lindsey invited us to Mikkie's birthday party a month ago. She's trying to figure out how to reconcile them. Dad didn't go to the party, which was one more thing on Jeff's list of stuff Dad did wrong. The list starts with Dad leaving his mother for mine, and the fact that their marriage didn't work either doesn't make him any less mad. Apparently stubbornness runs in the Simmons family." She pointed at the picture of Mikkie. "She's a handful. That's us at her birthday party this year."

"The cake on her face gives it away," he said. "Why didn't your dad go?"

"His medications weren't quite right then," she said, but it was an excuse, and she'd bet he knew it. "Can I have a sandwich, please?"

They divided up the food. Abby ate with the extra red fleece blanket draped across her lap, but the breeze chilled her back and sent goose bumps racing down her arms. "I should have brought a sweater," she fretted. Last year a picnic like this would have lasted all afternoon, with reading material, conversations, and maybe a nap. She had her flash cards for microbiology, but this chilled she'd be home in half an hour.

And it shouldn't matter. *This isn't what you wanted Sean for anyway, and he's breaking the rules. He maneuvered you into this.*

But it's such an excellent opportunity to prove that you're over him. Sex is one thing. A shared meal is more intimate. So do this. Eat with him, talk to him. He'll leave knowing what was so meaningful before is completely casual now. It's just a question of finding the right time to walk.

He stretched out on his side, head braced on his palm. "Come here," he said.

Suspicious of his intentions she sat with her back to his abdomen and draped the red fleece blanket over her legs. He pulled a book of poetry, of all things, from his backpack, so she started working her way through her flashcards, murmuring lists of virulence factors to herself. After a few minutes he asked, "What are you studying?"

"GI bugs," she said, refusing to feel embarrassed about studying pathogens that caused diarrhea. The very young and the very old were highly susceptible to diseases a healthy adult's immune system fought off. This mattered. Long term, that was what mattered.

She felt his gaze on her cheek like the caress of his fingers, and risked a glance at him. "What?"

"Nothing," he said.

She ignored the quiet admiration in his look and went back to the flashcards she'd made, but when her head drooped for the second time, his arm came around her waist. "Come here," he said.

Without protesting she lay down beside him. "Thirty minutes," she said. "That's all."

He tucked the blanket around her. His body heat, trapped in the blanket, quickly warmed her. "I've got you. Go to sleep, Abby."

She did, awakening to his hand at her waist. Keeping his movements slow and subtle, he untucked her shirt from her skirt and slid his hand up to her breasts. She gasped when his fingertips found her nipple, stroking the hard nub through the silk of her bra. Electricity coursed from her nipple to form a deep, dark ache between her thighs. The tension doubled when he treated her other nipple to the same torture.

"Sean," she whispered as she rubbed her ass against his tantalizingly unavailable cock.

"I promised you we'd have sex on this picnic," he murmured against her ear. "Tell me no if you've changed your mind."

A little nervous about such a public seduction, she glanced around the park, but the cloudy skies and cooler air kept the park fairly empty. Still . . . "We can't have sex here," she said.

"So we'll have foreplay here."

His hand left her aching, throbbing breasts and skimmed her abdomen, over her hip to the hem of her skirt. He tucked that up to her waist, then she lifted her bottom hip so he could do the same with the rest of the material. His fingers trailed lightly over her abdomen, tracing the elastic edge of her panties, just above her mound. With an unfocused gaze she looked down her torso, but the blanket hung loosely enough that she couldn't see his hand move, only feel it. Once again his fingers slipped under the elastic on her upper hip and tugged, then repeated the move at her lower hip. It took three attempts to get the material down to the tops of her thighs. He left them there.

"Take them off," she said, feeling less dressed that if she were totally bare.

Behind her, he shook his head as his hand stroked over her curls. "Too much movement."

She gave a pleading little sigh. He slipped one booted foot between her ankles, creating just enough space between her thighs to admit his hand. They were just a couple lying on a blanket, covered by another blanket, only their shoes exposed. So what if their feet were tangled up together? No one would guess that the silk of her underwear stretched taut around her thighs and his fingers were parting her swollen pussy lips to delve into the wet heat he aroused.

Stroke . . . stroke . . . stroke . . . slow and imperceptible. Getting a man off required an obvious movement. Not so for a woman. A woman could be driven out of her mind by motions so tiny and discreet that no one would suspect she was being touched. His hand barely moved, just the tip of his middle finger against her wet, swelling clit.

Heat flicked through her, drying her mouth and stealing her breath. She closed her eyes and drifted deeper into sensation from the slow circles his finger made around her clit, so arousing, yet not enough to get her off. Not hard enough, not fast enough, not precise enough.

None of it was enough.

"I want to feel you," she said, undulating against his hard shaft to make herself clear.

His hand left her clit to throb as his hand went to his button fly and popped it open. A few furtive movements, and his erection pressed against her bared ass, hot and silky smooth.

"Where do you want it? Here?" he asked. She felt his knuckles bump against her tailbone and the rounded flesh of her ass as he stroked it under the blanket. "Or here?" With those words he tucked the shaft between her legs so it nestled against her hot, wet folds.

"There," she whispered. His fingers resumed their slow circles, and the heft and thickness of his shaft, so tantalizingly close to where she really wanted it, ramped up the hot, syrupy tension even more. He was hard and hot between her legs, his shaft clasped between her thighs while the dark blond thatch of hair rasped against her bare buttocks.

The risk made her need profound. His fingertip slid through her slick heat and dipped into her swollen channel before returning to her clit. He thrust into the slick grip of her thighs. She gasped, breathy and high, unable to control the noise, or her face, then bent her arms at the elbow and closed her eyes. Maybe she'd look like she'd fallen asleep again under the blanket, not like she was quivering with need.

A low, rough chuckle rumbled in Sean's chest. "You just lie there. I've got you."

He did. He had her in every sense of the word. Emotionally, physically, mentally, right now she belonged to him. With the tip of his finger he left her clit and dipped down to stroke the soft, slick skin of her sensitive opening. "You're so wet," he said.

"We shouldn't do this here."

"Tell me what you'd do if we were somewhere private."

"One part of me wants to shove you back, climb on top of you, and ride you until I come."

His cock throbbed as he bent his head and bit down on the delicate curve of her ear. Edgy restraint was in the move, which sent liquid fire streaming down her nerves. "So fucking sexy to watch you take what you want from me," he growled. "What's the other option?"

"Roll over and spread my legs for you," she said.

The hand between her legs stopped moving for a second, just long enough for him to press against her mound. A shudder rumbled through him as he ground against her. "Which do you like better?"

His hand wasn't moving, so she could think a little more clearly. "I'd come in about five seconds if I was on top," she admitted. "It takes longer when you're on top, but it's a hundred times hotter when I'm totally helpless under you, spread for you, taking every thrust. I know I'll come, but it's not in my control like it is when I'm on top. You control it. Sometimes you make me wait and sometimes you drive me there so fast and hard and hot I see stars, and all I can do is cling to you and take it and beg—"

Where did that come from?

The hand bracing his head reached around to cover her mouth. "Abby. Stop talking." He was thick and hard between her thighs, her juices slicking up their bare skin as his cock throbbed once, twice, before he got himself under control again, and started breathing. "Fuck," he said. "Just . . . fuck."

She turned her head just enough to see his face, which made her pray to the gods who protected Marines on leave that no one would stroll past them. Heat burned on his cheekbones, and his blue eyes burned with unmistakable male intent. There was no way a passerby would think this was innocent. She was crazy to think it was meaningless.

Knowing surrender was in her every move she faced forward and let the dark, hot undertow of his touch close over her head. Every muscle in her body was drawn tight with pleasure as his circling fingertip picked up the pace, almost immeasurably. Soon she was stifling little cries in the back of her throat. His hot breath gusted over her jaw as he curled around her. It was slow, slight, subtle, and it was tearing her apart.

Almost there. She tipped her head back, trembling, *almost-therealmostthere*, felt his teeth close on the tendon in her neck. "Beg," he commanded. "Beg like you would if I had you on your back and at my mercy."

"Please." The word was nearly soundless, forced from her tight throat by a need powerful enough to overcome fear. "Please, Sean. Please."

The hand supporting his head once again covered her mouth, pulling her back against his bunched shoulder. One little thrust, then a second, both in time to the relentlessly circling finger on her clit, and she came. His hard hand stifled the involuntary cry that tore from her throat as the leading edge of the crest slammed into her. Wave after wave of pleasure swept from core to fingers and toes, again and again. If he hadn't held her together, one arm anchoring her hip while his fingers drove her insane, the other around her neck and face, she would have disintegrated into brilliant, white-hot shards right there on the hard, leaf-strewn ground.

The all-consuming passion ebbed from her body, leaving room for her to come back to herself, now soft and limp in his hold. Behind her he was still rigid in every sense of the word, from his cock nestled between her thighs, the trembling muscles of his abdomen, the rock-hard planes of his shoulders and chest. Desire poured from him in waves, physical, emotional; the sheer charisma of Sean swamped her, dragging her under. On the edge of tears, she buried her face in her folded arms, breaths shuddering into the air, snagging on the rough edges in her throat.

Damn him. *Damn him.*

A year ago she'd been young enough and stupid enough to believe in Prince Charming, in love at first sight. Experience taught her otherwise. Well-meaning friends said *Forget about him, that's the way his type is, just chalk it up to doing your patriotic duty and move on,* but the emotion remained. She couldn't forget him until she'd seen him again, finished the ending he'd begun, but on her terms. She would not quit. Point of honor. Point of pride. He'd started it, she would finish it, right to the bitter, bitter end.

Behind her Sean bent his head to that sweet spot at the nape of her neck. Heat arced through her like the flame from her father's blowtorch. She whimpered, tightening her thighs around his cock. To her surprise he put space between them and buttoned up, then tugged her panties up as best he could. Still reeling, she moved automatically, straightening her skirt as he stood. Cool air swept over her heated skin as he pulled the blanket away and began folding it briskly into a neat square.

"That's it?" she asked from her kneeling position. With his erection at eye level, she'd bet not.

"Pack up the food," he said and reached for the bottom blanket.

She fitted lids back on half-full containers and stacked them in the cooler, shoved the trash into a plastic bag. He shouldered all their gear, took her hand, and set a brisk pace back to the path leading to the parking area.

His Mustang wasn't the only vehicle in the lot anymore, but the other cars appeared empty, their occupants meandering the trails. When they reached the car he dumped everything in the back seat, opened the driver's door, and slid in. It took a second to turn the battery on, then he powered the driver's seat all the way back and hauled her in to straddle him, one knee on the side of the seat, the other foot planted in the dirt outside the car.

Off-balance, she looked out the wide-open door. "We can't have sex here!"

"The fuck we can't," he said, all command. "This won't take long."

The need burning in his blue eyes sent sparks skittering deep into her belly. In the time it took him to get a condom from the console and smooth it on, she'd steadied herself, one hand holding her skirt up, the other gripping the back of the seat.

With no preliminaries at all he tugged her panties aside, centered her over his straining shaft, and guided her down at the same time he thrust up. His thick cock stretched her, opened her, until she came to rest against his pelvis. Despite her resolve, the connection when he pushed in halted her breathing.

And his. A moment of breathless awareness hummed between them, crackling and snapping like a live current.

"Oh, fuck," he ground out. His head dropped back, but his gaze held hers. "Ride me."

In hindsight there never was any question that she'd do this, and not with her mouth, or her hand, but with her body. Quarters were close, the car's low roof bending her head forward. She looked down and saw his ridged abdomen flex and release as she took him deep. His hands tightened on her hips, guiding her, using her. She clenched around him, tilted her hips, seeking the right combination of angle and force, knew she found it when his eyes dropped closed and he jerked.

His grip tightened, but in this position—under her, at her mercy—there was nothing he could do but take what she gave him. He pushed against the floorboards and lifted his hips, tendons in his neck standing out as he ground his head against the headrest. The movement lifted her so she bumped her head on the roof and her ass on the steering wheel, but she had the power and the leverage, forcing him back down. A second groan choked from his throat. One hand left her hip to grip her hair and pull, hard, but she didn't relent. She jerked away from his fist, made him hurt her to hold her as she rode him hard and fast, making him take it, take her, and his surrender, the moment when his hand opened and cupped her skull to bring her mouth to his, was so fucking hot.

Soft, swollen, heated lips edged with blond stubble, abrasive and sexy, his tongue against hers as release jerked through him, like she'd reached into his body with her fist and yanked it from him. Her heart went into triple time just before orgasm hit. She leaned forward, her cheek pressed to his, the stubble chafing her heated skin. Slowly the tension eased from their bodies, leaving Abby with a second uncomfortable insight.

Was this how he felt, all cylinders humming as she grew more and more helpless, unable to control her response to him? Was this how he felt on top, this overwhelming, possessive tenderness . . . ?

Don't go there.

With a grunt he pulled her leg all the way into the car and

slammed the door. She continued the motion and separated their bodies, shifting off him, to the passenger seat, pushing her skirt down her thighs in case someone wandered by. He dealt with the condom in businesslike fashion, adding it to the bag of trash from the picnic, zipping up, then stalking across the parking lot to the garbage can. When he got back in the car he started the engine and turned the AC on full blast, then reclined in the driver's seat and closed his eyes.

Overwhelming, protective tenderness. She turned her attention to the stand of beeches across the parking lot before she spoke. "Don't expect me tonight. That should hold me for a few days."

He flinched. The movement was involuntary, a tremor through the muscles under the skin of his face almost but not quite mistaken for the play of sunlight and shadow from the leaves overhead on his skin, but she saw it.

"Whatever you want, whenever you want it," he said.

It was her turn to flinch, but thankfully, he wasn't looking at her. "This isn't like that, and you know it."

At that his eyes opened, the brilliant blue unsoftened by the intensity of what just happened. He looked at her, his gorgeous, combat-hardened body sprawled in the driver's seat, the smell of what they'd just done not yet dissipated by the AC. The shrapnel in her throat scratched as she swallowed hard, unable to look away until he spoke. "I know that, Abby. The question is, do you?"

For that she had no answer. She broke under the strength of his stare and turned to look out the front window. "Take me home, please."

Chapter Six

The ride to Abby's house was silent. She once again refused to look at him, staring out the passenger window until he pulled into her driveway. He unfastened his seat belt to help her with the salad bowl and the blanket.

"Don't," she said, still not looking at him. "Just . . . don't. I've got it."

If he'd learned anything in the last year it was that nine times out of ten the factor that fucked the best-laid plans was the human factor. Someone wasn't where he was supposed to be, missed a signal, froze when he shouldn't, or worse, attacked when he shouldn't. Unfortunately, the converse was even truer. The only thing, the *only* thing that saved a fucked mission was the human factor. A Marine took the lead when he'd never walked point before, raced under fire to save wounded men, located the unforeseen sniper's nest and took it out. People were un-fucking-predictable, but until life was totally automated, they were the only game in town.

In a neat little turned table, she'd blown his mind in the car, stripped his skin and left him defenseless. He loved doing that to her. He never felt closer to her than when she was sweating and trembling under him. But she'd done it to him when he was beginning to doubt whether she'd handle his vulnerability with any care.

Just so, he thought. Just like he'd fall for her, and she'd break his heart.

She slammed the car door and stalked up the front walk without a backward glance, the bright blue salad bowl balanced against one hip, the picnic blanket tucked under her arm. His heart squeezed tight. He loved her. He loved her and wanted her back, and she wouldn't look at him. He reversed out of the driveway and drove home. Nerves and uncertainty roiled in his belly, demanded physical release so he exchanged his cargo pants and T-shirt for swim trunks and a USMC shirt, then laced up his running shoes. He drove through town to East Beach, parked, and walked down to the beach against the tide of families and teens making their way home at the end of a day in the sun. He found a clear spot, shucked his T-shirt and shoes, and waded into the surf. When the water reached his waist he struck out for the horizon.

Abby didn't like the beach. Cursed with a redhead's pale skin she burned in a matter of minutes, and she was sensitive about the sun darkening the freckles he loved so much. Last year he'd bought an artist's fine paintbrush and a jar of high-quality hot fudge sauce, heated it up in the hotel room's microwave, and dotted it on every freckle from her lips to her thighs. Then he'd licked it off, freckle by freckle, counting while Abby giggled, then smiled, then went deeply, intently silent as he used his lips and tongue and teeth to worship her skin until she'd come in a series of shuddering, gasping waves. Later, after she'd rested up a little, she'd painted his cock with hot fudge sauce, using her fingers to swirl it around his shaft in thick, dark streaks. The next morning the jar was three-fourths empty. It was a miracle neither of them had lapsed into a sugar coma.

It was so easy last year, so hard this year, and that was entirely his fault. It was also reality. There was a reason why marriage vows included better or worse, sickness or health, richer or poorer. That was the span of human existence, and a lifelong commitment included all of the above. Even if he hadn't broken up with her, this year would have been harder. The home front was just a different kind of struggle.

The rhythmic movements and breathing ocean swimming demanded occupied his brain, leaving his subconscious free to send up thoughts in bubbles. In his opinion their strongest connection last year was sexual. They talked books and movies, a little about their families, and a fair amount about his deployment. How long, where, his duties, why he'd requested the transfer into an infantry unit.

But not about fear. Not about the fear that ruled his days, drove him to read and study and analyze to prepare for any contingency, and made sleep almost impossible. Beyond a simple exchange of *Are you scared? Of course; only fools aren't scared*, she hadn't pressed for more. In an effort to look strong and tough, he'd kept it from her. Some days knowing he'd see Abby smiling, watching him with those alert, alive green eyes was the only thing that kept him from vomiting up his guts in sheer terror, and he hadn't even set boot to Afghanistan's dirt yet.

His dishonesty made it easier to end things. He could see that in hindsight, but how much honesty could a fledgling relationship survive?

He slowed, treading water as he turned in a circle. The beach was a barely visible sliver of white between ocean and sky. The setting sun burnished the water in red and orange. The exercise worked, loosening his muscles, regulating his breathing. He turned back for the beach, emerging to find his shirt and shoes exactly where he left them. He pulled both on, ignoring the sand in his shoes, and set off down the sand at a fairly brisk pace. He alternated sprints with slower runs, veered into the water, pushing himself through sand and surf until he felt his muscles protest. Then he ran harder. Only when he felt on the edge of stumbling did he slow down. He walked the last mile back to his car, now the only one left in the parking lot.

He sat down heavily on the driver's seat, the same seat that hours earlier Abby used to strip away the defenses he hadn't even known he kept up. Fifteen months ago he'd purposefully made her that vulnerable, used her body's white-hot responses to him to turn her into a quivering puddle of flesh and bone, but he'd never stopped to think how she would feel afterward. Because he'd never let her do that to him.

Today she'd done it. She hadn't asked first, just trapped him between her body and the seat he now sat in, and she'd made him take what she would give him, when she'd give it to him. And he'd bet his Mustang she had no idea she'd done that to him.

He was in over his head. None of this was going the way he'd planned, but the only way out was through. He'd set events in motion, but he wasn't in charge of the results, much less in control of them. All he could do now was wait.

At least nothing would happen tonight. He had a late surveillance shift, then he'd go home and get some uninterrupted sleep. Tomorrow, the battle for the home front went on.

No Limits was rocking, the post-Halloween crowd even bigger than the year before. Abby hurried up to the bar and slipped between Lisette and another waitress.

"How's it going with your Marine?" Lisette asked.

"He's not my Marine," Abby replied. "Scotch neat, Scotch rocks, two Shiner Bocks, Cosmo, G and T," she called as she keyed the order into the computer.

"Who's drinking the G and T?" Lisette asked, wrinkling her nose.

"Some British girl who looks like she'd rather be anywhere else," Abby said.

"He sure looks like he wants to be your Marine."

"He doesn't want me. He wants the girl I was a year ago, and that girl's gone."

Lisette stepped aside to let another waitress up to the computer, then said, "Don't be too sure about that. The girl you are now, Miss-I-Sleep-With-A-Cop-On-My-Terms, might be just right for your Marine."

"Stop calling Sean my Marine," Abby said. "Why would I be just right for him now?"

"Because I saw him here with another guy and a woman, and the way they were dancing, I don't think your guy was looking for sweet and innocent."

Lisette set her drinks on her tray, but Abby stopped her before she disappeared into the crowd. "What are you talking about?"

"Your Marine—"

"He's not just a uniform. He's got a name. Sean."

Lisette lifted an eyebrow and cracked her gum. "*Sean* was here two weeks ago with another guy and a woman. They danced. Together. By *danced* I mean *simulated hot, sweaty, borderline kinky sex* to the point where they had the entire dance floor's attention and half the main room's. All three of them, not Sean and her, then her and the other guy, the three of them at once, front, back, side to side. The other guy was hot enough to melt steel, by the way, no daylight between bodies, let alone the phone book the nuns used to put between us to keep prepubescent pelvises apart. Just before Linc was about to kick them out to get a room, they left. Very, very to-ge-ther."

Lisette stretched the word into three syllables, and Abby's

stomach dropped six inches, but before she could question Lisette again, she vanished into the crowd and Linc loaded up Abby's tray. Tray held at head-level she wedged herself into the crowd. Noise and bodies buffeted her equally, but the turmoil inside her had her stumbling on her heels.

Sean . . . dancing? A year ago he would dance, if she smiled and pleaded prettily, and thanks to hours of drilling on the parade grounds could keep the beat in a way that wasn't embarrassing, nothing more. But . . . Sean? *Dirty dancing* . . . with a *couple* . . . at No Limits . . . two weeks ago?

Two weeks ago he'd been replacing her battery by day and driving her wild by night. And on the nights she'd forced herself not to show up at his borrowed house, had he gone out looking for other company?

After she delivered the drinks she pushed through the crowd, looking for her blond coworker. "Lis, when was this exactly?"

Lisette waved vaguely. "I don't know," she said. "It was a Friday, I think. Or maybe a Saturday. A weekend for sure because we were slammed from five on. Weren't you here?"

"I don't remember seeing him," she said, but then again, she'd missed him once before until he was right behind her. "I was late for work one Saturday because Dad was sick."

"I remember now . . . that's why we were slammed," Lisette said. "We were short a waitress on a Saturday night. I made money by the fistful until you came on at eleven. All I had to do was show up at a table with a drink, not even the right drink, and I got tipped."

If it was that Saturday, that was the night after he saw her in Ben's parking lot. She'd gone home, gotten a few hours of sleep, done homework, housework, and yard work, and was on her way out the door for paying work when her father turned a terrifying shade of blue. Between that awkward scene in Ben's parking lot and Sean showing up at No Limits again, full of intention and purpose and unrestrained sexual need. And here she'd been bragging about how grown-up she was, and once again he trumped her in his understated, modest way. Never drawing attention to his *accomplishments*, always letting the other person shine.

She stopped short in the middle of the big room, lights blinking and flashing, people shouting, a table surrounded by drunk guys doing rounds of shots to her left, the bar to her right, the dance floor that most nights rivaled a Girls Gone Wild show, where he and two other people somehow made enough of a spectacle that everyone noticed.

What had he done?

Possibilities flashed in her mind, each one hotter than the previous image. Apparently, the old Sean had new tastes, new interests. She should have guessed. Sex last year was an unhurried, subtle exploration of her body, their responses together. Sex this year had an edge to it, one she'd attributed to the aftermath of a year overseas and her own needs. But maybe he'd grown accustomed to the highly addictive combat adrenalin, sought it out in bed. Maybe that made her hot as hell.

Maybe this was exactly what she'd been looking for, something that would drive a final wedge between them, something that was here and now, immediate, not leave last year, not breaking up ten months ago, but right now.

Something moist, fleshy, and smelling vaguely of sweat moved slowly in front of her face, but the brisk, officious snap right in front of her nose jerked her back to the present. A pudgy, solemnly drunk man peered deep into her face. "Earth to Red," he said, followed by a long pause. "Hey . . . ?"

"Red?" she supplied helpfully. The other guys at the table laughed like she was the funniest thing ever.

"Yeah. Red. Earth needs Heineken."

Earth was already about a six-pack of Heinekens to the wind.

Afraid the reeking beer breath would knock her unconscious, she took a step back and found her smile. "Of course. Anything else?" she asked the rest of the table.

Tray tucked under her arm and order in hand, she trotted back up to the bar. So what if she'd told him not to expect her tonight. He'd given her a key. That sinking feeling in the pit of her stomach was relief she'd just found the best way to slam the door on her unruly emotions. Make it sexual. Stiff-arm him back where he belongs, tonight.

After she found out exactly what he'd done when he left No Limits.

Chapter Seven

A shadowy figure stepped between the bed and the thin curtains covering the window. Adrenaline poured along Sean's nerves, and he was off the bed, in a fighting crouch, knife in hand when the feminine shriek and the light from the full moon silvering the figure's red hair brought him fully awake.

"Jesus Christ," he said as he straightened, his heart rate out of the red zone and heading for the stratosphere. "Jesus *Christ*, Abby! You said you weren't coming over!"

"You gave me a key," Abby said, her voice high and thin, her hands spread like he was holding a weapon on her. Which . . . he was. "You gave me a key! Why did you give me a key if you freak out when people come in unexpectedly?"

"I didn't know I'd freak out," he said, and sat down on the edge of the bed. Goose bumps rippled under the fine sweat on his skin. "No one else comes over. *Fuck*," he ground out.

For a few seconds their irregular, stressed breathing was the only sound in the room. "Are you okay, Sean?"

The distressed tone in her words cut into him. "That's not a PTSD thing, Abby," he said quietly. "That's a Marine thing."

"That's a really big knife, is what that is."

He looked at his hand, his fingers still wrapped around the leather-washer handle of his KA-BAR fighting utility knife, the seven-inch blade long enough that keeping it in his boot was technically a violation of Texas's concealed carry law. He carefully replaced it behind the alarm clock, noted the slight tremor to his hand. That would take a while to subside. Even though he'd put the knife down she stayed where she was, just inside the room, so he shifted backward on the bed until he leaned against the headboard. "Standard issue combat knife," he said. "No big deal. C'mere. I'm harmless." That was as much for himself as her.

She stayed where she was, in the doorway, her hands slowly dropping back to her sides. "No, you're not, Sean. You are absolutely lethal."

His brain jerked into high gear as he scanned from her head to toe, but with her back to the window her face was hidden from view. She was here, when she said she wouldn't be. "I would never hurt you, Abby," he said.

At least she dropped her bag, stepped out of her heels, and crawled onto the bed. Then she straddled his body, her knees outside his, her hands by his hips, and kissed him, openmouthed, provocative. When she nipped his lower lip fight-or-flight adrenaline cracked into sexual response. His cock hardened painfully, and suddenly the only thought in his brain was getting Abby spread for him. He fisted one hand in her hair and gripped her hip with the other, ready to roll her when she resisted.

"I want to ask you a question."

Her tone was challenging, the look in her eyes even more so, and the urge to fuck her doubled. "After," he said.

"Now," she replied.

His cock throbbed. For the first time in his career as a Marine he was in a position to relieve combat stress with something other than a combat jack, and she was arguing with him? They'd discuss the immediacy of reptile brain male physiological responses later. Much later. "During," he said.

At that her mouth softened. She bent forward and placed her soft, open mouth against the pulse pounding under his jaw. Meticulously but rapidly she made her way down his throat to his collarbone, then along his sternum to his abdomen.

Fuck, yeah.

He shifted up so just his shoulders and head were braced against the headboard, brushed her hair back from her face and wound his fingers in it, all the better to watch. Abby gripped his cock in her fist and took the head in her mouth.

Three minutes ago he was sound asleep. Sound fucking asleep, beyond dreams. His eyes dropped closed as Abby swirled her tongue around the head, went down until her lips met her fist, then came back up again with enough sucking pressure to make his hips buck. She did it again, again, then backed away and licked the tip.

"I was talking to Lisette tonight," she said.

Who? Waitress. No Limits. Blonde, with a malicious sense of humor. "Uh-huh," he managed.

"She said you were in No Limits a few weeks ago with another guy and a woman."

And just like that, his past caught up with him. He went still, prey-still, like she did their first night together. His eyelids lifted enough to see Abby looking up at him innocently as she closed her pretty pink lips around the head of his shaft and flicked her tongue against the bundle of nerves just below. He groaned, shifted his hips up while he used the fist in her hair to urge her down.

"Tell me about that, Sean," she murmured when she came back up.

Okay, so he didn't know the protocol for this situation, but she was asking . . . and she was going down on him while she asked, so . . . she wasn't mad? He had nothing to be ashamed of here. She'd told him she was over him. "A friend called me and asked me to meet him and his girlfriend at the bar. So I did."

Abby sat up and put her fingers to the buttons of her blouse. "What else did you do?"

He watched her take off her shirt, then her bra before he answered. "The things you do at No Limits. Drink." Ass in the air she went down again, and he groaned. "Dance. Jesus, Abby."

"I heard about the dancing," she said, a cat's smile on her face. "Lisette said it was very hot. All three of you at once. And then you left together."

His cock throbbed, and whether it was from the memory of that night with Ty and Lauren or Abby's teasing sucks and licks, he didn't know. When he kept quiet, she pushed. "Did you do something naughty, Sean?"

"No," he said. *Naughty* was Abby in her No Limits uniform, teasing him with glimpses of her cheeky panties. What he'd done with Ty and Lauren . . . fuck, he had to choose the right word during a blow job?

She paused and looked at him, eyebrows cocked expectantly. "No, you didn't do something naughty?"

"We did something erotic," he rasped, scrambling for an answer so she'd continue. "Adult. Carnal. That's the right word. *Carnal.*" It came from some hot, dark place inside him, a place unlocked by the adrenaline and Abby's tight, wet mouth, and just thinking about it tightened his balls. Heat pooled at the base of his shaft, began to climb.

She wrapped her hand around his spit-slicked cock and began to jack him, slow but hard enough to retain that erotic edge. "When?"

"The night after I found you at Ben's."

"What did you do?"

Tell the truth. All of it. "We drove to her place and had sex with her just about every way you can have sex with a woman."

A blink, a curious tilt of her head. "Oral," she said, but it wasn't a question. "Vaginal?"

He nodded again, not sure how she'd take that, but she didn't seem fazed at all.

"Anal?"

"Not me. Ty did."

She took him deep. At the slick pressure of his cock against the back of her throat he tensed, clenched his fists in the sheets to avoid clenching his fists in her hair and bucking up into her mouth until he came.

"Why?"

Why what? He struggled for the trailing end of their conversation, latched onto it. *Why did you do it?* That was the subtext under the single word, and Abby's beguiling mouth, wet and tight and purposeful, was stripping his ability to filter his responses. "Because I found you at Ben's."

"Did finding me at Ben's make you mad?'

Finding her at Ben's broke his heart, but he wasn't about to tell Abby that. "And," he said, driven to honesty, "because odds aren't good I'll get another offer like that again."

A smile, knowing and amused, curved her wet, pink lips. "You really have no idea how hot you are," she said. "You could walk into No Limits and walk out twenty minutes later with any two girls in the bar."

He was the exception to the rule about the sex appeal of Marines. Women didn't emerge from the woodwork and hurl themselves at him. Even in uniform. They asked him for directions, trusted him to drive them home without violating them when they were shit-faced, cried on his shoulder when their boyfriends screwed their friends and broke their hearts. "You're crazy."

"You're arguing with me?" she asked coquettishly, and took a firmer grip on his cock. "I must not be doing this right."

She practiced assiduously for a few moments, and just when release seethed in the tip of his cock, she lifted her mouth again. He groaned.

"Poor baby. Have you done that before? Anal sex?"

The question, combined with a particularly hot moment of lips and teeth and pressure applied to the tip of his cock sent his orgasm climbing his shaft. "No."

"Do you want to?"

That got his attention. He opened his eyes and focused on her face. "Whatever you want, whenever you want, Abby."

"I want," she said.

Sweet Jesus. "Later," he said. "I'm too turned on to take it slow now." Slow was key.

Her cat-green eyes flashed a provocative challenge. "That's not all I want," she said.

It took him a second to get it, because she'd taken up that torturous siege on the tip of his cock. When her words formed meaning in his brain he slid his hand under her jaw to lift her face.

Maybe you should have thought about what she meant to you before you did it.

His conversation with Ty when the ménage with Lauren was over flashed into his brain. Then, he couldn't understand why he'd share a woman he cared about with another man. Now . . . it turned him on to think about it. Now . . . he remembered the look on Lauren's face, and the look on Ty's, when they shared that experience together. For a long, charged moment he looked deep into Abby's eyes. She meant it. Her truth was in her eyes, the flush on her skin, in her pouty, swollen lips. The explanation, a rationale beyond *whatever, whenever,* wasn't as forthcoming.

You just made it sound hot as hell, you moron. Abby won't need a rationale beyond that.

"Come here," he said, lifting his chin.

Still innocently obedient she let his cock slap against his belly and shifted her weight up to straddle his hips. With his eyes focused on hers, he worked his hand under her skirt and found slick, wet heat. Her eyes went heavy-lidded, and her lips parted on a soft sigh. With his wrist twisted awkwardly he sought and found her clit, swollen at the top of her sex. He stroked both sides gently, and heat flared on her collarbone and in her cheeks.

Time to turn the tables on her. "What turned you on, Abby? Giving me a blow job, the thought of anal sex, or the thought of a ménage?"

"All of the above," she murmured. "I'm not the girl you left behind, Sean."

Her hips tilted forward, seeking more contact. "Ah, ah," he said, heard the edge in his tone. "Do you have someone in mind?"

"Ben," she said, high-pitched, soft.

No surprise there, and if Abby thought she could drive him away by bringing her lover into their bed, she was wrong. Right now it didn't matter. He wanted Abby back here, going wild with him, not lost in her mind. "Turn around," he said.

When she did, moving slowly, awkwardly, he tugged her cheeky panties down and off, then flattened his palm between her shoulder blades. At his not-quite-gentle push she peered over her shoulder at him. "Suck me, Abby."

Then she got it. She aligned her sex with his mouth. When her hand gripped his cock and her mouth took him deep he delved his tongue into the juicy folds and followed her rhythm, circling her clit in time to her wanton sucking. It didn't take long. Her thighs stiffened and her hips tilted, then her throaty cries reverberated through his cock as her clit fluttered under his tongue. He shifted his hips back, telling her he was about to come, but she braced her forearm across his pelvis and kept a firm grip on his cock with hands and lips, and he couldn't stop. His orgasm pulsed from his cock, and a stuttering groan from his chest.

A minute later she shifted her weight across his chest and collapsed on the bed, her head by his feet. He should take off her skirt, the only article of clothing she still wore, get her a glass of water, get her under a sheet. But she was already falling asleep, and it was hot enough that he'd turned on the ceiling fan. It turned lazily overhead, the shadows from the blades flashing in the dim moonlight.

He was half asleep himself when Abby's voice came into his dream. "Do you want me to ask him, or will you?"

This wasn't in his plan. None of this was in his plan, but when it came right down to it, the squared up, black lines and white squares of his strategy were disappearing into the complex, difficult, edgy, confident woman Abby had become. Last year she'd been fun. Sweet. Uncomplicated. Now . . . now he could spend a lifetime exploring Abby, and never get to the end of her.

"I'll do it," he said.

Sean took the stairs two at a time. The sounds of a football game came through the door. He knocked twice and waited through a couple of seconds of nearly inaudible breathing behind the peephole. When the door opened he was looking right into Ben's eyes. His first impression wasn't far off—the vest added to his bulk, but not by much. His second impression was that Ben had worked the street long enough to learn the art of not reacting. He went physically still even as his gaze flickered over Sean, assessing details. Expression, hands, stance, back to expression.

"You get new stickers for your plates?"

"Yeah. Sean Winthrop," he said by way of introduction.

"I know." Ben must have decided Sean wasn't any more of a threat than Sean thought Ben was, because he stepped back and gestured Sean into his apartment with the hand holding a bottle of beer. Sean stepped onto the tile square doubling as a foyer and looked around. A flat-screen TV on a black stand faced a brown leather sofa. A glass coffee table strewn with paperwork and a bowl of half-eaten macaroni and cheese occupied the space between the TV and the couch.

"She's not here," Ben said. "Hasn't been since that night. And for the record, she said she wasn't seeing anyone."

Set the tone up front. "She wasn't. And she's been with me since then," Sean said.

Ben shot him a glance, then tipped the bottle to his mouth. "If you're here to gloat, don't bother. We were never exclusive."

"I'm not here to gloat," Sean said.

The crowd noise rose to a roar, and they both glanced at the television. The opposing team's corner sprinted down the sidelines, ball tucked securely between his arm and side, offensive linemen lumbering after him. The beaten wide receiver fought off the corner's stiff-arm and shoved him into the sidelines, preventing the pick-six. Jeers rained down on them both.

"I don't know who we have to fuck in this league to get a decent offensive coordinator, but whoever it is is playing hard to get," Ben observed without heat.

Sean huffed in agreement. "This is last week's game," he said.

"I know. I miss the games most weeks because I'm working. Too many cop, ME, and lawyer shows on these days. I DVR games for background noise when I'm prepping for trial." He swallowed the last of his beer, looked at the empty bottle, then at Sean. "If you're not here looking for Abby, why are you here?"

"Got another one of those?" Sean asked with a nod at the bottle.

To Sean's amusement, Ben actually looked abashed at the lapse in manners. "Yeah. Sure." He went into the kitchen and returned with two bottles. Sean perched on the arm of a matching leather chair, followed Ben's lead and tossed the bottle top on the coffee table, then swallowed some liquid courage.

Ben just looked at him. "What's this all about?"

"Abby wants to have a threesome," Sean said bluntly. "With you," he added, in case Ben thought he was gloating again.

Ben's dark eyebrows rose. "Abby does, or you do?"

"Abby," Sean said patiently. "If this were my deal I wouldn't be asking you."

The eyebrows took on a faintly amused air. "One ménage wasn't enough for you?"

Clearly Ben knew about him, Ty, and Lauren. "You saw me leave No Limits with another couple," Sean said.

"I did. Heard about it, too."

"You didn't tell Abby."

"None of my business," Ben said with a shrug. "She's not my girlfriend."

He didn't need Ty's radar to get the *I don't give a fuck* vibe loud and clear. "This is her deal. Ask her yourself," Sean said.

"Oh, I will. Be sure of that," Ben replied. A faint smile quirked the corners of his mouth. "Why me?"

"Ladies' choice," Sean said ironically.

"You're local," Ben said, but again, he wasn't asking. Sean's vanity plates were easy to remember, and Ben probably hadn't been in his car five minutes before he knew all about Sean Winthrop. "You don't have a friend to ask?"

The goal was to win Abby back. If they were going to do this, the other guy needed to be someone she knew, trusted, and could avoid for the rest of her life if she had any regrets.

Except Abby wouldn't have regrets. The new Abby was living life balls to the wall.

"Abby wanted you."

"And what Abby wants, Abby gets?"

"In this situation, yes."

Ben looked at the television, then back at Sean. "When?"

"You working Sunday night?" When Ben shook his head, Sean picked up a pen and a notepad from the pile of paperwork on the coffee table and said, "DVR the game and come over to my place."

Ben waited until Sean wrote out the address, then said, "Why?"

"Because Abby still lives with her father, and we're not doing this here," he said brusquely. His girl, his turf, no exceptions.

"Interesting," Ben said lightly, and Sean kicked himself, "but not what I was asking. Why does Abby want a ménage?"

Because I told her I had one. Because I'm in love with her, and God help me, I want her to have what she wants.

"Abby's feeling adventurous these days."

Ben's gaze returned to the TV. "I don't get her adventurous," he said evenly. "I get her frantic. Once a month or so. She's so tightly wound when she comes over here she goes off like a rocket. And then she's asleep in seconds. That girl's under enough stress to snap steel. You fuck her up, and I'll find you and fuck you up."

"Is this where I tell you I'm only going to Virginia, not deploying again, so if I hear word one that *you've* fucked her up, I'll be back to teach you how a Marine fucks someone up?" He bared his teeth in something that might pass for a smile. "Or can we end the pissing contest now?"

Ben eyed him judiciously. "Yeah, we're good. See you Sunday."

Sean let himself out and went home, his brain turning over this new information. She was in Ben's bed once a month? She'd been with him fourteen nights out of the last twenty. What did that mean?

She showed up on his doorstep five hours later, at one in the morning. Half-asleep and wearing only his boxers, customary condom in hand, he unlocked the door and let her in, but before he could ask her about her arrangement with Ben, she dropped her purse and stepped into his body, rocking him off-balance. In her No Limits heels she was tall enough to rub against him, hip to hip, breasts pressed to his bare chest, mouth tipped open and wet to his. To regain balance he shifted his weight forward, fisted his hands in her hair, and drove her into the wall. Air rushed from her lungs, and she inhaled sharply when he ground his hardening shaft against her belly. She pushed him back just enough to yank his boxers down and free his erection. Skirt up, sexy cheeky panties down to the floor, lift her knee, and find wet heat.

He groaned. Her nails stung his shoulders as she gripped for balance on her heels. "Jesus, Abby."

"Been thinking about you," she gasped. "All. Night."

The soft exhalation deepened into a moan as he pushed inside. He'd never been so hard, because he'd been thinking about her all night, too. His heart rate shot into the stratosphere, and his balls tightened almost unbearably. Hot sparks streamed down his spine as she whimpered and shimmied. He couldn't take the movement. He tightened his grip on her hair and pulled her head back hard enough to rap against the wall, then shoved his hips forward. Pinning her. Holding her helpless against him, mouth open to his, breasts flattened against his chest, legs spread for his hips, his cock. He began to move, short, hard thrusts that rammed her tailbone to the wall, his pelvis against hers, and drove sharp cry after sharp cry from her arched throat.

It wasn't pain. Her closed eyes, the nails in his shoulders, the way her thigh trembled against his forearm sent all the right subconscious signals to *keep going don't stop more more more*. In response he ravaged her mouth, then dragged lips and teeth and tongue along her jaw to her ear.

"You like it?" he growled. "You like taking it?"

A sharp, helpless cry was his answer. A blood flush swept up her throat, heating the cheek pressed to his, and she came. He slowed, the better to feel the tight, slick contractions around his cock, then pulled out.

"What?" she gasped.

He gripped her arm and dragged her down the hallway to the bedroom, then shoved her face forward on the bed. He covered her before she could do more than get to hands and knees, and her desperate cry of surrender shot straight to his balls. She dropped forward, braced on her forearms and spread knees while he flipped her skirt up over her ass and plunged roughly inside. Then he hooked an arm around her torso and hauled her upright against his chest.

"What were you thinking about?" he growled as he made swift work of her shirt buttons. Two quick jerks and he tossed it toward the floor, then unfastened her bra and pulled it off. His movements were rough, demanding, careless. His purpose was anything but.

"This," she gasped as he flattened one palm between her shoulder blades and pushed her forward again. The sheets, still warm from his body, muffled her next words. "You. You make me so hot. You make me want you so much."

She didn't sound happy about it. He pulled out slowly, pushed back into the clinging, slick walls even more slowly. "Good," he said. A pause, totally inside her, every inch of her tight pussy gripping his cock, then he pulled out again. "Were you thinking about Ben?"

A pause. He thought she'd lie to him, but she didn't. "Yes."

Glide in. "That's what got you hot?"

She looked over her shoulder, up at him, her eyes glazed with awakening lust. "You, me, and Ben," she admitted. "Him watching you and me . . . you watching him and me . . ."

Looking into Abby's eyes while he was balls deep inside her electrified every cell in his body. "Want to know what he said?"

"Later," she gasped. "Now . . . fuck me."

He braced his fists on the bed in front of her thighs, holding her still for his pounding thrusts, and hunched over to set his teeth to the sensitive curve between nape and shoulder. She writhed under him, but he used his whole body to keep her in place. His legs controlled hers, his arms trapped her, his mouth on her nape and his cock inside her reminded her in the most primitive way possible that right now, she was his. Only his. It was hot and wet and frantic, slippery with sweat in the darkened, still room.

Orgasm hit him like a freight train. Only dimly aware of Abby's ecstatic cries, colored fireworks went off behind his clenched-shut eyelids. He jetted into her trembling body with enough force to obliterate all thought from his mind.

Reality returned, but slowly. He pulled out and eased onto his back while Abby just lay down on her stomach beside him.

"Why'd you yank me down the hall?" she said sleepily. "Against the wall was plenty hot."

That's not the question he'd thought she would ask. "After sex you fall asleep in seconds," he said. "I didn't think I could get you to bed without bumping your head again."

"Oh," she said. Still on her stomach she reached for the button and zipper of her skirt, unfastened them, and lifted her ass to get the skirt off. He disentangled the sheet under their bodies and covered her. "What did Ben say?"

"We're on for Sunday." Like they'd made plans to go to the movies with a friend. "You knew he'd say yes."

Her heard her smile in her sleepy voice. "Ben's got quite the reputation," she murmured.

Sean gathered her in, one arm around her waist, the other under his head. She said something indistinct and cuddled into him, but her body was lax with sleep long before he was even able to close his eyes.

Chapter Eight

Sunday evening the shower shut off, the pipes thunking in the wall as the pressure eased. A few minutes later Abby emerged from the bedroom wearing a pair of jeans and a hip-length sleeveless blouse in a soft jade green with a standing collar. She'd dried her hair and parted it on the side hanging mane-straight to just below her jaw. A hint of mascara darkened her lashes, but otherwise her face was bare. The effect was sophisticated and simple, far from the college girl she'd been when they met at No Limits.

His heart began a slow, thudding rhythm against his breastbone. She looked at him, ducked her head, and tucked her hair behind her ear. "Do I look okay?"

He rose from the sofa and beckoned her over. When she stood in front of him he lifted one hand to her jaw and stroked her cheekbone with his thumb. Her freckles stood out against the pale skin. Absently he remembered how the blood flush of arousal consumed the freckles like dawn overtaking the starry night sky. "You're the most beautiful woman I've ever seen," he said.

Her eyes softened, green going mossy, then a sharp rap on the door, and she stepped out of his caress. "Even off-duty he knocks like a cop," she said.

Sean got up to answer the door. Ben stood on the other side, dressed in jeans and a Western shirt. They looked at each other for a long moment, then Sean stepped back to admit him. Abby had seated herself on the short, square leather ottoman, her legs spread, heels of her hands braced between her thighs as she looked first at Ben, then at Sean. The movement sent her hair sliding forward to cover one eye.

"Hey," Ben said. He gave Abby a slow smile that didn't quite mask the tension implied by the way he flipped his key ring around his index finger to thud against his palm.

"Hi, Ben," she said. "Thanks for coming over."

Flip-thud. "He said this was your idea," Ben said, jerking his chin toward Sean.

"He's telling the truth."

A beat passed, another flip-thud, then Ben said, "Fair enough," and shoved his keys in his pocket.

More than a beat passed. But still he waited, watching Abby look up at the two of them, facing her across the room. Patience was a virtue, even in circumstances that dripped vice.

"I'm ready," she said with a bright smile.

Something about her tone triggered a warning deep in Sean's gut, some incongruity, some crucial piece of the puzzle that was the new Abby he was missing, but her words shut down the analytical part of his brain working away at the Abby-cipher.

Without looking at Ben, he spoke. "She says she's ready. You think so?"

Ben just shook his head and split to Sean's left. They strolled toward Abby, approaching her from either side, and the smile faltered, then disappeared. Ben went down on one knee behind her just as Sean did the same in front of her. It was a shooter's stance, boxing her between their torsos and bent legs. Abby's eyes widened, and suddenly she didn't seem to know what to do with her hands, rubbing them over her thighs. Ben gave a rough chuckle as he gripped her hands and put them palms down, one on his knee, the other on Sean's knee, and covered her hands with his, holding them in place.

Abby blushed and looked down. As if it were the most natural thing in the world, Ben slid his big hand into Abby's hair and tipped her head back for Sean's mouth. The perfect launch point for the assault on the girl who loved to kiss, that sensitive, full mouth. He hadn't known what Lauren liked and had been more than happy for Ty to take the lead with her, but he surely knew what Abby liked, and Ben did, too. Ben might even know things Sean didn't. Between the two of them they could bring vast experience to bear on the slender, pale woman between them. They could take their time, layer pleasure over her until the air around them melted.

He started with one corner, just pressed his open lips to that delicate spot, felt her breath ease from her mouth. Her tongue reached for his, so he slipped lower, nibbling along her lower lip to the other corner for another pause. With the tip of his tongue he traced the curve of her upper lip to return to his starting point. He pulled back and looked at her. Her eyelids drooped, and a soft pink flush stained her cheeks under the freckles, but if she felt any embarrassment at being kissed so intimately while Ben watched, it didn't show.

"He knows what you like," Ben said, rough amusement in his voice. His dark head was bent over Abby's, and she sagged back against his chest, hands on their knees. Her nipples pressed against her blouse, and somehow her spread legs weren't defiant. They were open, eager. His senses went hyperalert, noticing little details. The sound of Ben's fingers closing in Abby's hair, holding her head while

Sean kissed her. The pressure of both Abby's and Ben's hands on his knee, the way heat crawled from the connection of mouth and hands to his shaft and balls. The moment nervous tension shimmered from Abby's body as longing crowded in, and her legs spread a little farther.

"I'm just getting started," Sean said, looking at Abby. He bent to her mouth again, this time giving her the lip to lip contact in soft, sweeping movements of his mouth over hers. She whimpered and leaned forward, chasing his mouth, but Ben's hand fisted in her hair stopped her.

"Wait for it," Ben said. "You'll get it."

"And more," Sean said against her mouth. His own mouth tingled with electricity from the teasing contact, and he could only imagine how Abby's felt. He pressed a little harder, flicked his tongue against the tip of hers, waited for the moment her tongue chased his, then pulled back. "When I'm ready to give it to you," he said.

He made her wait, used lips and teeth and tongue on the line of her jaw, the tendons running down her throat to her collarbone before covering her mouth with his and kissing her long and hard and deep. When he lifted his head her mouth was wet, her eyes glazed. Ben tugged her head back to rest on his shoulder, taking more of her upper body weight against his chest. Sean reached for her hands, flattened them at her hips, and covered them with his own while Ben's fingers worked down the front of her blouse and spread the fabric to expose her breasts and belly. She wore a silk and lace bra in a deep blue green that turned her skin milk white and made her eyes glow.

Sean pressed kiss after leisurely kiss into Abby's henna-starred skin, where her pulse pounded under her ear, the hollow of her throat, the bumps of her collarbone, then down her sternum to between her breasts. Abby shifted restlessly, but with her weight leaning back and her hands trapped, she lacked the leverage to get his mouth where she wanted it. Instead he explored the scalloped lace edge of her bra cup, from the clasp to the outer curve of her breast and back down again, this time with his tongue under the lace. He repeated the movements on her other breast, and her hips lifted, brushing against his shaft, straining against his zipper, but she couldn't sustain the lift.

"Sean," she whimpered.

Behind her, Ben chuckled as he lifted his hands to her bra straps and tugged them down to her upper arms. "Think she's ready yet?"

"She's getting there," Sean said. With his hands still pinning Abby's to the leather ottoman he bent to her nipple, taut and pressing against the silk cup of her bra. He took it between his teeth and laved the tip with his tongue, forcing wet silk against sensitive skin until pleading, animal gasps rasped from her throat. When she twisted between them he released it and moved to the other nipple, once again subjecting it to the same torment.

He sat back to survey her, then flicked a glance at Ben, who unfastened the front clasp of her bra and pulled the fabric to either side. Ben cupped Abby's breasts in his hands, offering them to Sean, and Abby let out a low moan. Once again Sean bent to her nipples, this time using tongue and lips on the overstimulated tips. They gleamed when he pulled back for a moment to watch Ben pinch and roll them. Abby writhed in their grip, her hips arching, but Ben let up only when she subsided. Sean opened his mouth over the now-red tips, breathing softly on them, lapping at them, feeling Abby's pleading sobs with his mouth as much as he heard them.

Ben leaned forward a little, and his hands went to the button and zipper fastening Abby's jeans. "Lift," he said.

Abby obeyed eagerly, but from his position behind her Ben couldn't get her jeans and panties any lower than her hips. Sean let go of Abby's hands and tugged her jeans to her ankles. As he did

Ben sat back on his heels until Abby reclined against him, her hips and ass on the ottoman, legs spread to either side. Her arms dangled, and Ben left them there.

Slow kiss after slow kiss, from sternum to belly button, then down to her mound while Ben slowly massaged her breasts. Sean worked his hands between her ass and the leather and lifted her. He opened her folds with his tongue, tasted hot desire as he dragged his tongue up to the swollen bump of her clit. The first fluttering lick made her flinch. At the second her legs dropped wide as she braced the balls of her feet against the floor and pushed up against his mouth.

With a rough growl he worked one hand over her hips to splay across her lower belly and hold her down, and two fingers of the other into her soft channel. Another low cry and Abby began to thrust against his mouth and fingers.

Above her, Ben spoke. "It's good?" It was the tone of a man asking a rhetorical question but expecting an answer.

"So good," Abby gasped.

"As good as getting fucked?"

She laughed, desperate and dark. "I'm not complaining."

"Is it as good as a man inside you, when he spreads your legs and pushes in? When he holds you down and fucks you? Tell me."

At Ben's words her clit fluttered under Sean's tongue, the walls of her slick pussy gripping at his fingers in rhythmic movements as she came. "No," Abby said, the words almost soundless. "That's better."

Sean leaned over her and traced her lips with his wet fingers. Her tongue flicked out and tasted her juices. "Now you're ready."

Abby felt Ben's rough chuckle reverberate through his hard chest even as the low, amused sound rasped against her ears like a cat's tongue. Once again, she'd underestimated him, misjudged his ability to strip away the protective layers. He was right. She'd asked for the ménage, suggested the third man, agreed to the time and place, prepared herself for them. That constituted one level of ready—worldly, intellectual, informed consent.

This was another level entirely. Physical. Animal. Raw. This was her body turned on by two men who each knew her well enough to fuck her into a screaming, breathless orgasm. And she wanted it. Needed it. Before she'd agreed in a casual way. *Yeah, sure, let's have a ménage. Ménage is the new bi. Whatever.*

Now she would do things she'd never dreamed she could do, like spread her legs for Sean as he went down on her while she leaned against Ben. And she would do more, before the night was over, arouse and satisfy one lover while the other watched.

And Sean, damn him, knew it.

Heat pulsed in all her hot spots, melding with Sean's dark words, driving her to up her game. She drew a deep, shuddering breath and pushed herself upright. Ben stripped her blouse and bra down her arms. As he got rid of the encumbering clothes she leaned forward and kissed Sean, put every ounce of passion and longing into the press of her lips against his, tasting her juices, then his surprise at the bold move.

"Let's get you two ready," she said.

She turned to kiss Ben, and Sean stripped her jeans and underwear off as she did. Another turn, and she was on her feet, towering over Sean, still on one knee in front of her, and for one bewildering, tilting moment a long-suppressed fantasy of him in that exact pose but with a ring box in his hand settled over reality like a sheet over a bed.

To shove the image into the darkest recesses of her brain, she reached down and laid her hand along Sean's jaw, then swiped her thumb across his wet mouth. Without breaking eye contact he got to his feet and bent to kiss her. The tips of his fingers trailed down her spine, the touch light, teasing until he got to her ass. Then he gripped and pulled her against him, deepening their kiss.

Behind her Ben seated himself on the leather ottoman. Growing dizzy with lust and options she turned once again, intending to kiss him, too, but he skated his palms up her rib cage and cupped her breasts, then captured one nipple in his mouth, flicking his tongue against the hard tip. Abby shuddered, laced her fingers through his hair, and tipped her head back to rest against Sean's shoulder. He nuzzled into her hair, found the sensitive curve of her ear, his breathing steady but shallower than normal as he stroked her lower ribs, then her hips. His erection pressed hard and insistent against her ass, and Ben's talented mouth made her undulate against him.

This wasn't what she wanted. She wanted both of them as hot and needy as she was, so she trailed her fingers along Ben's cheekbone until he opened his eyes. "Stop," she said.

Sean's fingers tightened on her hip bones, and his breathing halted midinhale. At Ben's lifted eyebrows she added, "That cube will hold me but there's no way either of you will be comfortable on it . . . much less all three of us."

Both men relaxed. Ben stood, then slid his hands into her hair and kissed her, his demeanor rougher, more casual, more demanding. She made a helpless, whimpering sound, and his hands cupped over her ears amplified her heartbeat and breathing. Sean's fingers tightened once again on her hips and he stepped into her body, crushing her between the two big, powerful men. Need once again thumped in her veins. "Let's go," she whispered, and linked her fingers with Sean's.

Ben preceded them down the hallway, stripping off his shirt as he walked. He sat with his back to the headboard, forearms on bent knees, while Sean closed the door. The tall trees in the backyard blocked the rising moon so the room was fairly dark until Sean turned on the light in the bathroom and cracked the door.

Lazy heat simmering in his eyes, Ben gave her a pure cop, palm up, all four fingers beckoning *c'mere* gesture, and she crawled forward, between his legs. His cock strained against his zipper, but he made no move to release it.

The bed shifted as Sean settled in behind her. He swept her hair to the side and put his mouth to that oh-so-sensitive spot right where nape met shoulder and back. Heat simmered in Ben's eyes, then he touched his fingertip to his lips. "Start here. Work your way down."

She leaned forward, braced her hands on Ben's chest, and kissed him, nipping and licking at his finger when he didn't move it. As the kiss deepened Sean's mouth moved down her spine, his tongue tracing each bump of her backbone, lingering when the connection between mouth and nerve endings made her shiver. She made her way across Ben's jaw and down his throat to his pectorals, then lingered over each nipple. Below her his cock surged against his jeans, as if the submissive pose aroused him as much as her mouth on his body. She kissed her way to the denim and brown leather belt, and Sean shifted with her, his mouth growing more insistent. More wicked. A swift nip followed the gentle brush of lip against skin, then his tongue soothed the spot. His tongue traced her lower back, then nuzzled at the base of her spine. She moaned and arched her back, but he began to work his way up her back, leaving her aching for more.

Her attention shifted when Ben set his hands to his belt. Hot, languid desire prompted her to kiss his fingers and knuckles as he unfastened the buckle. Her tongue darted between his fingers as he worked to get his jeans down far enough to free his shaft and balls, then nibbled and licked at his knuckles as he gripped his cock and stroked it.

"Don't tease, sweetheart," he said.

A rough laugh from Sean, who was back at her nape, one strong leg on either side of hers, keeping her knees pressed together. "Go on, Abby. Get him ready. Make him hot for you."

He looked plenty ready to her, a sheen of sweat on his torso, his cock thick and swollen, but she pressed a sweet, closed-mouth kiss into the tip. Sean bit down on her nape, sending electric desire sparking along her nerves; in response she gasped and opened her mouth. From there it was only natural to lap at the head of Ben's cock, swirling her tongue to gather the moisture collected on the tip, then taking him into her mouth.

Ben's firmly muscled abdomen tightened, then relaxed as air eased from him on a guttural sigh. On the next downward glide she took Ben an inch deeper. Her saliva slicked his shaft as she found a rhythm that pleased him, fist firmly gripping the base while she lavished attention as far down as she could. Ben tucked her hair behind her ear then trailed his fingers along her jaw. Behind her, Sean groaned, his fingers gripping her hips as she bent over Ben. Tension thickened the air, heated it to the point where it pressed against her skin, seeped inside to coat her nerves and pool in her breasts and pussy. Then Ben tugged at her hair and lifted her chin with his finger at the same time.

"His turn, sweetheart."

She turned once again to Sean. He sat back on his heels and crooked his finger at her. His gaze dropped to her mouth while she unfastened the buttons of his shirt, taking her time exposing the hard, planed muscles of his shoulders and chest. While Ben had the hard-muscled build of a man frequently called on to run down then restrain drug-crazed offenders, Sean was lean, taut strength, deceptive until she bared his body, revealing muscle and bone held together by sinews visible under his skin. When she eased his shirt from his shoulders and put her mouth to the hollow of his throat, she felt blood pulsing into the very surface of his skin.

She focused on the planes of his chest and shoulders, and this time her path to Sean's cock held a little more urgency, a little more need. He went up on his knees when she tugged at his belt, helped her unfasten the buckle and release his straining shaft, then stayed there when she leaned forward and took him deep into her mouth.

The feedback loop humming between her and Sean, the one she couldn't seem to break no matter what she did, kicked into high gear, shutting down her rational brain. Through the haze of arousal in her mind she heard a condom wrapper tear, then after a moment's pause, Ben situated himself between her legs and aligned the head of his cock with her soft opening.

Pleasure spiked along her nerves, and she moaned as Ben pressed deep. He held still for a second, gently caressing her hips, until Sean slid his fingers into her hair and lifted her face to his. "Now it begins," he said.

The rough growl eddied over nerves already stimulated into anticipation. Ben timed his thrusts to Abby's mouth on Sean's cock, a slow, deep sensory overload that felt like more than she could take . . . until it wasn't enough. This was a battle for control, not just a pleasure-drenched evening, so she sat back and wiped her mouth with the back of her hand. "You know what I want," she said.

Sean nodded, a blue-white flame burning deep in his eyes. "Sit back," he said to Ben, who withdrew and leaned against the headboard as Abby turned to face him. Behind her another condom wrapper tore, then Sean snugged up against her, chest to her back, erection urgent against her ass.

"Watch," Ben commanded.

She bit her lip and shook her head. She didn't want to see Sean's face, or for him to see what she feared she'd be unable to hide.

His brown eyes darkened with a lazy, sensual heat. "You have to watch," he said, and turned her to face the mirror hanging from the open bathroom door. "It's very, very hot."

The reflection made her gasp. Ben leaning tanned and sexy against the headboard, his erect cock straining from its thicket of dark hair between his legs. Herself straddling his hips, a heated blush staining her freckled skin, her mouth wet and swollen. And Sean at her back, the Marine Corps emblem tattooed high on his shoulder, a tube of lubricant in his deft hands. He flipped open the lid and coated his fingers, then began to circle her anus with the tip of his finger.

No hesitation. No regrets. Tonight Sean was all in, and she couldn't face what she'd begun.

She let her head drop back and moaned. Ruthlessly Ben turned her to face the mirror. As she stared at the tableau, Ben cupped her breasts, squeezing the soft flesh, pinching her nipples. Her mirror-mouth opened on a low sigh, and Ben chuckled. "Oh yeah. Show us, sweetheart. Show us how you feel when he does this."

Oh, no. No, no, no. The only thing that made this bearable was having her back turned to Sean so he *couldn't* see what he did to her. Because this wasn't just about pleasure, or about new experiences, or even the old experiences. This was about feeling more than she could afford to feel for a man who'd broken her heart once already. This was rapidly becoming about feeling more than she could afford to feel, period.

But if she focused just on her body, on the purely physical connection, it was . . . shockingly good. Scarily good, the pressure just enough, then tantalizingly not enough, then deeper, and more, until one finger slid easily into her anus. She threw her head back and moaned. Ben laughed again, that low, rough laugh, then one hand dropped and formed a fist. Ever so gently he stroked the side of her swollen clit with his knuckles. Each caress sent eddies of pleasure chasing each other along her nerves until her entire body was aflame.

Sean added a second finger, and she moaned. "Yes," she gasped. "Oh, yes."

Ben kissed her cheek, her jaw, the sensitive corner of her mouth, flicking glances at her in the mirror as he did. "It's good," he said, the light in his eyes dark, knowing.

"So good," she said faintly.

His melted dark chocolate eyes went heavy-lidded. "It gets better," he whispered.

Then Sean settled the head of his cock against her anus. Abby gazed at his reflection in the mirror, the set line of his jaw, the blue flame in his eyes as he pushed, pushed, and breached the tight ring of muscle. She moaned, let her eyes drop closed to absorb the sensations. When she opened them again Sean still watched her in the mirror. Without breaking eye contact he pushed all the way inside.

"Oh, God," she gasped.

He bent forward, chest to back, and left a trail of kisses from one shoulder to the other. When he reached the shoulder closest to the mirror he nuzzled his cheek against hers and once again met her gaze. "Okay?" he asked softly.

She refused the connection implicit in his question. He waited, infinitely patient, his stubble grazing the heated skin of her cheek, until she nodded jerkily. Then he kissed the corner of her mouth as he gave an easy, slow withdrawal and thrust. Sparks skittered along her nerves, made her moan. Then Ben nudged into place. When Sean pulled back, Ben pushed in, and the slow glide over aching nerves and flexing movement of his hips and abs triggered another rush of heated sparks to her core. Her head dropped back against Sean's shoulder as she sank into the dark, heated pleasure, kissed his throat at the spot where stubble gave way to soft male skin. Tasted sweat. Sean gripped the headboard with one hand and wrapped the other around her waist to hold her. Ben cupped her breasts, rolling and pinching the nipples, drawing her into the slow, submissive currents eddying in the room.

This wasn't about pounding or plunging into her, hard or fast or dirty. This was about a slow, steady rhythm, one that forced her to feel every stroke, every pause, hear every gasp and grunt and shuddering exhale. Neither man touched her clit, instead relying on the unavoidable, erotic internal stimulation and their devastating tag-team approach to nudge her up the slope. She'd been prepared to be physically vulnerable to them, but not for the total destruction of the walls holding back everything she felt. Waves of pleasure and emotion surged at the edges of her skin, eroding the shell she'd built around her heart. The girl in the mirror, the sweet-looking redhead getting thoroughly fucked by two hard-bodied men, was her. Sean was there, accepting the woman she'd become without him. He'd changed, she'd changed, they weren't together, and she couldn't take the vulnerability any longer. She closed her eyes, but that only intensified the cascade of feeling inside her.

Emotion and pleasure wound together, braiding and knotting, pussy, ass, stomach, nipples, heart, throat, mind. Blindly she slid her palm along Sean's outstretched arm and curled her fingers around the top of his hand, then braced her other palm on Ben's hip. His hands dropped from her breasts to her hips, and the slow flex and thrust of his body under hers shoved her right to the edge. Another stroke in from Sean, then Ben's cock glided over the aching bundle of nerves inside her, again . . . again . . .

She threw her head back, high-pitched gasps tearing from her throat as the black hole of orgasm sucked her into the whirling vortex. Ben shuddered under her, his fingers tightening on her hips as he succumbed, but it was Sean's mouth on her nape, Sean's helplessness in release that extended her orgasm almost unbearably.

And when it was over, when the physical tension eased to the point where she could breathe again, when she felt Ben's hands slip to his sides even as Sean's grip tightened and he bent to kiss her shoulder, the knots remained. She stayed still, clinging to the sharp-edged fragments of her shell as Sean withdrew. As soon as he sat back she lifted herself off Ben, then curled up on her side facing the closed bathroom door. Reflected in the mirror there was a flushed, pale woman, her red hair pooled against the white sheets. Ben's dark hand stroked her hip, the movement hypnotic. "You okay?" he asked quietly.

No. Not even close to okay, but that wasn't Ben's problem. "I'm fine," she said.

Sean pushed the bathroom door open, and her reflection disappeared. The bed dipped as Ben got up, then the mattress swayed when Sean lay down on her opposite side. The bathroom door closed again, and this time Abby saw herself with Sean curled protectively around her. He brushed her hair back from her face and kissed her jaw. "Go to sleep, Abby," he murmured.

She drifted in a haze to the sound of Ben dressing, jeans against hair-rough legs, shirt tugged on, belt buckled. Of course she would. Because that's what she did with Sean, have amazing sex and fall asleep in his bed. But this had to end. She would use this to prove she was over him, that he meant nothing more to her than . . . well, than Ben did.

"I'm heading home," she said. "This all started because you had a ménage. I'm ending it with one. Now I'm leaving."

Chapter Nine

Good thing he was already lying down. Sean took Abby's verbal roundhouse kick but couldn't fall any further. Air rushed from his lungs as Abby scrambled off the bed and hurried down the hall to the living room without a backward glance. "Hold up, Ben. I'll walk out with you," drifted back to Sean's disbelieving ears.

Sean hurled himself out of bed, snagging his shorts and pants from the floor on his way to the living room. Abby stood by the ottoman. She stepped into her panties, then shrugged into her bra and fastened the clasp between her breasts.

"What the hell is going on, Abby?" He reached for her arm, but she jerked away from him, picked up her jeans, and shook them out.

"Nothing's going on, Sean. This is just the logical conclusion to what we've been doing for the last three weeks."

"The fuck it is, Abby," he said flatly. "You're not leaving."

"If she says she's leaving, she's leaving," Ben said evenly from his position next to the door. He finished lacing up his shoes, then straightened to study Abby, and from the look in his eyes he'd figured out that this wasn't just a happy-go-lucky night of sexual exploration.

Focus on the goal. "Abby. Please stay," Sean said, every ounce of command he could muster in his voice.

She pulled on her jeans and spoke as she zipped up. "I don't have any reason to stay."

"Sure you do," Ben said from across the room. "I know what you're like at this time of night, and you're not safe to drive. The adrenaline will wear off in the car, you'll drift over the centerline or into a tree, and I'll get a call that you've been in a wreck."

Abby blinked. "Why would you get a call?"

"Because I would." Ben dug his keys from his pocket. "If you want to leave, I'll take you home. We'll get your car in the morning. I suggest you stay. You two have unfinished business that goes way beyond what we just did."

"Fuck you," Abby said, her voice shaking. Hunched over slightly, she wrapped her arms around her torso, as if to stop the tremors rolling through her body as she fought with Ben.

Sean's awareness slipped into tactical crystal clarity. Fought with Ben. No goose bumps, just shakes. The kind of adrenaline shakes he saw in Marines during combat. Combat stress, the human body's reaction to intense, unavoidable situations where emotional responses were delayed, or suppressed, or both.

The kind of reaction he'd never seen in Abby.

Because he wasn't around to see it?

"That option is closed to you until you get your shit together," Ben said. "I'll hook up. This was just for kicks. I draw the line at fucking someone long-term who's in love with another man."

Abby went white. The sexy flush drained from her face and neck like a vampire had latched on, drawing blood and life from her. "I am not in love with him!"

Air huffed from Ben's chest in something that was too painful to be amused. "It's against the law to lie to a cop, Abby. It's just plain stupid to lie to yourself."

She jerked like he'd slapped her, then reached for her blouse and shoved her arms into the sleeve holes. "What the fuck do you know about love?" she jibed.

Oh, that wasn't Abby. That wasn't Abby at all. Sean watched. Waited.

A muscle jumped in Ben's jaw. "Staying with him or going with me?"

"I'm leaving in my own car, and you can't tell me otherwise," Abby snapped.

This wasn't about the ménage. This was about the slow-motion trench warfare that was Abby's daily life, something devastating that had to be suppressed so she could go on, do what had to be done.

Devastating. Suppressed.

Oh, Jesus. In all of his planning, his strategizing, his tactical analysis of their situation, he'd assumed Abby had been angry with him, but she was over it. He'd never taken into account the possibility that *she'd never dealt with it at all.*

When would she? You were gone. Her dad got sick. She couldn't find a job. When would she deal? And if she couldn't deal, how could she move on?

You've screwed this up from the first move, Winthrop. Like the Chinese fortune cookie joke, you read her perfectly . . . in bed. You unearthed, explored, and satisfied her every need . . . in bed. Emotionally, you missed the boat, the bus, the point. Everything. You missed everything.

She and Ben were still jabbing at each other, if he could call Abby lashing out and Ben standing there like he'd been carved out of rock jabbing.

"The badge says I can," Ben said. "Pick up those keys and I'll call dispatch. You'll be pulled over in less than a mile."

"On what charge?"

Ben's smile walked a fine line between edgy and mean, like maybe he'd had enough. "The traffic ordinance book is two inches thick, Abby. Any cop with a month on the street will find something."

In all of Sean's strategizing to get Abby back, casting her uniformed lover in the role of bad cop never occurred to him. This was clearly an abject failure of imagination on his part. But Ben wasn't her target. Time to shift her attention.

"Abby."

Still shaking like she would fly apart she jerked around to face him, and he felt a moment's anguish for what was coming, what it would likely do to them—finish them like they should have been finished ten months earlier. No matter the consequences for him, she had to get loose from this, to walk into the future she chose to create.

With or without him.

"Stay. Please."

She was white with rage, her freckles standing out like burning stars from her hairline to the waistband of her jeans. She didn't say anything, just buttoned her blouse with trembling, jerky fingers, but it was clear from the way she refused to look at Ben that she wisely wasn't going to put his ultimatum to the test.

Ben nodded at Abby's keys, still on the tall, square table by the door. "If she leaves before she's gotten some sleep, call me." He stepped through the front door and closed it quietly behind him.

The shaking intensified. Abby probably didn't realize she was doing it, or what it meant, because she'd had no support, no CO or sergeant to watch over her, no friends with deployed boyfriends or husbands, a disinterested mother and a self-interested father. No boyfriend/fiancé/husband checking in on her mental state. That was his fault, his failure. Or so he assumed.

Time to stop making assumptions and start getting the story from the boots on the ground.

"Abby, tell me how you felt when you got my e-mail."

"That's old news," Abby said. Her fingers refused to function on her shirt buttons because she couldn't slip the green pearl button through the hole. She flicked her fingers to get them working again. "I felt then what I do now. A little disappointed, then nothing. It's over and gone, in the past."

"No it's not," he said. He stood in front of her, shirtless, his cargo pants riding low on his hips, legs braced, hands shoved in his pockets, his face grave. "It's in this room, right now, between us. How you felt a year ago is at the heart of what we just did, and why. So tell me."

She stopped, swallowed hard against the lump in her throat. Truth be told, it made her sick to think about it. Her stomach churned. Funny how a ménage with two men—so dirty! so bad! so wrong!—left her limp with pleasure, near peace, and remembering how she felt when she got an e-mail turned her guts to water.

Then she realized that this was the final nail in the coffin. This was the best way to prove to him that she was over him, by rehashing this like it was no big deal. She shoved her sweaty, tangled hair behind her ears and folded her arms across her chest. *Be specific. Use details.*

"I was sitting in the front parlor," she said. "Reading e-mail on my laptop, looking out the front window. This is important because I'd gotten the biggest yellow ribbons I could find, the kind with the big bows and rosettes on them, and tied them around the trees in the front yard. You know how your mind drifts when you're just hanging out . . . you hadn't written for a couple of days, and I was worried about you, and the men in your platoon . . . and thinking about those ribbons and wondering what they'd look like after a year.

"And then there was an e-mail from you. No subject line. I was so disappointed when I opened it because it was really short. When you were in training, you sent me two single-spaced pages, full of description and funny stories about your men. Then you deployed, and it dropped to a page, then a couple of paragraphs. Then this. Four sentences. *Abby, I think it's better if we end our relationship. You're in a transitory stage in your life, with a lot of growing up yet to do. It's not fair to ask you to support me through the next year when I'm not able to make the same commitment to you. I wish you all the best in the future. Sean.*"

"I had a long response written that I just deleted, because me telling you that I'd hung yellow ribbons and joined the local group for wives and girlfriends of deployed personnel wouldn't make a difference. And when I thought about the time we'd spent together I realized I was just a distraction. I didn't think about it when we were together, but you're a Naval Academy graduate. A Rhodes Scholar. A lieutenant in the Marine Corps. And I was just out of college, a fun fling for a few weeks, but not enough for you long term. If you want to know how I felt, that's how I felt. Stupid for believing that it would work, that ribbons and social events and e-mails and video chat would get us through, that maybe you'd come home and mar—"

Her mouth shut with a click, and the now-silent air rang with the echoes of her raised voice. He'd never said anything about marrying her, never even said he loved her. She was the one with the fairy-tale dreams of love at first sight. She hunched into her folded arms, looked away, then back at him.

"The support group would have fixed that, though. I admired those women so much. Some of them were going through second or third deployments with little kids to care for, working and raising families and taking care of houses and yards, and they were so strong. They served something bigger than themselves just like their husbands and boyfriends and fiancés. I could have grown up in their company. I knew the deployment would be hell for both of us in totally different ways, but sometimes you grow up because you go through hell, and you keep going, and when you emerge you're stronger and wiser and more mature. I know I wasn't then, when we met, but I could have been. You deprived *us* of the chance to go through that *together*, to let the experience shape *us* and make *us* stronger. You quit on *us*. You said Marines don't quit, and you did."

Her voice was now almost silent in the dimly lit room, and she was proud of that. She wasn't yelling at him, just calmly stating facts. "I loved you. I'd fallen head over heels, passionately, completely, and totally in love with you, with your brains and your sly sense of humor, how scared you were, how much you cared, how strong you were despite your fear. I loved you, and when that e-mail sank in, I hated you. I hated you so much. I went to the front yard with my mother's pinking shears, and I cut the ribbons off the trees. Then I cut them into tiny little pieces and threw them in the trash. Do you want to know what happened to the paint on my back bumper? I used nail polish remover to peel off the bumper sticker, the one that said *Forget Prince Charming, I have a U.S. Marine* on it. . . ."

At that he looked away. For the first time in the weeks since he'd been back, he broke eye contact first. There was no victory in the achievement. She went on, because she had to finish this.

"I loved you, Sean. I could have loved you forever, but now I hate you. I hate you as much and as fiercely and as passionately as I loved you. I know you got me a new battery and mowed the lawn because you're trying to get me back, and I love you but I hate you, too, and it's all just so tangled up inside I can't figure out how to breathe around you."

She really couldn't breathe. Panic set in, air in short supply, as she looked around for her purse, found it on the table by the door. "I have to get out of here," she said, and shocked herself with how matter-of-fact and rational that sounded. She turned for the door, but in the blink of an eye Sean was across the room, palm flat to the door.

"You're not leaving," he said. "Not in this condition. You'll wreck, or wreck someone else."

"I'll walk."

"It's miles to your house, Abby," he said rationally, implacably. "Please. Stay. You can't go out like you are right now."

"Try to stop me," she said, and dug her fingernails into his wrist in an effort to get his hand off the doorknob.

He put his whole body between her and the door. "I'll call Ben," he said.

She shoved him, but he wouldn't move away from the door. His face was ravaged. This was no stoic Marine. Her words raked grooves around his mouth, hollowed his cheeks, darkened his eyes, pulling down the mask he'd worn for the last few weeks; behind that curtain was a man who'd used every tactic in the book to gain his objective—her—because he wanted her. Desperately. Completely.

A second shove, this one hard enough to force the air from his lungs, but he didn't try to hold her or contain her, just wouldn't move from the goddamned door, and finally she gave up, spun on her heel and stalked down the hallway to the master bedroom.

Where the big, wrecked bed confronted her, making her face what she'd just done, and with whom, and why. She'd just had the most amazing, intimate sexual experience of her life, with Sean, and she'd used it to destroy whatever remained of what they had.

They were finally over.

She slammed the door behind her, not caring if Sean was in the doorway, in the hall, or still standing in the living room. Then she sank down to the floor, buried her face in her bent knees, and sobbed like she hadn't when she'd gotten the e-mail ten months ago, as if her heart was breaking.

Because it was. All over again.

Chapter Ten

So much for the most expensive, elite education the American taxpayers could provide. A decade's worth of tactics training and he'd just made the most basic mistake a young officer could make, and he didn't even have the excuse of youth. He'd failed to turn the map around and consider things from Abby's perspective. He'd assumed she was ready to be won back, that if he showed her how much he cared she'd understand he was sorry, and regretful, and wanted a second chance. He forgot about emotions, about all the steps they skipped going straight from seeing each other to bed. Abby didn't play sophisticated sex games. That first night in the No Limits parking lot she'd as good as told him to back the fuck off, she wasn't ready to be wooed, let alone won, and he'd missed the signals entirely.

What a mess. What a fucking ugly sewage pit of a mess he'd just spent his leave stirring.

Abby fled down the hall in full-fledged retreat, then the bedroom door slammed hard enough to crack drywall, and he flinched.

Again. Her sobs from the bedroom were heartbreaking to hear, full
of the passion lacking in her flat recitation of events from ten months
ago, but he forced himself to walk over to the sofa, sit down on it,
and listen. She was here, she was safe, and that would have to be
enough for now. In the morning he would . . . they could . . .

You idiot. It's over. You lost.

When the bitter, wracking sobs tapered off, water ran in the
bathroom, sending the pipes knocking against the wall again. Then
the sheets rustled, followed by a single, shuddering sigh, then silence.
Half an hour into the silence he stood, walked silently down the
hallway, and used a pen to unlock the bedroom door. Abby slept
in a tight ball on the far side of the bed, her tear-ravaged face turned
to the bedroom window. He closed the door, then walked through
the living room to the sliding door that led to the deck. In the yard
he pulled one of Camilla's chaise lounges to the spot on the grass
where the tree branches didn't block the sky, where the low, gray
clouds hid the stars. He stretched out on the chaise, folded his arms
across his chest, and stared up at the sky until dawn turned the
clouds pearl gray.

Then he went back into the house and started coffee, because
Abby's life would go on without him. A few minutes later she emerged
from the bedroom, but even with her face downcast to the carpet he
could see her swollen, red eyes and cheeks. He stepped back and
shoved his hands in his pockets as she hurried by him, a washcloth
in her hand. In the kitchen she dumped ice into a bowl, ran water
over the ice, then immersed it into the bowl. When it was saturated
she wrung it out over the sink, came back into the living room, lay
down on the sofa with her head on the middle cushion and her feet
dangling over the arm, and put the cold cloth over her eyes.

He sat down on the ottoman, braced his forearms on his knees,
and waited. There was no point in rushing now. Despite the fact
that she hadn't headed right for the front door, it was over.

One hand massaged her temple while the other held the cloth tightly against her eyes. "I don't really hate you," she said finally.

"Oh, I think you do," he said. His own voice was raw, thick, scored with exhaustion. He cleared his throat, and waited some more.

"When Dad got sick I just pushed it all away, deep down inside, so I could cope with what was in front of me, which sounds very much like what you did when you broke up with me." She paused. "Funny how you can do something that seems so right at the time and have it be all wrong."

"Yeah," he offered quietly, then kept waiting.

There was another longer pause, then she said, "I'm not over you."

"I'm not over you, either."

"If I was really grown-up and mature, I would have said something rational like *Sean, I'm really angry with you and I can't get past that, so you need to move on.* But I didn't know I was still angry. It was almost a year ago. Who stays angry for a year?"

"Someone who's badly hurt?" A bitter laugh huffed from his chest. "I could have been more mature about this, too. Who goes after a woman like she's an epic battle with the fate of the world in the balance?"

"It's probably romantic if she's in the right frame of mind. But everything I feel for you is this big tangled ball of barbed wire around my heart. Hate and love, longing and resentment, anger and admiration. Sometimes I can't bear to look at you, but that year you were gone, I was half alive. I never stopped loving you. I realized that last night. I just . . . don't trust you."

"Right." He exhaled through his nose. "After what I did, I wouldn't trust me, either. I quit. I got scared, and I quit."

"You did what you had to do."

"I'm sorry," he said. "I'm sorry I was such an unforgivable, egregious jerk to you ten months ago when I broke up with you, and I'm sorry for the last month. I never, ever should have come on to you like I did, shown up when you asked me not to, done things you could have done for yourself. I had a plan. I'd won you once in four weeks. I could do it again. Except last year you wanted to be won, and now . . . you wanted to be left alone. I should have honored that, and I didn't. I treated you like an obstacle to overcome, or a game piece, and I'm sorry."

She licked her dry, cracked lips. She needed lip balm—God knew he was a connoisseur of lip balm after a year in Afghanistan's dry air—and water. Probably a handful of aspirin, but he wasn't doing a thing until she asked. He wasn't stupid. He had two world-class degrees and the accolades to prove it, goddammit. He would get smart about this. He would.

"Why did you break up with me?"

The question was tentative, as if she didn't dare ask. Answering honestly would be like showing up naked on the parade ground for a full review. "You nailed it last night. I was afraid. Terrified. The thought that I'd make a mistake and get one of my Marines killed . . . I was so fucking scared I'd fuck up everything, and I sacrificed you for them."

There. That was the truth, the ultimate dishonor revealed. "Because what matters is the guy on your left and the guy on your right," she said.

He lifted his gaze from the floor to her face. Her eyes still obscured by the icy cold washcloth, she said, "I understand, Sean. I didn't want to be the most important person in your life. I just wanted to be in your life."

"You deserve to be the most important person in someone's life, Abby," he said.

Air huffed from her. "I'm done with fairy tales. What I deserve is to be a part of something bigger than myself. Like you are. You serve something. Your life means something. I wanted to be a part of that."

"You're on that path, going to nursing school."

"I wouldn't have quit on you," she said. "I know lots of women don't last the deployment. I wouldn't have quit on us."

"I know that now. I'm sorry I did."

I'm learning, Abby. Please don't quit on me. But he didn't have any right to ask her for that now. Maybe ever.

There was a long silence, then she held out the washcloth. "Would you wet that down for me again?" she asked, keeping her eyes closed.

He took the proffered cloth, soaked it in the ice water, wrung it out carefully, and came back to her side. He draped the cloth over her puffy eyes, then sat down on the floor with his back to the sofa. After a minute her hand patted his shoulder gently, then came to rest.

"Thank you."

"Did you really want to do any of the things we did? Anal sex, the ménage, any of it?" Not that he didn't deserve it, but he hoped Abby had done that because she wanted it, not out of some dark, twisted place he'd created.

Another heavy inhale. "Oh, yeah. I'm not the woman you left behind, Sean."

Not unlike gunfire and combat terror, knowing he would never get back what he'd thrown away clarified his thinking like a crucible clarified metal. He loved her. He'd fallen as hard and fast as she had, but that love, tender, new, and unfamiliar, went unacknowledged and unvoiced in the whirlwind of preparing for war, then sucked into the vortex of fear. He had nothing left to lose, so he told her. "I love you, Abby."

"I still love you, too, Sean."

She still loved him. He still loved her. In the fairy tales, that would be enough. In reality, two people could love each other and still have the odds stacked against them.

Fuck the odds. They were going to beat the goddamn odds if it was the last thing he ever did. The tactics decision tree winnowed through options in his head like a slot machine spinning up gold. *Dinner.* A quiet dinner, somewhere nice but not romantic was the right move here. He almost put his hand on her knee and asked her out to dinner.

Almost.

This time he waited.

She sat up and neatly folded the washcloth. "I have to go," she said, balancing the cloth on her palm, then offering it to him.

He took it. The chill seeped into his skin. "I know."

"I have homework, and about a year's worth of housecleaning to do." She looked down at her hands, then up at him.

It was awkward, standing up together, his throat tightening while she got her keys and purse together. "Can I call you before I leave town?" he asked.

She shook her head, the movement slight but unmistakable. "I need some time to think, Sean. Can I call you when . . . if I'm ready?"

"Anytime, Abby," he said.

She let herself out quietly. Her car started without a hiccup, and purred off down the street. When silence fell, it was his turn to cry.

Abby hurried through the front door of her house, dumped her backpack on the tile, and headed up the stairs. She'd just finished another review session in the lab and had barely enough time to shower and feed herself and her father before heading to No Limits for the Saturday night rush. True to his word, Sean made no attempt to contact her since that night. No surprise appearances at No

Limits. No knocks on her front door. No new bumper for her car, or even a bumper sticker. She'd asked for time, and he'd given it to her.

After a quick shower she toweled off, slathered lotion over her entire body, and pulled on a simple pair of capris and a T-shirt. She was on her way down the stairs to tackle dinner when the doorbell rang.

Sean.

A wide smile on her face, she opened the door not to Sean but to Jeff, Lindsey, and Mikaela. Her smile disappeared as Abby glanced over her shoulder at unvacuumed floors, undusted surfaces, the clutter of medical paperwork and unopened mail on the dining room table, her father's unmade bed in the office, and her face flushed. "Jeff . . . Lindsey."

"Hi, Aunt Abby," Mikaela said.

"Hey, sugar lump," she said, and gave the little girl a hug. "What's up?"

"We brought Grandpa some cake," she said, and held out a paper plate with a piece of white birthday cake with white frosting and pink roses on it. The plastic wrap was wrinkled, and one corner of the cake was smashed into the plate. "Grammie Ruth couldn't come to my party because she had a cold, but we took her some cake. I wanted to bring Grandpa some cake. That's fair," she said with a seven-year-old's certainty.

Grammie Ruth was Lindsey's mother, the grandma who babysat every Saturday night. Abby looked down at her wide-eyed niece, then at Jeff and Lindsey. They both jerked their gazes back from the disaster in the dining room to her face.

"Is now a good time?" Lindsey asked. "We called, but didn't get an answer."

"I was at school," she said. "Dad doesn't answer the phone. It's fine. Come in."

She took Mikkie's hand and led her down the hallway. "Dad, there's someone here to see you," she said.

Her father turned to face her, then his eyes widened. Little Mikaela confidently dropped Abby's hand and walked over to him. "Hi, Grandpa," she said, and held out the cake. "I brought you some cake."

Her father looked at the cake, then at Abby, his expression so flabbergasted Abby almost burst out laughing. "Do you want milk to go with the cake?"

"Yes, please," Mikaela answered for them both, then sat down on the sofa next to her grandfather. "What are you watching, Grandpa?"

"The History Channel," he said.

"I like the Cartoon Network," Mikkie confided, "but Mama won't let me watch it. It's in-a-pro-pri-ate."

Jeff and Lindsey stood in the doorway between the living room and the kitchen. "Dad," Jeff said noncommittally. "Hello, Stan," Lindsey added.

"How about PBS?" Abby suggested as she went into the kitchen for forks and milk. Her father switched the television to a show about a talking dog. Abby brought two glasses of milk to the table by her father's end of the sofa. Her father looked from Jeff to Lindsey to little Mikaela, then back to Jeff again. Tears shone in his eyes, and his lip quivered. He cleared his throat and put his hands on the arms of his recliner to get up. Lindsey gave Jeff a little nudge, and her husband crossed the room.

"Don't get up, Dad," he said and sat down on the hearth. "Who did the cool design in the lawn?"

Lindsey looked at Abby. "Do you want something to drink?" Abby asked.

"Water," Lindsey said. Abby got two glasses of ice water and led Lindsey into the dining room.

"Sorry about the clutter," she said as she cleared off two chairs. "I'm a little behind on the housework."

Lindsey looked around the disorderly, dusty room, then at Abby. "At Mikaela's party you said you guys were doing fine," she said.

"I wouldn't call it a lie," Abby said. "Wishful thinking, maybe. I wanted us to be doing fine. I wanted to be able to take care of him on my own."

"Why?" Lindsey said candidly. "From what Jeff's said and my own experience with your dad, he's difficult on a good day and mean on the rest. Why would you be able to?"

Because she had something to prove to someone who was ten thousand miles away. "I don't think it was actually about him," Abby admitted. "He and Jeff don't exactly get along."

"He may not be easy to deal with, but that doesn't mean we won't do right by him," Lindsey said firmly. "Family is family. He looks bad."

"He's a horrible patient," Abby said. "He won't take his meds. He won't eat. He won't exercise or practice any of the breathing exercises. It's exhausting. This disease doesn't have to kill him next year, but at the rate he's going, it will."

As she spoke Jeff appeared in the doorway, then stood behind Lindsey's chair. "You can't control him, Abby," he said gently. "But you can break your heart trying to. He'll choose to live as long as he can, or he'll choose to die as soon as he can. It's Dad's world, and we're just living in it."

"I know," she said.

"What do you need? Meals? Someone to take him to the doctor? A housecleaner? Backup?"

"You and Lindsey are already so busy. You have a house, and you both work," she started.

"Standing right here, Abby, offering to help," Jeff said a little stiffly.

An excellent point. "I had a thing about not giving up," she said.

Jeff looked at her more closely, then loosened his tie. "It's not giving up to ask for help."

He was the spitting image of her father as a young man, and Mikkie had their dark hair and eyes. She took a deep breath. "All of the above," she said. "All of the above, but would you start with the lawn? I hate mowing the lawn, and he's so picky about it."

He smiled at the intensity in her voice. "Lawn care. We'll start there. I'll call Cody, get him over here, too. I can't copy your Marine's work, though. I'm a straight rows kind of guy. Maybe diagonals."

"He's not *my* Marine," Abby said automatically, then amended her statement. "Yet. He's not my Marine yet."

"I'll come over next weekend and see if we can get some of this paperwork organized," Lindsey said. "Mikkie can spend some time with her grandfather."

"Thank you," she said.

The talking dog show over, Lindsey carried Mikkie down the hallway. Her father was actually out of his chair, gasping with the effort to follow the dark-eyed little girl. As soon as Lindsey realized he was trying to keep up with them, she slowed down and turned so Mikkie could see her grandpa. "Did you like my cake, Grandpa?" she asked imperiously.

He nodded. "I did," he said, then coughed.

"Can Grandpa come to my dance recital?" she asked her mom. "I wear a pink tutu and a crown!"

Her father had no interest in girl stuff. Princesses, ponies, stars, fairies, crowns, makeup, glittery shoes, dances, party dresses, none of it. "We'll see how Grandpa's feeling," Abby said. "Maybe your dad could record the recital and we could watch it here?"

"I'll be fine," said the man who'd never once seen her cheer in high school or college. "I'll be there."

From the expression on Jeff's face, he was familiar enough with their father's frequently broken promises to temper Mikkie's expectations. "Let's see how you feel, Dad," he said easily.

Jeff and his family left, and the house suddenly felt empty. "Pretty little girl," her dad said, his breathing loud in the silence.

"She looks like Jeff, and you," Abby replied. "She's going to be striking when she grows up."

A grunt, then her father shuffled back down the hallway. When he turned for the family room and his recliner, Abby said, "Hey, Dad? The recital's in four weeks. If you want to be able to go, you need to do some of those breathing exercises."

He paused for a long moment, then turned for the kitchen and the breathing machine.

Abby smiled. A lifetime of broken promises, hurt feelings, missed events, and yet there was always a new start. Someone walked through a door with a piece of cake, or offered to mow a lawn. She remembered her heart's response to a knock at her door, and found that the terrible, wild night with Sean burned away her anger. New shoots of love pushing through the devastated earth of her soul.

But she waited. First she helped her dad with his breathing exercises and fixed him a plate for dinner, then she called one of the part-time waitresses at No Limits and offered up her prime Saturday night shift. The girl jumped at the chance. Abby changed into jeans and a decent blouse, then scuffed her feet into flats.

"I'm going out, Dad," she said.

"Okay," he said.

"I left you a plate in the fridge," she said.

He looked at her. "Thank you," he said gruffly.

"You're welcome, Dad. See you later."

When she got to Sean's borrowed house and rang the doorbell, a woman answered. "Can I help you?"

The bottom dropped out of Abby's stomach as she looked into the woman's eyes. "I'm looking for Sean," she said.

"I'm Camilla," the woman said. "He's gone home for his last night before he leaves for Virginia."

"Oh," she said, disappointed. "Okay. Thanks."

"Are you Abby?"

She turned back. "I am."

"He said if you came by to tell you to come over to the house. I think his mother planned a tailgating party to disguise his going-away party. Knowing Sean, he's probably desperate for a break. He's so outnumbered by girls at home. He said to tell you he'd be waiting for you."

Her heart knocked so hard against her breastbone she reached for the railing to steady herself. "Okay," she said inanely. "Thank you. I'll go over."

Camilla closed the door. Abby got in her Celica and floored it.

Chapter Eleven

Sean had to admit his parents knew how to throw a party. He'd refused to have a big fuss made over leaving for Quantico, so his mother covered it as a Saturday football tailgating party that started at eleven and at five in the afternoon was only picking up speed going into the Texas game at seven. Half the neighborhood was watching television on the flat screen set into the brick patio wall, and his four sisters were there. Bronagh and Bridget drove down from Houston with several friends from work, and Kiera and Naeve invited a whole pack of girlfriends from high school and college that thankfully did not include the girl from the drive-through at Wendy's. Between friends of his sisters and his mother, women outnumbered men in the house and in the yard three to one. He did his best to cope politely with the press of chattering females ranging in age from fifteen to sixty, but when the chips, beer, and hard lemonade ran low and his father nudged him and asked him if he wanted to run to the store for fresh supplies, Sean jumped at the chance.

"You drive," he said to his dad, and tossed him the keys to the Mustang on the way down the steps. "Take the long way around."

His dad just laughed. Sean slumped in the passenger's seat, letting the engine's rough purr lick over his nerves like a mama cat's soothing tongue. They stopped at a superstore on the outskirts of town and loaded a grocery cart full of chips and salsa, sandwiches, salads, drinks, an array of alcohol that would have made an entire platoon whoop for joy, and a big cake. There was a brief skirmish over wallets when the checkout clerk rang up the total, but Sean got a few twenties into her hands before his dad could stop him. They filled the trunk with the contents of the shopping cart, keeping a bag of Doritos for the drive, and slid the cake into the backseat.

"How're you doing?"

Sean tore open the bag of chips as he considered how to answer that question. All things Marine considered, he was fine. He was home, his men were home, everyone was alive. No one seemed to be struggling, but he'd keep in touch with all of his men for . . . well, forever. But not a word from Abby since she walked out of Camilla's house days ago. "Fine," he said. "I guess."

"Want to talk about it?" his dad asked as he headed south on the Gulf Freeway.

He pulled his cell phone from his cargo pants pocket and ran his thumb over the screen. Nothing. "I screwed something up," he said. "Then I screwed it up worse, trying to fix my first screwup. Now I just have to wait and see what happens."

"Takes a strong man to admit his mistakes," his dad offered stolidly. "Is this about the girl from last year?"

"Yeah."

"You want my advice?" His father wisely didn't wait for an answer. "After thirty-six years with the same woman and fathering four girls, my advice is to be patient. They usually come around, but you can't rush them if they're not ready to be rushed."

"Where were you weeks ago when I started all of this?" Sean muttered as his cell phone rang. "Probably Mom, wondering where we are," he said as he pulled it from his pocket. But the picture on his screen wasn't of his mother crossing the finish line at the Houston marathon.

It was a smiling bright-eyed redhead on a picnic blanket. "Abby?" he said.

"Where are you?" she demanded. In the background he heard the noise and laughter of his parents' party. "Because I'm in your parents' backyard with about sixty other people. I have a beer and a sandwich, and I'm under orders to sit here until you get back. One of your sisters, Bridget or maybe Bronagh, told me not to leave until you got here. She's really quite fierce, and a little scary."

"That'd be Bronagh. I apologize for Bronagh. I'll be there in less than five minutes," he said, and gestured to his father to hurry the hell up. "Don't leave. Please."

"I'm not leaving," she said. "I'm going to eat a sandwich and drink this beer and pretend there aren't fifty women looking at me out of the corners of their eyes. But hurry. I really want to see you."

"We're on our way." He hung up, sat up straighter in his seat. "Step on it," he barked before he remembered the man beside him was his father, not the lance corporal who usually drove him.

"Patience," his father said. "This car's a cop magnet. If Bronagh's got her, she's not getting away."

They pulled into the driveway, and his dad loaded him up with four cases of beer and two bags of groceries stacked on top. He came through the front door of the big white house to a rousing round of cheers, set everything on the kitchen counter, looked around for Bronagh, but found only Naeve.

"Backyard," she said as she dug through the chip sack. "No Cheetos? You didn't buy Cheetos? Sean! How could you?"

He chucked her the keys to the Mustang and his wallet. Her

squeal of delight followed him through the sliding glass doors to the expansive brick patio, where he found Abby sitting on a chaise, Bronagh sitting next to her, both of them pretending to watch the pregame show. When he appeared Bronagh stood up to make room for him. "You're welcome," she said, and swept into the house.

"Hey," he said. "Want a burger? Potato salad? We have chips now."

She looked at him, wry amusement shining in her eyes. "You're always showing up and surprising me. I thought I'd turn the tables. I was going to leave when I figured out you weren't here, but Bronagh felt I should wait for you." She looked around, then leaned a little closer. "It's like being in a fishbowl. Everyone's watching us."

"I have four sisters," he whispered back. "They find my personal life very interesting."

"Do they know about us?"

"They know I broke up with you and I regret it," he said. "Nothing about what happened this month."

She looked at him, no challenge, no shutters, just Abby in those spring-green eyes. "About that . . . I know you don't have much time left with your family, but can we go somewhere else and talk? Just for a little while?"

"Yes," he said without hesitation. "But you have to drive. I just gave my sister Naeve the keys to the Mustang to get her off my back about forgetting Cheetos."

He took her hand and towed her through the melee, out the front door, where he found seven teenage girls trying to cram into the Mustang. He took a moment to ruthlessly evict all of the girls except Naeve, then leaned into the passenger window. "One passenger, Naeve."

"I can't choose between my six best friends," she wailed.

Behind him, Abby stifled a laugh. Sean took a deep breath, counted to five, then turned to the gaggle of girls clustered on the front lawn, twisting hair and whispering. "Throw for it," he said.

Fifteen seconds of rock paper scissors and a preening brunette slid into the passenger seat.

"Seat belts," he barked as the Mustang backed out into the street.

"You sure you're okay with this? We can wait until she gets back," Abby said.

"She's a good driver," Sean said. "I taught her to drive a stick in that car. She'll be fine. It was the six chattering BFFs with cell phones that worried me."

After the party and his sister's friends, the silence in the Celica rang in his ears, but still he waited. Abby drove them to the park. "You want to go for a walk?" he asked.

"Not really," she said. "I just want to talk to you. I want to know why you came looking for me at Ben's."

She looked at him, and in her calm, serious gaze was Abby, ready to be wooed again. Very, very slowly. He pointed at her foot and beckoned. She shifted in the driver's seat so her back was to the door and her feet rested in his lap. He tugged off her flip-flops and dropped them on the floor, then put his thumbs to the soles of her feet in slow, rhythmic strokes. "Because even though I cut you out of my life, I couldn't cut you out of my soul. I could keep you out of my mind for days," he said as the sun set. "Then I'd be on night patrol, looking up at the stars. They lay in a swath across the sky because there's no light pollution, and every time I looked up they reminded me of your freckles. And I felt better. Less alone. Less lonely."

"It's hard to forget someone when the night sky reminds you of her," she said.

"It's hard to forget someone when she's carved into your soul," he replied. "The stars just reminded me of what I'd thrown away, and what I wanted back."

She gave him an absent little smile. "Now tell me everything that happened after you broke up with me," she said.

"Everything?"

"As much as you want to tell me," she amended.

"That's everything," he said. "This could take a while."

"All night?"

He slid her a quick glance. Abby was flirting with him. Very gently. Very tentatively. Flirting. "At least," he said.

"Better get started," she said lightly.

So he did. He told her everything he could remember, impressions and sounds and stories about life on base, patrols, his men, their families, missions, the details that comprised *everything* while night fell around them. During the foot massage she'd gone boneless in the seat as she watched him. When the darkness registered in his awareness, he checked his watch.

"Do you need to get back?" she asked.

"No," he said. "I just realized I've done all the talking."

"I think you needed to get some of that out," she said.

To her. To the woman he wanted by his side forever. "I think you're right," he replied.

Another flashing little smile in the dusky light. She opened the door and got out of the car, stretching with a soft, satisfied sound. "You've got more stories, right?"

He walked around the hood of the car and stood in front of her. "I do. Do you want to hear them?"

"I do," she said.

"So we're not done?"

"We're not done," she replied.

"Then I need to talk to you about something," he said. "John Langley, the former Marine who owns Langley Security, offered me a partner position in his firm. Another guy from the Corps is coming on board to head up personnel. They want me for research and strategy. It's here in Galveston. There'd be travel, but at least I wouldn't be stationed in Virginia while you were here."

She blinked. "Are you asking me if I think you should resign your commission and go into the private sector?"

"That's what I'm asking, Abby. At the very least, I want you to know the option is there."

"Go to Quantico," she said without hesitating. "The whole point of deploying was to gain insights into modern-day warfare, then apply them to help keep Marines alive. That's who you are."

"Are you sure?" he said, peering into her eyes for any hint of resistance.

"Yes, I'm 100 percent sure I don't want you to give up your dream, your plan, and your future just because I'm here and you're there," she said tartly. "We would have survived you deploying to Afghanistan. We'll surely survive you living in Virginia while I finish school. After that, we'll figure it out."

He wanted to race in a circle in the parking lot, jump in the air, and pump his fist. Instead, he kissed her, soft and sweet, and felt her melt against him. "Yes, we will," he said softly.

She smiled at him, then looked up at the night sky. "That's what you saw that reminded you of me?" she asked.

"Too much light pollution," he said, and he didn't even need to look up to know that. "I saw something much more amazing."

"Pretty romantic," she said.

He stepped close and pulled her into his arms. "After this month we can both agree I suck at the Prince Charming stuff," he said.

She tipped her head back and smiled at him, her eyes gleaming. "That's okay. I'll take my U.S. Marine."

Epilogue

Towering evergreen trees waved their spiny branches in Abby's face as she waded knee-deep in snow behind Sean. The day after she arrived in Virginia a major storm dropped fourteen inches of heavy, wet snow on the region, and Prince William Forest Park at seven in the evening was dark and still.

"It's all very pretty," Abby commented to Sean's back, a few feet up the trail from her, "if you're inside, drinking peppermint cocoa. With marshmallows. In front of a fire."

He turned around, his blue eyes dancing under his pulled-down black watch cap as he reached for her hands. "You cold?"

"Let's see," she said as she pulled down a fleece scarf. "I'm wearing wool socks, boots, silk long underwear, flannel-lined jeans, snow pants, a turtleneck, a wool sweater, a parka, gloves, and a scarf." The clothes were her Christmas present, doled out item by item during a few hours of a whirlwind leave between Christmas and New Year's, and nestled in one boot was a round-trip plane ticket to Virginia during her winter break in January. The card tucked in the plane ticket read *You'll need this for continued conversations under the stairs.*

She'd been overwhelmed by the number of expensive items, considering that she had one gift to give him, but his reaction when he saw the hardcover photo album reassured her. She'd secretly contacted his gunnery sergeant and asked for his help gathering digital photographs of the men in his platoon in Afghanistan, then spent hours arranging the photos, using the stories the men sent with the pictures as the captions.

The memory of Sean's expression when he opened the box, then lifted the cover, would stay with her forever.

"Abby," he said, and his choked voice made her tear up. "How did you do this?"

"I copied Gunny Sandoz's e-mail address from your phone," she said. "Repayment for when you broke into my car to replace my battery."

He was silent, slowly turning pages, giving little huffs of laughter at some of the pictures, shaking his head at others. "I'm speechless," he said distractedly.

"I'm glad you like it," she said. "They sent in the stories that went with the pictures. I hoped you'd tell me what you remember about them, too."

He lifted his gaze to hers, tears shining in his eyes before he swiped at them with his shirtsleeve. "Thank you."

Now she stood in the middle of a very dark, very snowy forest, testing all her brand-new winter gear. "No, I'm not cold. It's just hard work, slogging through all this snow. Where are we going?"

"Up," he said quite seriously, and pointed. His clothing was similar to hers, minus the scarf and the long underwear, and he showed no signs of being affected by the heavy snowfall.

"I can see that," she said just as seriously. "Uphill, on a snow-covered trail, at night. The question is, why?"

"Because there's something I want you to see," he said. "It'll be easier on the way down."

He broke the trail, his breathing even and hardly labored while she waddled along in his wake. "I'm out of shape," she panted.

His back still to her, he went down on one knee in front of her. "Climb on," he said.

"You can't be serious. I weigh a hundred and thirty pounds. You can't carry me up that hill in the snow."

"You weigh about as much as the pack I humped through Afghanistan on patrols," he said without turning around. "And you're softer."

She giggled, then climbed on piggyback style. He looped his arms under her knees and shifted her higher on his hips, then set off up the trail again.

"You're not even breathing harder," she observed after a minute.

"This actually feels a little more natural," he said. "I got used to the extra weight. Your job is to keep branches out of my face."

"I'm on it," she said and extended her arm determinedly.

Twenty minutes later they broke through the forest at the top of the ridge. He crouched to let Abby down. "Okay," she said. "What did you want me to see?"

He pointed again, this time straight up. She tilted her head back, and felt her breathing halt. "Oh," she said almost soundlessly.

The Milky Way spread in an arc through the sky like someone with immeasurable wealth took fistfuls of diamonds and flung them on black silk. She turned in a slow circle, her mind unable to take in the vast expanse, the stark, indescribable beauty.

"That made you think of me? It's beautiful," she said. Having turned in a complete circle, she stopped, a little dizzy, and reached for Sean to steady herself. He held out his hand, and something in the tight grip through thick gloves caught her attention. She looked down to see diamonds sparking in his black-gloved hand, glittering like he'd plucked them from the night sky and set them in a band of moonlight.

"Marry me, Abby."

"Oh," she whispered. "Oh, Sean."

"You don't have to say anything now. I'm just letting you know that I'll never quit on us, or on you, again. If . . . when you decide you want to wear my ring, it's yours."

"How long will you wait?" she asked. "How long until you have to have an answer?"

"I'll wait forever," he said intently. "Until one way or the other you tell me to stop waiting."

Life was one huge risk, she thought. Service was a risk, taking a chance that giving yourself to something bigger wouldn't use you up for nothing, and even if it did, the daily act of fidelity to people, causes, places, beliefs, values, principles would transform you. Half a dozen logistical issues loomed in front of her, an intense, consuming year of nursing school and her father's illness not the least of them. She blew them all away with a puff of breath into the frosty air.

"Oh, Sean," she said, and pulled off her glove. "We've both waited long enough. Yes."

He extracted the ring from the box. Trembling, she held out her hand, palm down, fingers spread just a little. The ring slid easily onto her finger. She spun it with her thumb and watched diamonds glitter in a circle.

"It's an eternity band," he explained. "Do you mind that it's not a typical engagement ring? We can exchange it."

She turned it again and thought of how she'd remember this night forever, stars moving in a slow, eternal spiral overhead, diamonds encircling her finger. "We'll do no such thing. It's absolutely perfect."

His lips were warm against hers, soft, then firm and demanding as she wrapped her arms around his neck and pressed her body to his. "We must be wearing too many clothes," she said into his mouth. "I can't feel you at all."

He laughed. "Nobody gets frostbite on my watch, so we'll keep our clothes on until later," he said, and tugged her glove back on over the ring. They stretched out on the snow on their backs, faces turned to the glittering night sky.

"I feel like I'm spinning," she said after a few minutes.

"You are," he said. "A little less than a thousand miles an hour."

The precise answer, so Sean, so geeky Marine, made her smile. "This is what you saw."

"This what I saw," he repeated. "And every time I felt you beside me."

"Now I am," she said simply. "Forever."